Kylie & The Kelly Gang

C.R. Cummings

Also By
CHRISTOPHER CUMMINGS

Kylie & Skip
The Boy and the Battleship
The Green Idol of Kanaka Creek
Ross River Fever
Train to Kuranda
The Mudskipper Cup
Davey Jones's Locker
Fourteen
Air Cadet
Below Bartle Frere
Bowling Green Bay
Airship Over Atherton
Cockatoo
The Cadet Corporal
Stannary Hills
Sugar & Spice
Coast of Cape York
**Kylie and the Kelly Gang*
Beyond the Barrier Reef
Behind Mt. Baldy
The Cadet Sergeant Major
Cooktown Christmas
Secret in the Clouds
Mischief at Mingela
The Word of God
The Cadet Under-Officer
Through the Devil's Eye
Barbara in the Bush
Barbara and the Smiley People
Barbara at her Best
Barbara's Bivouac

Kylie & The Kelly Gang

C.R. Cummings

This 3rd edition Published 2023 by DoctorZed Publishing

DoctorZed Publishing books may be ordered through booksellers or by contacting:

DoctorZed Publishing
10 Vista Ave
Skye, South Australia 5072
www.doctorzed.com

ISBN: 978-0-6458591-6-4 (hc)
ISBN: 978-0-6458591-7-1 (sc)
ISBN: 978-0-6458591-8-8 (ebk)

National Library of Australia Cataloguing-in-Publication entry

Author: Cummings, C. R., author.

Title: Kylie & The Kelly Gang / Christopher Cummings.

ISBN: 978-0-6458591-6-4 (hardcover)

Target Audience: For young adults.

Subjects: Adventure stories, Australian.

Queensland--Fiction.

This is a work of fiction. Names, characters, places, events, and dialogues are creations of the author or are used fictitiously. Any resemblance to any individuals, alive or dead, is purely coincidental. The views expressed in this work are solely those of the author and do not necessarily reflect the views of the publisher, and the publisher hereby disclaims any responsibility for them.

Cover image Girl Riding Horse © Bowie15 | Dreamstime.com
Cover design © Scott Zarcinas

DoctorZed Publishing rev. date: 25/08/2023

Dedicated to

The Officers of the
The Queensland Police Service
and in particular
The Queensland Mounted Police
Who for the last 160 years have served with courage
and dedication to duty
And
Who have provided the framework of law and order
On which the State of Queensland was built.

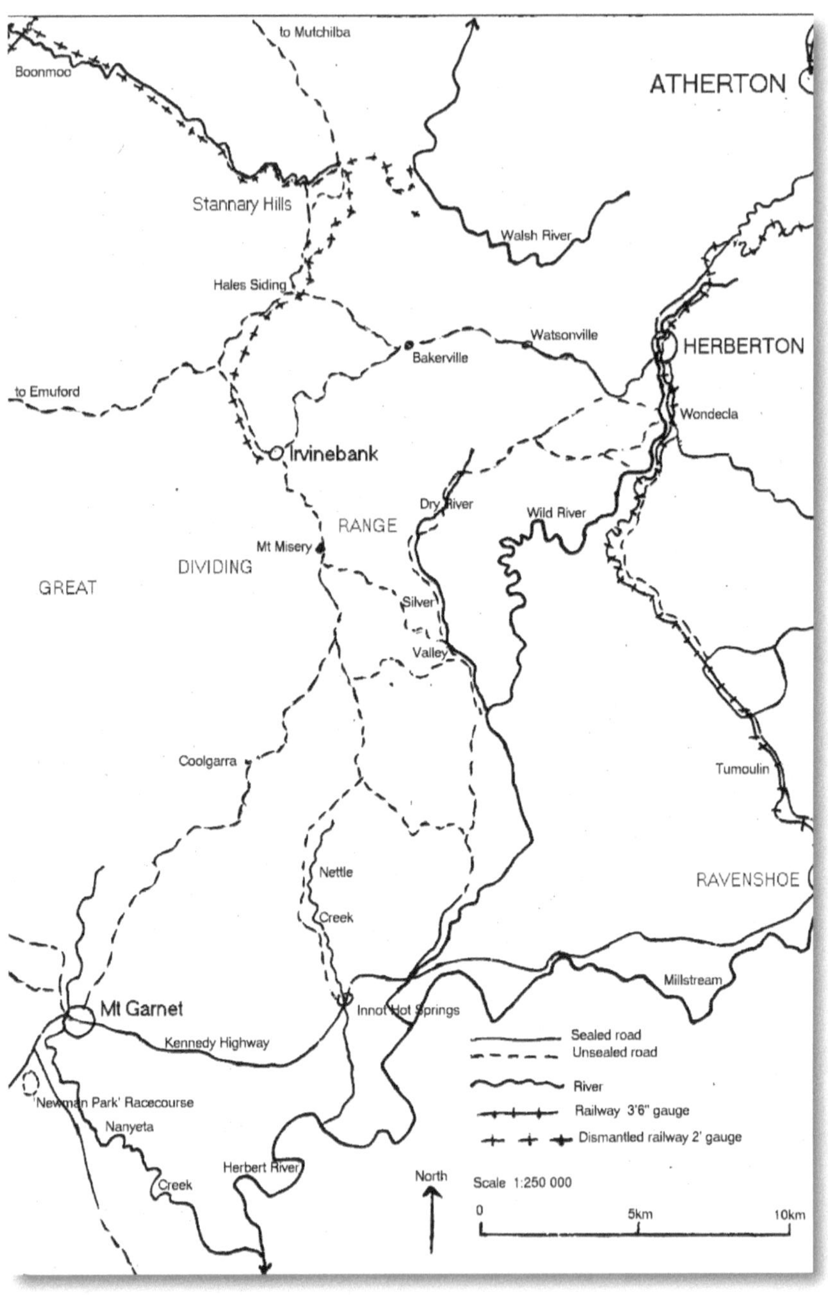

to Mutchilba
Boonmoo
ATHERTON
Stannary Hills
Walsh River
Hales Siding
Watsonville
Bakerville
HERBERTON
to Emuford
Wondecla
Irvinebank
Dry River
Wild River
RANGE
Mt Misery
DIVIDING
GREAT
Silver
Valley
Coolgarra
Tumoulin
Nettle
Creek
RAVENSHOE
Millstream
Mt Garnet
Innot Hot Springs
Kennedy Highway
Sealed road
Unsealed road
River
Railway 3'6" gauge
Dismantled railway 2' gauge
'Newman Park' Racecourse
Nanyeta
Creek
Herbert River
North
Scale 1:250 000
0
5km
10km

Chapter 1

RAIN ON OUR PARADE

Wednesday 26 April, 0950hrs
Herberton, North Queensland
The Railway Station
Overcast and starting to drizzle.

Kylie Kirk, 13 years old, stood against the southern end of the old wooden railway station building, pressed in between her friends and a growing crowd of locals and tourists. In front of her was an open area of sandy 'platform', ending in a small garden bed. This was also crowded by spectators. Beyond them several flat-bed trucks were parked, allowing even more people places on which to stand and observe. On her right were the empty rails of the old railway and drawn up on her left was a company of army cadets ready for a ceremonial parade.

The army cadets were mostly from her own high school in Cairns and out the front stood the Company Sergeant Major, who also happened to be her big brother Graham. He was two years older than her. Graham had just marched the company into position and 'Right Dressed' it. He now stood the cadets 'at ease' and then did an about turn and stood at ease himself.

"Isn't he handsome?" whispered Margaret, Kylie's best friend and Graham's devoted admirer.

He is, Kylie thought, studying her big brother and noting the straight bearing, firm chin and tanned, good-looking face. In his camouflage uniform, with scarlet sash, black belt and 'slouch hat' tilted at a slightly rakish angle, she thought he looked the very image of an Aussie 'Digger'.

But Margaret's comment also made her smile. "You are just biased," she said.

"Oh poo!" Margaret muttered, her freckled cheeks mottling with a blush. "He is better looking than Peter."

That caused Kylie to swivel her gaze to the sergeant standing in front of the closest platoon. He was Peter Bronsky, one of Graham's friends.

Peter was also two years older than her and, like Graham, a Year 11 at school. In contrast to her brother with his fair colouring and blue eyes Peter had brown eyes and dark hair. To Kylie he looked very manly and attractive. For several years now she had been half-hoping that Peter would notice her and again this wish crossed her mind.

The sight of the other sergeant standing in front of the second platoon had the opposite effect. That was Graham's other friend, Stephen. She did not like him much, having heard a few stories that bothered her about his morals and behaviour.

Stephen is not nearly as handsome, she considered, noting his smaller stature, freckles, and glasses.

At that moment, a few people walked along the edge of the platform in front of the cadets. One of these was a very attractive teenage girl with dark hair. She wore a cheque shirt and hip-hugging jeans which outlined a very shapely figure. Kylie saw Graham's eyes light up with interest and then follow the girl till she vanished among the crowd behind Kylie. *Silly boy!* she thought. She was very aware that her brother was now extremely interested in girls.

A drizzle of rain caused Kylie to bite her lip and glance up at the low clouds drifting overhead and clinging to the surrounding hilltops.

"Oh, I hope it doesn't rain on the parade," she commented.

Margaret nodded. "Yes, it would be a pity after all their preparations," she agreed. "Oh, I wish I was on parade," she added. Margaret had joined the cadets a few weeks earlier, but Kylie knew that the new recruits had not been allowed to join the guard.

The fifty cadets had been doing extra drills for the last six weeks, ever since the invitation to take part in the ceremony had been received. As the cadets were only a part-time volunteer organisation which normally did a two hour 'Home Training' parade each week the extra afternoons had been quite a sacrifice of their spare time. The event itself was the handing over of a large government grant at the same time as the commissioning of a new steam locomotive. This was to be placed in service by 'RailCo', the private company that now ran the tourist railway between Atherton and Herberton. The railway had been completed way back in 1910 and to make the event more spectacular the committee had organised a re-enactment of the opening ceremony. This was to be complete with speeches, dinners, and a ball, all attended by VIPs.

It was the Easter school holidays and Kylie knew it had taken an effort to muster such a large number of cadets. This year Easter had been very late in April and had joined onto the Anzac Day holiday. Preparation for traditional Anzac Day guards and marches had helped motivate the cadets. The previous day the cadets had all marched in Cairns and the members of the ceremonial guard had then travelled up to Herberton to rehearse. They had spent the night at Woodleigh College and been up early for another rehearsal.

Margaret studied the guard with a critical eye. "I'm glad I joined the cadets," she said.

Kylie smiled. "You just want to be near Graham," she replied.

"I do too!" Margaret answered.

Kylie shook her head. "I can't see you crawling around the bush in camouflage," she commented.

Margaret grinned and made no reply. She then stood on tiptoe and craned her neck to look around. "I've never seen a real live duke," she said. "I hope I get to see him."

"Nor have I," Kylie agreed. The Chief Official Guest was a visiting British Lord, The Duke of Fitzwater. He was billed even ahead of the State Governor and the Premier. It was stated in the advertising and on the programs that the Duke and his entourage would be wearing appropriate 'period costume' and that was something that Kylie wanted to see. Many of the crowd had also obviously made an attempt to dress for the occasion as she could see quite a number of old-fashioned ladies bonnets and parasols, and more than a few top hats. That most of these were only hastily stuck together from black cardboard was not obvious at a distance but she could see that the steady drizzle was starting to bring some of these creations unstuck.

The cadets had also made an effort to dress for the occasion. Apart from wearing their best uniforms and their good Hats KFF with gold badges, the sergeants and CSM all wore scarlet sashes and the officers their 'Sam Browne' belts and swords. Graham had his CSM's cane in his right hand and the front rank of the cadets all held old .303 rifles. For weeks they had been learning the old-fashioned drill with these and there had been a full rehearsal that morning. To Kylie's eyes they had looked very proficient and smart when they marched on.

A tall, slender girl wearing a long 'period costume' dress, complete with gloves, handbag, muff and bonnet, edged in against Kylie as another spatter of raindrops sprinkled the waiting crowd. For a moment Kylie eyed her with a slight feeling of envy, wishing she had worn some sort of costume rather than just jeans and shirt.

The tall girl looked up at the clouds then said to the woman next to her, obviously her mother, "Oh dear! I hope it doesn't rain."

The mother also looked up. "Yes, it will spoil the photography," she said.

Kylie could only agree with that. Both she and Margaret had cameras and she noted that almost everyone in the crowd seemed to have one. As well there were TV cameras from four different stations, all mounted in various locations to capture the event from different angles.

Margaret studied the steadily growing crowd. "It's certainly a big event," she said.

"My word yes! The advertising seems to have really caught on," Kylie agreed. Initially she had not been fussed over attending, being more interested in the horse-riding holiday that was to follow, but a compromise had been reached. As soon as the ceremony was over and the cadets were dismissed, Graham and his three friends (Tubby Roger was just visible in the rear rank of the second platoon) were to join them for a five-day trail ride with a local horse-riding group.

The idea of a horse-riding expedition during the holidays had been Kylie's. She had seen an ad in the local paper and, as she and Margaret were trained in both the care and riding of horses, she had persuaded her parents it was a good idea.[1] Graham and his friends were less enthusiastic but as they had nothing else planned had agreed to go along. As their father, a ship captain, was away at sea, their mother was taking the opportunity to visit her sick sister in Toowoomba. She was to drive back to Cairns and fly out that afternoon.

Kylie breathed deeply of the cool, moist, mountain air and sighed. "I'm really looking forward to the trail ride," she said. "I hope they have good horses."

At that, the tall girl beside her turned to look at her. "Excuse me, I didn't mean to eavesdrop," she said. "Are you going on a trail ride this afternoon?"

Kylie nodded. "Yes, with a group called 'Conroy's Equine Explorers'."

---

[1] Read *Kylie and Skip* by C. R. Cummings

The tall girl gasped and then shook her head in amazement. "Why, that must be with us! I'm Norah Conroy and I am to guide a group called the Kirks."

Kylie's mouth opened in delighted surprise. "Oh! That's me, Kylie Kirk. We go to the to .. er… to your place, straight after lunch."

"That's right," Norah replied, her face breaking into a lovely smile. She turned and said, "Mum, this is Kylie Kirk, one of the girls who will be on the trail ride this week."

"Well I never!" Mrs Conroy replied. She then made a fussy welcome. Kylie was thrilled and pleased. *I like Norah,* she thought. *She seems to be a lovely person.* She gestured to Margaret. "This is my friend Margaret Lake. She is coming with us too."

Margaret was warmly greeted, the greetings being interrupted by Graham coming to attention and bawling an order in his best 'sergeant major's ' voice.

"Companeeee... Atten... Shun!"

Kylie pointed. "That's my brother, Graham. He is coming too."

Norah nodded. "Oh good. Gee, he's good looking, isn't he."

The comment sent an instant chill through Kylie, and she glanced at Margaret, just in time to see an anxious look cross her face.

Oh dear! she thought. *I hope Norah isn't going to be competition for Margaret.*

Margaret had been in love with Graham for years, but he often just ignored her, or took her for granted. Of late he had taken to having hopeless 'crushes' on beautiful girls who did not even know he existed. And there were the rumours about that red-headed cadet in the front rank there, Barbara Brassington. Worse still there were stories about some blonde girl in Townsville who was reputed to be a nudist and a cheap tart.

The cadets had taken part in a 'commando' exercise the previous month against the cadets from Townsville and during it the blonde girl, Chloe some-one-or-other, and a friend, had been kidnapped. There were fantastic tales about how she and her friend had escaped and run naked along the beach. It was obvious that Graham had seen them naked and that made Kylie embarrassed and concerned, which in turn made her feel guilty and annoyed at herself for being a hypocrite because both she and Margaret had joined Graham in the bath as recently as two years before.

It was the knowledge that Margaret was a 'Plain Jane' with a slightly chubby figure that really bothered Kylie. She didn't mind Graham seeing Margaret nude (as long as they didn't do anything silly!) but she thought Margaret would find it hard to compete with sexy girls with good figures.

A surreptitious glance showed her that Norah, while tall and willowy, did not have big boobs. That was something, Kylie decided, well aware that her brother was starting to be attracted to girls with such attributes.

Still, Norah is very pretty. Oh I hope there's no ill-will, she thought.

Out on the platform there was a bustle of movement. One of the Cadet Under-Officers, a tall, thin Year 12 girl named Coralie Bates, had marched forward, sword in hand, to take over from Graham. He saluted, cane under his arm, then turned and marched towards them, to end up standing one pace to the right of the Right Marker. CUO Bates then about turned and ordered the other officers to fall in.

Swords swept up and down in graceful salutes, their blades shimmering in the watery sunlight. A very pretty dark-haired girl, CUO Sheila Sherry, marched out to replace Peter in front of 1 Platoon. CUO Grenfell, a chunky, handsome lad, took over from Stephen in front of the second platoon. Both sergeants marched around to the rear of their platoons. When all the officers were in position CUO Bates called the parade to the 'Slope Arms' and then ordered, 'Present Arms', and 'March on the Flag.'

As she did, a buxom old lady in period costume near Margaret made a proud aside to her friend, "That girl out the front is my granddaughter, Coralie."

Kylie glanced at her with interest and then joined the remainder of the assembled audience in standing straight when the Master of Ceremonies called on everyone to stand to attention for the marching on of the Australian flag. Marching music began and a Flag Party consisting of CUO White, (A Year 12 Kylie did not like because of rumours about his attitude to girls), and three sergeants, all resplendent with red sashes and white gloves and carrying rifles at the 'slope', came marching on from beyond the flower garden. They turned on the march, wheeled in between the two platoons and halted. After turning to face the front they also presented arms. The music changed to the first part of the National Anthem, the ANF salute. The cadets were then ordered to 'Order Arms' and 'Stand at Ease'.

The crowd then relaxed and the buzz of chatter resumed. Margaret smiled and said, "That looked good."

"Yes, they did it well," Mrs Kirk replied.

At that moment, a chubby captain in khaki ceremonial uniform, with Sam Browne belt and a row of medals, strolled by. Kylie knew him well. Captain Conkey, OC of the cadet unit, was also her Geography teacher. He stopped and began to chat to Mrs Kirk, expressing the hope that the rain would not spoil the parade.

Mrs Kirk nodded. "I hope not," she. "It seems to be clearing a little."

Kylie glanced up and noted that her mother was right. A couple of tiny patches of blue sky were showing through and a beam of watery sunlight began to play on the swords and polished brass and badges. These sparkled and the whole effect: of glitter, red sashes, white gloves and the red, white and blue of the flag made the whole scene look very pretty.

A portly gent in top hat and tails walked over to Capt Conkey. "Your chaps look splendid captain. Thank you very much for offering their services. They are really making this look excellent."

"Why thank you Mr Chairman," Capt Conkey replied. Then he looked up and turned. "Ah! Is that the train I hear?"

It was. A thrill of anticipation ran through the crowd. The crowd surged and jostled against the barriers. The officials and a couple of police were kept busy keeping them back. The shrill whistle of a steam locomotive echoed around the valley and Kylie heard someone, presumably a local, say that the train had just passed through the small tunnel under the main street. Then the sound of it huffing and chuffing came clearly to her, along with the ringing of a bell.

The ground began to vibrate, and Kylie hopped with excitement. The train sounded its whistle again, so loud and so close that she jumped with fright. Then it rumbled past five metres away, the old steam locomotive billowing spurts of white steam. The engine was painted a glossy black with red trimmings, and it had shiny brass bands around its boiler. Flags and bunting were fastened all over it and it looked a real picture as it slid slowly to a stop. A broad yellow ribbon had been strung across the tracks at the end of the platform near the truck with all the TV cameras on it and the locomotive came to rest with its front only a couple of metres from that.

The platform was so short that the locomotive and its tender took up most of the space. Only the end of the first passenger carriage was visible to Kylie. There followed a few minutes of bustle and confusion while officials and the police moved people back from the platform beside the train. During this the cadets were called to attention and then sloped arms.

Kylie saw the portly official in period costume sweep off his hat and bow and Capt Conkey stand to attention and salute. Into view came the Duke. He returned the salute, then shook hands with both men. Kylie almost danced with excitement. The Duke fulfilled all her expectations. He was tall and thin and much younger than she had expected. Apart from a moustache, which she wasn't fussed over, she thought he looked quite handsome. His ceremonial uniform was a sight to see; tailored dark blue cloth embroidered and crusted with gold braid and patterns. Gold and silver epaulets sparkled in the sun and medal ribbons made a bright showing on his chest. He wore a gold-lined, fore-and-aft bicorn hat bedecked with a billowing white plume. The hat came off as the Duke bowed gracefully to a lady.

The lady (The Shire Chairman's wife?) flushed with pleasure and simpered and giggled. There were more introductions. Into view came the State Governor, a refined looking gent in top hat and tails. For a moment Kylie felt slightly ashamed that she did not even know his name. Then a face appeared that she did recognise, the very aggressive and active red face and thinning fair hair of the State Premier. With the men were wives in long dresses with bustles and hoops and wearing large hats adorned with feathers and flowers. Then an army officer with much gold braid and a senior police officer in his dress uniform moved past. More officials and ladies edged forward.

The VIPs and officials made up such a crowd they filled the whole space and Kylie found herself being jostled between Margaret and Norah. A large woman with a high hat covered with flowers almost obscured her view. To Kylie there appeared to be a few moments of confusion and then Capt Conkey stepped forward and guided the Duke to a small dais placed beside the engine. Capt Conkey gestured with his open hand and the Duke stepped up onto the dais.

At a nod from Capt Conkey CUO Bates called the cadets to present arms. As the swords swept down in salute the municipal band struck up a tune which Kylie did not recognise but which her program told her was the British Anthem: 'God Save the King'. A choir from the Mount St Bernard Girls Boarding School sang this. After a pause the band changed to playing 'Advance Australia Fair'. The choir also sang this and many of the crowd joined in. Kylie knew the words well but felt embarrassed singing in public so only hummed and mumbled. Beside her Norah sang loudly and confidently, her voice very melodious and clear.

Again Capt Conkey appeared to take control when flustered officials dithered. He signalled to CUO Bates, who returned the cadets to the 'slope arms', then ordered arms. She marched across and halted a few paces in front of the Duke and saluted. The Duke returned the salute and then leaned forward to listen to what she was saying. Kylie saw the Duke nod and smile. He stepped down and walked across with CUO Bates to inspect the guard.

"Look at all those other 'Big Wigs'," the lady near Margaret said. "They don't like being left out of the limelight."

Kylie looked and noted the Premier and his wife both appearing a bit concerned and annoyed. The Governor and his lady just stood in dignified calm and watched. The first cadet the Duke inspected was Graham and it gave Kylie deep pleasure to see the Duke smile and nod with what appeared to be approval. He then made his way along the front rank with CUO Bates beside him and Capt Conkey following, obviously stage-whispering directions to both. Photographers, both TV and still, scuttled and jostled to get the best shots.

Margaret nudged Kylie and whispered, "I'm glad the sun has come out."

It had. Kylie hadn't noticed but now saw that at just the right moment a strong beam of sunlight had lit up the cadets and their parade. To Margaret's murmured approval the Duke saluted the flag as he passed in front of it and CUO Bates brought her sword to the 'Recover'. Capt Conkey, who was following as 'Host Officer' also saluted. The group moved on to inspect the second platoon. At the end of the front rank there was a moment of confusion, again apparently resolved by Capt Conkey's advice. CUO Bates saluted the Duke and Capt Conkey escorted him back to the dais. The cadets were stood 'at ease' and the Duke adjusted the microphone to make a speech.

The Duke began by pointing out quite humorously that he doubted if they had such fancy, new-fangled gadgets as a sound system back in

1910. Then he read an excerpt from the original opening speech and added a few comments of his own, including a particularly glowing commendation to the cadets for their drill and turn-out. That pleased Kylie and she warmed to the Duke, knowing that Graham and his friends would particularly appreciate the praise.

Then it got a bit more boring. The Governor said a few words of thanks to the local officials and also added a few kind words for the cadets, and for the detachment of Mounted Police. Kylie hadn't noticed them but now saw that five Queensland Mounted Police sat on their horses just beyond the truck with the TV cameras on it. There was a line of official cars parked there in the station yard, waiting to take the VIPs up to the hotel for lunch. Having never seen Mounted Police in their ceremonial uniforms Kylie looked at them with interest. They wore white sun helmets of the old 'Solar Topee' or 'Pith Helmet' type; dark blue tunics, white jodhpurs and highly polished black leather leggings, boots and belts. Across their chests they wore a single white cross strap which supported their sabres. The one with officer's 'pips' on his shoulder straps had his sword drawn but the other four had long lances tipped with glittering silver spear points. Blue and white pennons fluttered from the lances.

They certainly look the part, Kylie decided, noting that one particularly large sergeant sported a most impressive 'mutton-chop' moustache.

Then it was the turn of the politicians, and the speeches became tedious and went on and on. Kylie became bored and started to fidget. The clouds came back over and a fine, misty drizzle started. The crowd became restless and only brightened up when the Premier presented the cheque for track repairs to the chairman of the railway. Kylie joined in the polite applause but now she just wanted it to end. Worse still the cooler weather had caused her to feel an insistent need to go to the toilet.

"Oh hurry up!" she muttered as the politicians posed for the cameras.

The Duke was then moved back to centre stage by the shire mayor. He was led forward to the front of the engine, the other VIPs crowding behind and almost completely blocking Kylie's view. Here there was another short speech and the Duke was handed a pair of large scissors, with which he ceremoniously cut the ribbon, symbolically re-opening the railway.

Kylie hardly saw any of this but she joined in the applause and stood on tiptoe to try to see. There were cheers and then a sudden silence and a sort of whispering murmur, followed by gasps and then loud cries.

Margaret leaned forward to look. "What's going on? What's happening?" Being even shorter, she was having difficulty seeing.

It was Norah who answered. Being taller she was able to see.

"There's a man with a green mask over his face holding a gun to the Duke's head," she said.

Chapter 2

THE KELLY GANG

Kylie stretched on her tip-toes and got a glimpse of the Duke. She saw that Norah was right. A tall man with a green 'bandanna' tied over his lower face was holding the Duke by the arm and pointing a pistol at his head. Instant fears of seeing an assassin about to commit murder made Kylie's heart palpitate in apprehension.

The situation became a confused swirl for a few moments, and she glimpsed burly men in suits stepping in front of the Premier and Governor and pushing them down and out of sight, along with their wives. The senior police officer and the army aide-de-camp both elbowed their way forward through the crowd to shield the governor.

Then the man with the green mask and gun yelled out, his voice amplified electronically. "Stand still and be quiet! Nobody try anything stupid or His Nibs gets it!"

As he did, two more figures appeared from around the front of the locomotive. At the sight of them Kylie was at once amazed and puzzled. One glance at the cylindrical metal helmets with flat tops and a single, horizontal eye slit, and at the metal shoulder straps and breastplates and images of Australian History filled her mind.

"The Kelly Gang!" she muttered in amazement, along with most of the crowd.

She now saw that the first man also wore the metal (steel?) body armour. Both newcomers also carried guns but theirs were shotguns. Comments rose from all around, echoing her own thoughts: 'Is this part of the historical act?'; 'Is this a joke?'

The first of the 'Kelly Gang' now boomed at them, his electronic amplification screeching and squawking but carrying his message loud and clear for all that. "This is no prank! We mean business. These guns are real and they are loaded. Watch this."

One of the other Kellys pointed his shotgun up and pulled the trigger.

Bang!

There was the sound of breaking glass as the locomotive's headlight was smashed. A few pellets struck the steel of the engine and went hissing and whistling through the air. Kylie winced and felt an urge to run, along with most of the people around her. The crowd began to edge back and several people cried out in fright.

Next to her Coralie Bates' grandma gasped. "Oh! The police! Why don't the police do something?" she asked querulously.

Kylie had been wondering the same thing as she watched the Duke go very pale and look shocked. Then her eyes noted movement over at the Mounted Police detachment. They had been about to move forward but were now looking back over their shoulders and raising their hands. A momentary glimpse through a parting in the crowd showed another of the dull black helmets.

There is another Kelly there, she noted. *He has snuck up behind the police.*

Lances were dropped and the police put their hands up, the officer showing furious humiliation as he threw down his sword.

Margaret nudged her. "Who are these people?" she asked. "What do they want?"

Norah answered. "It's the Kellys," she began.

"I can see that, but who are they?" Margaret persisted. She was looking so pale that her freckles stood out like coco-pops.

"The Kelly family," Norah started to explain again. "That is Phil Kelly holding the Duke."

Before she could elaborate Phil Kelly stepped up onto the garden bed, still gripping the Duke and holding the gun to his head. "None of you coppers try to be heroes," he warned in a broad Australian accent. "If you shoot at me, then Duke what's-his-name here gets shot."

Now that the initial shock was over most of the crowd stood silently watching, waiting. But not all. A few began edging away. Near Kylie there was a flurry of movement and she saw the Premier and his wife being hustled through the crowd by several plain clothes police. One of them had a pistol in his hand and another had a small radio. The plain clothes police gestured furiously to the people blocking the platform to get out of their way. This resulted in a crush which pushed Kylie and Margaret hard up against the wall and CUO Bates' Grandma.

By the time the press eased apart and allowed her to see a bit, Phil Kelly had begun speaking. He was so angry and spoke so quickly that she did not get more than the gist of what he was saying. It was all about fair play, rights for the little people, justice, and official corruption by some local official.

As Phil Kelly spoke, Kylie saw that the TV crews were still filming and that he and his gang were making no attempt to stop them. *A political stunt,* she thought. *They are doing this for free publicity.*

Phil Kelly shook the hand holding the gun in the air and screamed, "We demand justice! Free our father, and our big brother, and you can get these people back!"

At that, he gestured to the Duke and the nearest VIPs and guests.

Mrs Conroy gasped and put her hand to her mouth. "Oh no! They are taking hostages," she cried.

Phil Kelly looked around, his gun now pointing at the crowd. "Where's that rat of a Premier? Come out, you cowardly bastard!"

At that, the Governor shook off the restraining hand of his army aide-de-camp and stepped into the clear space that had now developed near the dais. "Take me as a hostage, but let these other people go," he said, his voice very educated and calm.

"Why you? Who are you?" Phil Kelly snarled.

The Governor told him. Phil Kelly shook his head. "Never heard of you! We aren't interested in governors. We want that low, thieving rat of a Premier. Come out you sneaky dog!"

The crowd edged back even more, and Kylie found that many of the people who had been on her left had now slid off around the corner of the building and were gone. She was able to stand without being jostled, and she could see more clearly. What now bothered her were the cadets. They stood in their ranks, not moving but plainly nervous. She could see that Graham was watching every move with intense alertness. To Kylie he gave the impression of being tensed ready to spring.

Oh, I hope he doesn't do anything stupid trying to be a hero! she thought anxiously.

To her relief, Capt Conkey walked out in front of the cadets and stood near CUO Bates. He deliberately turned his back on the Kelly Gang and said, in a quiet voice that carried, "Cadets, stand fast. If there is any shooting, drop flat."

Phil Kelly waved his gun at him. "You shut up Fatso!" he yelled. "Any trouble and we will start shooting."

Capt Conkey turned to face him and drew himself up with great dignity. "These are only kids. Shoot me if you must but don't blacken your name by murdering children. And I'm not fat thank you, just a little tubby."

This last was said with such injured dignity that a murmur of laughter and approval swept round the crowd. Phil Kelly glared at Capt Conkey but then turned his head to look at one of his gang who had turned towards him. Only then did Kylie see the earpiece and lead going to Phil Kelly's left ear.

They have little radios and are talking to each other, she decided.

Somehow, she knew that the other Kelly had told him not to harm the cadets and she felt a bit easier.

The Governor also stepped closer and called loudly, "You have made your point. Now don't harm any innocent people and spoil your cause. Take yourselves away while you still can."

Kylie was filled with admiration. Margaret mirrored her thoughts by saying, "What a brave old man he is!"

Phil Kelly glared along the platform at the other VIPs and guests. "We want the Premier! He is the man we want. When he gives himself up, you can go."

The Governor shook his head. "He is gone already. You won't get him without bloodshed."

Kylie saw Phil Kelly's dark eyes blaze and she was sure he was grinding his teeth. He shouted, "If it's bloodshed you want, I'll bloody well give you some!"

He gestured with the pistol, aiming it at the shire mayor, who took a pace back but then stood his ground, trembling and gripping his wife's hand but still looking defiant.

At that moment, more Kellys came into view from along the railway line. They were riding horses and looked very menacing. All carried rifles which they held vertically by one hand. To Kylie their dark steel armour had a dull sheen to it which gave it a more sinister aspect than if it was really shiny. There were three more Kellys and she saw they were leading a string of horses.

She saw Phil Kelly's head shake and his lips move and she knew the gang were talking to each other on their radios.

They are having an argument, she sensed.

Phil Kelly again faced the crowd. "The Premier! We want the Premier!"

To Kylie's surprise the Duke now spoke, his voice a cultured English drawl. "It looks like you can't have him, old chap, so you'd better make do with me."

"Oh, we will OLD CHAP!" Phil Kelly snarled, his anger and frustration plain in his tone of voice. He shook the Duke, causing his ceremonial hat to fall off.

There was another minute of tense stand-off while the gang appeared to argue. Suddenly Phil Kelly swore and stepped down, dragging the Duke with him. The other two Kellys followed him, edging backwards, their shotguns still swivelling to threaten the crowd. By then the riders and horses had arrived near the front of the locomotive. For a few moments Kylie was unable to see what was happening, but then saw the Duke being pushed up onto a horse, his hands tied or handcuffed. He then sat there, his face quite calm.

Oh the poor man, Kylie thought, admiring his self-control and poise.

The other members of the gang began mounting. Just once there was a snarled, "Back off!" by one, who threatened a TV cameraman with his shotgun when he came too close. Then Kylie saw the Mounted Police dismount, their faces masks of angry shame. The Mounted Police moved off out of sight with their hands held high. Then the Kelly who had been guarding them climbed onto a police horse and began gathering up the reins of the others.

By then Phil Kelly was mounted. He turned to face the crowd. "Just remember, we want justice, and we want our dad and our brother set free. Then this Pommie bastard might be let go." He indicated the Duke, whose lip curled ever so slightly.

At that, Phil Kelly signalled and the gang wheeled their horses around and began moving off. Two armed Kellys went last, their shotguns still pointed menacingly at the crowd. The Kelly with the police horses was joined by two others who each took a set of reins. Then they were off. Kylie watched in an agony of suspense, fearing that even now there might be shooting and people hurt. But within a minute the whole gang had vanished from view along the old overgrown section of the railway leading south.

There was a moment's silence, then the crowd burst into excited chatter and began to mill around. The uniformed senior police officer now stepped forward. Hurrying to the dais he seized the microphone.

"Everyone please stay where they are for the moment. We will move the VIPs to safety." He gestured to the Governor, indicating he should move to the cars at once. The Governor nodded, but turned to Capt Conkey and held out his hand.

"Thank you for your support, Captain. Very bravely done. And congratulations to your cadets for the way they stood firm."

"Thank you, sir. Cadets! Companee... Atten... shun!" Capt Conkey bellowed.

The cadets came to attention and Capt Conkey ordered them to slope arms and then to present arms. He then saluted. The Governor took off his hat and bowed, then turned to take his wife's arm and the pair made a very dignified withdrawal through the crowd. Capt Conkey ordered the cadets back to the slope, then to the order while the senior police officer fumed and fussed, directing VIPs and police.

A couple of minutes of shouted orders and bustling about had all the other VIPs shepherded over past the garden bed to the line of waiting cars. Kylie glimpsed the Premier hurrying by, surrounded by bodyguards and staff. The now dismounted Mounted Police retrieved their lances and swords and were used to hold the crowd back. Plain clothes security men, looking deeply annoyed, seemed to appear in numbers.

As soon as the VIPs were gone the senior police officer told Capt Conkey to move the cadets away. Capt Conkey fell the officers out and handed back to Graham. He marched smartly out and saluted. As soon as Capt Conkey had stepped back Graham called the company to the slope arms, turned them to the left and gave the order 'By the right, Quick march!'

The cadet company marched off, to swelling applause from those of the crowd who remained. That pleased Kylie and she and Margaret joined in clapping enthusiastically. She felt very proud of her brother and his friends. She was also very conscious they would now be on TV that night as most of the TV crews were still at work, having been held back from following the VIPs.

As the cadets marched away along the sandy station yard to where they were to hand back their rifles, flag and so on, Kylie turned to Margaret and both began talking at once.

"Wasn't that exciting," she cried.

Margaret nodded. "I was so scared," she replied.

It had all been so interesting that Kylie realised she hadn't thought of being scared but she did not say so. She turned to Norah and asked, "Did you know that Kelly fellow?"

Norah shook her head, "Not really. I've seen him about, that's all."

"So what was that all about?" Kylie asked.

"Oh, some sort of legal trouble with their farm," Norah replied. "I don't know the details, but I think they lost their farm for some reason and the eldest brother was found shot dead. They claim it was murder, but others said it was suicide."

At that moment, Mrs Kirk interrupted. "Sorry children, but we must fly, or at least I must fly. I've got a plane to catch, so we must go and have lunch, then get you to the Conroy's."

Mrs Conroy shook her head. "I hope you weren't planning to buy lunch at the shop," she said, indicating the crowd which was now streaming uphill out of the station yard towards the main street.

Mrs Kirk shook her head. "No, we thought of that. We brought a picnic lunch and planned to go to the Wondecla Sports Ground to eat it."

Mrs Conroy nodded. "That's a good sensible idea. We live not far away so you can do that, or come and eat it at our place."

"I wouldn't like to impose," Mrs Kirk said.

"Nonsense!" Mrs Conroy replied. "The children will be with us tonight anyway so you may as well. We have to collect a couple of others, that's all."

"Thank you. As soon as the cadets have handed in their gear and been dismissed then," Mrs Kirk replied.

"You know how to find our property?" Mrs Conroy asked.

"Along the Flaggy Creek Road past Tepon isn't it?"

"That's right. You can't miss our place. The turn-off has a big sign," Mrs Conroy replied.

At that moment, a small, wiry girl of about twenty, dressed in tight jeans and silk blouse, stopped in front of Norah. She scowled, then said, "Well, look who it is! Beanpole. Are you still planning to race that broken down nag of yours next weekend, Conroy?"

Kylie saw Norah purse her lips and stiffen, then nod. "Of course I am," she replied quietly.

The wiry girl's lips curled into a mocking sneer. "Huh! Won't do you any good. You may as well give up now and save yourself the trouble."

"I'll be there," Norah replied coolly.

The wiry girl gave a harsh laugh and walked on. As she did, Margaret turned to Norah. "Who is that horrible girl?" she asked.

"Doris Peagreen," Norah answered. To Kylie she looked flushed and annoyed.

"What was that all about?" Margaret asked.

"She has a horse, called 'Silver Streak'. She is racing him in the main race at Mt Garnet next Saturday," Norah answered.

"Are you riding against her?" Margaret queried.

Norah nodded. "Yes, I am, a horse named 'Romantic Ruby'."

Knowing that the horse ride they were to do would be at the Mt Garnet races on that day caused Kylie to say, "Good. Then we will be there to see you win."

"I hope so," Norah replied. "We really need the prize money."

Mrs Conroy patted Norah's arm and said, "You will win dear, now it is time we went."

After a few more comments Mrs Conroy and Norah hurried away. Kylie followed her mother along past the still hissing steam locomotive to where the cadets were now lined up to return issues. Because of the excitement this was a bit noisier and more disorganised than usual but was all done within fifteen minutes. By then Kylie was needing to go to the toilet quite urgently. Luckily several portable toilets had been positioned for the ceremony, so she was able to nip away and deal with this. By the time she returned she found the station yard all but deserted except for a few cadets, a few railway people, and some police busy photographing the locomotive's broken headlight, and a few interested spectators.

Kylie found her mother telling Capt Conkey what a good job he and the cadets had done, and how brave she thought he was. Graham, Peter, Stephen, and Roger were standing to one side with Margaret.

As soon as Kylie returned, Mrs Kirk said, "Right, let's move! Back to the cars."

Chapter 3

THE CONROYS

Except it wasn't as simple as that.

As the group walked up the hill away from the railway station, they found the streets still crowded with people and a jam of motor vehicles. The buzz of gossip was all about the Kelly Gang and their daring raid, and speculation about where they had gone and whether they would get away. The few police were in a bad mood and were as busy trying to locate their humiliators as they were attempting to sort out the confusion.

As the group reached the main street a police car went past heading south with its siren wailing. Stephen jeered and called, "Bit bloody late!"

Peter watched the car as it vanished over the rise. "I wonder if they have found them," he said.

Graham shook his head. "I'll be they haven't," he replied. "They are on horses. They won't be riding along roads where police cars can chase them. They'll be off in the bush somewhere."

"They can't be far away though," Margaret offered.

Peter looked at his watch. "Been more than twenty minutes now, nearer half an hour. They could be five or six kilometres away."

"Can horses travel that fast?" Roger queried.

Kylie could answer that one. "Yes, they can. They can easily trot or canter at about ten kilometres per hour."

"Yes, but how long can the keep that up?" Peter asked.

Kylie wasn't sure. She could only shrug. The only guide they had was that horse races like the Melbourne Cup, run over a couple of kilometres, winded the horses considerably.

Graham was in a light-hearted and facetious mood. "They can't get all that far," he said. "Poor Old Ned Kelly must be so old he will need a rest."

Peter chuckled. "I thought he was dead," he added with a grin.

"He is," Stephen said. "He was hung; no hanged."

"When was that?" Margaret asked.

Stephen shrugged and shook his head. "Not sure. Back in the Gold Rushes of the Nineteenth Century sometime."

"Anyway, it wasn't Ned Kelly," Kylie said. "His name was Phil Kelly."

Peter grinned again. "How do you know? I didn't know you were on such close terms with a bushranger," he teased.

Kylie snorted and stuck her nose in the air. "Oh poo to you! I don't know him. Norah Conroy told me."

"Who's Norah Conroy when she's at home?" Graham asked.

"She is the girl who is to be our guide on the trail ride," Kylie explained. "She was down at the railway station."

She was about to add that she was sure they would like her when that niggling worry about them possibly liking her too much crossed her mind, causing her to glance at Margaret.

The group scurried across the main street and made their way up a side street to where the cars were parked. The topic of the Kelly Gang was temporarily forgotten while they sorted out who was to sit in which car. In the end Graham, Kylie and Margaret went in the back of Mrs Kirk's car, with Roger in the front, while Stephen and Peter went with Peter's mother. Kylie knew that Margaret had wanted to sit next to Graham, but he had contrived to sit next to her instead, so Margaret was on her other side.

Oh silly boy! she thought. *When will he realise that Margaret is the girl for him?*

They set off, turning left in the main street and heading south. As they drove along Kylie looked out, partly admiring the quaint old architecture of the town, and partly wondering if the Kelly Gang were even now riding up one of the tree-covered hills she could see. The town was certainly worth a look, being a collection of 19th and early 20th Century buildings mixed with a few newer structures and all scattered over the forested slopes among the trees. It still had that indefinable air of being 'historical', of belonging to that great age of the 'Pioneers' and the gold rushes (or tin in this case).

The road went down across a small valley, then up over a rise and from there on the houses thinned out until there were none, just dry savannah woodland. After curving down to the right the road passed between a hill and the end of a rough embankment. A police car was parked there and an armed policeman in a bullet proof vest was standing watching. He signalled them to a stop and looked into the car. Only after checking the names and identity of everyone in the car did he wave them on. As he did, Kylie noted a second armed policeman standing in the edge of the scrub.

Graham pointed up. "That is where the old railway used to run. There was a bridge over the road here."

Roger twisted in his seat to look. "Then those bushrangers might have ridden this way," he suggested. "They rode south along the railway."

Mrs Kirk shook her head irritably. "Stop talking about the bushrangers. If they did come this way then it might not be safe for you to go on this horse ride."

At that, Graham snorted. "Oh fair go Mum! We aren't likely to run into them. It's a big country. Even if we saw them, they would hide."

Mrs Kirk sighed. "Oh I don't know. You children have a disconcerting knack of getting involved in whatever trouble is around."

The thought of the riding holiday being cancelled dismayed Kylie. She spoke up, trying to sound light-hearted, "Oh Mum, that is only the boys. This time we girls are here. We will make sure they behave."

"I'm not worried about their behaviour," Mrs Kirk replied. "It's what those terrorists might do."

"Terrorists?" Kylie echoed, further dismayed by the term.

Mrs Kirk nodded and looked grim. "Yes. That was some sort of political stunt to gain publicity, and as it involves some Irishmen and a British lord then it could well be a terrorist action."

"Why do you say that, Mum?" Kylie asked, now genuinely worried.

"Oh Kylie! I wish you would watch the news a bit more. The Irish have been fighting with the English, or, I should say the British, for hundreds of years."

"But he sounded Australian to me," Kylie replied, puzzled and feeling quite young and ignorant.

"He might be, but the name Kelly is Irish, and I don't doubt there will be a family attitude," Mrs Kirk replied.

By this time they had driven through the small settlement of Wondecla, passing the sports ground where they had planned to have lunch. Now they sped on, crossing the railway line and going on south. After a few minutes they arrived at a road junction and turned right along the Flaggy Creek Road. This was a good bitumen road to begin with and they made good time. The road curved left around the Tepon airstrip and sports area. Here the houses ended and there was only dry savannah bush on both sides of the road.

After crossing the concrete bridge over Flaggy Creek the road became gravel. A few minutes later they reached the turn-off to the Conroy's, clearly marked with a sign. A few minutes of driving along a dirt side road brought them to the homestead. As they got closer Kylie studied the cluster of buildings and horse yards and decided she liked the place. It was snuggled down near the trees lining a watercourse and all looked clean and in good repair. There was a large paddock off to the right with a dozen horses grazing in it, then a set of yards with more horses. Beyond the yards were stables and store sheds and some sort of bunkhouse. The actual homestead building was at the end of the road with a circular drive sweeping around a large shady tree.

As the car approached, dogs began to appear, barking and running forward. The sight of these made Kylie quite anxious but as the car stopped the largest, a big blue heeler cattle dog, rushed over and stuck his nose in at the window and snuffled and licked in a friendly way. Even so the dogs were so noisy and active that none of them felt like opening a door.

Norah appeared from the house and seized one dog by its collar. "It's alright," she called. "They will lick you to death before they bite. Down Spotty! Down Peg!"

Norah had changed out of her period costume and now wore a shirt, jeans and riding boots and that concerned Kylie slightly as these showed off her slim figure to perfection. That she had cause for concern was immediately apparent to her as she watched Graham's eyes light up with appreciation and interest as he was introduced.

The dogs were shooed away. Everyone climbed out of the cars and introductions began. Mrs Conroy, also changed back to shirt and jeans, came out to join them. It was instantly apparent to Kylie that both Peter and Stephen were impressed by Norah, and both began clumsy attempts to show off. Even Roger tried to be nice to her. Their interest was so obvious that Kylie saw Norah blush, the blood mottling her lovely, tanned complexion.

Oh, she is pretty. I hope Graham doesn't hurt Margaret, she thought.

That got her wondering how old Norah was. *Seventeen or eighteen,* she decided, hoping that the age difference might prevent any romantic notions by Graham. *And Peter,* she added as a wistful afterthought.

Introductions over Peter's mother cautioned Peter to be careful and then took her leave. As she drove away, they began unloading gear. While they were doing this the sound of an approaching vehicle came to them. They turned to look and a white police 4WD came into view. The sight of it sent Kylie's heart rate up with anxiety.

Oh no! Not more trouble, she thought.

The vehicle braked to a standstill and Kylie saw it had two policemen in it. A large, radio antennae quivered and wobbled from an attachment on the front fender of the vehicle. A young constable in his twenties climbed out, his eyes quickly scanning the group. Kylie noted that his lower legs were encased in shiny black leather leggings and that he wore a pistol on his right hip.

Mrs Conroy spoke. "Why, Constable Lonergan, what brings you here?"

"Sorry to bother you Mrs Conroy, but there was an incident in town a while ago and I have been sent to check on your horses," Constable Lonergan replied.

"We know. We were there," Mrs Conroy said. "We have just returned."

Constable Lonergan eyed the cadets in their uniforms and then quickly glanced at Kylie and Margaret. He did this so swiftly that Kylie felt quite miffed. Then she was amused when he almost bowed as he spoke to Norah. "Hello Miss Norah. How are you?"

"Fine thank you, Constable," Norah replied, blushing even more.

There's a story here, Kylie mused, watching the by-play of eyes.

Constable Lonergan looked at the boys and said, "You boys were with the cadets at the railway station?"

Graham nodded and answered. "Yes. We saw everything."

Constable Lonergan nodded. Mrs Conroy said, "You were with the Mounted Police weren't you Frank?"

Kylie saw anger and embarrassment mottle the young policeman's face as he nodded. "Yes," he said shortly. "Now, have you checked your horses to see if any are missing?"

Mrs Conroy looked anxious. "No, we will do it now. Come with me Frank. Norah, would you find Dingo and Old Neville please and ask them to join us?" she replied. She turned to Mrs Kirk and said, "We won't be long. Please, make yourselves at home on the veranda."

While Mrs Conroy led Constable Lonergan away and Norah vanished towards the stables the others lugged their gear across the short stretch of lawn to the veranda and seated themselves on the chairs and benches there. Mrs Kirk called Kylie to help with the picnic lunches and they distributed sandwiches and cold cordial and sat down to wait. As they ate Kylie saw Norah re-appear with an old man and a youth of about her own age. The youth was clearly an Aboriginal and she realised he must be the 'Dingo' Norah had been asked to find. They walked off towards the horse yards.

Ten minutes later Mrs Conroy, Norah, Constable Lonergan, and the Aboriginal youth came walking back. They were met by the other policeman, who had been talking on the radio. The whole group walked over to join those on the veranda.

The other policeman from the 4WD said to Constable Lonergan, "They have found what they think are the horses the gang used, or some of them, over at the Alma Mine."

"Where's that?" Constable Lonergan asked.

"On the south side of St Patricks Hill. The boss thinks they have switched to vehicles and gone east across the Hugh Nelson Range towards Upper Barron. He wants us there pronto, to see if we can identify the horses."

Mrs Kirk asked, "So they are not coming this way?"

The other policeman shook his head. "We don't think so. We think they are going east. That is where the Kelly's farm was."

"That's a relief. Maybe we can allow these children to go ahead with their ride. What do you think, Mrs Conroy? Is it safe?" Mrs Kirk asked.

She directed this as much at Constable Lonergan as at Mrs Conroy, and it was he who answered first. "I should think so. I can't imagine what interest the Kellies would have in a bunch of kids, even if they did bump into them."

As he said this Kylie couldn't help noticing that his eyes met Norah's and that she blushed. Mrs Conroy now added, "I think they will be safe enough. They are going the other way and they will be a big enough group, especially with Dingo with them."

At that, the Aboriginal youth, who had been standing fidgeting at the back, gave a big grin and said, "Too bloody right! I'll look after them, Mrs Conroy. No bloody bushrangers are going to bother us."

Once again Kylie noted the byplay of eyes and was almost sure that Dingo had met Norah's eyes and she was sure that made her blush again.

Dingo must like Norah too, she decided. Now she studied the youth more carefully. *Not bad looking,* she decided, *but not a full-blood Aborigine.* She tried to decide what the other racial mix might be, settling for part European and part Asian. *Chinese or something like that?*

Mrs Conroy said to the two policemen, "Would you boys like a cold drink before you go?"

Kylie was sure the other constable was annoyed at being called a boy, but Constable Lonergan smiled and said, "We'd love one, but we have to gulp it down and get moving thanks."

Once again there was that glance at Norah, confirming Kylie's earlier supposition.

Mrs Kirk now said, "Here, we have cold cordial. Have a cup." She quickly poured the two policemen drinks and they drank them gratefully.

Constable Lonergan licked his lips and placed the cup down. "Thanks. See you then. Take care."

As he said this, his eyes again flicked to meet Norah's and Kylie wondered if she had also seen a tightening around Dingo's eyes indicating jealousy, or resentment. Dingo's look certainly turned to a cold stare when Constable Lonergan added, "You stay out of trouble, Dingo, eh?"

The two policemen then walked to their vehicle and got in. As they drove off Stephen asked Norah, "Is he the local copper?"

Norah shook her head and blushed. "No. He's in the Stock Squad. We had a couple of horses stolen a few months back and he was sent to try to find them."

At that, Kylie asked, "Did you get them back?"

Norah shook her head. Stephen said, "The Kelly Gang have got them, obviously."

"Oh piffle!" Mrs Kirk snorted. "Now stop talking about them." She then re-opened the question of whether the expedition should go ahead. To Kylie's relief, Mrs Conroy was of the opinion that it should. Mrs Kirk obviously was still uneasy about it but finally consented and then said, "Well, I had better go. I've got a two-hour drive."

Graham then asked, "Mum, can you get Alex to tape the news on Channel Nine tonight please?"

"Yes, I'll do that."

At that, Stephen said, "Mrs Conroy, can I use the phone to ring my Mum? She will freak out when she hears about today."

"Get her to tape the Channel Seven news," Graham added.

"All you children had better phone your parents," Mrs Conroy said.

Roger looked glum and was obviously less than keen but Mrs Kirk and Mrs Conroy both insisted. They finally did so, with the urging by Graham for them to get their parents to use their HDDs to record the other two TV channels so that they could watch the incident at the railway station after they got back from their expedition.

The phone calls took half an hour and Mrs Kirk and Mrs Conroy both got called in to reassure anxious parents that the children had been in no danger and were safe. To Kylie's relief, everyone was still allowed to go on the expedition.

Mrs Kirk then packed up the picnic basket and took her leave, giving Kylie a hug and, to Graham's embarrassment, kissing him too. With a chorus of 'goodbyes' and 'take cares' she drove off.

As the dust settled, Mrs Conroy stood up and said, "Well, you children had better get organised if you are going to get any distance today. You have the dance at the Mt Garnet racecourse on Saturday night and I don't want you pushing the horses too hard to get there on time."

And that got Kylie up and moving. As part of the holiday 'package' they were offered a trail ride with quiet horses to see old mining areas, a genuine 'Ghost Town', a visit to a cattle station, and camping under the stars. As an added bonus they were also being offered attendance at the May Weekend Picnic Race meeting and the dance that followed it. The idea of that dance had grown in Kylie's imagination, with various romantic possibilities to go with it, until it had become quite as important as the horse riding.

That it was important to others was also made apparent when Norah replied. "We can go slow Mum. It doesn't matter if we miss the dance."

Mrs Conroy made a face and said, "I think young Colin Costello might be a bit disappointed if you aren't there."

Once again Kylie saw Norah blush and she was pleased. She thought, *If there is a young man waiting for Norah in Mt Garnet there is much less likelihood of Graham falling for her and thereby hurting Margaret.*

Norah's mother then added, "Besides, you are down to ride in the two-kilometre race at 4 p.m. that day, so you need to be there well before then to get organised."

Norah made a bit of a face at that but nodded. "If you think I should," she replied.

"Of course I do! You have every chance of winning this year. Romantic Ruby is in top condition. You should romp it in," Mrs Conroy replied.

"Yes Mum," Norah answered, but she did not sound very happy about it to Kylie.

The group were all issued with plastic safety helmets and bridles, then led across the dusty yard to the horse yards by a surly Dingo. When they reached the railings, he climbed up and then gestured to the horses standing there.

"There they are. Best mob of horses in the district."

"Can we take our pick?" Margaret asked, her eyes dancing with pleasure at the sight.

Mrs Conroy shook her head. "Sorry, no. We took on board what your mother said about your experience, and we have allocated horses to each one on that basis."

Peter chuckled and said, "In that case I should have a rocking horse."

Roger and Stephen both laughed, and Roger replied, "I couldn't even ride one of them. I reckon one of those bronze horses you see as a monument in a park would be about my type."

"Which one is mine?" Kylie asked, her gaze running over the small herd with intelligent interest.

Norah pointed to a lovely brown mare with a white blaze on her nose. "That one, the chestnut mare. Her name is 'Blazer'."

"Oh good!" said Kylie, and she felt her heart leap.

Instinctively she liked the mare, and she could hardly wait to meet her and to start riding.

Chapter 4

ON THE TRAIL

In all there were 12 horses ready for the ride. Eight of these were saddle horses to be ridden by the group. Two were spare horses and the other two were pack horses to carry the camping gear and food. After the boys had changed out of their cadet uniforms the group were given bridles and then taken by Old Neville into the yard to meet their horses and to start getting them ready. For Kylie and Margaret this was easy. Both had been properly trained to look after horses and to prepare them for riding. Not so in the case of the boys.

Dingo took them aside and demonstrated how to slip on the bridle and fasten it. They then did this to their allocated horse, after first being introduced to it. Kylie watched all this with some amusement, not to mention satisfaction. It wasn't often she could demonstrate superior skill to her brother! She had immediately made friends with 'Blazer', rubbing and patting the mare's nose and neck. To her it seemed as though the liking was mutual as the mare seemed to give her a kindly look and stood quite calmly while she was patted and then while she slipped the bridle over her ears.

"Good girl!" Kylie whispered to her as she did up the buckle. Then she turned and met Margaret's eye. Margaret was grinning with pleasure after quickly fastening the bridle on her own horse, a brown mare named 'Socks', presumably because she had white fetlocks. As she did, this another horse came over and nuzzled at her in a friendly way. "What is her name?" she asked.

"His name. He is called 'Pesky'," Norah replied. Then she went red. "Though he isn't anymore," she added, "Not since he was.. er... doctored."

Kylie mentally winced at the idea of cutting off a stallion's testicles and blushed to match Norah's delicate blush. To change the topic she nodded to Norah's glossy black stallion and asked, "What's his name?"

Norah fondly stroked the stallion's nose and said, "This is 'Whiplash'. He's my favourite."

"Is he fast?"

"Yes, but not as fast as my mare 'Romantic Ruby'," Norah replied, pointing to a horse out in a paddock across the entrance road. She added, "Mum will be taking Ruby to Mt Garnet by horse float, and I will meet her there."

Kylie indicated Romantic Ruby and said, "This is the horse that horrible girl talked about?"

"Doris Peagreen? Yes. She has been trying to beat me for years and has got quite nasty about it," Norah replied.

Margaret admired 'Romantic Ruby'. "She looks a beauty," she commented. Kylie studied the distant horse and had to agree. Even from a hundred metres away the horse looked a champion.

Norah nodded and replied proudly, "She is."

"But you aren't keen on this race?" Kylie ventured to ask.

Norah made a face and nodded. "Not really. There has been some unpleasant rivalry in the past and I am only doing it because Mum needs the prize money to help clear our debts here."

"Rivalry? With that Doris girl?" Kylie hinted, not wanting to probe into the Conroy family's financial situation.

"I'd rather not talk about it," Norah replied. "Let's see how you girls can ride."

The girls led their horses out of the yard and across to a rail fence near the stables. On this were placed saddles, blankets and saddle bags. The girls proceeded to saddle their horses while the boys tried to bridle theirs. By the time the boys came walking towards them, leading their horses, this task was almost completed.

By now Kylie was bubbling with excitement. She loved the feel and the smell of the horses and the smell of dubbin and leather, and even of fresh manure, all added to her pleasure. She and Margaret had been taking riding lessons at a property near Mareeba for three years and she felt quite confident.

But obviously the boys didn't. Roger was shown by Old Neville how to swing the saddle onto his horse and asked, "Is it quiet?"

"She. She's a mare," Mrs Conroy replied. "Of course she is. They are all as tame as could be. It will be just like riding a wooden horse on a roundabout."

Roger wrinkled his nose and looked sceptical. "A big, smelly, wooden horse that moves," he said.

Kylie could see that Graham was not looking happy either. His horse was also a mare, a speckled grey one named 'Sugar'. As he stepped cautiously away from the snuffling horse while trying to tighten the girth strap he said, "I don't know about this. I have a feeling that I prefer the infantry to the cavalry."

Peter grinned. "A second-rate ride is better than a first-rate walk," he suggested, but he was also obviously quite unsure and anxious.

Kylie was enjoying the scene by this, and she noted that Dingo was watching with what appeared to be sardonic amusement. "Can we mount?" she asked Mrs Conroy.

Mrs Conroy nodded. "By all means, but no galloping. I want to see how each of you rides before you set off."

Lifting herself lightly into the saddle Kylie felt her spirits lift even more and she could only smile with happiness. Blazer stood quite still until she had her right foot settled in the stirrup, then the mare turned her head to look at her. Kylie smiled even more and reached forward to pat the mare's neck. "What a good horse!" she said, already liking her.

Margaret also mounted. The two girls then dismounted and spent a few minutes adjusting the length of their stirrup leathers. That done they remounted and urged their horses into motion, walking them clear of the group. For a minute or so Kylie just got the feel of Blazer but instinctively she felt the horse and her were going to be a good team. Emboldened, she tapped her heels on the mare's flanks and Blazer broke into a gentle trot. Kylie guided her off along the entrance road. Margaret followed. It had always secretly peeved Kylie that Margaret was a better rider, could even ride bare-back and still look as though she was stuck on by glue, and she saw that this was still the case. Margaret was following close behind her, busy laughing and talking to Socks who seemed to be snuffling and tossing her head in agreement.

"Oh this is going to be fun!" Kylie cried as she urged Blazer into a steady canter.

The girls only rode as far as the front gate. Here they reined in and stood to pat their horses and to exclaim how good they were. They were joined by Norah. Norah took them to the gate into the big open paddock and opened it. She then led them through, closing the gate after her, all without dismounting, for it was a sensible gate and she was a good rider on a good horse.

The next ten minutes were pure pleasure for Kylie. Norah had them walk, trot, canter and then, after she was sure they knew what they were doing, allowed them a short gallop. The girls then rode around in a circle, Margaret singing and whooping with the sheer delight of it. There were jumps in the paddock but, even though she was tempted to ask, Kylie refrained.

When they came to a halt in front of her Norah looked at them with approval. "You two are good, much better than the group we had last week. My, you stick on well Margaret. You just seem to balance there."

Margaret beamed at the praise. "I told you we had been properly trained. Mrs Lucas was very strict with us."

"Mrs Lucas?"

"At 'Corwa'. It's beside the Barron River near Venture Creek," Margaret explained. "We go there on weekends."

"Oh I think I know her. Does she do show jumping and equitation?" Norah asked.

"Yes, she does. Oh, look at the boys!" Margaret replied, breaking off to point and gurgle with laughter.

Kylie looked and also giggled. On the other side of the fence the boys had at last managed to saddle their horses and were now trying to mount. Roger had managed to get half up and was lying across the saddle, his right leg waggling in the air. Stephen made an even more comical spectacle. He had managed to get his left foot into the stirrup but then, every time he tried to hoist himself into the saddle, the horse sidled away and he had to hop after it, all the while clinging to mane and saddle and trying to get the spring to get up.

Norah smiled and said, "That's 'Darby'. He's been like that ever since he lost his stones. Maybe we had better get that boy another horse."

Kylie had several malicious thoughts which she later felt bad about: that it was nice to see Stephen being made a fool of as he so often put people down with his tongue; that he might be nicer if he lost his 'stones'.

Peter was first to settle in the saddle. Roger finally got his leg over but had trouble finding the stirrup. Graham managed to get into the saddle but looked very uneasy and gripped the front of the saddle with both hands. At last Stephen managed to spring up and get himself seated. At that, Dingo gave a sarcastic whoop and clapped. He had been sitting on his horse, a big yellow stallion named 'Jupiter', watching with obvious amusement. There was then another delay of several minutes while Old Neville went from horse to horse, adjusting the stirrups.

When that was done Mrs Conroy opened another gate and Dingo led the boys into the large paddock. For fifteen minutes they were required to walk around in single file, the girls joining the end of the line. This was a bit frustrating to Kylie but she could see that the boys needed at least some familiarisation. Next Norah demonstrated how to trot. The teenagers were then required to trot the length of the paddock to where Norah waited.

This almost resulted in several accidents. Stephen kicked back too vigorously and Darby resented that, bucking instead. Stephen was almost flung off. He clung on, half out of the saddle, his glasses all awry. However the horse settled, and he was able to claw his way back upright. He looked deeply angry, and for a moment Kylie feared he was going to lash at the horse but he just sat there and told Peter to try.

Peter managed it alright. Roger was then told to go, and Kylie had to smile when Margaret whispered, "He looks like a bag of potatoes bouncing around."

Then it was Graham's turn and Kylie was dismayed when Graham got his horse to trot, only to have it break into a canter when he urged it on. Then it swerved and Graham suddenly went over the side. For a fearful moment Kylie feared his boot would catch in the stirrup, but then she saw him rolling on the ground. The horse came to a stop and stood looking back at him as though wondering what had gone wrong.

To Kylie's relief, Graham stood up and dusted himself. He looked embarrassed and gave a sheepish grin before walking over to the waiting horse. After a moment's hesitation he mounted and again got the horse moving, but this time clung on like a limpet with legs, knees and hands. Kylie could tell he was not really controlling the horse at all. She felt sorry for her brother, but also experienced again the satisfaction at being better at something than him.

The girls all trotted over to join the boys, arriving in a laughing, chattering group. Norah then offered them all some advice. In particular she commented to Graham and Roger not to be scared of the horses. "Show them you are the boss," she said. "If you are afraid, they can tell and they will take charge. Now, let's ride back to the yard and get the gear loaded on."

The group rode slowly back to the horse yard and dismounted. Norah then insisted they all pat their horses and lead them over to a horse trough for a drink. "You have to look after them and let them know you care if you want them to give their best," she explained.

This had all been part of Kylie's training and she was happy to do so. Already she felt at home on Blazer and was sure they would get on well together. She happily chatted to the horse when she put her muzzle down to drink. All the while Kylie patted, stroked and talked, the horse twitching her ears and meeting her eye as though she was trying to answer.

"Oh, good horse!" Kylie muttered, giving her neck a big hug. Having done this, she noticed that Mrs Conroy was watching and she blushed.

Mrs Conroy smiled and nodded. "That's right dearie. That is the way to build trust and to get the best out of a horse. You are doing very well."

Dingo gave a grunt. "Huh! Dunno about these boys though," he muttered. "Maybe we need to get out the rocking horses after all."

The horses having been watered and relaxed, the group was shown how to fasten on saddle bags and a roll of bedding, this latter strapped tightly at the back of the saddle. While they did this Dingo saddled the two pack horses and, helped by Norah and Old Neville, loaded on the leather and canvas valises of camping gear and food. This all took nearly half an hour and by then it was close to 2pm. Mr Conroy looked at her watch and said, "You children had better get moving. You are a couple of hours behind schedule and you want to be at Dry River before dark."

There were a few more minutes of preparation. Kylie quickly visited the toilet, knowing she would have to squat in the bush for the next few days. They all quaffed a cup of cold fruit juice and then Mrs Conroy urged them into the saddle. With much waving and wishing of good luck they set out, Norah leading.

As they rode down a side track between the house and the bunk house, Kylie turned and looked back and was thrilled. Peter was obviously enjoying it too.

"Like an expedition of explorers back in the old days," he said.

"Bloody Burke and Wills," Graham added, still looking anxious.

"I hope we do better than them!" Roger cried. "Anyway, they weren't in this part of the world, were they?"

Kylie hadn't paid that much attention in History but Graham had. "No," he replied. "Kennedy was the first explorer through here."

"And look what happened to him," Dingo said.

At that, Kylie turned sharply to glance at Dingo, remembering that Edmund Kennedy had been speared by the Aborigines. *I wonder what he meant by that?* she pondered, unsure if Dingo thought it a good thing that a white explorer had been speared to death. *No,* she decided. *It was too long ago, a hundred and fifty years or more.*

When she thought about it the 19th Century explorations seemed an impossibly long time ago, but then she looked along the line of riders, dressed and equipped in almost the same way, and had an amazing feeling of immediacy. This was added to when thoughts of the Kelly Gang flitted across her mind.

This is silly, she thought. *This is the 21st Century! We are exploring Space. The Kelly Gang were back in the Gold Rushes a hundred and fifty years ago.*

But it was nice to be a little bit romantic and to imagine they really were explorers setting off into the unknown. She was sure that was what Graham would be thinking.

Once past the house they rode in single file, following a dirt vehicle track down towards the streamline. Norah led, followed by Graham, Margaret, Roger, and Stephen, then Peter, Kylie and Dingo. He led the two pack horses and the spare saddle horses. To Kylie it all looked very exciting, and she decided it really did look like one of the old time exploring parties setting out.

Apart from the white safety helmets, she added.

The track led them down through a belt of trees, She-Oaks mostly, which whispered in the breeze. There was an almost dry riverbed, more sand than stones and easily crossed. Then they went up the other bank, through another belt of trees and out onto a gently rising slope covered with savannah woodland. The grass here was still partly green from recent rain but the overall impression to Kylie was of dry bush: the black trunks of the ironbarks and occasional termite nests and grass trees.

The group moved at a steady walk. Kylie noted that both Graham and Peter had maps in their hands and that made her smile. She knew that her brother had a passion for knowing exactly where he was, and for accurate navigation. As they were following a marked horse-riding trail, and being led by a guide who knew the way, she found this amusing.

"Never mind," she told herself. "We are on the trail at last."

Chapter 5

FIRST NIGHT

For the first hour the group rode slowly but steadily. Norah kept dropping back to check on how each person was going. After riding up a long, gentle slope through open bush they halted for fifteen minutes to adjust all the things that now required fixing. Already Kylie was feeling the strain on muscles unaccustomed to riding and she knew that some of the others, even less experienced than her, must also be feeling the beginnings of soreness.

Both Graham and Stephen grumbled a bit and rubbed their calf muscles and backs and Graham again muttered about preferring the infantry. That peeved Kylie as she both enjoyed riding and loved horses. She frowned and said, “Stop talking army for a minute, can’t you? This is a holiday.”

Graham’s resulting scowl told her that her comment had been both accurate and resented. She at once regretted it but got no chance to make it up. After adjusting bridles and saddles they all mounted again and continued on.

What did please Kylie was the good temper and willingness of the horses. They were obviously very placid and experienced animals, trained to accept indifferent and even bad riders. The horses loped along at a steady walk which made it easy for her to relax and look around. To her it all looked like more bush, but she did note a few larger hills showing through the treetops in the distance.

These hills became more and more pronounced as they got closer to them. After riding for a few more kilometres they came to a graded dirt road which led northwest between two of the hills. She knew it was that direction as the afternoon sun was already low and shining strongly in under the tiny brim of her helmet onto the left side of her face.

They passed the first signs of old mines: a few rough heaps of weathered earth and rocks, mostly overgrown with grass, and a couple of bare areas littered with a few rusty sheets of corrugated iron and rotting timber posts. She looked at these with some curiosity, very aware of the intense interest the boys were showing in them. It made her feel better to see Graham studying his map and pointing at the ruins, his face again animated with interest.

After a while they came out on a much wider and better maintained road. This was graded gravel with a few marker posts at bends.

Peter showed Kylie where they were on the map. "The Silver Valley Road," he explained.

They halted to have a drink and to allow the horses to have a short spell. Norah walked along, checking each horse and the fit of its saddle. "It is nearly five," she said. "We will stop in about half an hour to camp."

"Oh, I hope so," Roger moaned. "I'm starting to get a bit sore."

Norah smiled. "You will for a day or two, but you will get used to it. That's why we don't want to push it too much on the first day."

With a few groans about growing stiffness they remounted and rode on. Norah insisted they keep well over on the right and that they keep in single file. "This is a public road and some of the locals drive very fast," she explained.

No sooner had she said this than a vehicle appeared from ahead of them. It barely slowed as it raced past, leaving them enveloped in dust. That scared Kylie as she could picture what might happen if another vehicle came along behind them, travelling too fast in the dust.

The road curved to the right around the side of a hill, with an ever-steepening gully on their left. Black rocks showed all along the sides and bed of the gully and the summits of the hills beyond it were very stony. In places there were quite extensive sheets of exposed rock. Clumps of boulders stuck up out of the dry grass. Abruptly, or so it seemed to Kylie, they found themselves at the top of a steep slope, the road dipping down sharply and curving out of sight as it hugged the side of a steep ridge. In front of them was a large valley several kilometres across, its bottom already bathed in shadow. Beyond was a quite forbidding tangle of rugged hills and mountains which seemed to stretch on endlessly.

Peter looked up from his map. "That's the valley of Dry River," he said, pointing down into the valley.

Graham twisted in his saddle and pointed off to the right. "One of those mountains over there is Mt Misery," he said.

The name sounded ominous to Kylie, and she replied, "I hope we don't go there."

"We do," Norah replied. "On the way back. That's when we go through Irvinebank."

Kylie had a vague mental image of a dry, dusty and very poor little town hidden away among dry, barren hills. The houses she remembered had all appeared to be a hundred years old and made of corrugated iron, all set in dusty yards with a few straggly bushes for a garden. She had only been there once on a drive with her parents, and she had not paid much attention, being both bored and thirsty.

It meant much more to the boys and they began chattering about the amazing little narrow-gauge railway that had once wound its way through the dry ranges to the town. They had done an expedition to the area the previous year and were busy reminding each other about it.

"Stannary Hills is that way," said Graham, sighting through the compass he carried tied to a buttonhole of his shirt.

Norah raised her eyebrows. "Have you been there?" she asked with genuine surprise.

"Last September holidays," Graham replied. "We got into a bit of bother."

"Bit of bother!" Margaret cried. "You were nearly all killed!"

Graham just grinned and shrugged. "Not me, only Steve and Pete. I just got a broken ankle bone."

Margaret shook her head and said, "And walked all night with it."

Norah raised her eyebrows. "How did that happen?"

Kylie saw Graham blush and knew he would not boast. Instead he said, "It's a long story."

Norah nodded and said, "Tell me about it later. We had better push on or we will be camping in the dark."

As the hills on the other side of the valley were already mostly shadows on their western sides, Kylie could only agree. The group started down the steep section of road. That was an experience that Kylie found trying but which the boys openly complained about. The grade was so steep they kept slipping forward in their saddles and had trouble keeping their seat. Even Kylie found it tiring on her leg and lower back muscles. The experience was made worse by two motor vehicles passing them, seemingly at the narrowest, most dangerous bends.

Finally, Graham could stand it no longer. "I can walk as fast as this," he grumbled, "And it couldn't be any less tiring."

To prove his point he dismounted and proceeded to march along, leading his horse. In that fashion they reached the bottom of the hill after twenty sweaty minutes. As they reached the lower slopes they passed from sunlight into shadow, which Kylie found a distinct relief. She also noted a very definite drop in temperature.

Along the road at the bottom Norah kept them riding, pushing the speed up to a trot for ten minutes. Graham had to remount and hurry to keep up. The road ran in a deep valley with a dry stream bed on their right and a ridge covered with fairly dense savannah woodland beyond. On their left were steep slopes which Kylie saw had sections of cliff and bare rock on them. The afternoon sun was still shining on those upper slopes, and it looked very wild and picturesque.

Graham gestured to the rugged hillsides and said, "Well, if I was a bushranger in the old days, this would have been the place to hold up the stagecoaches."

The boys all began discussing the best place for an ambush and this quickly moved to a discussion of modern military tactics on that terrain, to Kylie's decided annoyance. She made a face at this which Margaret returned.

Silly boys! she thought. *Why do they have to think about such horrible things as wars and armies all the time?*

Margaret dropped back to ride just ahead of her. She turned and said, "I wonder if the police have caught the Kelly Gang yet?"

Roger heard this and he said, "We can listen to the radio and find out." Then he added, "But this area would make an ideal hideout."

Kylie glanced at all the bush and rugged hills and felt a sudden chill. *It would too,* she thought. To reassure herself she said, "Didn't the police say they went the other way?"

Roger nodded. "Yes, across towards East Barron on the Tablelands," he agreed.

Quite suddenly the scenery changed. The road dipped across the dry stream bed, then curved to the right around the tip of the tree-covered ridge. They came out into a small, fairly open plain dotted with a scattering of tall, white gum trees. The flat was carpeted in a thin layer of green grass. A few beef cattle could be seen grazing on it in the distance. The place was hemmed in by the steep, rocky slopes but still had a feeling of being open and airy.

A hundred metres out on the flat they came to a much larger watercourse. At first Kylie thought it was dry, as all she could see was sand and rocks but then she realised that a thin trickle of water was flowing along it and that there were a few pools in under the trees which dotted its banks. The trees were mostly large paperbarks and there was very little of the thicker undergrowth often found along such streams. All in all it was a very pleasant place and Kylie was pleased when Norah led them across the stream bed and pointed to where a 4WD and horse trailer were parked a hundred metres further along, on a grassy area beside the river. Near the vehicle Kylie saw Mrs Conroy working at a portable barbeque.

Norah turned to them. "This is the Dry River. We are going to camp here," she said. She then led them off the road and across the short grass.

As they reached the vehicles, Norah swung herself out of the saddle and greeted her mother. She did it with such lithe grace that Kylie felt a distinct niggle of jealousy.

Mrs Conroy smiled a welcome and asked, "Any problems?"

"No Mum."

"Good. Now all of you get off those horses and have a drink of cold cordial," Mrs Conroy said.

Graham moved to dismount and then groaned. "Ah! Thank heavens for that!" he cried as he lowered himself to the ground. He put his hand to his back and appeared to straighten up with difficulty. He was not alone. All the boys grumbled and complained about sore muscles. Kylie had them too and was feeling decidedly worn out but not for anything would she admit it. She did a stretch, but then she breathed deeply the cool evening air and felt very happy.

It was also a relief to remove the safety helmet. The thing was just heavy enough to have caused her neck muscles to ache and it also fitted so tightly that her hair was all damp from perspiration. The boys all grumbled about them and happily removed them as well.

The boys then got another shock when Norah insisted that the horses were looked after first, before any thought of setting up camp. Saddles and bridles were removed, being replaced by rope halters. Once the saddles were neatly placed on a log near a stone fireplace the horses were rubbed down, then combed and brushed. Only when they had cooled and been groomed were they led across to a pleasant pool of waist deep water and allowed to drink.

There was a nice sandy beach and good access down a low bank only a metre high, so it was all very easy. Kylie enjoyed rubbing and brushing Blazer, for whom she had already developed a strong affection. She stood happily patting her while she drank. Then she led her back and Dingo proceeded to place hobbles and bells on her. Mrs Conroy, Norah and Dingo carefully examined each horse and seemed satisfied with their condition.

Once the horses were turned loose Norah ordered various tasks to be done. The boys were sent to collect firewood while the girls unpacked small tents and began erecting them. These were little nylon bubbles with flexible frames and were only big enough for two people.

"I don't want to sleep in one of them," Graham said as he dumped an armful of firewood.

Mrs Conroy raised an eyebrow/ "Where are you going to sleep then?" she asked.

Graham glanced up at the sky, then said, "Under the stars next to the fire will do. It isn't going to rain."

"It could get cold," Norah said, a frown creasing her face.

Graham shrugged. "All the more reason to camp close to the fire."

Norah looked anxious. "That could be dangerous. You might roll into the fire in your sleep."

Graham shook his head. "We do it all the time. We are used to it. We go camping a couple of times a month."

Kylie knew this was true so wasn't worried, except that she suspected Graham was just trying to impress Norah with how tough he was. She was not surprised when Peter also opted to sleep beside the fire. By then she and Margaret were placing their gear into their tent.

As she knelt to push her bag inside the tent Margaret gave a glance towards where Graham was dumping his army pack. "It might be nice to sleep beside the fire," she said.

Kylie couldn't help herself. She laughed aloud and said, "You mean beside Graham, don't you?"

"Oh poo to you!" Margaret replied, but her face crinkled up into a mischievous grin. Kylie smiled in reply and held her tongue. For years now Margaret had been in love with Graham, and she knew that on several occasions they had been a bit naughty. That only bothered her if they went too far and got Margaret into trouble. What worried her more was the thought that Graham might not return Margaret's love. Seeing the way Graham was talking to Norah brought those fears to the surface. He was flirting, there was no doubt of that.

And he's not the only one, Kylie thought, noting with a stab of hurt how Peter was also acting towards Norah. Then she was pleased to note both Stephen and Roger joining in. Dingo was working nearby, setting up the surround of a portable toilet. He then began unpacking food, casting a few sour glances at them as he did. *They all think she is nice,* she decided, again feeling a surge of jealousy which she then regretted as she really wanted to like Norah.

Margaret had noticed as well and was also looking a bit worried. However she shook her head and whispered, "This could get interesting."

Kylie could only nod. She unrolled her groundsheet and sleeping bag in front of the tent and sat on it to relax. "Is there anything else you want us to do Mrs Conroy?" she asked.

Mrs Conroy shook her head. "No. Make yourself comfortable. Dingo is the cook."

She and Norah then busied themselves lighting a small fire in the circle of stones. Kylie found the flicker of the flames very comforting, and she stretched and sighed. It was now so quiet and peaceful that she felt very relaxed. Apart from the boys talking the only other sound was the tinkle of the horse bells and the munching sound of them cropping the short grass. She looked around to look at the horses and was quite surprised at how dark it had become. The twilight was almost over and the light of the fire emphasised this.

Norah stood up and brushed her hands, her pretty face lit up by the flames. "We usually get here an hour or so earlier," she explained. "We usually eat in daylight."

Graham answered that. "Doesn't bother us. We often camp in the dark on army cadet exercises."

"Sometimes we don't even camp," Peter added. "We just stop to eat, then keep marching all night."

Stephen now joined in, "And sometimes we stop in the middle of the night and just lie down on the ground for a few hours, then get up and keep marching."

Norah wrinkled her nose and sniffed. "Oh you Cairns mob! You think you are so good! I know what cadets do. I was a cadet."

The boys were astonished. Peter spoke first. "What unit were you in?"

"Atherton. Mum used to drive us down on Monday nights."

Mrs Conroy looked up from turning sizzling steaks on the barbeque, "And both her brothers before that. I've driven a few miles for cadets."

Graham was puzzled. "When was that? I don't remember seeing you."

"Two years ago," Norah said, poking more twigs into the fire.

Kylie knew that the boys were Third Year cadets, and she could see them doing the mental sums. Pete worked it out first. "That was when we were First Years," he said, as though this explained things.

As the two units only met on occasional camps and on the annual promotion course Kylie could understand why they hadn't known her.

Stephen pushed his glasses up and asked, "How old are you Norah?"

Margaret cried out, "Oh Stephen, you don't ask a lady her age!"

Kylie agreed but she sensed it was a very important question to the boys. Norah obviously sensed it too because she blushed and hung her head for a moment before saying, "Nineteen."

That fact seemed to hang in the air, laden with significance. Kylie did the calculations herself and took some comfort in the fact that Graham was only 15.

And Peter is only sixteen, so she should be too old for them.

Then Peter twisted her anxieties another notch by saying, "You look younger. Do you still go to school?"

Norah smiled at the implied compliment and returned Peter's smile, then shook her head. "No. I am doing Second Year University. I'm going to be a vet."

They talked about this for a while, then the conversation came back to cadets. It was Stephen who asked what rank Norah had been.

"I was a Cadet Under-Officer," Norah said shyly, obviously not wanting to boast.

At that, Kylie felt even better, *Oh good!* she thought. *She outranks them. Now maybe they won't flirt with her.*

The conversation shifted to cadet camps and exercises. Norah told them she knew people like Capt Conkey quite well, as well as some of the Cadet Under-Officers of the Cairns unit. The subject kept the conversation going but Kylie could see that Dingo wasn't looking very happy. He was now placing cooked sausages and steaks on a plate and had almost finished preparing the meal.

Norah turned to the girls. "We should stop talking about cadets. You girls must find it boring."

Margaret shook her head. "Not me. I'm a cadet."

Norah looked mildly surprised and turned to Kylie with a raised eyebrow. Kylie shook her head. She had never felt any desire to join any military organization, being quite happy with Guides. "Not me. I do dancing and Guides," she explained. She suspected, but did not say it, that the only reason Margaret was in the army cadets was to be near Graham and to try to get him to like her more.

"Why weren't you in the guard of honour?" Norah asked Margaret.

"Because I'm only a recruit and they only let the older cadets take part," Margaret answered.

Kylie watched the by-play with mild amusement. She could see the boys trying to readjust their ideas now that they had learned that Norah wasn't just a simple country girl. Her own admiration had also grown. As very few cadets ever reached the rank of Cadet Under-Officer she was impressed. The fact that Norah was bright enough to not just to get into university but to study veterinary science made her even more admirable.

The conversation was interrupted by Mrs Conroy calling them over to the folding table to collect their food. The aroma of sizzling steak had already worked on Kylie's saliva glands, and she was hungry and ready to eat a big meal. She selected a bread roll and steak and added salad and onions to it, then sat on a folding chair to eat, before hastily changing to a leaning forward position to prevent greasy juice dripping onto her clothes.

The billy was boiled and they drank tea or coffee, then ate more food. After half an hour Kylie sat back, wiping her fingers on a tissue. She sighed with satisfaction. The food had been delicious and she was feeling very happy. It was getting cool, but not cold and she saw that the sky was quite clear, a brilliant pattern of stars.

Mrs Conroy set Norah and Dingo to cleaning up. Margaret offered to help but Mrs Conroy shook her head. "Thanks for the offer Margaret, but you are paying guests. You can sing instead." So saying she reached into the vehicle and took out a guitar. "You can have the full tourist treatment," she said.

"Oh fair go Mrs Conroy!" Graham cried, his face a mixture of embarrassment and annoyance. "We aren't tourists! We are locals."

Mrs Conroy realised she had offended them, but she still laughed and replied, "Not out in this country. I'd like you to sing with me anyway."

Stephen made a face and said, "Have you heard Graham try to sing Mrs Conroy? It is too painful for words. You should spare us."

Mrs Conroy smiled and said, "I'm sure Norah would like a bit of accompaniment."

"Do you sing Norah?" Peter asked.

Norah nodded and smiled, then made herself comfortable on a chair. Her mother handed her the guitar, and she began strumming and testing her chords.

"I'd appreciate some help," she said.

Put like that they found it hard to refuse. Mrs Conroy made it all but impossible by handing them all song books and lighting a pressure lantern, so they had enough light to see the words. Kylie was secretly delighted, and she and Margaret joined in with gusto. She was amused to note that all of the boys actually tried to sing and, once they got into it, they seemed to enjoy themselves. The songs were a mixture of 'traditional' Australian songs and 'Country and Western'. Kylie knew most of them and the only sour note was Stephen's teasing comment, "I see you have both kinds of music out here, both Country and Western!"

It turned into a very enjoyable evening and the singing was followed by a supper of hot chocolate or Milo. Kylie opted for the Milo, and it warmed her nicely before bed. Bedtime was early, 9:30pm. As she snuggled down in her sleeping bag Kylie was very conscious of Margaret peering out at where the boys were bedding down beside the fire, her eyes glistening in the reflected firelight.

"He will be alright," Kylie teased. "No monster will drag him off in the night."

Margaret gave her a smile and snuggled down, still looking out. Kylie lay back and hoped that Graham would find love for her. Then Kylie stared out at the fire and knew that she was lonely and unhappy herself. One thing at least was very obvious to her: Peter was not showing any interest in her. In fact he seemed to have eyes only for Norah and, with a pang of jealousy, Kylie saw him saying goodnight to her.

Rolling on her side to hide her unhappiness Kylie bit her lip.

Oh, I hope I find love! she thought wistfully.

Chapter 6

DRY RIVER

Kylie did not have a good night's sleep. Unused to sleeping on the ground, or next to another person, she kept waking. Then she would roll over and wriggle to find a more comfortable position. Each time she woke she looked out of the tent. All she saw were the lumpy shapes of the boy's sleeping bags around the red glow of coals. Deep sleep only came in the last few hours of darkness.

Even then she woke before dawn. She changed position, tried to get comfortable and closed her eyes again. But sleep would not return. After a while she rolled onto her back and stared at the roof of the tent, moodily wondering if the reason why she didn't have a boyfriend was because there was something wrong with her. But her self-analysis produced no answer. She knew she was pretty, and she was satisfied that her body shape was normal for her age.

"So why?" she muttered.

She rolled on her side and looked out at where Peter slept. All she could see was a dark shape, the fire having completely burnt itself out. Then she shrugged and had to admit that he really didn't spark any great passion in her.

He's nice, but I'm not in love with him, she told herself.

Wondering if she was interested in him more out of anxiety and desperation she finally crawled to the entrance and looked out. Outside it was very quiet. There wasn't even a breeze to rustle the leaves. In the starlight she could see quite clearly. Then the snuffle of a horse came to her, and she saw the dark shapes about 50 metres away.

Deciding that she would not sleep any more she changed from her pyjamas to jeans and shirt, then struggled into a pullover as it was chilly. Doing this without waking Margaret called for some care. Several times Margaret moved and murmured and once she rolled on her back and lay with her mouth slightly open. She looked so young and relaxed that Kylie had to smile.

I'll bet she's dreaming of Graham, she thought.

Pulling on socks and boots Kylie crawled out, to immediately discover that the grass was damp from dew. Then she made the unpleasant discovery that she was much stiffer and sorer than she had thought. She groaned and rubbed her back and bottom, then walked slowly over to the portable toilet. After that she made her way towards the horses. The horses heard her and stopped eating to lift their heads and look. For a moment she thought they might take fright, so she spoke quietly, calling Blazer by name.

The horses went back to nibbling the grass. Blazer watched Kylie approach, allowing her to walk right up to her. Kylie gently stroked the horse, surprised how warm she felt and enjoying the horse odour. Blazer looked at her and sniffed, testing to see if she had any little treat in her hand. Finding none the horse resumed munching the grass.

"Sorry Blazer. You are a good horse aren't you?" Kylie said, patting her neck.

As she stood there, Kylie looked around, breathing deeply and feeling very well and content. She noted a faint lightening in the sky over the mountain top across the river and realised that daybreak was not far away. Leaving the horses to their feed she strolled over to the bank of the river, going slowly just in case a snake might be slithering around.

Kneeling on the sand she rinsed her face, noting with surprise that the water felt quite warm. Then she shivered as it dried on her skin. That woke her up and she wondered what to do next. Not wishing to wake anyone else she seated herself on a folding chair, discovering too late that it had dew on it which wet her bottom. For the next twenty minutes she sat, thinking about her life, and savouring the stillness. Very slowly the light increased until she could determine colours and see right across the valley. In the distance a kookaburra began to chuckle and laugh.

Faint electronic beeping from the large tent told her an alarm was waking someone and soon afterwards Mrs Conroy emerged, pulling on a jumper. Seeing Kylie she raised her eyebrows and smiled. "Good morning, dear. Couldn't you sleep?"

Kylie shook her head. "I'm not used to sleeping on the ground."

"We can give you a stretcher or an air mattress," Mrs Conroy said.

Kylie shook her head. That would only provoke the scorn of the boys, who imagined they were tough. "No thanks. Is there anything I can do?"

"You can wake Dingo first. He is in that tent over there, then you can help Norah and I get breakfast if you want," Mrs Conroy replied.

Kylie did that. By then Norah had also appeared, wrapping a jacket around herself as she did. They began setting out food and cooking utensils. Mrs Conroy lit a gas stove and began heating water. Kylie was aware of the increasing chatter and twitter of birds but almost jumped with fright when a kookaburra suddenly started its call from the tree above her. The noise and movement obviously woke the boys as they began to stir. Peter was first up, then Graham. Stephen snorted and, to Kylie's embarrassment, farted. This was so loud that Graham went and stirred him with his boot.

"Not so loud Steve, you'll frighten the horses," Graham said.

Kylie was even more embarrassed, but Mrs Conroy laughed. Margaret poked her head out and the kookaburra broke into its maniacal chuckles again.

Graham said, "See what you've done Margaret? Go back inside the tent."

At that moment, the kookaburra laughed even louder. Margaret went red and Kylie could see that her feelings had been hurt. Margaret gave Graham a reproachful look and came over to join Kylie. Kylie glared at her brother, but he thought his little joke very funny. Then he prodded Roger's sleeping form. After a minute of this Roger angrily pulled his sleeping bag off his face and snarled, "I'm awake! How could anyone sleep with you buffoons making so much noise?"

"Get up," Graham replied.

"No. It's cold," Roger said. He rolled over and covered his head again.

Graham began to nudge him again and Stephen joined in, but Mrs Conroy stopped them. "You boys do something useful," she said. "Go and wash your faces and hang those sleeping bags up to dry."

The boys did as they were told. Roger grumpily sat up and struggled out of his sleeping bag to join them. By then Mrs Conroy had hot water ready and she and Norah made up warm drinks for them. Kylie opted for Milo again and stood holding the cup with both hands to warm her fingers. The boys and Dingo joined them. Then Kylie was annoyed even more by the very obvious way the boys were all paying attention to Norah.

Mrs Conroy noted this and looked thoughtful, then said, "You children can go and check your saddles and bridles and polish them. Dingo will show you what to do. That way I can get on with cooking breakfast."

The boys grumbled a bit but followed Dingo over to the log where the saddles were. He removed a plastic sheet which had covered them and then explained what to check and what to look for. Then he produced cans of dubbin and cloths and got them all seated and polishing, rubbing the saddle soap well in. Kylie enjoyed doing this. She liked the smell and she enjoyed the thought that she was making the leather supple and prolonging its useful life.

While they worked Graham grumbled about the amount of time wasted looking after the horses. Kylie was annoyed by that but just made a face and went on with her polishing. As she did, she smelt the frying bacon and began to salivate. *Oh, that smells good!* she thought hungrily. Normally she only ate a light breakfast of cereal and fruit but now she was more than ready for a full meal when fifteen minutes later Mrs Conroy called them over to eat.

It was very enjoyable meal: bacon and fried eggs on toast, fruit juice or hot drinks, Weetbix with warm milk (or as Graham ate it, dry with butter and honey). While they ate breakfast Kylie noted the sunlight lighting up the hilltops across the valley and that seemed to make her shiver. Another cup of warm Milo helped warm her up and she sat back and wiped her fingers and lips and just relaxed and enjoyed watching the sun's rays light up the treetops. A few wisps of mist drifted up from the river and the dew drops on a spider web among the branches sparkled as the light shone through them.

This is really nice, she told herself, her spirits lifting even more.

She would have been even happier if the boys (particularly Graham) hadn't continued to flirt with Norah and try to show off to her. This almost reached the ridiculous when Norah, who was packing the food away, turned and said, "Would one of you please bring that box over here?"

All four boys moved at once. Stephen and Peter almost sprang to the box, both bending to pick it up at the same moment. The result was their heads bumping together. They glared at each other.

"I got it first!" Peter snapped.

"I did," Stephen snarled.

Mrs Conroy interrupted. "There's no need to fight over it. There's plenty more to do. Make sure your sleeping bags are hanging in the sun, then pack up."

Peter and Stephen both glared at each other and kept a grip on the box for a few more seconds. Then Peter shrugged and let go, casting a hopeful look towards Norah as he did. That hurt Kylie, but so did the fact that Graham had also moved.

I can't compete with Norah, Kylie thought. She then mentally flailed herself about her looks, her personality, her figure, and her age. *Peter must think I am just a little baby,* she thought unhappily.

The next half hour was taken up with packing. Graham and Stephen both shaved, a process which fascinated Margaret. She kept casting curious glances at them. Chores such as washing up, rolling up bedding, striking and folding tents, and packing the stoves and cooking gear, kept them busy for another twenty minutes.

While they were working Dingo turned on a small radio, "To get the weather forecast," he explained.

Roger called to him, "Listen to the news and see if the cops have caught the Kelly Gang yet."

They hadn't. Neither the 7:30 local news, nor the 7:45 national news had anything to add except that the police were still searching and were following several leads.

"They won't catch them," Stephen commented.

They returned to packing up. Kylie took the opportunity to go to the toilet again in the camp 'Portaloo', an experience she didn't enjoy. While she was strolling back to the camp afterwards, she detoured over to the horses. While she was talking to them, she heard an unusual noise and looked around. The noise became a deep vibration, and she realised it was an engine. A blue and white helicopter buzzed into view from behind the mountain top. It flew straight on over them in a westerly direction and was soon gone from sight. As helicopters were widely used for mustering on cattle stations, she thought no more about it.

By then it was time to get the horses ready. They were led down to the river for a drink and then the halters were swapped for bridles. Saddle blankets and saddles were added. Then saddle bags and bedding were strapped on. All this was under the watchful supervision of Mrs Conroy and Norah. They both came along and checked that the saddle girths were tight, but not too tight.

Mrs Conroy looked at her watch. "After half past eight. You lot had better get moving. So get those helmets on and mount up." This last was particularly directed at Graham and Stephen, both of whom were wearing old felt hats. They all picked up the white helmets and buckled them on, but not without some grumbling from the boys.

Mrs Conroy did a check that everyone was ready then added, "I'll just finish tidying up here and then load 'Topsy'. I'll catch you up. Start going."

Topsy was the spare horse Mrs Conroy had brought 'just in case' and she was tethered to a nearby tree. As the others began moving, Topsy whinnied and tried to pull free.

Poor horse, Kylie thought. *She doesn't want to be left behind.*

The route led on southwards across the flat. After a few hundred metres they crossed a sandy creek with a dry bed. The road then swung left and dipped to re-cross the Dry River. It had a bed of sand and small, rounded pebbles so they took it slowly. What really impressed Kylie was the way the steep, rugged hills began to close in on either side until the road and river ran along the bottom of a gorge. The slopes on the left were the most impressive, with areas of sheer rock high up near the top. The vegetation remained open, with few trees and almost no undergrowth along the banks of the river.

As they got into the gorge the road ran on a bench cut a few metres above it. This allowed a good view of its bed and Kylie decided it was a nice river, and that the rugged scenery was quite picturesque. She particularly liked the trees with white trunks that lined the riverbank.

After dipping to cross a small dry gully, the road went on as before. Graham suddenly pointed across at the rocky slope opposite. "An old mine."

Kylie could just make out the difference caused by the disturbed rocks. Stephen laughed and cried, "Don't go near it, Roger!"

"Don't worry, I won't," Roger replied with feeling.

Norah twisted in her saddle and said, "You should stay away from old mines. They are very dangerous."

"You don't have to tell me!" Roger retorted.

When the other boys burst out laughing Norah looked quizzical and said, "What happened?"

Roger made a face. "I fell down one. Last year, when we were exploring Stannary Hills."[2]

---

[2] Read *Stannary Hills* by C. R. Cummings

"Did you get hurt?"

Roger shook his head. "Just a bit stunned and bruised."

Norah was obviously intrigued. She asked, "How did that happen?"

"We were being chased by crooks on trail bikes. I ran through some bushes and didn't see the hole till it was too late."

"Crooks? Did you get away?"

Roger shut his eyes and shuddered. Then he nodded. "The bloke chasing me didn't see where I'd gone."

"So then what? Did you climb out?"

Roger shook his head. "I couldn't. I had to go through a tunnel. It was the scariest thing I have ever done. You won't get me into a mine again, not for any money."

"What were the crooks doing?" Norah asked.

Peter answered. "They were hiding stolen goods in an old mine tunnel. We found it."

"That's when Graham broke his ankle," Margaret added.

Norah looked even more interested. "Tell me more."

So while they rode along the story of the expedition to Stannary Hills was described. Kylie could see that Graham appeared to be quite embarrassed when Peter revealed that the boys had a large model railway and that the expedition had been to research to build an extension of it.

He doesn't want Norah to think he is a little boy who still plays with trains, she thought.

The story telling was interrupted when they came to the ruins of a building right beside the riverbank on their right. Beside it were large heaps of crushed gravel. Otherwise all that was there were concrete slabs, a few rotting posts, and some rusty corrugated iron sheets.

"This was the Newelton Battery," Norah explained.

"What is a battery?" Margaret asked.

"It has big steel stampers or hammers that crush rocks dug out of the mines. That way they can get the silver or tin ore out of it easier," Norah explained.

They stopped and dismounted and spent a few minutes looking around. There were more signs of old mines on both hillsides and the boys wanted to go exploring but Norah said there wasn't time. Reluctantly the boys remounted.

They rode on, passing through the narrowest part of the gorge. Now the road had a very steep slope up on the left. On their right was a steep bank which dropped down to the sand of the riverbed. Fifty metres away, right on the other side of the dry sand, a rugged, stony bluff rose up. The river was squeezed between the two hills.

"Another good spot to hold up the stagecoach," Graham suggested.

"I think there was a town here in those days," Norah said, gesturing ahead.

All Kylie could see was the dry riverbed doing a sharp curve, first to the right so that it flowed at the base of the steep bluff, then to the left so that it again crossed in front of them. The road ran across a small flat at the lower end of a spur and then went across the river again. There was almost no undergrowth or grass, the ground cover being as much leaf litter and deadfall as bare sand or tufts of grass.

As they began to cross the riverbed, Kylie noted that it was now mostly composed of cricket-ball-sized black stones, rounded smooth and coated with some sort of whitish powder. She also noted that the trees along the bank had given way to mostly sheoaks. On the other bank the road went up through quite a thick belt of them and onto a dry, open plain. She also noted that the river had now almost lived up to its name. The flow had decreased to a mere trickle a metre wide and only centimetres deep, barely visible among the stones.

"We will let the horses have a drink," Norah said. "The road goes away from the river for a few kilometres now and this will be the last water they get for a while."

They stopped and allowed the horses to put their heads down, the line closing up and bunching.

Suddenly, from the trees twenty metres ahead, came a loud command.

"Stop! Get off your horses and put your hands up!"

Chapter 7

FRICTION

Kylie's heart leapt into her throat in fear. *Bushrangers!* she thought, then told herself that was ridiculous.

This is the 21st Century, not the 19th!

The others had jerked upright, equally surprised and alarmed. Then the voice came again, loud and directly in front of them. "This is the police! Get off your horses and put your hands up."

The police! Kylie's mind raced and she experienced a surge of relief. She immediately dismounted, as did most of the others. Stephen, Graham, and Dingo remained on their horses, their eyes searching the tree line.

The voice boomed out again. "Get off your horses! You are being covered by armed police. Do not try to run away. Put your hands up!"

Kylie looked anxiously at her brother. "Graham! Get down please!" she called.

By now she was half-heartedly raising her hands, feeling quite silly as she did so. To her relief, Graham made a face but obeyed. Slowly both Stephen and Dingo dismounted as well.

The voice then called, "Walk towards me, away from the horses."

Feeling decidedly anxious Kylie dropped the reins and obeyed. The others moved with her. As they did, another voice called from off to their left, "It's okay Sarge. This isn't them. It's the Conroy's horse rides. I know them."

"You're sure?" queried the 'Sarge'.

"Definite," the voice replied.

The young, mounted policeman who likes Norah, Kylie thought.

She was right. A moment later Constable Lonergan stepped out from behind a tree, rifle in hand but lowered. Two other police emerged from cover as well. Kylie saw that one of them was the sergeant with the mutton chops whiskers she had seen at the Herberton railway station.

The police walked over to face them. Kylie was astonished, then annoyed to find that two more armed policemen were on the other bank behind them. The police had lowered their guns but still looked watchful.

They wore black bullet proof vests over their blue shirts and had modern automatic weapons. They also had radios hooked on their web vests and the sergeant called on his as he approached. Then he turned to Constable Lonergan.

"Who is who? Introduce us please."

Constable Lonergan gestured to Norah, an embarrassed smile on his face. "Sorry for giving you a fright Miss Norah. Norah, this is Sergeant Healey. Sgt Healey, Miss Norah Conroy."

Norah gave slight bow of her head but obviously wasn't amused. "Why did you hold us up like bushrangers?" she asked.

"Sorry, Miss Conroy," Sgt Healey answered. "Our helicopter saw a group of horsemen and we thought you might be the Kelly Gang. You know what happened yesterday in Herberton, do you?"

"We were there," Norah replied. "We saw it all. And we spoke to Constable Lonergan yesterday afternoon at my place."

Constable Lonergan went redder and said, "Sorry Norah. It never crossed my mind it might be you. I didn't realise you were going on a trail ride."

At that, Norah relented slightly. "I suppose we should have told you. It never occurred to me."

Stephen now spoke up, "So this means the Kelly Gang have given you the slip then?"

The policemen all looked irritated and embarrassed. Sgt Healey turned on Stephen. "And who are you sir?"

"Stephen Bell," Stephen replied.

A frown crossed Sgt Healey's face and he looked hard at Stephen "I've heard that name before. Why would I have?"

At that, Kylie got all anxious again and she wished Stephen had kept his mouth shut. She knew that Stephen had been in trouble with the police a couple of times over the years but did not know the details.

Stephen returned the sergeant's hard look and said, "We helped you catch some crooks at Stannary Hills last year."

"Yes, I remember that," Sgt Healey replied, but he did not sound happy or convinced. He looked at the others. "Who is 'we'?"

The others were all introduced. When Dingo was named Sgt Healey pursed his lips and said, "Yes, I know young Dingo."

Dingo scowled at that and earned Kylie's sympathy, at the same time arousing her curiosity about what he might have done to be 'known to police'.

At that moment, Mrs Conroy arrived in her 4WD. She got out and joined them, not realising what a drama had just taken place. Once the situation was explained, she said, "I thought you were chasing the Kellies over the mountains towards Malanda?"

"That was the direction they first took," Sgt Healey admitted. "They rode up over St Patricks Hill, but it seems they then dumped the horses. We think they switched to cars and drove quickly out of the area."

Mrs Conroy then echoed Stephen's statement. "So you don't know where these bushrangers have gone?"

"No Mrs Conroy," Constable Lonergan replied.

"Do you think it is safe for these children to continue with their trail ride?" Mrs Conroy asked.

That dismayed Kylie even more and she was relieved to hear the sergeant say, "I don't see why not. I doubt if the Kellies would bother them. Why should they?"

"Then you can keep going kids. I will get on and get things organised for tonight. I will see you at lunch time," Mrs Conroy said. Norah nodded and said yes.

Mrs Conroy climbed back into her vehicle and drove on. The police all trudged back across the riverbed while the group recovered their horses. They stood and allowed them to drink while they discussed the incident.

Margaret was happy and excited. "I nearly wet myself," she said. "I was sure it was the bushrangers."

Stephen curled his lip. "What did you think they would do to you?" he asked.

"Take our horses, and maybe take the girls as hostages," Margaret said.

Again Stephen sneered. "Oh, dream on!"

"We can live in hope," Graham added unkindly.

That comment made Kylie angry as she could see that Margaret's feelings were hurt. She was further annoyed when Stephen started telling a joke.

"The Kelly Gang held up a stagecoach," he said. "Ned Kelly gets all the people out and says, 'Men over there, women over there. Now boys, rob the women and rape the men.' When one of the male passengers hears this he questions it. He says, 'Don't you mean rob the men and rape the women?'. 'No,' says one of the bushrangers in an effeminate voice. 'You shut up mister. Ned Kelly's robbing this coach, not you!'"

Graham laughed, then went red as he noticed the disapproving looks on Norah's and Margaret's faces. Kylie was also not amused. "That's enough of that sort of talk, thank you Stephen Bell!" she snapped. Then she felt a surge of satisfaction at the way Norah curled her lip and turned up her nose up at Stephen.

Good! she thought. *Norah doesn't like him either.*

"Let's mount and get moving," Norah said coldly.

As Kylie mounted, she was again cheered up to glimpse a look of contempt for Stephen on Dingo's face. *He isn't amused either. Good, that's put him in his place.*

The group rode on across the riverbed and up the bank. A hundred metres on they saw the police clustered at two vehicles, both of which had double horse trailers hooked on behind. Two more police were sitting in them. As the horse riders passed them Constable Lonergan looked up and gave a friendly wave. Kylie returned it but noted that his eyes were only for Norah.

He likes her alright, she decided.

Once they were out of earshot Peter said, "The coppers are making a big effort to catch the Kelly Gang alright. It's not often you see so many police all at once."

"I think their pride was badly hurt," Norah suggested.

Peter nodded. "It was a very public humiliation," he agreed, "What with the Premier and the Governor and all those TV cameras."

"Don't forget the Duke," Graham added. "There must be some real political pressure to find him and get him back."

Kylie had forgotten the Duke. When Margaret piped up and said, "Poor man, I thought he was really handsome," she agreed.

Graham curled his lip. "You can have him then!" he retorted.

"Fine, I will!" Margaret snapped back, plainly hurt.

Kylie gave her brother a furious glance. *What's bothering him?* she wondered. He was normally much more tolerant of Margaret, affectionate even. Then it clicked. *He is scared that Norah will think he is Margaret's boyfriend.* That annoyed her even more. *Surely he doesn't think he has a chance with her?* she wondered. But it was obvious from the way he spoke and acted that he did fancy his chances. Kylie found it both distressing and annoying.

For a time the group rode on in silence. The road now ran across a wide, open plain, the valley opening out so that the larger, more rugged hills were several kilometres away on both sides.

"Silver Valley," Norah explained.

The road was straighter and wider, so they had less trouble from the couple of vehicles that passed them, having enough time to turn the horses off into the bush.

For several kilometres the road ran up and down over long, mostly bare ridges with a few trees on them. Kylie noted that the ground was half bare, the grass cover being sparse and yellowed. Both the soil and the rocks had a reddish hue. It became so hot and dry she found herself licking dry lips. Perspiration dampened her back and armpits and she shifted uncomfortably in the saddle as the previous day's aches and pains returned.

Apart from occasional glimpses of corrugated iron shacks off among the trees there was almost no sign of settlement. There were no beef cattle and only an occasional vehicle. Kylie enjoyed the scenery, which had a sort of barren grandeur to it, but she also found it hotter than expected.

It's April, she thought. *It should be cooler than this by now.*

April in North Queensland was the end of the Wet Season. Over Silver Valley there wasn't a cloud in the sky. Kylie knew enough about the local geography to understand that they were now west of the Tablelands and the main ranges of mountains, so were in a 'rain shadow'.

Probably still raining back in the mountains near the coast, she decided.

Their original plan had been a ride that went south to the Evelyn Tablelands and Ravenshoe, but Mrs Conroy had changed that plan as the weather had worsened. Kylie was now glad that they had, although she had to admit the scenery wasn't as pretty.

They halted after an hour for a short break and to have drinks. There was very little conversation and that bothered Kylie. *This is supposed to be a fun holiday,* she thought.

What concerned her even more was that all of the boys, even Roger, still seemed to be trying to impress Norah. She found it almost a relief to resume the ride.

By now she had settled into the rhythm and was feeling much more relaxed. She was more than happy with Blazer as a mount and felt like she had known her for years. At frequent intervals she patted the horse's neck, ruffled her ears and told her how good she was. Each time Blazer tossed her head and looked back at her, as though to answer.

At 10:30 they turned right along a rough vehicle track that led up a long ridge. The track twisted and turned around trees and rocks and the ground dropped away on both sides to dry, rocky gullies. At times the slope became so steep that they had to dismount and walk, the horses scrabbling to get a grip on the loose gravel. This was solid exercise for Kylie as she wasn't used to walking. She found she was perspiring freely.

Graham and Peter both seemed to be enjoying it and Kylie noted that both still frequently referred to their maps. At the next rest stop Peter dug around in his saddle bag and extracted another map. He held it up to Kylie.

"We are off that map," he said. "We are on the Ravenshoe map now."

He showed Kylie where they were, and she was surprised at how far they had come. "How far to Mt Garnet?" she asked.

Peter did some calculating and said, "About thirty kilometres."

Kylie knew they weren't due to arrive there till the next day so she happily accepted this and tried to engage Peter in conversation. In this she was unsuccessful and after a few minutes he excused himself and walked over to where Graham and Stephen were talking to Norah. That little rejection really hurt Kylie and she felt quite miffed.

She wasn't the only one. Margaret looked quite down and kept glancing towards the group clustered around Norah. Kylie knew what the problem was but could not immediately come up with a plan to deal with it. She found it almost a relief to remount and ride on.

The route went on along the ridge, ever further into a seemingly formless maze of hills and gullies. The country was very dry and rugged and in places there were no trees, only stunted bushes and tufts of tough, spiky grass. The only real things of interest were the numerous old mine sites. Some were just slumped in depressions with eroded mullock heaps next to them, or a few rusting pieces of machinery or old iron sheets. Others still had quite deep, timber-lined shafts. The group stopped to look at a couple of these, leaning carefully over to peer down.

Norah wasn't happy with this and kept warning the boys to stay well back and to be careful. Roger looked into a couple, but without enthusiasm. The other boys kept talking about the mine tunnels at Stannary Hills that they had actually explored, particularly one whose roof had almost collapsed, and another which had been drilled and blasted out of solid granite.

"It was a lot of bloody hard work for a bit of tin," Stephen summed it up.

"Or silver," Graham added.

"Garnets maybe," Peter suggested.

"What are garnets?" Kylie asked.

Norah answered. "Semi-precious stones. A bit like opals. You have to polish them up to make them look really good."

Kylie nodded, feeling slightly foolish. She had actually known that. Now she looked at the dry, reddish rocks around her and was amazed. *How could anyone have walked around such barren country looking for precious stones or minerals?* Her admiration for the early pioneers went up another notch.

Peter mirrored her thoughts. "They must have been tough people, those old fossickers," he said.

"They are," Roger agreed. "Remember Old Zeke?"

"My word yes!" Peter agreed.

Norah looked from one to the other. "Who is Old Zeke?"

Roger answered. "The miner whose mine I fell down. He saved us last year."

Norah nodded, "Tell me more."

So the boys added more of the story of their adventure at Stannary Hills the previous September. Kylie knew the story well but she was getting just a little peeved by the way the boys kept telling Norah about their adventures. Not wanting to be left out of the conversation she added, "Don't forget old Mr Donaldson."

Norah turned to her and looked interested. "Who is he?"

"A gold miner we met in the jungle down in the Mulgrave Valley," Kylie explained.

Margaret nodded. "Last year, when we found our gold mine," she added. Then she looked at Graham and said, "Well, not really ours to begin with. It was really the Kirk family secret."

That got Norah interested so they had to relate the finding of the gold during the January holidays. As they got into the story Norah gasped and cried, "I heard about that. It was a mine called 'The Jeweller's Shop'."

"That's the one," Graham agreed.

"That's how we can afford touristy holidays like this," Peter added with a grin.[3]

When the story had been told Norah shook her head and said, "You kids certainly have some adventures."

That pleased Kylie because she could tell the boys were not amused at being called kids. *Good, that's put them in their place,* she thought.

The ride went on. Half an hour of hard riding and walking up the ridge brought them to a road junction. The other road had a roughly North-South alignment and was in better condition and obviously more frequently used. Norah pointed along it.

"This is Deadman's Road. Irvinebank is up to the north on the other side of Mt Misery. The other way goes back down to the road we were on this morning, the one along Silver Valley."

It was easier going now and they even trotted for a while to make up for the time lost talking. They passed a side road going off westwards and Norah said they could have taken that road. "It goes down to Nanyeta Creek and near an old ghost town called Coolgarra. We will see it on the way back."

"Ghost town?" Roger queried, his voice sounding to Kylie just a shade anxious.

Norah nodded. "Yes, a real ridgi-didge ghost town, with all these deserted old buildings in the bush. It is a great place."

The mention of the ghost town in the advertising brochure had been one of the main reasons Kylie had pushed for this particular trail ride and the knowledge that it was quite close helped get her interested and lift her spirits. They needed lifting because she could see that Margaret was looking quite miserable. To a stranger she would just have looked quiet and calm, but Kylie could tell that her best friend was hurting.

That stupid brother of mine, Kylie thought.

Soon after that Graham gave her more cause for annoyance. They came to a pleasant dry creek bed shaded by large paperbarks and found Mrs Conroy parked there. It was lunch time. Mrs Conroy said, "Saddles off children and give the horses a good rub down, then you can eat."

---

[3] Read *Below Bartle Frere* by C. R. Cummings

As he dismounted Graham grumbled openly. "Saddles off! These bloody horses take a lot of looking after."

"Yes, they do," Mrs Conroy replied coolly.

Graham knew he was being rebuked and looked truculent. "We have only come about fifteen kilometres. We could have walked just as far in that time," he said to no-one in particular.

"I couldn't have!" Roger said, groaning as he climbed stiffly down.

Kylie let her annoyance boil over. "Then why did you come?" she snapped at Graham.

Graham opened his mouth to snap back but then glanced at Norah and shut it, looking angry.

There was a few moments silence then Peter called to Dingo to help him loosen the girth strap on his saddle. The saddles were removed and placed on a tree trunk. Then the horses were wiped and rubbed and tied to a rope strung between two trees. Mrs Conroy handed around cups of cold fruit juice and began organizing lunch. As she did, Kylie saw Margaret heading off down the bed of the creek. Presuming she was going to the toilet she let her go, but when she had not returned after a few minutes she became concerned.

She drained her own cup and followed the direction Margaret had taken along the stream bed. It was easy walking, mostly sand but with some patches of rocks. Trees overhung most of it but it was all very dry. Fifty paces downstream there was a sharp bend. She rounded this and was about to call out, not wanting to catch Margaret in the act of going to the toilet. To her dismay, she spotted Margaret sitting with her back to her, head down and obviously crying.

Hurrying over to her she said, "Margaret, are you alright?"

Margaret raised a tear-stained face and nodded. She tried to wipe away the tears and smile, but it didn't work. Kylie sat down on the same rock and put her arm around her friend's shoulders.

"It's Graham, isn't it?"

Margaret nodded and sniffled, then cried, "And Norah!"

"Norah?" Kylie echoed. "What's she done?"

Just then there was a sound behind Kylie and she looked over her shoulder to see Norah standing there. Norah's smile vanished and she put her hands on her hips.

"Yes," Norah demanded. "What have I done?"

Chapter 8

TRAIL RIDE

There was a moment of tense silence. Norah's face went hard. "What have I done?" she demanded to know.

Kylie was appalled and tried to think of a suitable answer. However, Margaret spoke first. "Nothing, Norah. It's not you. It's those stupid boys."

"Why? What have they done?" Norah asked, her face relenting slightly.

Margaret shrugged, the movement clear to Kylie, who still had her arm around her shoulders. "You are so pretty that the boys spend all their time trying to impress you," Margaret explained.

Norah blushed at the compliment and Kylie could only agree. She was very pretty. Norah then shook her head, "I'm sorry. I don't quite understand."

By now Kylie had gathered her wits. She gestured to Margaret. "It's Graham," she explained. "He is ignoring Margaret while he shows off to you."

Norah nodded. "I'm sorry. I'm not trying to encourage them," she answered.

"You don't have to do anything," Kylie said. "You are so... so good looking and so nice they just... just act like the idiots they are."

Again Norah blushed, the embarrassment mottling her complexion to a beautiful shade of honey and peach. "Is... is... Oh it's none of my business," she stammered.

Margaret shook her head and answered for her. "No, Graham's not my boyfriend. I just want him to be, and... and (sob)... I love him so!"

Norah's face changed to concern. "Oh Margaret! You are such a nice person. I'm sorry. I didn't realise. From now on I won't encourage him at all."

Margaret lifted her tear-streaked face and smiled. "You are such a kind person, Norah. We really like you and want to be your friends."

Now Kylie could see that Norah was really embarrassed. Norah nodded, then said, “Thank you. I’d like that too. Now, let’s go back and have lunch and see if we can come up with a plan to put these silly boys in their place.”

“Oh don’t hurt them!” Margaret cried. “They can’t help themselves.”

Norah smiled at that. She then made Margaret laugh by saying, “Remember what my mother says: boys go for the pretty faces because they can see better than they can think.”

Kylie wasn’t sure if that implied Margaret wasn’t pretty, but she had to laugh as well. “That’s what my mum says too,” she added.

The three girls walked back to where the boys and Mrs Conroy were sitting around on the sand eating sandwiches and biscuits and drinking cold cordial or fruit juice. Mrs Conroy gave them a quizzical glance, but the boys did not seem to notice. The girls collected food and drinks and moved to seat themselves as a group away from the boys. When Stephen, and then Peter, moved to join them they were frozen out of the conversation by a lot of ‘girl talk’. Baffled, the boys retreated to rejoin Graham and Roger. Dingo remained seated to one side.

Kylie was moved to go and talk to him. While she had seen Aboriginals all her life, she rarely spoke to one. There were a dozen or so at her school, but that was out of a thousand students. There were none in her class, so she had little day-to-day contact with them.

“Is your name really Dingo?” she asked.

Dingo smiled and Kylie noted the curious yellowing of his eye ‘whites’. He shook his head. “Just a nickname,” he said. “My dad liked Graham Connors’ songs. My name’s George.”

“Do you mind people calling you that?” Kylie asked.

Dingo shrugged. “Sometimes. Depends on their tone of voice.”

“You speak good English.”

“Why shouldn’t I?” Dingo snapped. “I went to high school, same as you.”

Kylie blushed and felt foolish for making the statement. To keep the conversation going she asked, “Which school was that?”

“Kalkadoon State High, in Mount Isa,” Dingo replied.

“Mount Isa. I’ve never been there. What’s it like?”

For the next ten minutes Dingo amused her, and Margaret and Norah, who joined them, with his description of Mount Isa. As he talked Kylie studied his very dark, black hair, and the interesting shape of his lips and nose. It was Mrs Conroy who ended the talking by looking pointedly at her watch and saying, "Time to start packing up and saddling up people."

By the time they resumed the trail ride Kylie was feeling much happier. Norah was now busily ignoring the boys or giving off-hand answers, while at the same time being very nice to Margaret and her. Even so Kylie still felt a bit flat in her emotions.

I would like a bit of romance, she thought, but was puzzled about how such a state of affairs could possibly develop out here in the bush if Peter wasn't interested. It was obvious to her that he still had eyes only for Norah, even if he was a bit puzzled about the way she was speaking to him.

The only incident of note was Mrs Conroy and Norah both having to remind Graham and Stephen to put their safety helmets on.

"Aw Mrs Conroy!" Graham grumbled. "They don't protect us from the sun. They need a brim on them."

Kylie had to agree with that, but she knew that the real reason was that the white plastic helmets did not fit in with the boy's image. 'Too dorky looking!' Stephen had quietly commented. But the helmets went on and the ride resumed.

Once again Mrs Conroy drove on ahead to set up for the next camp. The riders followed at a steady walk. The going was relatively flat and just ordinary Australian 'bush', savannah woodland. After a couple of kilometres they came to another side road. This was just two wheel ruts winding off towards the southwest. Norah led them along it after first checking that all the horses were alright, and that all the saddles were properly fixed.

For the next hour they rode slowly along this track, trending southwest but with many small deviations. The country began to change, and Kylie noted that the track was now running along the crest of a wide ridge, undulating from one rise to the next. Off to the right, a few kilometres away, was a vast and rugged jumble of hills that seemed to go on forever away to the West. On her right was an ever-deepening creek line which steadily developed into a regular gorge. Beyond the gorge were more hills but with a hint of the ground dropping off abruptly to the south.

They halted on the next hilltop for a rest and Kylie was able to see that they were now right on the edge of quite a deep valley. This was very rough and studded with rocks. A dry stream bed ran along its bottom. The vegetation changed back to the stunted bushes and gnarled little trees with silver-grey leaves which shimmered in the breeze.

She was glad of that breeze because the sky was still clear of clouds and the sun was very hot. That was in contrast to the long line of grey clouds she could now see over the mountains back to the east. It was obviously raining back around Herberton and Ravenshoe, but the rain shadow effect of the lower western ranges meant it was dry and hot where they were.

After ten minutes the ride was resumed. Most of the time they rode in single file and in silence. Graham and Peter did the most talking, pointing out features they had identified on their maps or to relics of old mines.

The group rode slowly down a rough section of track and then past the top of a very steep-sided re-entrant which led down into the valley on the left. Then it was up over a bare little knoll studded with red boulders and clumps of stunted bushes and trees. Peter called it '910' and it took Kylie a moment to realise he was giving its height in metres above sea level. There was a gentle, tree-covered stretch beyond that, but this led to a much steeper and higher hill. Kylie eyed this with some apprehension, as it looked too rugged for horses and she could not see where the road went over it.

She discovered that it didn't. The track led past a couple of old campsites and mullock heaps before turning abruptly left. It then went over the side of the gorge. Norah made them all dismount and check their saddles. The horses were rested for ten minutes and given a drink and the boys wandered around exploring the old mining area.

"This is a lot easier than looking for those old mines in the jungle near Bartle Frere," was Peter's comment. It was something Kylie could only agree with, remembering with distaste the tangle of jungle with its vines, wait-a-while and leeches. In spite of that Kylie considered the rain forest better. She found the drabness, dryness, and vastness of this 'outback' country somehow intimidating.

The next hour was hard, slow work. They went down the side of the mountain on foot, leading the horses along the old road. In many places the road had been eroded or partially blocked by landslips and it took care to avoid stepping into a washout or pothole. Many stretches of the steep downslope had a surface of loose gravel, and these were tricky to negotiate safely too. The horses, with four feet, seemed to find it easier.

On a dozen occasions one or other of the group slipped but only Roger actually fell. He landed hard on his bum and sat for a while with tears in his eyes. Kylie was glad they weren't riding down that part of the route.

The saving aspect was the scenery. They now had a view out to the south along a large valley. The view seemed to go on forever, the valley giving way to an immense plain studded with hills. Away off to the southeast, Graham pointed out a sharp-edged, flat-topped peak which he said was Arthurs Seat.

"Named after the one in Edinburgh in Scotland," he explained.

Peter stood, map in one hand and the other, reins looped over his elbow, at his brow. "I reckon we can see for a hundred kilometres," he estimated.

Studying the vast plain which extended southwards to a hazy horizon Kylie was prepared to accept that. For a few moments she felt a strong feeling of 'being there' as one of the first European explorers and she knew she now had a much better appreciation of all that 'explorer' stuff she had learnt at school.

Stephen articulated this by saying, "Now I know how all those blokes like Leichhardt and Dalrymple and so on must have felt."

"Too right!" Graham agreed. "All this huge area of unexplored bush, and all those wild Aborigines."

As soon as Graham said that, Kylie was embarrassed and glanced around to see if Dingo had heard him. He had and he met her eye and gave a sardonic smile.

"Too bloody right!" he commented. "We remember that Leichhardt fella, and Kennedy and Gilbert, and a few more."

There was a moment of embarrassed silence as no-body quite knew if they had offended Dingo or not. To Kylie's relief, he grinned and said, "It's alright. I admire them fellas too. They were tough men, but I resent what followed. Just remember who was here first and whose land this really is eh?"

Kylie nodded and was granted yet another strong image of what the past actually meant. Norah restored the situation by telling them to keep moving. After that the view vanished quickly enough. They only had to go down for about a hundred metres and they were below the level of most of the surrounding hills and another short descent had them down at the level of the tree canopy and that blocked most of the view.

To everyone's relief they reached the bottom after another ten minutes and from there on the going was easy, a grassy flat studded with ironbarks beside a dry creek bed. This was joined by an even larger dry stream from a rocky gorge to the East.

"Nettle Creek," Peter said.

Norah nodded. "Yes. Only another hour to our camp," she said. "We will have another rest and check the horses."

They dismounted and Norah and Dingo went along and lifted up every horse's leg to check their shoes. While they did this the others grouped in the shade of a stand of sheoaks beside the creek bed. Stephen was busy discussing whether the rock types might be suitable for finding minerals other than tin when he suddenly stopped and looked up. Kylie followed his gaze and then heard the vibration.

"Helicopter!" Peter cried.

With a buzzing clatter a blue and white helicopter swept low overhead. It had flown low down the valley of Nettle Creek, so they had not heard it till it was almost overhead. As Kylie watched she saw it tilt on its side, then abruptly change direction to swing round in a sharp circle. On its side the word POLICE was clearly visible. She saw faces peering down at them and felt a distinct chill when she noted that at least one of the black-clad people in the helicopter appeared to be holding a weapon. Another raised binoculars to his face.

"Looking for the Kelly Gang still," Peter commented.

He smiled and then waved. The helicopter swept around again, low overhead while the people in it subjected the group to a close scrutiny. That made Kylie feel distinctly uneasy and she experienced a sense of dislike at being spied on. Even so she waved as well.

Stephen jeered and looked up. "They are being a bit more careful after their stuff-up this morning," he said.

"I hope so!" Margaret cried. "That gave me a real fright."

"Not as much as being held up by real bushrangers would have," Stephen replied with a laugh.

The helicopter abruptly steadied on a course which took it away from them down the valley. It quickly vanished from sight and almost as soon the sound of its engine died away.

Kylie watched it go with an uneasy feeling. "I wonder if they have found the Duke yet?" she said.

"I doubt it," Graham answered. "If they had they wouldn't be flying round the bush in circles."

"We can listen to the radio when we get to camp," Norah said. She had been holding two of the horses by their bridles, the animals having been upset by the helicopter. "Here, take the reins," she said to Graham, handing him a set.

The group remounted and continued with the ride. It was hot and still by then, not a cloud in the sky and the sun's rays trapped and reflected by the stony hillsides on either hand. It was only after a few more kilometres, when they entered more forested country and the valley opened out, that they felt the vestiges of a breeze.

The vehicle track crossed Nettle Creek and ran across a pleasant, well-wooded flat on the left bank for a few more kilometres. By the time they reached a junction Kylie was starting to feel very stiff and even a little chafed. She could tell by the way they kept fidgeting and adjusting their position in the saddles that most of the others were feeling the same way. The trail ride began to imperceptibly shift from a pleasant expedition to a bit of a physical ordeal.

The group took the right fork and re-crossed Nettle Creek across an old, overgrown mining area. The whole floor of the valley was a jumble of small hills of soil and scooped out hollows, some full of knee-high grass, others filled with muddy rain water, and others bare, dry scars of reddish clay.

Peter indicated the area and asked, "What happened here?"

Norah answered him. "Tin mining, with a dredge. About forty years ago. I never saw it but mum showed me pictures. The dredge was like a huge floating factory about five stories high and it floated in its own lake. It had all these enormous buckets on a revolving chain and as it moved along it scooped up all the topsoil, processed it to remove the tin, then dumped all these heaps of tailings behind it."

"Made a bit of a mess," Roger commented.

"They wouldn't be allowed to do it these days," Dingo put in, "Not with all the environmental controls."

"They shouldn't have been allowed to do it then," Stephen commented with some heat. That surprised Kylie a bit as she hadn't put Stephen down as being a person who cared much for the environment. But she had to agree, the old mined area was an unpleasant wasteland. She found it a relief to get out of it and back into ordinary bush, although she kept getting glimpses of it through the trees on her left as they rode along. As Norah pointed out, the tin dredge had worked its way right up the creek for ten kilometres or more, leaving a trail of devastated bush in its wake.

After a couple more kilometres they came to a locked gate. Norah had a key for this and let them through. By then Kylie was in real pain and just wanted the day's ride to end.

"How much further?" she asked, trying to make it sound casual.

"About one kilometre," Norah replied.

That was a real relief to Kylie, and, she guessed, to most of the others. She gritted her teeth and set herself to ignore the aches and rubbing. The group rode on. A few hundred metres further along they passed a road junction and Kylie saw several houses among the trees to her left. After crossing another overgrown area of mined land they came up a slight rise to find more houses and fairly open country.

Norah pointed towards the houses. "This is the town of Innot Hot Springs," she explained.

"Town!" Stephen jibed. But Kylie was relieved and studied the place. On the left were several grassy paddocks dotted with a few trees and several horses. On the right was pleasant open savannah woodland with long grass and tall eucalypts with very few bushes or small trees among them. The next open paddock on the left had a dozen horses in it, all clustered over at a trough at the far side. A black-haired girl in jeans was busy there, adding feed to a bin.

Waiting at the gate to the second paddock along on the left was Mrs Conroy with the vehicle. Beyond there was a cluster of buildings and then more open areas. Topsy was already in the paddock and walked along the other side of the fence whinnying. Mrs Conroy held the gate open for them and told them go across to the far side. They did so and arrived at a horse trough under a spreading tree. Norah told them to dismount and off-saddle. To Kylie that was a real relief but she managed to hide it. Margaret seemed to be quite unaffected by the day's ride and chattered away happily, springing down from her horse and walking around apparently without any sore muscles.

Not so the boys. They all groaned and winced, and Kylie noted that they all seemed to be walking very gingerly. *Chafed, poor things!* she deduced.

Mrs Conroy drove the vehicle across and parked nearby. The horses were tethered in a line along the fence. Saddles were removed, then carried to the vehicle and stowed in the trailer. As they did this, both Roger and Peter limped and repeatedly groaned, much to Dingo's sardonic amusement. The horses were rubbed down and watered and only then did Mrs Conroy tell them to remove the bridles and let them go.

"Where to now?" Margaret asked.

Mrs Conroy pointed to the buildings a hundred metres away. "To the camping ground at the caravan park," she replied.

"Oh bloody hell! I don't know if I can walk that far!" Roger cried in dismay.

They set off walking along the fence in a straggling group, their bridles slung over their shoulders or arms. Kylie found she was hobbling but bravely tried to pretend she wasn't hurting. Peter and Roger both made no secret of being sore but both Graham and Stephen walked in silence. To Kylie it was clear they were both determined not to admit they were feeling any pain.

A gate allowed easy access to the back of the camping ground. Norah led the group across a lawn past several caravans to a line of timber huts beside a large grassy lawn. The lawn was dotted with trees and included children's playground equipment and a swimming pool. Beyond them was the back of the office and store.

Norah pointed to three rooms. "These are yours. Two to a room. Girls in the third one, boys in the other two. Your gear is inside. We are in the next row of huts. Showers and toilets over there," she explained.

None of this was any surprise to Kylie as the booking had included bunking in cabins and she was now yearning for a hot shower. The doors to the huts were open and had keys dangling in the locks.

Graham pointed to the swimming pool. "What about a swim?"

"Be bit cold," Peter suggested doubtfully.

"Aren't there hot springs here?" Stephen asked.

Norah pointed to the creek, whose sandy bed was just visible a hundred meters away. "The hot springs are over there, just behind the hotel."

Kylie looked and noted a shallow flow of water and was not impressed. "Hot bath for me!" she cried, hurrying towards the doorway of her hut.

Norah laughed and called, "Tea is at six, barbecue, so don't be late."

Margaret joined Kylie and they went in and examined the room. To Kylie's relief, it smelt very fresh and was nice and clean. Her suitcase and bag were there on a sideboard. Nodding with pleasure she went to them and began digging out a change of clothes.

A few minutes later she made her way out with clean clothes and towel over her shoulder and thongs on her sore feet. Margaret followed, wrapped in a big dressing gown. The shower block was twenty metres away along a concrete path. Inside it had nice clean tiles and separate cubicles.

As Kylie studied the layout, one of the cubicles opened and out stepped a teenage girl slightly older than herself. The girl had lovely rich black hair which she was still rubbing dry. Even wrapped in a dressing gown, a strikingly pretty one of dark green silk, it was obvious she had a very shapely figure. The girl looked surprised, then nodded and gave a weak smile before making her way past them.

Where have I seen her? Kylie wondered as she made her way into a shower cubicle.

Then she shook her head and forgot about the girl in the sheer sensual bliss of the hot water. There was some tingling and itching of her chafed inner thighs and a few small cramps and aches in numerous muscles, but she felt so good she just sighed and rubbed.

Twenty minutes later, she came back out of her cabin feeling much refreshed. Her whole body felt a tingling tiredness, but the worst of the sore muscles were eased and the chafing was temporarily soothed. She joined Margaret and Norah at the BBQ out on the lawn.

"Where are the boys?" she asked.

Norah pointed to the creek. "Over there, swimming in the hot pools."

Kylie was surprised and it must have showed on her face because Norah gave a wry grin and added, "There are some young women there and they aren't wearing very much."

"That figures!" Kylie snorted.

She glanced at Margaret and decided she was trying not to look unhappy. Now that she focused, she saw the boys splashing and lying in the shallow water. It was obviously only knee to thigh deep as they kept standing up and running around. Near them were the young women: four of them and all wearing tiny bikinis. One in particular, a blonde, seemed to be very well endowed and to have a very skimpy bikini top.

"Showing off!" she snorted.

"Playing the fool, anyhow," Norah agreed.

Margaret said nothing but concentrated on getting the fire alight. Kylie helped set out food, slice onions and arrange salad in bowls. Mrs Conroy joined them and then Dingo. Steaks, sausages, and onions were placed on the hot plate. Cooking proceeded with a lot of happy chatter about the day's ride and horses.

Mrs Conroy turned a steak and then said to Kylie, "This is nearly cooked. Would you go and call those boys please?"

Kylie did as she was asked, getting some malicious amusement by noting that the bikini girls had wrapped themselves in towels and walked away to the hotel. The boys came straggling out of the water and dried themselves, then followed her back to the camping ground. Graham and Stephen both picked up prickles from walking barefoot and that made Kylie shake her head in exasperation.

Her exasperation increased when Graham started flirting with Norah as soon as he arrived at the BBQ. He wore only shorts and Kylie was sure he was deliberately showing off his muscles. She conceded that her brother had a very attractive body, with good muscle tone, but it was annoying to see that Margaret was being ignored. Then another of those petty incidents which peeved Kylie so much happened. The black-haired girl she had last seen in the shower came walking along the concrete path from the shop at the front of the campground. Now she wore tight jeans and a flannel shirt tied in a knot to expose her midriff. Kylie recognised her as the girl who had been feeding the horses when they rode in.

The boys all turned their heads to watch the girl walk past and Kylie noted a look of what could have been despair cross Margaret's face. She knew that Margaret was very anxious about her slightly chubby build and lack of really obvious female features and that she felt she could not compete with older, better developed girls.

The black-haired girl was certainly attractive, even beautiful, Kylie conceded, but that did not help ease her annoyance at Graham's blindness to Margaret's love. All she could do was sigh and wish as she watched the girl go into the room next to hers.

The black-haired girl had no sooner gone when Dingo looked towards the front of the campground where the sound of engines could be heard. He shook his head and muttered, "Here's more trouble!"

Chapter 9

TENSION

Kylie looked around in alarm.

Trouble! What kind of trouble? she thought.

Then she saw what Dingo meant. Three policemen had come through the back door of the shop and were walking along the pathway towards them. They were mounted police and wore khaki jodhpurs and black leather leggings. All were carrying duffle bags. As they got closer, Kylie recognised Constable Lonergan as the second one.

The leading policeman, a Senior Constable by the single chevron on the epaulet of his blue shirt, saw them and veered across the lawn towards them. In his free hand he had the key to a room, but he now slipped this into his pocket and moved his hand to near the pistol holster on his belt. To Kylie he looked a surly brute, and she felt a twinge of guilty anxiety.

The senior constable stopped facing them. He nodded to Mrs Conroy, then ran his eyes over the group before settling his stare on Dingo. After a moment he grunted, then said, "G'day Dingo. Keeping out of trouble?"

"Yes, Mister Grogan," Dingo replied in a very respectful voice.

"And who are all you people?" Snr Constable Grogan asked. Once again, his eyes swivelled to look at each in turn. They were hard, flinty grey eyes, Kylie noted, and she shivered slightly, glad that her conscience was clear, yet perversely annoyed that the man made her feel guilty.

Constable Lonergan saved them from answering as he arrived. "This is the Conroy's Trail Ride, Senior," he said. Then he smiled at Norah before saying to Mrs Conroy, "Hello again Mrs Conroy. How was the day's ride?"

"Fine thank you, Frank," Mrs Conroy said. "And how was your day?"

"Tiring," Constable Lonergan replied, his face again breaking into a friendly grin. Kylie noted that his gaze kept shifting to Norah and that she was blushing. She also noted that the mounted policemen all looked tired and dirty.

Mrs Conroy smiled back. "Have you caught the Kelly Gang yet?" she asked politely.

Constable Lonergan smiled and laughed while Snr Constable Grogan scowled. The third policeman joined them. It was Constable Lonergan who answered. "Not yet. That's why we are here."

Norah spoke next. "Are you staying here?" she asked, her face blushing red as she did.

Constable Lonergan nodded. "Yep. The pub is full up, or it is now that Inspector Moriarty and Sgt Healy have booked in."

Stephen made a face. "I thought the Kellies were hiding in the Herberton Range," he commented.

Constable Lonergan smiled, Snr Const Grogan scowled, and the third policeman snorted with annoyance and walked off towards another row of huts. Constable Lonergan gestured towards the barbecue.

"That smells good."

Mrs Conroy nodded. "Would you like some? We've got plenty."

Kylie did not like that idea but was too polite and nervous to say anything. But she did see Dingo frown and look unhappy, and Stephen grunted.

Constable Lonergan shook his head. "Thanks very much, but no. We are booked in for a meal in the hotel dining room." He glanced at his watch and added, "That is in twenty minutes. We had better get a wriggle on if we are going have a bath and change."

Margaret spoke next. "Where are your horses?" she asked.

"In the paddock across the road from yours," Constable Lonergan replied as he started walking. He gave a last smile to Norah and said, "Enjoy your meal."

Snr Const Grogan looked hard at Dingo and added, "You keep out of trouble Dingo. Stay away from the pub."

Kylie saw a look of dislike cross Dingo's face, but he made no reply as the policeman walked away. There was a tense silence until the policeman was out of earshot, then Stephen tactlessly asked the question that was on Kylie's mind. "What have you done to make such good friends with the police Dingo?"

Dingo grunted angrily and scowled, then replied, "Nothin'. I'm black, that's enough for some people."

There was an embarrassed silence for a few seconds, broken by Mrs Conroy saying, "Now start eating you people, before these steaks go cold."

The food eased the situation. There were enough tables and chairs for everyone to seat themselves and Kylie sat beside Margaret at the same table as Graham and Roger. The food was good and after a day of fresh air and unaccustomed exercise she felt quite hungry. The tension eased away and the conversation became general, ranging over the day's ride, horses, the weather (clouds had come across and looked threatening) and cadets.

Seeing the policemen walking to the front of the campground where their vehicle was parked moved the conversation to speculation on whether they would catch the Kelly Gang and rescue the Duke.

Dingo sneered and said vehemently, "I hope they don't!"

Margaret looked up sharply. "Well, I hope they do," she commented, "I thought the Duke looked a very nice man."

Graham snorted. "Huh! You can have him. He will be just another stuck-up, toffee-nosed Pommy lord."

Peter laughed. "You'd know all about them, having met so many," he teased.

Kylie had been nettled by the insinuation that Margaret could look elsewhere so she now replied, "It's because Graham thinks he's Lord Muck."

Graham shot a hurt look at her and opened his mouth to respond. Norah beat him to it and asked who wanted desert. That eased the situation and they settled to eating tinned peaches with custard and condensed milk.

By the time they were finished it was dark and a few spits of rain made them quickly pack away and clean up. Mrs Conroy reminded them that it was a 6 o'clock rise for an 8 o'clock start in the morning and told them all to be in bed early.

Kylie then went to the shop. There was a pay phone against the back wall, and she tried ringing her mother to tell her they were alright. However the phone at the other end was engaged and she could not get through. When she tried again later, she was told that her mother had gone out to dinner with relatives.

"That's alright. I will ring again in the morning at seven," she said.

She then went and did her washing in the laundry, making the boys do likewise. There were tumble driers so that problem was easily solved. In between loads of washing the evening was spent watching TV in the small recreation room, or playing snooker in the annexe. For

Kylie two hours of that was more than enough, so when her laundry was done she took herself to bed. It was only 9:30 but she was tired and her bed very comfortable and pleasant. Margaret came in a few minutes later and, after changing and cleaning her teeth, climbed into her own bed. The two friends lay and talked for half an hour until they drifted into deep sleep.

* * *

Mrs Conroy woke them by knocking on the door. "Wake up girls. Get packed up. Breakfast in half an hour," she called.

The girls rolled out of bed and hurried to the toilet and shower block. A wash woke them up and Kylie noted that it was a cool morning and that the sky was overcast. Back at the room she dressed ready for the day's ride and then packed her bag. That done she went out to help prepare breakfast. This was another BBQ: bacon, sausages, and fried eggs with toast. There was also a variety of fruit and cereal and plenty of orange juice. Mrs Conroy and Norah cooked the breakfast. Roger came out to help, the other boys not yet having appeared.

"Seven o'clock," said Mrs Conroy. "Roger, go and hurry them up. We need to be out of here in thirty minutes."

As Roger went off to the boy's dormitory Kylie remembered that she wanted to speak to her mother. She excused herself and hurried to the telephone. As she arrived, she saw that the black-haired girl was ahead of her and was speaking on the phone. As Kylie arrived the girl looked around in alarm, then made a face and covered the phone with her hand.

"Sorry, you startled me. I won't be a moment," she said. She then looked away and continued speaking. "Yes, that's right, at about five o'clock, heading east. Goodbye."

The girl then hung up, turned and held her dressing gown tightly around her and hurried off back towards her room. Kylie went to the phone and made the call. This time her mother was there, and she was able to tell her all the news.

Her mother said, "So you are enjoying yourselves?"

"Yes Mum. It is great, well, for Margaret and me anyway."

"Why? What do you mean?" her mother asked.

"I don't think Graham is enjoying it. Oh, he likes the bush and the camping and exploring but I think he got very chafed and saddle-sore yesterday. So did Roger and Peter but they admitted it," Kylie explained.

Her mother agreed, then added, "I've been worried about you children."

"Why Mum? We are safe. Mrs Conroy and Norah are very nice and look after us very well," Kylie replied.

"Oh it's this Kelly Gang business. I see on the news that the police haven't caught them yet," her mother replied.

"No," Kylie agreed. "There are some police staying here, mounted police they are, and one of them likes Norah I think."

"You are at Innot Hot Springs, aren't you?" her mother queried.

"Yes Mum."

"So why are there police there? I thought the Kelly Gang had gone into hiding at Upper Barron?"

That really got Kylie anxious. "I don't think the police know where they are Mum," she answered, while thinking, *If Mum isn't happy she might cancel the trip!* To forestall this she added, "Anyway, we ride along near the main highway today and will be at the Mt Garnet Racecourse this afternoon. It will be fine Mum."

"Yes, alright," her mother answered doubtfully. "Alright then, but you ring me again tonight from Mt Garnet please."

"Yes Mum. Say hello to Aunty Frances for me, bye."

As she hung up Kylie heard the roar of an approaching vehicle. It was a police 4WD and it skidded to a stop in the driveway. The sergeant with the mutton chop whiskers, Sgt Healy, jumped out, slammed the door and hurried across. He wore only his trousers, boots and a T-shirt.

"Which rooms are my men in?" he asked.

"Six and seven," Kylie answered. A thrill of excitement ran through her as the sergeant ran past her along the path. *They must have information,* she decided. This was confirmed as she heard the sergeant pounding on the door of Unit 6.

"Come on you slugs! Out of bed and get moving!" he bellowed.

The door opened and Constable Lonergan's face looked out. "What is it Sarge?" he asked.

Kylie did not hear the whole conversation as she walked across the lawn to rejoin the others at the BBQ but she did overhear Sgt Healy say, "Report from a lady on a farm of five men on horses riding east from Tumoulin towards the Tumoulin Woods at about five this morning. So get a wriggle on. Get packed and have those horses in the trailer in twenty minutes."

"What about breakfast?" called a voice from inside.

Sgt Healy swore, then remembered there were ladies present and instead quietly growled his opinion of breakfast. He then turned and hurried back to his vehicle.

Kylie sat down to eat and saw Constable Lonergan dash across to the shower block in just a pair of shorts. On the way he passed Dingo, giving him a cheery good morning as he did. Dingo made a face in reply and came over to join them. "What are the coppers in a fluster about?" he asked.

Kylie answered. "Some report of men on horses near Tumoulin," she replied. "How are the horses?"

"Fine Missus," Dingo replied.

The four boys now appeared and were offered breakfast. Stephen gestured to the unit behind him. "What's all the excitement?" he asked.

Kylie related what she knew and the whole group watched with interest as the police hastily packed. Constable Lonergan came running back after an obviously hasty shower and shave, to re-appear five minutes later fully dressed in uniform. As he stood in the doorway buckling on his pistol belt, Kylie felt a little thrill of admiration.

Noting the straight nose, firm muscles and determined jaw she thought, *Oh, he's a good-looking man. I hope he doesn't get hurt.*

Norah obviously thought so too as she called to him as he hurried past with his bag. "Frank, be careful please."

"I will," Constable Lonergan called back. "Don't you worry Norah. Only the good die young." He gave a big grin and hurried on out of sight. Kylie glanced quickly at Dingo to see how he took this and noted a look of stony hostility on his face.

The other two police appeared soon after and went off in the same direction. As they did, Peter asked, "Where are the Tumoulin Woods?"

Norah answered that. "About thirty or forty kilometres east of here, just to the north of Ravenshoe."

"Oh I know where," Roger cried. "Where we went for that steam train ride a couple of years ago."

"That was at Herberton," Stephen said.

Roger nodded but replied, "Yes, but we also went on one at Ravenshoe. The train with the blue tank locomotive."

Stephen nodded and agreed. "Oh yeah, I remember. That was a great engine, really well looked after."

"Like 'Thomas the Tank Engine'," added Peter.

"Except that Thomas has only four driving wheels and that one has six," Graham replied. Then he glanced at Norah and blushed and Kylie guessed he was embarrassed to have spoken like a little boy who still played with trains.

Mrs Conroy now broke in and urged them to eat. "Hurry up. We want to be on the road. It is going to be a long day. You girls are on show at three and Norah's race is at four, so let's move. We still have about twenty kilometres to go."

The mention of being 'on show' caused Kylie to blush with embarrassment. She had kept this a secret from the boys and they all looked at her inquiringly. She just shook her head and bent to her plate. It was something she now half-regretted, but she and Margaret had both nominated to take part in the 'Fashions on the Field' and both had their dresses packed in their suitcases in the vehicle. It had been Margaret who had suggested it, then dared her. At the time, Kylie had thought it would be good fun. Now she wasn't so sure and felt a swirl of nervousness.

Urged on by Mrs Conroy and Norah they ate, washed up, packed away and then carried their bags out to the vehicle. Kylie lugged her bag out behind Margaret. Norah followed. The vehicle was parked to one side of the driveway, which was also a ring road with fuel pumps. There were two other vehicles there, one a white 4WD towing a horse trailer. Kylie paid this no attention but went to the back of Mrs Conroy's vehicle and handed her the bag. As she did, she heard angry voices behind her and turned to look.

It was the short, thin girl, Doris Peagreen. She was standing holding the nozzle of the pump in the fuel tank inlet, while looking over her shoulder. "You keep out of my way 'Beanpole'," she snapped at Norah.

"Don't you try cutting me off again, not like you did last year," Norah retorted.

"That broken down nag you were riding was getting in the way and holding everyone up," Doris said.

Just behind Kylie was the open back of the horse float. She looked in and saw the rumps of two horses; a chestnut and a grey. As Norah came towards her, her eyes flashing and her complexion red with anger, Kylie pointed and asked, "Is one of these 'Silver Streak'?"

Norah nodded and pointed. "The chestnut."

On hearing his name Silver Streak turned his head and Kylie had an impression of a very nice-looking horse. She took a step closer to get a better look. As she did, Doris snapped at her, "You keep away from my horses!"

"I just wanted to have a look," Kylie answered, blushing with hurt and embarrassment.

"Want to nobble them more likely," Doris retorted.

The accusation so shocked Kylie that she was unable to think of a reply. Norah did though. "That is very unfair!" she cried. "You don't even know her."

"If she's a friend of yours then she is bad news," Doris answered.

"At least I've got friends!" Norah cried.

At that, Doris went very red and called Norah a very-unladylike name. Mrs Conroy now intervened. "Norah, you and Kylie go and get your bridles. Now stop the name calling and get on with packing."

Kylie did as she was told but she went with seething emotions. Anger and dislike boiled in her and she felt hurt and humiliated. Somehow it felt like she was running away but arguing with Mrs Conroy would be even more undignified, so she obeyed. As they went around the corner she glanced back and caught a glimpse of a sneer on Doris's face.

"What a horrible girl! I really hope you beat her," Kylie said.

Norah shrugged. "She hasn't liked me ever since we were little."

"Have you known each other long?" Kylie asked.

"Since we were babies. Her brothers and mine are also rivals," Norah replied.

"What happened to make her dislike you so much?" Kylie queried.

Norah looked uncomfortable, then shrugged and said, "Oh, a dozen little things. I beat her in the Year Three spelling test, and I didn't invite her to my fifth birthday party, and she accused me of being the teacher's pet. And Colin Costello gave me flowers at a school dance, and she was in love with him."

She tailed off and shrugged again. Kylie had to smile at the sheer 'human-ness' and pettiness of it all but it was still quite unpleasant. It was on the tip of her tongue to add, 'and you are beautiful and she is ugly,' but stopped herself. They rejoined the others and the subject was dropped.

Having cleared the rooms they collected their bridles and followed Norah and Dingo through the back gate to the horse paddock. By then the sun had broken through and it was hot enough to get them all sweaty while they caught their horses and bridled them. Mrs Conroy drove in to the paddock with the vehicle and they collected saddle cloths and saddles and fitted them.

That cheered Kylie up and she pushed her anxiety aside. Just rubbing Blazer and talking to her made her feel more relaxed and happier. There was a moment's doubt as she swung herself up into the saddle and all of yesterday's sore muscles protested, but she bit her lip and settled herself firmly in a comfortable seat. Margaret just seemed to spring up but all of the boys made a drama of it. Graham was tight-lipped and silent, pretending it didn't hurt but the other three all groaned and moaned and fidgeted a lot.

Mrs Conroy gave them instructions for the next stop and then loaded Topsy and drove out. The group followed in a straggling line. Kylie and Norah led and as they walked along Kylie asked, "Where do we go now?"

"Through that other gate opposite and up across that paddock," Norah replied. She led the way through the gate and across the side road to the next gate. Here she dismounted to open it. Behind them Dingo dismounted to close the first gate. While they waited Kylie looked around and saw the black-haired girl walking along the far side of the paddock. She was carrying a saddle and bridle and appeared to be heading for the horses in the paddock beyond.

The group went through the gate and continued on across the next paddock. This was the one with waist high grass and dotted with a forest of tall eucalypts and it was very pleasant riding.

As the trail ride settled into its routine, Kylie relaxed and began to enjoy the day, her pleasure just slightly marred by niggling anxiety about the fashion contest.

Maybe I should withdraw my nomination, she wondered.

Chapter 10

GROWING ANXIETY

For the first twenty minutes the riding was easy. They followed a track beside a fence line up a long, gentle slope. The houses of Innot Hot Springs were lost to view among the trees behind them. Sore muscles eased as they warmed up but Kylie noted the first faint twinges of soreness in her chafed parts and hoped that it would not get worse.

I don't want to be limping around during the fashion parade, she thought.

Anxiety about that event now began to grow in her mind. What particularly bothered her, above any of the sneers of the crowd, was what her brother and his friends might think of her.

They will think I am a very vain show-off, she thought unhappily. Once again she considered pulling out.

The trail crested a gentle ridge top. Here they paused for a few minutes, dismounting to adjust saddles and clothing. While they did Kylie talked to Blazer and rubbed her nose, savouring the horse smell and the animal's obvious liking for her. She barely noticed when Peter pointed back to the east and commented on the fact that a long line of grey clouds was covering the mountains in that direction.

Norah ordered them to mount, and Kylie had to smile at the chorus of groans and wails from Roger, Stephen and Peter. Once again Graham remained tight-lipped but there was no doubt he was not happy. By now Kylie's stiffness had eased and she was able to enjoy remounting and settling comfortably into the saddle.

They rode down another gentle ridge through savannah woodland for 2 kilometres, reaching a creek line at 9 o'clock. This creek had also been heavily mined by tin dredges at some time in the distant past and for several hundred metres the going was through an ugly wilderness of bushes, mullock heaps and bare patches of clay.

"Battle Creek," Graham commented after studying his map.

"Who had the battle?" Roger asked.

Graham shrugged. "No idea."

Dingo called from the back of the line, "Black fellas against white fellas, back when the whites first invaded."

Kylie felt uneasy about that word 'invaded' and none of them asked who won the battle. It was all too obvious who had won the war. It was the first time in her life that Kylie had ever really confronted the issue of white settlement and its consequences and even though it had happened a hundred and fifty years before she was born she found it prickly on the conscience. She had learned about it at school of course, and had even taken part in debates about it, but now, actually riding across the bush in the same way the first European pioneers had done gave it a much more intense emotional edge. Her uneasiness made her a bit wary of Dingo.

The trail led them up another ridge covered with sparse grass and open woodland of ironbarks. The ridge ran west with Neds Gully on their right and Dempseys Hanging Pinnacle on their left. Despite peering often through the trees Kylie failed to sight the hanging pinnacle, a rock balanced on top of another. On top of the ridgeline they came to a gravel vehicle track and followed it southwest, down a spurline.

From ahead of them came the sound of vehicles on the Kennedy Highway and hearing the noises sent Kylie's anxiety back up. It meant they were getting closer to Mt Garnet and that embarrassing moment when she must disport herself in front of all those critical viewers.

Just before the riders reached the highway, they found Mrs Conroy and the vehicle. She had parked in a shady clearing and the riders were invited to dismount, ease their horses saddle girths and give them a drink, then have morning tea themselves.

"Halfway," Mrs Conroy explained. "Only five more kilometres to the town and the same again to the racecourse."

That was good news to Kylie as her anxiety about being chafed was again growing and she knew she had a few sore muscles developing. Her concerns were heightened when Margaret came over and said, "Oh goody! Won't be long. I am really looking forward to this afternoon."

Seizing this opportunity Kylie replied, "Aren't you nervous about showing off in front of a lot of strangers?"

"Yes," Margaret answered frankly. "But it is what the boys will think that bothers me more."

"Me too!" Kylie replied with feeling.

Margaret gave her a searching look. "Would you like to back out?"

Kylie really wanted to, but she replied, "Only if you want to."

"No. I'd like to do it," Margaret answered.

That wasn't what Kylie had wanted to hear, yet perversely she was glad, knowing she would despise herself if she gave in to her fears. She managed a smile and sipped at the cup of sweet tea. Then a sprinkle of rain made them all look up.

Margaret said, "Oh, I hope the rain doesn't wash out the event."

That became the straw that Kylie clung to. She did not really want rain spoiling the day for other people, particularly Norah, but she still felt anxious.

After the break, at 10:20, they remounted and resumed the ride. The next half hour wasn't very pleasant. To begin with they crossed the highway and then rode along parallel to it on the powerline clearing. This meant less shade and less pleasant views. There was also the traffic. Cars and trucks went past every minute or so and their noise became an almost constant background irritation. Adding to that the waft of burnt oil and diesel smells and Kylie wished they could get it over as quickly as possible. To achieve this Norah led them for some stretches at either a trot (which the boys hated and said so) or a canter.

Just after 11:00 the group reached the outskirts of the town of Mt Garnet. Kylie had visited the town before, so knew what to expect, but coming into it more slowly on horseback gave the place a whole new aspect. What struck her the most was how spread out it was, a straggle of buildings and large empty allotments that went on for several kilometres down a very long slope. The group rode on the grassy verge until they reached the 'business' section of town, two blocks with a scattering of shops and the hotel. Here they dismounted and walked, leading the horses.

When they reached an empty allotment next to the hotel Norah told them to tether the horses so they could have a drink. Mrs Conroy was there with plastic dishes and nosebags. She waved her hand around and said, "When you have looked after your horse you can have half an hour to go to the shop. Buy yourself lunch and be back here ready to go at eleven thirty please. I want us to be at the racecourse by one."

Kylie removed her helmet and wiped perspiration from her face, then moved to care for Blazer. Having cared for her horse Kylie waited till Margaret was also finished, then asked, "Where shall we go?"

Margaret shrugged and then giggled. "We are too young to go to the pub, so we had better go to that shop over there. I think they sell pies."

The girls walked to the very wide main street and looked both ways. After waiting for a car to pass they walked across. As they did, Kylie again looked up and down the street.

"Not very lively for a Saturday morning. There isn't a soul to be seen," she commented.

Margaret also looked around and laughed, then added, "Yes there is. There are those people with horses in the back yard of that house over near the bottom of the hill."

"Yeah, but not in the main street," Kylie insisted. She saw the two people Margaret meant, rubbing down several horses in a back yard. As she looked one of them, a young man, turned and started walking towards them. She noted the fact that he wore 'cowboy' clothes: riding boots, jeans, open-neck, check shirt with sleeves rolled up, cowboy hat; and that he was only a few years older than her. She also noted that he was very good looking. *A stockman,* she decided.

She lost sight of the stockman as she and Margaret went into the shop but her heart gave a little flutter of interest when he followed them in and stood beside them at the counter. Kylie found she was very aware of his presence. Out of curiosity she risked a peek at him, and found herself looking into a pair of very dark brown eyes.

The young man gave her a half-amused smile, then said, "Hi! You girls going to the races?"

Kylie was tongue-tied. *He is very handsome!* she thought, noting the firm jaw, lean neck, curly black hair and bulging arm muscles. All she could do was stammer and nod.

Margaret answered for her, while giving her a knowing look. "Yes, we are," she said.

"So am I," the young man replied.

Sixteen or seventeen, Kylie decided, aware that her heart was beating faster and that she was feeling flustered. Not wanting to appear forward she said, "My mother told me not to talk to strange men." Then she realised the word 'men' was a compliment to the young man.

He grinned and winked at Margaret. "Very wise," he said with a chuckle.

Kylie blushed and looked away, using the excuse that she needed to place her order with the girl behind the counter. Margaret giggled and asked the youth, "Are you going in any of the races?"

"Not me, but my brother is," he replied, directing his words at Kylie.

Kylie glanced at him, then hastily looked away as her heart leapt. Then she blushed and, knowing that she was blushing, blushed some more. She was saved from having to answer by the entry of a teenage girl who called to the youth from the door, "Brian, hurry up. We are late."

The youth, Brian, turned and called back, "Nearly ready, Sis. Just a few things to buy."

At the sound of the girl's voice Kylie glanced back at her. To her surprise she saw it was the pretty, dark-haired girl who had been at the Innot Hot Springs Campground. Their eyes met and the girl frowned, obviously wondering where she had seen Kylie. Then she nodded and turned to leave. As she did, Graham came through the doorway, followed by the other boys.

To Kylie's concern, she saw Graham's eyes take in the black-haired girl's beauty and then light up. "Sorry," he mumbled, all but ogling her. Hastily he stepped aside.

"Thank you," the black-haired girl said, giving Graham a sparkling smile. Then she turned and called again, "Hurry up, Brian!"

Brian glanced at Kylie, and looked a bit annoyed. "Yes, Kate," he called. "Won't be a minute."

Kate walked out after giving Graham another smile. That got Kylie really worried as she saw Graham's face light up and then the way his head turned and his eyes followed her. That Margaret saw this and was anxious was obvious.

Poor Margaret! Kylie thought, but then Brian spoke to her again and she forgot everything else. "She can be a bit bossy my sister," he said. Again he favoured her with a mischievous grin.

Once again Kylie looked away. Graham walked over beside her and said, "What are you buying Kylie?"

"Kylie, eh? That's a nice name," Brian commented.

"Oh humpf!" Kylie snorted, but secretly she felt pleased. *He is just so good looking, and he has really nice eyes,* she thought.

The shop girl gave Kylie her pie and she paid for it, then moved back to wait for Margaret. While she waited Brian turned to look at her and even winked. That so surprised Kylie that she got all flustered and had to look away. As soon as Margaret paid for her pie and moved to join her Kylie led the way outside.

Once outside Margaret gestured with her head back to the shop and said, "Isn't he hunky."

"Cheeky and fresh," Kylie snapped back.

Margaret laughed. "So you agree with me then. He likes you."

"He's just some bushy stockman," Kylie replied, biting into her pie to end the conversation.

As she did, Brian came out, carrying a bottle of cola and a chocolate. He looked towards Kylie and said, "See you at the races then."

Kylie blushed again and was rendered quite speechless. Brian grinned at her, then walked away around the side of the shop. For the next few minutes Kylie pretended she was concentrating on eating her pie, but her mind was racing with emotions, not least of which was hope.

Margaret fuelled these by saying, "How old do you reckon he is?"

"Sixteen or seventeen," Kylie replied through a mouthful of pie. "Too old for you."

"Oh, I don't know," Margaret said, giving Kylie a sly grin. "You are thirteen and will soon be fourteen."

Once again Kylie blushed. She was glad that Peter and Stephen came out with pies and sausage rolls and joined in the conversation. To change the topic Kylie gestured to a passing vehicle towing a horse float. "Lots of horses around here."

"Well, it is race day, and there is a gymkhana and a rodeo tomorrow," Peter answered.

Norah now walked across the street to join them. "Hurry up guys," she said. "Mum wants us to get moving. She wants me to have a practice ride before my race and also time to rest."

That got them walking back across the street. Graham and Roger followed. As quickly as they could, they ate their food and drank their drinks. Rubbish was then deposited in a nearby bin, and they moved to get their horses ready. As she tightened her horse's saddle girth Kylie noted Graham staring back across the street. Following his gaze she was concerned to see that he was looking at the black-haired girl: Kate. She had mounted a horse and was leading two others out onto the footpath. The look of hungry yearning in Graham's expression caused Kylie to bite her lip with worry.

Then she saw Brian appear, also riding and leading three more horses. She immediately forgot about Kate and stared intently at him. At the same moment Brian looked across at her and their eyes seemed to meet and lock. Brian smiled and waved, sending Kylie into a dither of confusion. Embarrassment froze her so she just gave a faint nod in reply and looked away.

Stephen added to it by saying, "Who's that joker waving to?"

Margaret giggled and neither she nor Kylie answered. Both pretended to be busy with their horse's furniture, while actually surreptitiously watching as Brian and his sister rode off down the main street towards the Nanyeta Creek bridge.

As Brian disappeared from sight down a side street to the left after crossing the bridge, Kylie shook her head and thought, *Now I think I understand what they mean by love at first sight.* Then she sighed and thought, *I hope I meet him again!*

Further romantic speculation was ended by Mrs Conroy telling them to get moving. "You've got five kilometres to go, and I want you there in an hour," she said.

Norah led the way, walking and leading their horses for safety. They crossed the street and then walked down the footpath, following the same route Brian and Kate had taken. Once down past the shops they crossed the bridge. Nanyeta (Return) Creek said the sign. The creek was nothing much, just an ordinary dry creek bed ten metres wide and with steep grassy banks. There was very little room on the sides of the bridge, and they had to go slow and wait for passing cars to be able to cross safely.

They were half across when a police car came down the hill. It was travelling the same way they were going. Kylie looked back and idly watched it, expecting it to just drive on. To her concern it slowed and then swung around to stop near her. Two hard-eyed policemen got out, one actually with his hand on the butt of his pistol.

"Who are you people?" he asked.

Norah answered, then showed the policeman some ID. By then all the others had crossed and stood in a shuffling line on the bank of the creek along the side street. The policeman looked them over, his gaze causing Kylie to feel a twinge of anxiety. Then his eyes noted Dingo and he walked across to him.

"Who are you? Show me some ID," he demanded in a harsh voice.

Dingo did as he was told, his face a mask of good-natured happiness. The policeman studied the cards Dingo handed him. Norah now intervened.

"Mister Woodhouse is one of our employees. He has worked for us for a year."

The policeman nodded and handed the cards back, but he did not smile, or apologise for his abrupt manner. Without any explanation the policemen got back into their car and drove off. As they went Dingo curled his lip and shook his head.

Stephen commented in a dry voice, "Well, I guess that means that they haven't caught the Kelly Gang!"

Graham and Peter both laughed but Kylie felt anxious. She did not want any more trouble on the ride. *I've got enough to worry about with the fashion contest,* she thought, her worries being given a new sharp edge by the realisation that Brian might be there and might see her.

On Norah's command they swung into the saddle, and she led them at a fast walk along the side street, keeping to the grassy verge. A few minutes later they passed the last house and were back into dry savannah woodland, more ironbarks. They came to Nanyeta Creek again and crossed it on a dirt vehicle track. The slope down was so steep that Kylie had to lean right back and felt as though she was going to slide forward out of her saddle and over her horse's ears.

This was too much for Graham and he muttered 'bloody hell!' a few times before jumping off and walking across while leading his horse. Going up the other side was just as steep, and this time Kylie had to lean so far forward her face was touching Blazer's mane. She didn't mind and patted the horse's neck as she did. Behind her she heard Margaret giving little whoops of delight.

Up on the far bank they stopped to allow Graham to remount, then set off along a dusty track across a wide, grassy paddock. This allowed them to canter for half a kilometre and Kylie enjoyed that, laughing and savouring the thrill and motion. The track then crossed the lower slopes of several small, stony hills which showed the workings of an extensive open cut mine. Speed came back to a walk as they wound their way among the trees, paperbarks now, growing in red soil.

A pipeline was crossed via a small mound of earth. Off to the right Kylie could see another open paddock, then the line of trees marking the bank of Nanyeta Creek. Beyond the creek she began getting glimpses through gaps in the trees of several old-style buildings.

"'Strathvale' homestead," Norah explained, "One of the first cattle stations in this district."

It looked like a very interesting place to Kylie, but she was granted only tantalising glimpses as they hurried on. The homestead vanished from view as they rode on into more bush around the foot of a larger, rougher hill. Ten minutes of trotting and fast walking through flat bush in a south westerly direction brought them again to the bank of Nanyeta Creek.

"We could have come round beside the highway," Norah explained, "But it is kinder for the horses to keep them away from the traffic."

"Nicer scenery too," Margaret commented.

They crossed the creek's sandy bed and rode on through flat country covered with waist high grass and large ironbarks. After crossing another small, dry creek a few minutes later they came to a gate and then a bitumen road.

Graham had his map out as usual and said, "The Gunnawara Road."

That meant nothing to Kylie, and she was now focused on her coming ordeal. They went through another gate and up a long, gentle slope through more open, drier looking bush. Then, a few hundred metres ahead, Kylie glimpsed movement and buildings.

Norah pointed and said, "There it is, Newman Park Racecourse. Won't be long now."

At that, Kylie's stomach turned over with nervousness and she swallowed. *Oh dear! Maybe I should admit I don't want to do this and pull out,* she thought.

Chapter 11

PICNIC RACES

As they got closer to the racecourse, Kylie looked in amazement at the scene that was revealed through the gaps in the increasingly open scrub and bush. A whole cluster of buildings showed through the trees. Parked amid them were dozens of large trucks and caravans and a general shimmer of movement. As they got closer, the movement was resolved into horses and people, lots of people. There was also a buzz of noise which rose and fell in waves and then became discernible as the blaring of loudspeakers and the murmur and roar of a crowd.

Oh my gosh! Kylie thought in mounting alarm. *This is a lot bigger than I expected.*

Seeing all those people in the distance caused a wave of uneasy nervousness. Once again she considered withdrawing from the fashion show.

Maybe it will be over by the time we get there? she thought. Then a slight sprinkle of rain got her hoping for more to cause a cancellation.

It was certainly raining hard a few kilometres off to her left and away behind her to the east. As they approached the racecourse boundary she looked back and saw that they had ridden up a long gentle slope and could now see out for quite a distance. For a few seconds she studied the rain, hoping it might save her. Then she shook her head.

No, that is selfish. A lot of other people don't want that. I will just have to go through with it, or maybe just withdraw my nomination.

The route Norah took them along led to the north side of the racetrack. This was a grassy oval half a kilometre long surrounded by open and straggly savannah woodland on three sides and the grandstand and cluster of buildings on the other. The buildings were all on the western side of the course. Along the northern side were a series of horse paddocks and yards. To reach these the riders had to pass through several gates.

As they did, Kylie had a better chance to look around. A race went thundering past, six horses, their jockeys all wearing brightly coloured silks. There were also riders busy in the paddock they were entering.

These were in ones and twos and were busy exercising horses. A group of riders was clustered over at the far side, dismounting near some yards under some large trees.

As the group approached the last gate a man came galloping across from near the sheds and parked vehicles. On arriving near the gate the man flung himself from the saddle and quickly opened the gate before Norah could reach it. Kylie saw that he was a typical stockman, dressed in open-necked, white and black checked shirt, broad leather belt, worn jeans and the inevitable elastic sided riding boots. On his curly black hair was a battered and much used 'Akubra' and on his freckled face a cheerful grin of welcome.

About twenty, was Kylie's estimate of the young man's age.

She then watched with interest as the man swept off his battered hat and looked up at Norah, saying. "G'day Nor. Glad to see ya. Was gettin' worried that ya mightn't make it in time."

"Hello Collin," Norah replied. "Is Mum here?"

"Yes Nor. She's over at the shed. She asked me to take you to where these kids are to camp. Old Neville is there setting up," Collin replied.

Norah then looked around at the others. "This is Collin Costello. He's a friend of mine, from 'Karwir' Station," she said.

Friend? Kylie thought, noting the young man's hopeful, but anxious, looks at Norah. *He's smitten by her,* she decided.

Collin gave them all an embarrassed but friendly grin. Then he vaulted into his saddle and set his horse moving beside Norah's. As the two moved off Dingo was left to close the gate and Kylie noted a sour look on his face as he glanced after the departing pair.

The group rode slowly across the paddock to where the set of yards stood under some large trees. In some of the yards there were horses. Collin led them to a gate into the furthest yard, saying in an apologetic tone that it was the only one they could get.

"Why didn't we get our usual one?" Norah asked in a peeved tone.

"The Peagreens have their horses in it," Collin answered.

Norah humpfed and looked irritated. "Oh them! I suppose they slipped the manager a few dollars to get that," she said.

"Just got here first I think," Collin countered in a mild tone.

At the gate to the yard Norah told everyone to dismount and off-saddle, sliding out of her own saddle as she did. Collin leapt off his own mount and held her horse for her, confirming Kylie's thoughts that he was in love with Norah. The group then led their horses to the fence.

Inside the yard were two beautiful horses. Kylie looked at them appreciatively and recognised one as 'Romantic Ruby'. "That's your horse there isn't she Norah?" she asked.

Norah smiled and nodded, then went to the fence and leaned across to stroke Romantic Ruby's nose. "Yes she is. Hello girl, ready for a run?" she said.

The other horse, a ruddy chestnut, trotted over and also wanted some attention. Margaret reached up and patted her muzzle and asked, "What's this horse's name?"

"This is 'Redgum'," Norah answered. "She is my stand-by in case Ruby can't race."

The two horses were admired and then the riders moved back to tending their own mounts. As Kylie loosened the girth straps of her saddle, she noted that the open area beyond the fence was crowded with cars, tents and people, dozens of people. *Hundreds of people!* she thought in amazement.

"I had no idea the races were such a big event," she commented.

Dingo answered her, saying, "Everyone and his dog comes from all the stations for this one. You get people from right up in the Peninsula and even from the Gulf Country."

Margaret pointed and said, "I didn't realise there were all these buildings."

Dingo glanced and nodded. "They'se the camps."

"Camps?"

"That's what people call 'em. Once they was camps but over time they bin turned inter buildings," Dingo explained.

Kylie looked and saw that there were actually dozens of buildings, so many it looked like a village in a third world country. She saw that the buildings were in fact mostly just rough sheds of posts and beams with sheets of corrugated iron nailed to them, though a few looked more like small houses or beach huts.

"Do we camp in one of them?" she asked.

Dingo shook his head and gestured across the fence. "Nah. We set up tents there. That's our truck just there and Old Nev has claimed a few spaces for us."

Kylie now saw Old Neville busy pitching a tent between the parked truck and the fence. That made her feel a little bit happier as the thought of camping in the dingy looking sheds did not really appeal to her. "What about showers and toilets?" she asked.

"Up that way," Dingo replied, pointing to the far side of the yards. "Permanent shower blocks and toilets there. Just make sure you take yer own soap and dunny paper."

"And wear thongs," added Collin.

Collin then reached forward to pick up Norah's saddle from the fence rail. As he did, Dingo reached for it from the other direction. Both men took firm hold and Kylie witnessed an exchange of sharp looks and an evident battle of wills. Collin then snapped, "Let go buster!"

For a second Kylie thought that Dingo would refuse but when Norah said, "Don't fight boys," he did so. That he was not happy was plain from the resentful and sulky look that clouded his dark face.

Oh dear! I hope there isn't trouble, Kylie thought as Collin gave Dingo a scowl then hoisted Norah's saddle onto his shoulder.

The saddles and harness were carried to the side fence and handed to Old Neville, who placed them in the trailer behind his truck. Having unsaddled the horses they rubbed them down, then fed and watered them. This led to another little incident. Collin moved to rub down Norah's mount but she shook her head.

"I'll look after my own horse thank you Collin," she said.

Collin immediately stepped back. "Sure. Just trying to be helpful," he said. Once again Kylie noted a sour look on Dingo's face.

He loves Norah too, she decided.

The horses having been tended and released into the paddock the group made their way around through a gate to where the tents were now set up in a row of four between the vehicles and the yard fence. On one side was a campervan and on the other two 'cowgirls' were busy cooking beside an open backed truck. The campers and their vehicles formed two long lines along each fence with a grassy 'lane' between them.

Graham looked around then asked, "What do we do now?"

"Have a look around," Norah said. "It is half past one now. The fashion parade isn't till three, so you have an hour or so to look."

"What are you going to do?" Margaret asked.

Norah checked her watch then replied, "I am going over to our camp to lie down for half an hour, then I'll take Ruby for a practice run to warm her up and get myself ready. After that we will both have an hour's rest before the big race. Now you lot go and see what the picnic races looks like."

The boys placed their safety helmets in the vehicle and replaced them with hats, then set off along the lane. Kylie and Margaret both stood for a minute or so, Kylie debating whether to change or not. Then, after checking their gear was secure, both girls also donned hats and set off in the wake of the boys. At once the variety of scenes and people seized Kylie's attention. It was immediately apparent that this was not the 'upper' class part of the races. It had lots of ordinary people camped in it. What was also apparent was the feeling of togetherness and friendliness of the place.

"They are nearly all real country people, aren't they?" was Margaret's comment.

With that Kylie could only agree. There seemed to be equal numbers of teenagers, young people in their twenties, and older people. Only a few small children were evident, but even they had the look of 'bushies'. The battered felt hats, the worn jeans and the scuffed riding boots all spoke of real stockmen, not show-off pretend 'cowboys'.

Into Kylie's thoughts crept the idea that these people were the 'real' Australians and that she was somehow an imposter and an outsider. She noted that the crowd was almost overwhelmingly white and of the Anglo-Celtic type. The accents were all those of the bush.

The sheer variety of tents, vehicles and dress kept her eyes busy as they walked along. There were middle-aged men just in shorts and singlets, teenage boys in jeans and with cowboys shirts, or with no shirt, girls in jeans with short tops that exposed their navels, a few jockeys in their silks and an occasional lair in a bright red or green silk cowboy shirt with tassels. The one thing many of the shirts had in common was that they had double press studs on their pockets rather than buttons and the long trousers all looked worn and not as clean as they might be. There was a lot of beer in evidence.

As they passed each 'camp' Kylie glanced in, noting the people crowed in around tables loaded with food and drinks, the bare rafters, clothes and bedding in piles and the general air of groups of friends having a good time. The lanes between the parked vehicles, tents and sheds were not straight and were almost blocked in places by vehicles parked at odd angles. It all gave her the impression of being a cross between the annual show and a refugee camp in Africa.

The girls passed the toilets and came out into a more open area. The main 'road' in from the front gate crossed this, leading across to some houses and buildings over on the left near the racetrack. Ahead were the fences and seating of the rodeo arena. Vehicles were coming and going so the girls had to wait to cross, then made their way towards the tall, corrugated iron wall that shut off the actual racecourse area and grandstand.

Rather than go in there, Kylie led the way around the rear, past many more sheds, tents and parked vehicles, to the far side. Here they found even more campers and vehicles and a completely different atmosphere. In this area most of the people were in their late teens or early twenties and there was a boisterous game of drunken football in progress in the grassy area between the rows of tents.

Not liking that sort of thing at all both girls turned away and made their way back towards the main grandstand area. As they did, one of the youths whistled and called out, "Hey girls, come and have a drink!"

Rude hints and leering looks accompanied this invitation. It all caused Kylie mixed emotions. She resented their crude implications but was flattered that she and Margaret looked attractive enough and old enough for such offers.

This time they went in through the gates and strolled around, still taking in all the sights. They located more toilets and a large open-sided shed with a concrete floor which they learned was to be the scene of the bush dance that evening. At the far end of this was the back of the grandstand and underneath this they found a series of food stalls.

Both being hungry the girls purchased hamburgers and sat at rough wooden tables to eat them. While they ate, they watched the passing crowd. Several times one or the other commented on the variety of dress and of people. Some people were very well dressed, the ladies with good frocks, gloves, high heeled shoes and fancy hats; the men in suits with ties and even several with grey top hats. At the other end of the dress code spectrum were the scruffy, unshaven males in old jeans, bare feet and dirty singlets.

Kylie was just finishing her hamburger, had crammed the last mouthful into her mouth, when a youth stopped in front of her and said, "Hi there! It's Kylie, isn't it?"

With her mouth stuffed so full she could hardly chew Kylie looked up and saw that it was Brian, the teenage boy who had flirted with her at Mt Garnet. She flushed with both pleasure and annoyance and struggled to chew and swallow as she nodded. Then she realised she shouldn't be trying to smile or to answer.

Brian grinned. "Struck speechless, eh? I have that effect on girls."

At that, Kylie did snort. She swallowed and glanced at Margaret for support, only to find that her friend's eyes were dancing with mischievous delight. Embarrassment at being caught not looking her best added to Kylie's confusion. But all she could do was shake her head.

Again Brian chuckled and then added, "I'm glad you are here. Are you going to the dance tonight?"

Kylie shook her head and was peeved to hear Margaret say, "Yes we are."

Clearing her throat at last Kylie turned to give Margaret a disapproving look before saying, "Margaret, I can do my own talking thank you; and I don't talk to fresh boys."

Brian chortled and his black eyes twinkled. "Good. That means I won't have much competition."

"Oh... Oh!... Oh!" spluttered Kylie, quite at a loss as to how to save the situation. Never having met a boy as forward or as bold as Brian, she was unable to do more than gasp and snort. Still embarrassed by having to wipe sauce and crumbs from her mouth and cheeks she could only shake her head.

Brian added to her discomfiture by adding, "You missed a bit... here." He pointed to the side of his mouth.

Kylie dabbed at the place, then blushed again as she realised he meant the other side, the mirror image. Then she stood up and said, "Come on, Margaret. Let's watch the horse racing."

Brian raised his eyebrows and said, "Margaret, eh? That's a nice name."

Margaret also blushed but Kylie was peeved to notice that she was not offended and was actually enjoying the situation. To her relief, Margaret also stood up and followed her, but then annoyed her further by saying to Brian, "Bye."

"See you later!" Brian called after them, then laughed.

As they made their way through the crowd Kylie turned and said accusingly, "You didn't have to encourage him, Margaret!"

"Isn't he hunky!" sighed Margaret, quite unmoved by her annoyance.

"He is just fast and fresh," Kylie snapped back.

By then they had come out at the side of the grandstand and were near the grassed enclosure where the horses were paraded before and after each race. Kylie walked over to the chain wire fence surrounding the enclosure and leaned on the steel pipe which topped it.

Margaret looked back, further aggravating Kylie. "What are we doing now?" she asked.

Kylie pointed to the horses. "I am going to watch a horse race," she said.

"Are you going to bet?" Margaret asked.

"We should, but I'm not sure if we are allowed to," Kylie answered. "It is probably only adults that can do that."

"You'll just lose your money anyway," Margaret commented.

At that, Kylie determined to bet and to prove her friend wrong. Luckily at that moment she saw Mrs Conroy walking past, now clad in a very attractive floral print frock. "Mrs Conroy, excuse me but would you place a bet for me on one of the horses?" she asked.

Mrs Conroy stopped and looked at her with an amused smile on her face. "A bet eh? On which horse and at what odds?"

Those questions made Kylie feel even more foolish. She did not know the names of any of the horses in the next race and she certainly did not understand the betting odds. Blushing at her own ignorance she gestured to the horses. "Which horse would you recommend?" she asked.

Mrs Conroy smiled even wider. "I will get you a list. If you really are going to win at this sort of gambling you need a lot of knowledge of horses, and a lot of background on the history of each horse in the race."

That made Kylie feel even more like a little girl who knew nothing but perversely she became stubborn. "Please Mrs Conroy," she asked.

Mrs Conroy joined them at the fence and pointed to the first of five horses being led around. "These are all two-year-olds. That is 'Mountain Man'. He is a proper racehorse and was trained by Jake Morris. He has won two races this season. The next is that gelding Lucky Streak. It came second at the Ewan Races last September. The third is only a station horse and is called 'Fantastic Legless'. This is the first race meeting he has been in. Then we have the mare there, the one led by the girl in the blue. She is called 'Turquoise' and has been in six races but never won any. The last is another mare and her name is 'Supergirl'. She's not really as racehorse at all, just a girl's pet pony."

All that information flustered Kylie. Her first thought was to choose one of the mares, just based on gender bias. Then she thought that 'Turquoise' might be the one as she liked the name, but finally she decided that would sound silly so she chose 'Lucky Streak'. Having heard this decision, Mrs Conroy looked at Margaret with raised eyebrows.

Margaret shook her head emphatically. "No thanks, Mrs Conroy. I don't want to throw my money away."

"Wise girl. Now, come with me and we will place our bets," said Mrs Conroy.

She led them in under the open fronted shed where the bookilometresakers had their stands and placed a bet for Kylie at ten to one. Kylie put up $5 and felt both excited and silly as she did so. They then made their way out to the grass area fronting the grandstand to watch. The whole-time people kept saying hello to Mrs Conroy and she stopped frequently to chat to friends.

Now that she had very publicly committed herself Kylie felt quite emotionally involved. She watched anxiously as the jockeys mounted, noting with a mild spurt of disappointment that the jockey on Lucky Streak looked to be a bit on the big side and wore a purple silk which did not appeal to her. The horses trotted off around the track past the grandstand to the starting barrier on the far side of the field.

As she watched the horses lining up, the boys appeared. Graham came over and followed her gaze.

"What ya lookin' at, Sis?" he asked.

"The horses," Kylie said. "We came to watch the races, didn't we?"

Margaret then added, "She's just bet five dollars on a horse."

Graham laughed. "You'll be sorry. I'll bet you a dollar you lose."

Kylie turned her nose up and pretended to be unmoved, but inside she was now all a-flutter with tension and excitement. It was a revelation to her how exciting it all felt and how much she felt involved.

I hope I'm not one of those people who become addicted to gambling, she thought anxiously.

Then something happened which took her mind right off the horses. Two teenage girls walked past, and she saw Graham's head swivel to watch them. Both wore jeans and one, a big girl of about sixteen with large breasts, had an off-the-shoulder top which looked like it might jiggle off at any moment. That caused Kylie to wrinkle her nose in distaste, but it was the other girl that got her worried. It was Kate, the black-haired sister of Brian. Kate wore jeans and shirt and a cowboy hat and looked very much part of the local scene. But what disquieted Kylie was the way she glanced at Graham as she passed and the coy little smile she gave him.

Oh dear! she thought, worrying about Margaret.

Then she realised that her race had begun, and she transferred her attention to the racing horses over on the far side of the track.

Oh come on Lucky Streak! she thought, unconsciously gripping her hands and biting her lip.

Chapter 12

FILLIES ON THE FIELD

As the horses came around the far bend, Kylie began to jump up and down with excitement. She found that she was clenching her hands so tightly that her fingernails were digging into her palms.

Oh come on, Lucky Streak! she willed.

So unused to watching such a scene was she that she found it quite impossible to tell which horse was in the lead and even had difficulty in detecting Lucky Streak by his rider's purple silk. It was only as the horses dashed into the home straight and strung out that she was able to distinguish the placing clearly; and that was disappointing. Lucky Streak was clearly last!

'Amazingly Legless' won by two lengths. Even the favourite was left in third place. As realisation of her loss sank in Kylie blushed.

Margaret was good about it, just giving her a brief 'I-told-you-so' look. Graham was less sympathetic. "Done your dough Sis!" he laughed.

Kylie could only put a brave face on it and pretend that it did not matter, while feeling quite astonishingly disappointed. To change the subject she looked at her watch and said, "Oh, look at the time. It is ten past two. Come on, Margaret. Time to have a shower and get changed."

With chuckling jibes from the boys to hurry them along the two girls made their way across the front of the grandstand and past the enclosure to the north gate in the corrugated iron fence. From there they made their way past the back of a small police station and a house and across an open area at the end of the entrance road. Within another minute they had plunged into the bustling alleyway between the camps and parked vehicles.

On the way they checked out the toilets and showers. Back at their camp they went into their tent and found the suitcase containing their good clothes. This had been very carefully packed, and just as carefully kept from the notice of the boys, so as to limit their teasing comments. For a few minutes the two girls were in an embarrassed dither, lifting out dresses and good underwear and shoes but unsure what to do next.

A short discussion while holding their new dresses in their hands decided them that the thing to do was go and have their shower and then come back and change. Boots were pulled off and thongs put on in their place. Then, with towels over their shoulders and toilet bags in hand, the two friends walked back to the showers.

The shower was a pleasant surprise, being both clean and hot. To Kylie it was a welcome lift as her stomach was now a-flutter with anxiety and she was feeling quite stressed. But she knew it was now impossible for her to back out.

Margaret is going ahead and I can't let my friend down, she thought. There was also the certainty of comments and possible derisive teasing by the boys if she 'chickened out'.

So she washed herself and brushed her hair, uncomfortably aware that time now seemed to be flying. With a shock she saw that it was already 2:30 and that they were due to parade at 3:00.

"Come on Margaret, we will be late otherwise," she called.

The prospect of all that worry and then missing out by not being on time was all the spur Kylie needed. She hurried Margaret out of her shower and back to the tent. Here the two girls stood back-to-back and changed their underwear, both finding the situation an embarrassment even though they had often had baths together when they were younger. As quickly as she could Kylie slipped on her dress, then helped Margaret. Hair and make-up was harder to get done quickly and finally they had to just finish up and hope.

Standing face-to-face they pinned on and adjusted each other's hats. Kylie had only ever worn such a hat once and was quite unused to pinning one on. Nor was she used to high heels. She badly wanted to see herself in a full-length mirror but had to content herself with looking Margaret up and down and remembering what she had looked like during the practice dressing session back at home the previous week.

"Fifteen minutes. We had better go. It will take us more than five minutes just to walk back," she urged as Margaret twisted to get a better view of her back.

"How do I look?" Margaret asked with obvious nervousness.

Actually Kylie thought that her friend looked a bit like a little girl dressing up, but she did not say that. "You look really pretty, Margaret," she complimented. "What about me?"

Margaret looked her up and down and nodded. "You look really classy. Very stylish," she said.

That reassured Kylie a bit so, hoping she did not look overdressed or silly, she stepped out of the tent and began walking towards the enclosure. As she did, she felt she was horribly self-conscious, sure that everyone's eyes were on her, and that they would all be very critical eyes. There were people looking and now that she and Margaret were all dressed up in fancy hat, dress, stockings, and high-heel shoes she knew they stood out from the crowd.

Tugging on equally unaccustomed gloves Kylie set her back firmly and walked deliberately, trying to act cool and relaxed. But she did know they were very nice clothes, and she liked that 'stylish' comment by Margaret. The dress she had chosen was a tight-fitting, full length one of pale pink with a floral design of darker pinks and reds. It had bare shoulders and only two thin straps to hold the top up (which made her feel very daring and not a little anxious). The shoes were open, with red straps and gold buckles. On her head she wore a large, broad-brimmed white straw hat topped with masses of pink ruffles. To complete the arrangement she had white gloves and a pink satin handbag with a woven silk handle.

Margaret had also chosen pink but hers was only just knee length and with more patterns on it and a higher front. White shoes below and a very nice white and gold handbag set it off well. But it was her hat that was Kylie's secret envy. It was mauve, wide brimmed but turned down all round in a graceful curve and wrapped around the crown with pink gauze and held on by a big pink rose.

To appease her guilt at being jealous and to help reassure her friend Kylie said, "I love your hat, Margaret. It looks ever so pretty."

At that, Margaret positively glowed and neither girl really noticed the wolf-whistles from some half-drunk youths in stockmen's clothes. The two friends walked on side by side, feeling better by the second and both worrying about their shoes. That meant sidestepping muddy puddles and trying not to stir up the dust in other places.

A couple of minutes later they came out onto the big open area where the entrance road opened out into roads going both ways at the back of the police station and the caretaker's house. To Kylie's surprise there was a row of five police 4WDs towing horse floats parked there. Policemen, mounted police by their leggings and jodhpurs, were busy coaxing horses out of the floats and leading them away towards the paddocks to the north.

For a moment the girls hesitated but the shortest way was past the row of vehicles and Kylie was now anxious lest they be late, so she led the way towards them. As she did, she glanced to her left and stopped. Walking towards them was Norah, now dressed in her racing silks and leading Romantic Ruby. Behind her followed Collin Costello with another horse and Dingo leading a third.

Kylie waved and waited. As she stood there, she admired Norah's racing clothes: glossy black boots, tight, white moleskin trousers, a bright blue silk top and the safety helmet. *Gee, Norah looks the part,* she thought, knowing she was experiencing another spurt of envy.

She said, "Hi Norah! How did the practice go?"

Norah smiled back and nodded. "Good. Ruby is right at the top of her form. She should knock the socks off that Peagreen's nag. My, don't you two look a pretty sight. What do you think Collin?"

Collin came up and stopped beside her. He was now also dressed for racing and looked somehow younger and stockier. He nodded with approval and grinned. "Very nice," he commented. "I'm no judge of women's clothes but you both look as pretty as a picture to me."

Kylie felt a surge of pleasure at the compliment, but she also knew that minutes were ticking rapidly away. She gestured towards the enclosure and said, "We are on in less than ten minutes. We must fly."

"My race is still half an hour away. We will come and watch you," Norah said, clicking Ruby into motion again. The group, led by Kylie and Margaret, headed across behind the line of parked police vehicles. As they went to pass behind the last horse float in the row a policeman came around from the other side. As soon as he saw them, he stopped and gave a half bow, waving them through.

"Ladies," he said, raising his felt hat in an old-fashioned gesture that sent a thrill of pleasure through Kylie.

Then she recognised him. "Constable Lonergan!" she said.

For a few seconds Constable Lonergan did not recognise them. A quizzical frown wrinkled his brow and then his face brightened into a real grin. "My word! Sorry girls. I didn't recognise you. Golly gosh, don't you scrub up well. Oh!... Hello Norah."

Seeing the look on Constable Lonergan's face sent a real thrill through Kylie, instantly tempered by the 'girls' and by the fact that his real interest was instantly transferred to Norah.

Norah stopped and gave a dry smile. "Hello Constable Lonergan. What are you doing here? I thought you went to search the Tumoulin Woods for the Kelly Gang?"

Constable Lonergan gave a wry grin and said, "False alarm. There was no farmer that had seen them."

"So what about the phone call?" Norah asked.

"A hoax, or a ruse to decoy us away I reckon," Constable Lonergan answered.

"So what are you doing here?" Norah queried.

"Boss said to go and help the local boys keep order at the races, so here we are. You are obviously racing?"

"Yes."

"On Romantic Ruby?" Constable Lonergan asked, his gaze shifting to the horse with evident approval.

Norah nodded. "In the four o'clock race," she replied.

"I'll make sure I watch that one," Constable Lonergan answered.

During this conversation Kylie had turned to look back and saw looks of flint-eyed resentment on Collin's face and of downright stony-faced hostility on Dingo's. Even to her there was an awareness of the tension between the men. But Norah seemed unaware of it and gestured. "We must go. These girls are strutting their stuff in five minutes."

"And good luck to you kids," Constable Lonergan said.

That miffed Kylie and she turned and walked on. As she did, she heard Constable Lonergan say, "Hello Collin. How's your mum?"

She did not hear the rest but was aware that the policeman also spoke to Dingo as he passed. When she looked back from near the gate, she saw that the policeman was urging a big black stallion out of the back of the horse float.

Then concern over the fashion parade made her forget horses and policemen. As she and Margaret reached the gate to the enclosure her eyes took in the other girls waiting there and she almost froze in fright. These were the opposition and they looked ever so grown up and stunning. A perspiring middle-aged man in a jacket and tie met them, clipboard in hand.

"Names please. Age?" he asked.

Kylie told him but had trouble making her mouth work. Her lips had gone dry and her throat seemed to be all constricted. She recognised that she on the edge of a blue funk of panic and had to force herself to stand and answer the official's questions. All she really felt like doing was running away.

To her relief, the man found her name on a list and nodded, ticked it off, then handed her a white card with the numeral 6 on it. "Stand over there in your order please," he said.

Moving as though in a dream Kylie walked stiffly over to stand between '5' (in a stunning black and white swirl patterned dress) and '7' (in yellow jacket and black dress). She gave the other girls a thin smile but her eyes barely registered them as people. All she could see was blurry images of females who looked much more adult and much better dressed.

Oh! I wish I hadn't let myself be talked into this, she thought, burning with secret shame and bracing herself for the humiliations to come. Only vaguely did she note Margaret moving to 9th position. Then '3', in a hip-hugging black skirt, white frilly top, and perky little round black hat arrived and made her feel even more inferior. *Oh what have I let myself in for!* she thought.

As she stood there, stomach churning and now worrying she might throw up or faint, her eyes swept along the fence. Familiar faces registered on her flustered mind, and she saw it was the boys. Graham was grinning from ear to ear and gave her a thumbs-up, then endeared himself to her even more by calling, "Margaret, you look really pretty."

Standing on the other side of the enclosure stood three people: a middle-aged man in a grey 'morning suit' and grey top hat, and two overdressed ladies, one quite elderly and the other of middle age. Kylie supposed they were the judges and seeing them did nothing to calm her nerves.

After waiting for a few minutes she relaxed and focused a bit more, glancing at the faces along the fence. She saw Mrs Conroy smiling at her. Norah came to join her and then Collin elbowed his way through the crowd to stand beside her. Their obvious approval and moral support made Kylie feel happier. But this evaporated when her eyes moved on and met those of Brian. He grinned and she saw his eyes twinkle with what she instinctively knew was male approval. That sent surges of embarrassed heat coursing through her. His sister Kate was beside him and Kylie noted that she was glancing in Graham's direction. To Kylie's dismay she saw Graham notice Kate, then start to divide his attention between her and the girls in the enclosure.

There was then a cute and pleasant diversion as the 'littlies' fashion parade was staged. There were seven children aged 3 to 7. Two were boys wearing suits and two others were twin girls of 4 or 5 who made the cutest pair Kylie had seen in a long time. Both wore pink skirts and white cotton tops, pink cowboy hats and ankle length pink plastic cowboy boots emblazoned with gold patterns and silver horses. Their hair was done up with pink ribbons, causing Kylie to muse that pink must be the colour of the day. The twins took out an equal 1st Prize and Kylie thought they deserved it. One of the boys was runner-up and he looked quite hurt and upset at not winning.

Then it was the 8 to 12s. There were only four children in this group, all girls, and there were tears from two when they did not win. Seeing them upset made Kylie feel both sympathetic and anxious. She braced herself for bad news and defeat.

The loudspeaker then boomed, "And now! The thirteen to sixteens. Ladies and Gentlemen, move to the enclosure to see these young ladies showing up the adults on how to be well dressed. The first contestant is Mavis Mottram from Lynd Valley. Mavis is wearing a pale blue dress and hat and has matching accessories in cream."

At the urging of a female official, Mavis set out to walk along a ten-metre strip of carpet laid on the turf. Kylie watched her and felt her heart go out to her rival. The poor girl looked very awkward and embarrassed and had trouble walking. She stalked along with jerky motions, obviously embarrassed. She was a tall girl with a largish bottom and, as she turned to walk back, a drunken youth in the audience yelled, "Wiggle yer bum, Mavis! That might help the judges decide."

Kylie winced at the crudity and tensed, ready to endure similar vulgar comments. Poor Mavis mottled red with shame and hurried back to rejoin the group. Number 2 then took her place. Kylie noted the sleek, tight-fitting purple dress and the exaggerated wiggle of the girl's buttocks and went red with embarrassment again.

Why on earth did I let myself get talked into this! she wondered again.

Number 3 strolled languidly along the carpet, smiling and looking casually at ease. She moved with enviable grace and exuded confidence. Her whole presentation was band-box perfect, from the neatly cut black hair to her pale pink fingernail polish. The black-white-black-white effect was striking, and Kylie secretly thought she was the winner.

Number 4 was entirely different. Her dress looked like a crocheted tablecloth and her top had the appearance of a loose undergarment. The floppy white hat with a big pink flower hid most of her face and strands of loose hair hung down. The only thing Kylie really admired were her white shoes with white straps and lacings around above the ankles.

A bit cheap and tarty looking, was Kylie's unkind assessment.

Poor old Number 4! As she turned her high heel caught in the carpet and she stumbled, almost fell, recovered her balance with an effort and had to clutch at her hat. Clearly flustered she walked jerkily and red-faced back to the line.

Then Number 5 moved off, leaving Kylie trembling slightly with nervousness. Number 5 looked very attractive to her. The dress was a sort of swirl pattern of black and white that had the effect of emphasizing her nicely shaped figure. The hat was plain black and broad brimmed but set at a cheeky angle and her shoes were a lovely glossy black with silver buckles.

Oh dear! How can I hope to compete with that? Kylie thought in despair.

But then it was her turn. No 5 resumed her place in the line and Kylie heard her own name as though in a dream. Swallowing with anxiety she stepped forward and began walking along that strip of red. As she walked, she was barely conscious of anything but where she was going. She did not even glance at the crowd. What did help her was all those years of ballet. It came to her like some sort of revelation that she was able to walk with grace and rhythm. The turn at the end that had been Number 4's undoing she accomplished with a polished swirl. That went so well she even managed a smile and a wave of both hands. Feeling much better she walked slowly back to her place, even finding the courage to look at the crowd and managing to hold her smile.

As she resumed her place Kylie was aware of clapping and cheers from the boys, and of Brian's smiling face, nodding and filled with approval. *Oh, I've done it!* she thought, gasping with relief.

Number 7 then strode out, hips gyrating, with an exaggerated rolling motion. It looked so false that Kylie almost laughed aloud and had to cover her mouth. The effect was so overdone that Kylie was sure she looked better.

Number 8 was worse. She wore a black, knee-length dress that was bare at the back and open down the front almost to her navel. The two bodice pieces barely covered the girl's pointy little bosoms and the straps met behind her neck. To make it worse the girl stumbled several times and gave silly giggles.

"Drunk!" was the hissed comment from one of the severe old matrons in the audience.

Kylie now tensed again as Number 8 returned. Margaret's name was called, and Kylie did not want her friend to make a fool of herself. To her relief, she watched Margaret stroll along, looking happy and confident, smiling at the boys and waving to them. She paused after her turn and gave a sweet little smile, then seemed to wander gracefully back.

"Oh well done, Margaret!" she complimented as Margaret reached them again.

There was only Number 10 to go, a very stylish fawn two-piece suit and skirt with a fur collar and a broad-brimmed hat with a large dark brown crown festooned with long striped feathers. Kylie didn't hear her first name but heard she was 'Tamblyn'.

She looks very nice; very classy, she decided.

There was then the tense wait. This seemed to stretch on and on but her watch told her it was only about three minutes before the judges had their decision.

"First the Best Hat. This goes to Miss Margaret Lake of Cairns. Miss Lake, please come forward," Kylie heard the official say.

Margaret was amazed and very, very pleased. Smiling with delight she stood while a blue silk sash was secured over her shoulder. A bouquet of flowers was handed to her, and she then had to pose photographs. When she came back Kylie could not resist giving her a hug and a kiss on the cheek.

Hat Spectacular was next. It went to Miss Tamblyn from Townsville. The Young Trendsetter Award went to Number 5: Jasmin Someone-or-other. But these were only consolation prizes and Kylie stayed tense, still hoping in spite of all she had seen.

It was not to be. Her name was called next, for Best Young Model. Stifling her sharp disappointment and telling herself that any prize was better than none she placed a fixed smile on her face and made her way over to the judges. The middle-aged lady slipped the silk sash over her head and shook her hand. The bunch of flowers she liked but not the slobbery smooch on the cheek by the middle-aged male official who smelt of beer and tobacco. After posing for photos she made her way back, to a hug from a happy Margaret.

Number 3 was the winner, which now came as no surprise. The sheer symmetry and balance of her dress and accessories, coupled to her evident poise and grace allowed Kylie to accept that defeat without too much envy. Not so some of the others. Kylie smiled at Number 7 and got a smile in return, but one that did not reach the girl's eyes. These were hard and catty with jealousy and hurt. It made Kylie wonder if such contests weren't bad things that caused too much ill-will.

The contestants were then hustled out of the enclosure to make way for more horses. Kylie found her heart beating fast with the excitement and relief and could not help talking too much and too loudly as she joined the others outside the fence. Her pleasure was increased by Brian stepping out to speak to her.

"You look really beautiful, Kylie," he said, his eyes twinkling.

Kylie flushed with pleasure and nodded but could only say, "Thank you."

Norah hurried over to give her a hug and then kissed her. "Oh, well done, Kylie. You looked so graceful out there."

"Thanks," Kylie mumbled. "That's all those dancing lessons."

Mrs Conroy also congratulated Kylie and Margaret, then turned to Norah. "Come on Norah. Your race is on soon. You'd better go and saddle up."

"Oh yes!" Kylie cried. "Good luck, Norah. We will all bet on you."

Chapter 13

TURF ACTION

The group all moved away from the fence, heading towards the stables. The main grandstand area was surrounded by the high galvanized iron wall in the form of a hollow square a hundred metres wide by two hundred long. The open side was towards the racetrack with the grandstand and 'hall' being separated from it by a grassed area crossed by vehicle tracks. Around the inside of two of the three sides of the fence was a roofed area subdivided into open stalls for the horses.

Each stall was just big enough for one animal and had side rails and straw underfoot. Harness and saddles were draped over the side rails. It was all very basic and rustic but quite adequate for the event. Only a dozen stalls had horses in them.

As the group walked across the grassy area towards them Kylie saw that Constable Lonergan was in one of the first stalls brushing the sleek coat of a fine-looking black stallion. He gave them a nod and called, "I see you did alright. What'd you win ladies?"

The comment caused Kylie to blush and be very conscious of her sash, but she felt obliged to detour closer to answer. "I won 'Best Model'," she answered shyly, quickly adding, "Margaret got Best Hat."

Constable Lonergan looked at Margaret's hat and nodded. "It's a good hat alright, nearly as good as mine."

As he was wearing a battered blue police felt hat, his comment caused snorts of derision and some laughter. Kylie stopped to admire the stallion.

"He's a splendid horse," she said. "What's his name?"

"Black Knight," Constable Lonergan. "He's my primary mount."

"Are you going to ride him?" Margaret asked, indicating the saddle cloth and saddle on the rail.

Constable Lonergan nodded. "We've been requested to do a ride past with the official party before the presentation of the gold cup," he explained.

"Ride past?" Kylie queried.

"The Mounted Police do lots of official public duties," he explained.

"We provide mounted escorts for the Governor and people like that at parades and ceremonies."

Kylie nodded. "We saw you, at Herberton."

"Yes," Constable Lonergan replied shortly.

That instantly made Kylie anxious as she saw that the memory of their public humiliation rankled. To change the subject she said, "Will you be wearing that blue coat and white helmet?"

Constable Lonergan nodded. He was still smiling and brushing his horse but Kylie saw that Norah was fidgeting. She said, "Sorry, but I must get ready. My race is in a few minutes."

"Good luck, Norah," Constable Lonergan said, straightening up and looking her straight in the eye.

Norah blushed but smiled. "Thank you."

The group walked on, studying the other horses they passed. Then Norah suddenly stiffened and grabbed her mother's arm. "Look! There's that horrid Doris Peagreen standing at Ruby's stall."

Norah hurried quickly forward, calling out, "Hoy! Peagreen! Get away from my horse!"

Doris, now dressed for racing in an aquamarine silk top and white trousers, turned to look, then sneered. "Huh! I don't need to noble a broken-down nag like this. Silver Streak will be so far in front all you will see are his tail and hooves."

At that moment, Dingo came out of the stall. "It's alright, Miss Norah," he said. "I'm here. She was just trying to pick up a few pointers on how to get on a horse."

Doris snorted and curled her lip but stalked away towards where her own horse stood ready, saddled and bridled. For a second a horrible suspicion floated across Kylie's mind that perhaps Dingo was not a friend at all. She had heard tales about horses being drugged, 'doped', before races, either to slow them down, or to speed them up.

Norah now added a new and even more unpleasant twist to the idea. "I'd hate Ruby to be doped. When I win, the stewards might do a swab. If she has been drugged, we would be fined and deregistered and banned from racing and all sorts of horrible things. It would be a real disgrace."

"What a disgusting idea!" Margaret cried in genuine shock.

Dingo answered. "It's been known to happen. But Ruby's alright. I bin here all the time lookin' after her."

"Thanks Dingo. Now, can you help me saddle up please."

Collin now stepped forward and he said, "I can do that Norah."

Norah shook her head. "No. You get your own horse ready. Your race is straight after mine."

Collin did not look happy but nodded and went off. Kylie stood with Margaret and Mrs Conroy while Norah and Dingo put saddle and bridle on Romantic Ruby. To Kylie the horse looked just magnificent, all shiny coat and rippling muscles.

As Norah moved to back Ruby out of the stall, Doris came past, leading Silver Streak. "Get out of my way you kids," she snapped, scowling and striking her boot with a riding crop with a thwacking noise that made Kylie wince. She saw Doris and Norah exchange hostile glances.

Norah started walking towards the gate to the left of the clubhouse. "You girls should go and place your bets," she said.

Margaret answered. "We will, but we want to watch you lead Ruby around the enclosure first. She is a lovely horse to watch."

Norah gave her a winning smile and Kylie's heart glowed for her friend. *Margaret knows just the right thing to say,* she thought happily. Then she glanced at Graham, who had been strolling along with the group of bored looking boys. She saw he was looking sideways, and the object of his gaze was Kate. *Oh drat that girl!* Kylie thought.

Norah followed Doris out onto the track, then around the outside of the clubhouse and back into the enclosure through another gate. Kylie stood with the others at the enclosure rail to watch. The race was called 'The Nymbool Stakes' and there were only five horses in it. Luckily, each rider had different colours so she thought there might be a chance of keeping track of how the race was going. But she found seeing the other horses and Jockeys a worrying experience. In particular she did not like the look of a big chestnut named 'Cyclone' ridden by a thin girl in a yellow silk. The stocky looking stallion ridden by a plump little girl in red did not look much competition, nor did the horse ridden by the attractive blonde wearing the purple and gold silk.

For several minutes the horses were led around by their riders, walking in a circle on the bright green turf. Kylie could not help admiring Norah: her lithe, graceful form, the shiny black plait hanging down from under her safety helmet, the shimmering blue silk of her top. Then she watched with fascination as Dingo helped Norah to mount. As always it amazed Kylie at how the jockeys sprang up and then seemed to crouch right up on top of the horse's back, their polished boots fitted into the high-slung stirrups and the cloth of their trousers stretched tight by the way their legs were bent back.

Norah gave them a last wave, then turned Ruby and walked her out of the enclosure. As she did, she passed close to Doris on Silver Streak and for a moment Kylie feared the two horses might collide in the gateway but Doris reined in with a scowl to let Norah pass. Once out on the track Norah set Ruby into a gentle canter and was soon lost to sight.

"Come on, we must place our bets," Mrs Conroy urged.

"Should we leave these sashes on?" Kylie asked. She was now feeling very self-conscious about wearing it.

"Of course! You earned them. Enjoy your few minutes of glory," Mrs Conroy replied.

Kylie did but she still felt embarrassed, noting the looks she and Margaret kept attracting, some approving, others envious. The group made their way through the crowd to the bookilometresaker's stands and once again Kylie handed Mrs Conroy a $10 note.

"Only at two to one," Mrs Conroy commented.

"But that brown thing called the 'Chocolate Beast' is at a hundred to one," Margaret protested.

Mrs Conroy laughed. "That's because Ruby is the favourite."

"What about Silver Streak?" Kylie asked.

"Five to one," Mrs Conroy replied. This time Margaret also handed over a $10 note. When Mrs Conroy looked at the boys Graham shook his head. "Not me. Remember old 'Unlucky Legless'," he said.

Kylie snorted but the loss still irritated. Peter, Stephen and Roger all placed bets, Stephen surprising Kylie by betting $10 on Ruby and $5 on Silver Streak. She realised that was probably not such a bad idea, but it seemed somehow disloyal.

By the time they had done this the horses were at the starting barrier on the far side of the field. Last bets were called and then the betting stopped with the horses all in the barrier and 'under starter's orders'. Kylie stood on tip-toe to see over the heads of the crowd and bit her lip with excitement.

The loudspeaker crackled. "And they're off!" screamed the race commentator.

To see better Kylie stood on tip-toe and then jumped up and down. But that did not help. The distant horses were all in a multi-coloured bunch and she could not pick out Ruby by Norah's colours. Even when the horses started to string out along the curve it was no better because of the angle, making them all still appear to be a brightly shimmering blob. The colours were bright because the afternoon sun was shining directly on them, and they had a backdrop of dark grey rain and cloud, but she could not tell if Norah was first or last.

As the horses came around the last bend, it was hardly any better and the excited bellowing of the race caller was no help because he spoke too fast for Kylie to understand. Only as the horses began to stretch out on the home straight did she see the dark blue was definitely among the three leading horses.

But so was the aquamarine of Doris Peagreen!

Kylie now saw that Silver Streak and Romantic Ruby were racing neck and neck. "Oh come on Norah!" she shrieked, jumping even faster as the excitement mounted.

The horses came thundering along the straight in a tight bunch. Even the big brown horse was keeping up and worse still the big chestnut named 'Cyclone' was leading and then Kylie saw that Silver Streak was drawing ahead of Ruby.

As the horses dashed off around the bend away from her, Kylie noted that Silver Streak was definitely ahead of Ruby and she chewed at her lip with anxiety. It got worse. On the far straight the horses strung out so that Cyclone and Silver Streak were side by side and a good horse length ahead of Ruby. The only hopeful sign was that the big brown horse was clearly dropping back.

Then the horses rounded the curve for the final run to the finish. Kylie danced up and down with excitement and she blinked and rubbed her eyes to clear them as she tried to see which horse was winning.

As they came around into the home straight, the big brown horse was well behind but the other four were in such a tight bunch that Kylie could not tell if Ruby was still behind or not. Then she noted the shimmer of Norah's silk and saw that she was up among the leaders.

"Oh come on, Norah!" she shrieked.

As the horses entered the straight, it was clear that Cyclone was now behind both Silver Streak and Ruby, and Kylie cried with excitement.

As the two lead horses came thundering along towards the grandstand Kylie saw that Norah was on the inside and that she was standing up in her stirrups, urging her horse along with her voice and hand. Next to her was Doris and she was now flailing at Silver Streak with her whip. To Kylie it looked quite horrible and vicious, the whip rising and falling in rapid, hard strokes.

Oh, what a cruel beast! she thought.

She saw Doris glancing frequently towards Norah and saw that she was shouting at her, though what she was saying she could not hear above the roar of the crowd and the loudspeakers. But she did see what happened next. It was now plain to her that Romantic Ruby was pulling ahead, was quite definitely in the lead. Doris raised her whip and struck at Norah. It happened so fast Kylie wasn't sure she had seen it but then Doris did it again and Kylie distinctly saw Norah flinch and then put a hand to her face before bending lower and kicking with her heels to urge Romantic Ruby on.

The horses flashed past the winning post and there was no doubt, Romantic Ruby was the winner by nearly a whole length.

Margaret grabbed at Kylie's arm. "Did you see that?" she asked.

Kylie nodded. "That awful Doris hitting Norah with the whip?" she asked. "Yes, I did."

"Quick, down to the enclosure," Mrs Conroy cried. She looked furious and was muttering about stewards and disqualification.

The crowd was agog with a mixture of outrage and excited speculation. There was a general movement towards the enclosure, and it took a determined effort for the group to push their way forward. By the time they had arrived Norah was there, still seated on Romantic Ruby, who was led by an angry but happy Dingo. Even from a distance Kylie could see a red weal across Norah's face.

"She did hit her," she cried.

Margaret nodded. "Oh, I hope Norah doesn't get a scar from it."

That was an awful thought and made Kylie feel sick. She saw the judges and officials clustering to question Norah, and she dimly heard the loudspeakers calling for Number 3 to report to the race marshals.

More horses came in, led by their now dismounted jockeys, but Doris was not among them. Margaret craned her neck and looked in all directions but there was no sign of Doris.

"Run away," she concluded.

She had. Even though she was the runner-up Doris did not appear. That caused Kylie mixed feelings, all overlaid by happiness that Norah had won. Mrs Conroy pushed her way to the front and ran over to Norah, holding her face and carefully examining the red mark left by Doris's whip. Norah protested but her mother would not relax until a doctor had been called from the clubhouse to look and had nodded she would be alright.

The presentations then went ahead, Norah proudly posing for photos while holding a large silver trophy cup in one hand and Romantic Ruby's reins in the other.

"Doesn't she look the part," was Margaret's opinion, with which Kylie could only agree.

Norah and Dingo then led Romantic Ruby out and around to return to the stalls. Kylie joined the large group who pressed forward to congratulate Norah. There were more photos and hugs and Norah wiped tears from her eyes. She also tentatively fingered the livid mark left by the whip. Watching her do that caused Kylie fresh concern but she was also pleased and gave Norah a hug and then patted Romantic Ruby's neck.

"Good horse Well done!" she said, and Romantic Ruby seemed to look at her and nod.

Constable Lonergan was there next, shaking Norah's hand and then he paused and very gently put his fingers up to the weal. Norah shivered but stood still and let him lightly touch it. Then he leaned forward and murmured 'well done' and gave her a quick kiss on the cheek.

That drew stony glares from both Dingo and Collin. Collin angrily snapped, "You should get on that bloody horse of yours Lonergan, and go and arrest that little bitch for assault."

Constable Lonergan stepped back from Norah and looked at him coolly. "I saw what happened. So did a thousand other people. If Norah wants her charged, I am sure she will be but I can't help thinking she has already done herself more harm than that."

Norah nodded. "Oh yes. Poor girl! She has really lost everything now. Mum has complained to the stewards so I doubt if Doris will ever race again. She doesn't need me giving her any more grief."

She then turned to Collin. "Your race is on soon. You had better go,

Collin. Dingo will help me look after Ruby. You others go back and watch the races please. I need a bit of time by myself just now thanks."

Kylie could see she was trembling with emotion, and she thought that a very sensible idea so she urged the boys to go back and took Margaret with her while Dingo and Mrs Conroy went on with Norah. Constable Lonergan resumed buttoning on his tight-fitting ceremonial blue coat.

Collin hesitated, an anxious look on his face. "Is anyone going to bet on me?" he asked the group at large, but with his eyes on Norah.

Norah turned back to him and nodded. "I will. I'll just get Ruby rubbed down. Now get going."

Collin nodded, licked his lips and hurried off to where his horse stood in the stalls. Norah and Dingo walked Ruby along to her stall. The others made their way back to the enclosure. "So I can study the form," Stephen explained.

Peter chuckled. "What form would that be?" he enquired with a dry smile, indicating the young ladies in their twenties who were now lined up for another fashion parade.

Stephen just grinned and leaned on the fence. "They look pretty good to me," he commented.

Kylie thought they did too but she felt uneasy at Stephen's comments and leering look. She had heard too many whispered stories about Stephen and naughty girls to feel completely easy in his company. Margaret leaned on the rail beside her, squeezing in between her and Graham. Peter, Stephen and Roger stood on her right. Then someone moved in on her left.

"That one is really classy," said a male voice which sent a little thrill through Kylie. She knew instantly who it was, Brian, but she resisted the urge to look at him until he spoke again.

"Are you talking to me?" she asked, trying to sound off-hand and distant while a single glance into his eyes sent her pulses racing and made her throat and chest tighten up.

Brian laughed. "No. I was talking to those horses over there."

"You'll have more luck with them," Kylie answered.

Again Brian laughed. Kylie made no reply but pretended deep interest in the contestants. The young ladies were awarded prizes and then ushered off and an older group, all in their forties and fifties, went on. Most of them were wearing quite conservative outfits but one largebosomed lady had a very low cut, red dress with lots of ruffles and flounces. Her cleavage was very obvious and her large bosom quivered and bounced as she stumbled.

As she made her walk along the carpet, another large and obviously drunk lady of about 50 came up behind Kylie and shouted, "Show 'em yer tits, Merl. That might influence the judges."

Kylie stared at the lady behind her in embarrassed disgust. This obviously transmitted itself to the drunken lady, who put her hand to her mouth, then to her own ample bosom, before hiccoughing and saying, "Oops! Sorry kids!"

As she staggered away, Kylie murmured to Margaret, "Common baggage!" echoing an expression she had heard her own mother use.

The lady in red did not win, could in fact barely stand she was so drunk on wine. After she and the others had left the enclosure more horses were led in. Among these was 'Mulga Monster', Collin's horse. The stallion had a big barrel of a chest but to Kylie his legs looked too short and his haunches too small, so she privately resolved not to bet on him.

Norah joined them at that moment, easing in between her and Brian. She called loudly, "Good luck Collin."

Collin blushed with pleasure and smiled but Kylie could see it was a false smile. He did not look either confident or happy.

He was right not to. His horse came in last out of seven. When Collin dismounted at the end of his race, he looked both embarrassed and angry.

"Bloody useless neddy!" he fumed. "If the stupid thing had started promptly, I would have been in with a chance."

Norah shook her head. "Don't blame your horse, Collin. He did try. He's only a stock horse after all."

Collin seemed to wilt at those words, and he looked deeply unhappy. Without another word he turned on his heel and stalked away. Kylie glanced at Norah and noted the look of concern on her face. *But it's not love,* she decided. She also noted the welt across Norah's left cheek. It was now a vivid purple and red with tinges of green and brown around the edges.

"That was a real whack you got," she said.

Norah gingerly touched her cheek and nodded, still looking unhappy. To change the subject she said, "This is the main race coming up now, 'The Garnet Cup'. I am going to bet on 'Chillagoe Rocket'."

"Which one is he?" Kylie asked, eyeing the line of horses being led in by their jockeys.

Norah pointed. "That one, the one with the jockey wearing the gold and white."

Kylie studied the horse with approval, then noted the next, led by a fit looking man wearing emerald-green. "What's the name of the next horse? It looks really nice," she asked.

"That is 'Green Flash'," Norah answered. "I don't know anything about him at all."

"He's a fine-looking horse," Kylie commented, while at the same time thinking that the jockey, who was taller than average, was fine looking young man.

Brian now spoke. "He's the one to bet on."

"Then you go and do that," Kylie snapped, a little annoyed at his boldness.

"I will," Brian answered. He gave her a brazen wink, and grinned, then turned and made his way into the crowd.

Norah stared after him and frowned. "Who is that?"

Kylie could only shrug. "Some fresh stockman," she answered as off-handedly as she could manage.

"Where do you know him from?" Norah asked.

Again Kylie shrugged, but this time she blushed and she knew it, causing her to blush some more. "He just made a pass back in Mt Garnet at lunch time. He's here with his sister."

"What's his name?" Norah asked.

"Brian," she said, "Why?"

Norah frowned. "I've seen him somewhere before," she answered. Then she shook her head and resumed her study of the horses.

Kylie studied the man in green and experienced a vague feeling of also having seen him somewhere. After a few more minutes, when the jockeys began to mount and the horses were being led out onto the track, Norah said, "I'm going to place my bet. Are you girls coming?"

Kylie shook her head. "No thanks. I can't afford to," she answered.

"Didn't you win on me?" Norah asked.

"Yes, but only twenty dollars," Kylie answered.

Norah laughed and went off into the crowd. Kylie resumed watching, remaining at the enclosure fence as the most interesting place to watch from, even though half the racetrack was obscured by the clubhouse. The boys wandered off, causing Kylie to fret about Kate. Then the main race began, and she forgot her in her interest.

It was a good race, two kilometres, and that gave time for the field to space out so that it was possible to keep track of the leading horses at least. Kylie saw that Green Flash led all the way and she wished she had placed a bet on him, while secretly urging him on to win.

Green Flash did. He was led into the enclosure first, with 'Chillagoe Rocket' next, and a gangling looking piebald creature named 'Martian Moonscape' as third. As the horses were led in Kylie heard more horses close behind and looked back to see that the mounted police had led their mounts in and were standing in a group ten metres away. They were now dressed in their very best ceremonial uniforms: white sun helmets of colonial style, dark blue jackets with a white cross strap to their sabre, tight white riding breeches and glossy black boots with silver spurs. They held long lances with blue and white pennons just below the silver spear points. Constable Lonergan and Sgt Grogan were the leaders, their Inspector standing nearby tugging on his white gauntlets while chatting to an official in a suit.

Green Flash's rider dismounted and, still holding his horse's reins, moved to shake the hand of the official who held the cup. Another official took up a microphone and announced, "Ladies and gentlemen, the winner of this year's Mt Garnet Cup is Green Flash, ridden by Mr Michael Patrick of 'Home Rule' Station."

At that, Kylie heard a sharp grunt and looked over her shoulder to see the Inspector staring at the rider. The Inspector suddenly shouted, "By God! That's not Michael Patrick. That's Michael Kelly. Get him men!"

Chapter 14

MIXED EMOTIONS

Kylie stared in astonishment as Inspector Moriarty pushed his way forward to the fence.

"Get out of my way! Step aside!" he bellowed.

Kylie did. Inspector Moriarty sprang up onto the fence and went to jump down into the enclosure. As he did, the silver spur on his right boot hooked into the chain wire netting and when he tried to spring down he was caught and fell headlong. The attempt left him hanging with his head and shoulders on the grass, his white sun helmet rolling off, one booted leg kicking wildly and the other firmly snagged in the netting.

The hooked spur was right in front of Kylie, but she held back from trying to get it free, fearful of the rowel cutting her hand. Swearing and red faced with annoyance Inspector Moriarty broke free and rolled over on the grass. As he scrambled to his feet he reached out towards Michael Kelly and shouted, "Stop! You are under arrest!"

Michael Kelly did not stop. He dragged Green Flash's head around and sprang into the saddle. By the time Inspector Moriarty had regained his feet Michael Kelly had one boot in a stirrup and was swinging into the saddle. Inspector Moriarty dashed forward, reaching out to grab the horse's reins. As he did, the scabbard of his sabre swung between his legs and tripped him. For a second time he went sprawling on the turf.

Kylie clapped her hand to her mouth, torn between the desire to laugh at the policeman's predicament and sympathy for his humiliation and frustration. Inspector Moriarty rolled over and this time, seeing Michael Kelly kicking Green Flash into motion away from him, began clawing at the shiny black leather holster on his belt.

Oh no! Kylie thought, seeing the gun come out. *People could be killed!*

Inspector Moriarty rolled over onto his stomach and raised the pistol to aim it, shouting as he did, "Stop, Michael Kelly! In the name of the law, stop!"

But to Kylie's enormous relief, he didn't fire. By then Michael

Kelly had ridden Green Flash out of the far gate onto the racetrack and there were other horses, riders and officials in the line of fire. Inspector Moriarty scrambled to his feet a second time, fuming and swearing. This time he had the presence of mind to grasp the sabre scabbard before he started to run. He dashed forward, dodging through the horses and riders to the racetrack fence.

Margaret jumped up and down in wild excitement. "Oh! Will he get away?" she shrieked as Michael Kelly set off at a gallop back past the grandstand.

Beside Kylie a man's voice shouted, "Look out! Out of the way!"

Kylie jumped with fright and looked to her left. It was Constable Lonergan. He had swung into the saddle of his horse and was urging him forward towards the gate onto the racetrack. Kylie saw that he had discarded his lance and looked very red-faced and determined. The crowd parted and Constable Lonergan spurred forward, passing out of sight behind the clubhouse. A few seconds later he reappeared out on the racetrack, kicking his horse into a gallop as he set off in pursuit.

Other mounted police followed, some still with their lances and others without. They were slowed down as they crowded to jostle at the gate but then set off in a straggling group in pursuit. As they went past, Inspector Moriarty screamed at them to 'catch him!' and bellowed for one of them to bring him his horse.

As the crowd realised that something unusual was happening, the excited buzz grew to a roar. By then Michael Kelly was well past the grandstand and a hundred metres along the track, galloping fast. When Constable Lonergan went galloping past the grandstand the roar of the crowd grew to a shout, mixed with laughter. Kylie clearly heard several loud voices yell, "Go on Kelly! Give the troopers a run for their money!"

"My money's on the Green Flash!" yelled another man.

"Ten to one on the copper!" called another.

"Yer on!"

Bets, shouts of encouragement (nearly all for Michael Kelly, Kylie noted) and hoots of derisive laughter at the passing mounted police, all added to the uproar. This swelled again as Inspector Moriarty, now mounted on his horse, whacked his mount into a gallop and set off, a long way last.

All eyes now strained to follow the action. Kylie had to stand on tip toe, and even then found most of her view blocked by other people or by the judge's and announcer's boxes. She was able to glimpse the green silk of Michael Kelly as he rode fast around to the far side of the track. To her surprise he kept on going and vanished from her view, the clubhouse blocking her view. All the while she was expecting him to jump the fence and ride off into the bush.

Then the excited buzz of the crowd rose to a deafening roar, filled with cheers and laughter.

"What's going on? What is happening?" she asked.

The race caller answered that by bellowing in his most excited voice, "And here he comes into the home straight, Green Flash a good hundred metres ahead of Copper Number One."

"He's coming right round again!" Margaret squeaked, putting an excited hand to her mouth.

"The cheeky bugger!" Graham cried.

Michael Kelly on Green Flash suddenly thundered into view past the clubhouse and on along the home straight past the grandstand. As he did, he waved to the crowd, who burst into wild cheering and laughter. In Kylie's mind there was no doubt that he had the sympathy of the crowd and that did peeve her. He was, after all, a criminal on the run.

Constable Lonergan now burst into view, galloping hard in a determined attempt to catch up. He got a few cheers, and some yells of encouragement but even more laughter and shouted bets. But the remainder of the mounted police troop, and especially Inspector Moriarty, were bombarded by a storm of jeers and laughter which made Kylie wince in sympathy for them.

Norah shook her head and said, "Oh, how humiliating!" with which Kylie could only agree. Inspector Moriarty's angry red face seemed to underline this.

Michael Kelly rode on around to the far side of the track a second time. Then he stopped there for some reason and Kylie saw him bending down and his horse circling. She could not make out what he was doing. Constable Lonergan came dashing around in hot pursuit and she thought that Michael Kelly would be caught but then he went off away from her and out of sight down the slope to the east.

"What happened? What did he do?" she asked.

Peter answered her. "Opened a slip rail and left the racetrack."

Kylie watched as first Constable Lonergan, then the other police, Inspector Moriarty still trailing well to the rear, all turned and went through the same gap and vanished. They seemed to ride off into a wall of bush half hidden by a wall of rain. Sprinkles of small, cold drops began to wet the watchers. Kylie was left feeling quite unsure who she wanted to win. That bothered her conscience as she was normally a very law-abiding person who liked order.

Stephen had no doubts. "Those useless coppers won't catch him," he scoffed.

Another sprinkle of rain swept across the racecourse. "We had better find some shelter fast," Roger commented, hugging himself against the chill of the wind.

"Back to the tent and change," Margaret suggested.

That seemed a good idea to Kylie, so she and Margaret hurried away, more sprinkles wetting their hair and making their dresses damp.

"Wasn't that daring?" Margaret asked, alluding to Michael Kelly riding in the race when all the police were scouring the region for him.

Kylie could only nod and agree. "It was certainly cheeky," she answered, speeding her footsteps as a few real raindrops hit her.

"I wonder where that duke is?" Margaret speculated.

"I hope he is safe," Kylie answered, remembering how handsome and brave the Duke had been at Herberton.

"The police must get them now," Margaret said.

That was the consensus of most of the others when the girls, now changed back into jeans and shirts and with pullovers on, rejoined them near the grandstand. Only Stephen disagreed.

"The Kelly Gang will run rings around those coppers," he stated.

"I'll bet you ten dollars they catch them within twenty-four hours," Peter said.

"You're on," Stephen agreed.

The brazen exploit, and possible hiding place of the Kelly Gang, remained the main topic of conversation during teatime. The group, minus Norah, her mother and Dingo, ate hamburgers and hot chips at the food stalls under the grandstand. While they ate dinner several heavy showers of rain swept across the racecourse.

Hearing the rain drumming on the corrugated iron roof made Kylie think of the large pavilion that had been erected for the ball. Neither she, nor her friends, was going to the ball, the cost being well outside their limited budgets, but Norah and her mother were, and Kylie felt sorry for them.

"It won't be much fun being in that marque in this weather," she commented.

Margaret shivered and hugged herself. "No, it won't be. Not in a ball gown. Will we still be going to this dance?" she asked.

At that moment, Kylie saw Brian in the distance. He was walking along with several other stockmen, and he had not seen her. In spite of her mind saying she wasn't interested she felt her heart leap and knew she badly wanted to be with him.

"Yes, unless it gets really stormy," she answered.

Graham agreed. "Be better than huddling in a leaky tent," he said.

That got Margaret all hopeful and Kylie could see she was smiling at Graham. *Now, if only the dunderhead will realise she is the girl for him,* she thought.

When the dance began an hour later it was quickly obvious that he hadn't. To the distress of both Margaret and Kylie Graham at once began making eyes at Kate. From the moment she walked in he kept glancing in her direction. She wore a bright red shirt and new blue jeans and had a black cowboy hat set back on her head. The outfit showed off her figure remarkably well, adding to Kylie's sense of grievance for her friend. It did not help that her innate honesty made her admit to herself that Kate had lovely glossy black hair and that she truly did look very attractive.

Those blasted sparkling eyes, she lamented. *How can Margaret compete with them; or with those bouncy boobs?* It was all very annoying.

But then she completely forgot about Margaret and her troubles when she found herself staring into another set of flashing, bold eyes. Brian stood in front of her and bowed, sweeping off his black cowboy hat as he did.

"How about it then, Kylie?" he asked.

"How about what?" Kylie stammered, slightly stunned by the suspicion that Brian was about to make her what she had heard called an improper proposal.

"A dance of course!" he replied with a wink. "Why, what did you think?"

"Oh humpf!" was all Kylie could say.

Before she realised she had not answered either yes or no, she found herself walking out onto the concrete dance floor. She had no idea how to do the dance that was starting but Brian reached out and she took his hand, then allowed him to guide her steps. She was a bit anxious about that hand, worrying that it might feel sweaty and unpleasant. Apparently, he was satisfied as he kept a firm hold. His hand, she noted, felt warm and strong. She also blushed with self-conscious pleasure at the way his eyes shifted from her face to her body and then back to her face every time they stepped apart as they danced. From his expression she was sure he liked what he saw.

It was a real bush dance with a wide variety of music and dance styles. Some were old-fashioned, others were more traditional 'country', even 'folk'. There was 'Rock and Roll' for the grandparents who had enjoyed the sixties and seventies of the previous century, plus more modern pop, rap, hip-hop and other styles. To the intense amusement of Stephen there were even banjos and ukuleles in the very versatile band.

He mimed strumming a banjo and said in a 'hick' accent, "They'se got both kinds'a music out here: country and western!"

As Stephen often made jokes about 'country hicks' and 'hillbillies', that irritated Kylie even more. She really liked the country people and even much of the music.

"It is certainly toe-tapping stuff," she commented to Brian as they swung along doing a barn dance.

As she danced, she was acutely conscious of her body movements and worried that she might do the wrong thing and make a fool of herself. There was also the emotional test of letting him hold her in a traditional dance pose. That got her heart beating faster and she became concerned that he might smell her perspiration. But she enjoyed the experience. His grip felt warm and smooth and she liked the way he held her. It sent tingles through her, and she had to admit she was getting a bit of a crush.

I'd better be careful, she mused. *I don't know anything about him.*

She set about to remedy that, eliciting the information that his name was Brian Ross and that he and his sister were off a cattle station named 'Ivanhoe' out in the Gulf Country.

In reply, Brian asked, "Are you from around here?"

Kylie shook her head. "No. I come from Cairns."

"A city girl, eh? Oh well! What does your dad do?" Brian asked.

"He's a Master Mariner," Kylie said. Then, when she could see that Brian did not know what that meant she explained, "He's a ship captain."

"Oh, I see. What brings you to Mt Garnet then?" Brian asked.

"We are on a horse-riding holiday," Kylie explained.

"We?"

"My brother and his friends, and my friend Margaret," she answered.

"Brother?"

"That's him there," Kylie said, pointing to where Graham was dancing with Kate.

To her annoyance she saw that his face was flushed and that he was staring at her with big, love-struck eyes.

Oh drat, the bloody fool! she thought.

"Oh him," Brian said. "Yes, I saw him making a pass at my sister back in Mt Garnet."

"He did not! She made the pass at him!" Kylie replied heatedly.

Brian raised an eyebrow and then grinned. "If you say so. Let's not argue. Would you like a soft drink?"

As the band had just stopped playing, and as she had just danced four dances with Brian and she felt a little heated and out of breath, she said yes. He took a firm hold of her hand and led her towards one of the tables along the side where soft drinks were being sold. Having him do that both annoyed and aroused her. He felt so masterful and strong that she just knew she wanted to fall in love with him.

During the next dance the pair stood to one side chatting and drinking soft drink. Kylie knew she was flushed and happy and was already wondering what else might develop. *I hope he wants to kiss me,* she thought, her heart pitter-pattering at the thought.

For a while she stood watching the people, her mind on how to accomplish the next move. She knew she was having a good time and really enjoyed watching the people. It particularly amused her to watch the numerous children, many quite young, who were dancing on the edges of the crowd. *They look really cute,* she decided, noting the two little twin 'cowgirls' with their pink skirts and pink ribbons on their blonde plaits and pink cowboy hats.

Brian looked towards the open side of the shed and then walked that way. "I wonder if the rain has stopped," he said.

Kylie went with him and found herself beside him just outside, staring up at the sky. The rain had. She commented on this and then had her breath taken away when Brian suggested they go for a walk.

"A walk?" she queried, anxious but hopeful.

"Yes," Brian replied. Very gently he took her hand and Kylie found herself walking unresistingly away from the music, lights and people and into the darkness.

They didn't go far. In the shadow of a big tree Brian stopped and turned to face her, taking hold of her other hand as he did. After a moment's silence Kylie became anxious, more that he say what she wanted to hear than for any other reason. In the dim light she saw him swallow and then he said, "I think you are really nice."

Kylie could only nod. Somehow, she found herself in his arms being hugged and the next moment her eager lips were seeking his. She had never been really kissed by a boy before so did some inexperienced fumbling. The touch, and the scents, seemed to set her heart racing and her blood on fire. It was something she had read about, and which she had frequently daydreamed of experiencing, but the real thing she found even better. With a sigh of pure pleasure she relaxed into his embrace and began to kiss him.

For several minutes they clung together, kissing and sighing and holding each other tightly. Then he held her with her head on his shoulder and she felt his hands slide down her side and onto her buttocks. That caused her to stiffen in anxiety. It felt really nice, but she knew it could be the prelude to things that were very naughty and that she wasn't at all sure she was ready for.

Brian moved his hands back upwards and caressed her back, pulling her hard against him. He sighed and murmured that she was wonderful and kissed her again. *And hard is the word!* Kylie thought with a thrill, feeling his maleness pressing against her stomach. Having two older brothers she was well aware of how boys were made and what their bodies were capable of doing. It both excited and worried her. She found it flattering that she had the power to arouse but fervently hoped that Brian liked her for herself, and not just because she was female.

They kissed again, more passionately than before. Kylie began to worry about how to end it without stress. She need not have bothered. A shower of heavy rain sent them both scuttling back to the shed.

Even while they ran Brian kept a grip on her hand. They arrived panting and laughing under the roof. Brian's eyes were sparkling, and he smiled and said, "Drat the rain! I was just starting to enjoy myself."

Kylie had been too but decided it was not good tactics to appear too keen. She did smile but she said, "I probably shouldn't be going out into the dark with boys."

At that, Brian looked concerned. "Why not? Is your mum here?"

"No. Mrs Conroy is in charge of the trail ride," Kylie answered. That made her feel guilty as she knew they were at the dance on trust as Mrs Conroy was at the ball.

"Do you still go to school?" Brain asked, anxiety evident in his voice.

He wants to know how old I am, Kylie deduced.

It flattered her that he might think she was older than she actually was. She certainly wanted to know his age. Feeling rather anxious that he might drop her when he learnt the truth she was momentarily tempted to lie, but then she nodded and said, "Yes. I'm in Year Nine. Do you still go to school?"

At that, she fancied that a look of disappointment appeared briefly on his face, but he kept smiling and said, "Yes. I'm in Year Twelve, but I don't know if I am going to finish it."

"Oh, why not?" Kylie asked.

At that, Brian shrugged and asked what school she went to. Kylie named her school in Cairns and then asked the same question. Brian answered, "Atherton State High."

That puzzled her. "I thought you said you came from a cattle station?"

"I do. I board at Woodleigh College in Herberton," Brain answered.

Kylie actually knew where Woodleigh College was, Graham having pointed it out to her as they had driven through the town. "Oh do you? We were in Herberton the other day, when the Kelly Gang kidnapped the Duke," she said.

Brian nodded and said, "So were we. Where were you?"

Kylie described where she had been standing and Brian said he had been at the back of the crowd so had not noticed her, but when she mentioned Graham and the cadets he did say he had seen them. He did not seem very interested and changed the subject to ask her about her home. Kylie began telling him about her house in Cairns and her pets. As she talked, she saw Margaret sitting over against the far wall. She looked decidedly miserable.

Oh no, where is Graham? Kylie wondered. She looked around the room but there was no sign of either him, or of Kate's red shirt. *Oh no! I hope he hasn't gone outside with her.*

He had. As the next shower of rain drummed on the roof, she saw Graham and Kate come scuttling in, holding hands and laughing. To add to Kylie's worry, she noted her brother's excited look and guessed that he and Kate had been 'having a pash'. Knowing that she and Brain had done exactly the same made her feel like a hypocrite, but she still felt sorry for Margaret. She noted that when Margaret had seen Graham and Kate come in, she had gone every pale and Kylie was sure she was on the edge of tears.

But she could not think what to do about it. As she bit her lip with worry, the MC announced the next dance and Brian took her hand.

"Come on," he said. "This is my favourite dance."

"What is it?" Kylie asked, noting that Kate seemed to be leading Graham out to dance as well.

"A Pride of Erin," Brian answered.

"Oh I know how to do that," Kylie said. "We learnt it at school."

She had too, and she loved it. The rhythm and the closeness of Brian, and her own romantic thoughts mingled with the music to set her head twirling and her heart beating in the same way the music set her body whirling and her feet tapping. The only thing that spoiled her happiness was passing Graham and Kate and seeing the look of guilty defiance on his face; and noting Margaret sitting in silent misery.

When the dance finished Brian kept hold of her hand and then whispered to her, "Would you like to go outside again?"

Kylie very much did want to, but she was also quite anxious that nothing might happen to spoil her happiness. *I don't want things to go too far and get out of hand,* she thought. Then she blushed at the wicked thoughts that the concept of 'hand' conveyed.

"You won't do anything naughty please," she croaked, aware that her hands had gone sweaty and that her heart was suddenly hammering much faster.

"No. You can trust me," Brain replied. He looked very earnest and anxious and that helped to melt her resistance.

With that she nodded, and they walked hand in hand out into the darkness again.

Chapter 15

PUZZLING

As Kylie walked out into the darkness with Brian, she was very excited and hopeful, yet also anxious. She did not think Brian would try anything too naughty, but she had heard stories from other girls of what boys wanted and tried to do.

He will be alright, she decided. Somehow, she felt she could trust him. It was only a gut instinct as she was well aware she hardly knew him, but with the promise of more of those lovely hugs and kisses she was willing to take the risk. *Anyway, he must have worked out I am too young to try anything really naughty,* she mused.

But the nice tree where they had kissed earlier was now taken up by another couple, so they walked on, Kylie glancing at the pair with envy and curiosity. Brian led her around to the rear of the shed, but this was worse. It was lit up and there were half a dozen drunks there having an argument. To get away from them they walked on to the far side and found a dark corner near the back of the grandstand.

No sooner had they embraced and their lips met then grunting noises and a loud fart attracted Kylie's attention. She looked past Brain's shoulder (She wasn't quite tall enough to put her head on it) and saw two more drunks. They had detoured in against the wall and by the way they were fumbling with the front of their trousers she had a horrible suspicion about what they were going to do. She was right. The nearest, a man in his thirties, pulled out his penis and then leaned on the wall and began to urinate. Kylie had often seen her brothers doing a pee but this she found disgusting.

Brain wasn't amused either. "Sorry," he whispered, while obviously trying to shield her from the unpleasant sight.

The two drunks finished and then wandered on. But that place had now lost its romantic appeal to Kylie. If nothing else, it now stank of stale urine. She wrinkled her nose and muttered, "Let's go somewhere more private please."

Brian grunted with annoyance but agreed so they strolled on past the back of the grandstand and around to near the enclosure and clubhouse. Here they found another shady nook and snuggled into each other's willing arms. Once again Kylie relaxed and started kissing with as much enthusiasm as Brian was displaying. He was very keen and held her tightly, stroking and gripping her back and buttocks and setting her body on fire. Then his hands moved to stroking her side and she shivered in anticipation, suspecting that this was preliminary to him touching her breasts.

She wasn't quite sure if she wanted that yet, although she knew she did want it eventually, indeed expected it as part of a normal relationship. As his hand slid slowly up her side she stiffened and felt her heart rate increase.

Only to be interrupted again. This time it was by two men, both of whom came from the open area outside the gate. An angry call caused both Kylie and Brian to lift their heads apart and look. It was at once clear to Kylie that the men had not seen them and were intent on their own business. Then she felt a stab of anxiety as she recognised the voices. It was Dingo and Collin Costello.

Collin had run after Dingo and now caught up and grabbed his arm. "Don't walk away from me when I'm talking to you, you bastard!" he snarled.

"Let me go!" Dingo snapped, wrenching his arm free.

"You stay away from Norah, or else!" Collin hissed.

"Or what?" Dingo grated in reply, raising his fists as he did.

Kylie watched this with growing alarm but also with little surprise. *I was right,* she thought. *They both love Norah. Oh dear! I hope there isn't going to be a fight.*

There plainly was as neither man would back down. They circled warily, fists raised. Kylie gripped Brian's arm and muttered half to herself, half to him.

"Oh no! Stop them."

But Brian did nothing except put a protective arm around Kylie. She could only watch with dismay as Collin lunged forwards, fists swinging. Dingo stood his ground and met him, his own arms flailing. The sound of curses, swearing and hard smacks followed. Again Kylie called on Brian to intervene. Again he did nothing, except to start edging her away towards the side of the corner they were sheltering in.

To Kylie's relief, other people did intervene. Three men came running in the gate and grappled with the two men. For a few seconds Kylie feared they were going to join in and make it some sort of gang bashing but then she saw they were trying to pull the two combatants apart.

One of the three men called out, "Stop it you mad buggers! The cops are just out there and they are coming this way."

That calmed the two but before Kylie could look around Brian muttered, "Time we were gone. Come on!"

He took her firmly by the wrist and led her out of the corner and around the side of the betting shed. Being hustled that way annoyed Kylie but she did not resist and went with him. As they crossed the sawdust floor of the darkened betting shed towards the canteen area, she glanced back and saw four mounted constables come through the gate on plodding horses. By then the fight had apparently broken up and the men were all walking away towards the rear of the shed.

Kylie looked back again and this time pulled back to slow Brian. "That looks like Constable Lonergan and the others who went off chasing that Michael Kelly fellow. I wonder if they caught him?"

Brian looked back and his eyes narrowed. Then he shook his head and scoffed. "Doesn't look it. That's no victory parade. Those bloody troopers aren't good enough to catch a Kelly."

The remark puzzled Kylie and she wanted to go back and ask but Brian kept a grip on her wrist. She said, "We could go and find out."

"No thanks. I want to go back to the dance," Brian replied shortly.

Kylie didn't. She wanted some more kissing but sensed that Brian was now in an odd mood, so she accepted his decision and walked with him through into the crowded and well-lit canteen and then back in to the dance area. By then her romantic mood was half spoiled so she thought that being with the others in the bright lights might be for the best.

As soon as her eyes had adjusted to the lights, she looked around and was pleased to note that Margaret was no longer sitting against the wall. That got her hopeful so she looked around the dancers. After a minute or so she spotted Margaret, and her pleasure evaporated. Margaret was dancing with Roger. That got her looking even more anxiously around but there was no sign of Graham, or of Kate.

He is outside with her, she surmised, feeling annoyed and sympathetic towards Margaret.

That Margaret was not happy was obvious. She gave Kylie a smile, but it clearly did not reach her eyes. That made Kylie feel quite extraordinarily guilty as she was once again dancing with Brian and enjoying the strong tenderness of his touch.

Then she saw Graham and Kate. They had come in from the canteen and were holding hands and laughing. Seeing that sent another spasm of annoyance through Kylie as she saw a look of bleak misery flit across Margaret's face. Wishing somehow she could break up the evidently blossoming romance, Kylie cast around in her mind for a tactic.

To her surprise, Brian helped her by saying, "There's that sister of mine. Excuse me for a minute. I just want a word with her."

"She's with my brother," Kylie replied by way of explanation when she started walking with him.

Brian just grunted and then let her come. They walked quickly over to where Graham and Kate stood. As they got closer, Kate saw them and she gave Brian a smile and Kylie a frown. As they reached them, Kate said, "They didn't catch Michael."

Brian nodded, but Graham looked puzzled. "Who's Michael?"

For a few seconds Kate stood with her mouth open, giving Kylie a peculiar feeling she had said something she hadn't meant to. Graham repeated his question.

Brian shrugged, then said, "Michael Kelly, the man on Green Flash who the police were chasing this afternoon."

Puzzled, Kylie asked, "Do you know him?"

Brain nodded. "He used to work on our property," he said. Then he turned to Kate and said, "It is getting late Sis. We had better get going."

Kate nodded and looked wistfully at Graham. Kylie also felt dismayed. "Do you have to?" she queried.

"Yes, sorry," Brian replied. He took her hand and turned towards the side door.

Kylie walked with him, her mind racing with anxieties. *How can I stay in touch?* she wondered.

Brian was obviously thinking the same thing as he said to her in a low and urgent voice, "I would like to see you again."

Kylie nodded. "Me too. Can we meet again tomorrow morning?"

Brian looked unhappy and shook his head. "Sorry. We have to be on the road early." He looked at her intently in a way that made her heart thrill. To her great relief, he then asked, "Can I have your address and phone number?"

Again Kylie nodded. She stopped just outside the door and Brian took out an old envelope and the stub of a pencil. Kylie gave him her address and he wrote it down. She then asked, "Can I have yours?"

At that, Brian looked quite agitated. After a significant pause he shook his head. "Sorry. It's a bit difficult. We are in the process of moving house, and I don't know what the new number is. I will contact you when I do know. Is that alright?"

It wasn't very satisfactory but Kylie saw no option, so she agreed. She badly wanted to see this wonderful young man again. He led her a few more paces out into the darkness and put his hands on her shoulders and drew her to him. She sighed and allowed him to hug her. As she did, she was aware that Graham was kissing Kate beside her.

Kate asked him, "What are you doing tomorrow?"

Graham answered, "Riding back towards Herberton."

"Which way are you going?" Kate asked.

"Past some old ghost town called Coolgarra," Graham answered.

"Never heard of it," Kate replied. "Where is it?"

"In the hills to the north of Mt Garnet," Graham answered.

By then Brian had given a trembling and unhappy Kylie a kiss and eased her away. He then said, "Come on Kate. Say goodbye and let's move. We need to be back at camp soon."

"What's the hurry?" Graham asked. "It's only just past eleven. You won't turn into a pumpkin for another hour."

"We've got stock to look after," Brian explained. Then, with a last smile at Kylie, he turned and walked away. Kate followed, turning to wave and blow kisses at Graham.

Already upset, that annoyed Kylie further. As soon as Brian and Kate were out of sight, she turned on him, "You are a cad, Graham, hurting Margaret like that."

"Why? Margaret doesn't own me. I'm not married to her or anything," he replied defensively.

"The way you have been carrying on, kissing that Kate like that. Why, she is a complete stranger. You don't know anything about her."

"I do so!" Graham replied, his guilty conscience evidently sparking anger.

"Oh yeah! So what do you know?"

"Her name is Kate Williams and she lives on a cattle station called Lynd Vale on the road to Charters Towers," Graham replied.

That really puzzled Kylie. "I thought she was Brian's sister," she replied.

"She is," Graham answered.

"But he said his name was Ross," she said.

There was an awkward silence for a few moments, then Graham shrugged and said, "Might be one of those families with step-parents." Then he rounded on her, "And anyway, who are you to speak? Talk about the pot calling the kettle black! I saw you two. He had his hands all over you!"

"Oh he did not!" cried Kylie, blushing with guilt as she did.

"Did so! He's lucky I didn't knock his block off," Graham answered.

"Oh piffle! You and what army?" Kylie retorted, but then a tear trickled out and she fled back into the dance hall to escape.

Brother and sister did not resume the argument inside and Kylie kept away from Graham. She felt suddenly drained and unhappy, and also puzzled. She had an uneasy feeling that she had, if not been lied to, then at least not told the whole truth, and she did not like it. That clashed with her intense desire to fall in love with Brian.

And there was the problem of Margaret. She was clearly so unhappy that Kylie decided the only thing to do was to get her away from the dance to have a good cry. To that end she sidled over to where Margaret was standing talking to Peter and suggested they leave. To her relief, Margaret nodded and said, "Good idea. I'm tired and we have to be up early tomorrow."

But there were no tears from Margaret. As they walked back she kept a brave face and chattered about the horse races and about the dresses worn by various girls. A sprinkle of rain helped to speed them along. The two friends walked out through the canteen and the betting shed and across past the enclosure towards the gate.

As they did, Kylie saw a man walking towards them from the horse stalls. He was carrying a bundle of some sort. As he got closer, she noted jodhpurs and polished leather leggings shining in the lamplight. *One of the mounted police,* she surmised, relaxing a little as she did not want to meet strange males in the dark and rain.

It was Constable Lonergan. His course converged with theirs near the gate. After he had called a cheerful hello, Kylie wondered if she should ask if he had caught Michael Kelly. *It might rub salt in the wounds of his pride if they didn't,* she thought. So she kept her question unasked.

Constable Lonergan recognised them and said, "Have a good time at the dance?"

Margaret answered, her voice sounding cheerful enough. "Yes thanks. What about you?"

At that, Constable Lonergan gave a rueful laugh and hefted his burden to his other shoulder to be polite. Kylie now saw it was his saddle, saddlecloth and bridle. "No," he said, "I've had a jolly good long ride in the mud and rain. Have just finished giving poor old Black Knight a good rub down and a feed."

Once again it was Margaret who spoke. "So you didn't catch that cheeky man?"

"Michael Kelly? No," Constable Lonergan replied. "We lost his tracks down along the creeks beside the Gunnawarra Road when the rain came in heavy. He rode along the creeks and then got out at places where it was hard to pick up hoof marks."

"Rode along the creeks?" Margaret queried.

"Yes. They mostly have sandy beds here and the water was only knee deep. Got bloody... er. jolly wet," Constable Lonergan replied with a tired chuckle.

Kylie now saw that his uniform was soaked and splattered with mud. "Have you had any tea?" she asked.

"Not yet. That will be next after a good hot bath," he answered.

By then they had passed out of the gate. Constable Lonergan veered off to the right towards the police building. "Well, goodnight, ladies. You get home before the wicked witch turns you into a pumpkin."

"Oh poo!" Margaret snorted. "I'm not Cinderella. That's Kylie."

"Oh?" Constable Lonergan said, raising an eyebrow.

Kylie blushed when Margaret said, "She met her Prince Charming at the dance, but I didn't."

"Oh well, you are young yet," Constable Lonergan answered. "Good night."

"Good night," both girls chorused.

They turned and headed down the darkened dirt road towards their tent. As they did, a shower of rain swept over, sending them hurrying along, for which Kylie was thankful as it stopped the conversation. On the way they made a short visit to the toilet, then continued on. When they arrived back at the tent Margaret quickly changed into her pyjamas and slid into her sleeping bag, saying she was tired. By then Kylie was feeling both glad and unhappy. She wanted to talk about Brian, but did not want to upset Margaret by rubbing her own good fortune in her friend's face.

So she quickly prepared for bed and lay down as well. Outside the rain pattered on the tent and the sounds of drunken revelry came from several parties. These were mostly groups of youths in their late teens or early twenties and their loud voices and laughter kept Kylie from drifting off to sleep. Not that she really wanted to. She had a strong desire to dream about Brain instead and lay in a doze, fantasizing about what might have happened, and about what the future might hold.

The arrival home of the boys then kept her awake as they laughed and carried on with cheerful horseplay in the next tent. When she called out, telling them to be quite and go to bed, some of the youths at a nearby party all cried out in mock alarm and yelled at the boys to get to bed before mummy came and gave them a good smack.

Kylie could only grin and be thankful she was warm and dry. She was actually glad the boys were back because at one of the parties some obviously drunk youths had begun an argument that was threatening to break into a fight. There was a lot of crude swearing and threats and then sudden silence. That left Kylie wondering what had happened, but angry girls' voices gave her a clue as to how the situation had been settled.

Chapter 16

GHOSTS OF GLENROWAN

Kylie woke to a grey dawn and groaned. Mrs Conroy shook her to wakefulness. But waking up was the last thing Kylie felt like. Not only did she feel tired and stiff but she was enjoying a wonderful dream in which Brian figured strongly. The images left her feeling slightly guilty. Blinking sleep from her gummed-up eyelids she sat up.

"Hello Mrs Conroy. What time is it?"

"Six o'clock. Time to be up and about," Mrs Conroy replied cheerfully.

"Oooh!" groaned Margaret, who stretched, then pulled the sleeping bag clear of her face. "Do we have to?"

"Yes. The horses need attention and we have to get moving to keep to our schedule," Mrs Conroy replied.

Her head withdrew from the tent and a moment later Kylie heard her calling on the boys to wake up. With another groan, a stretch and a yawn, Kylie sat up and then climbed stiffly out of her sleeping bag. She slid on sandshoes and a dressing gown and hurried out to go to the toilet.

Outside was cool and grey with heavy overcast. It had obviously rained more during the night as the ground was slightly muddy and the grass wet. Treading carefully she made her way to the toilet block and back. On the way back she passed a bleary-eyed and grumpy Margaret.

Back at the tents she found the boys awake and Mrs Conroy in a bad mood. "Have any of you seen Dingo?" she queried.

A flashback to Dingo starting to fight with Collin made Kylie bite her lip. But rather than get Dingo into trouble she just said, "I saw him last night at about ten o'clock."

Norah joined them and said, "Has anyone seen him this morning?"

"No," Kylie replied.

Mrs Conroy looked annoyed and Norah appeared to frown. Mrs Conroy shrugged and said as Margaret returned, "Get dressed and then let's go to the horses."

Kylie quickly dressed in her riding clothes, keeping her back to Margaret as she did. The group then walked through to where the horses waited in the next paddock. Old Neville had rounded them up but he made only a wry face and gave a grunt expressing dissatisfaction when told no-one had seen Dingo. For the next half hour they worked in relative silence, feeding, watering, and grooming the horses. That was something Kylie always enjoyed and as she brushed Blazer down her mood improved.

The sun came peeking through the clouds and that helped to cheer her up as well because it was surprisingly cold for an April morning, and she found herself wishing she had worn a pullover. On their return to the camp she put one on and then helped with preparing breakfast.

By 7:30 breakfast was over and there was still no sign of Dingo. Norah looked worried and Mrs Conroy looked annoyed. "Where has he got to?" she asked. "He knows we have to get away early."

Helped by Old Neville the teenagers pulled down the tents and packed them into carry bags. These were packed into the trailer and then the cooking gear and personal belongings followed.

Norah looked even more concerned. "But now Dingo won't get any breakfast," she said.

At that, Old Neville snorted and replied, "Do the lazy bugger good! He doesn't need it. Anyway, he's probably still got a skinful of grog and won't feel like eating anything."

"Oh, there's no need to say things like that!" Norah answered.

Old Neville gave her a pitying look and snorted again. "Huh! If the cap fits, wear it."

Mrs Conroy shook her head and looked at her watch. "Nearly eight. You had better go and see if you can find him."

Margaret agreed. "We can ask the police. They might know."

At that, Old Neville snorted again and grunted, "They'll bloody know all right! They've probably got him locked up for drunk and disorderly!"

"Don't be horrible Neville," Norah chided, clearly not amused. She turned to the teenagers. "You boys go around to the other side of the rodeo ground and we will go to the police station and ask, then look around the stalls and the grandstand."

So Norah, Kylie and Margaret set off through the 'camps' along the winding track that led past the showers while the three boys walked straight along towards the front gate. As they walked, Kylie noted that at many of the camps people were busy packing up.

"There seem to be a lot of people leaving," she commented. "I thought there was another day."

"There is," Norah replied. "The rodeo, but that attracts quite a different type of clientele."

That much became quickly apparent to Kylie as the girls came out into the open area between the camps, rodeo ground and police buildings. The rodeo had begun but vehicles were still driving in. These were, she noted, mostly 'country' type vehicles: utilities and battered light trucks and 4WDs. The people were different too, younger and rougher looking. Most seemed to be in their late teens or early twenties and there were very few girls to be seen. There were also a lot more indigenous people.

A loud shout from the crowd now seated around the ring of the rodeo ground made the girls all look but they could not see what had caused it, only some rising dust. Kylie had never been to a rodeo and wasn't sure if she wanted to go to one now. The idea of people or animals possibly getting hurt just for sport or amusement did not appeal to her.

As they went to cross the dusty access track, a line of police vehicles came in from the highway. The girls stopped and waited as they went past. As the last one crawled by Norah let out a little gasp. Kylie looked to see what had caused it. She had noted that the last police vehicle was a 'paddy wagon' with a cage on the back but had not taken much notice. Now she saw that there were people seated in there, and one of them looked very much like Dingo!

Oh, I hope not! she thought. But Norah obviously did as she set her jaw and began striding determinedly after the vehicles.

It was Dingo. After the vehicle stopped, the same horrible policeman who had been rudely abrupt in Mt Garnet got out and came round to the back and unlocked the door. The men climbed out. Among them was an embarrassed and shamefaced Dingo. When he saw Norah, he blanched and his already pale complexion took on a pasty, yellowish look.

The policeman spoke loudly to the group of men, saying, "Get going you lot! And don't get into trouble again."

Oh dear! thought Kylie, *Old Neville was right.*

She found it quite sad, and Dingo was obviously ashamed. He stood and shuffled his feet and tried to straighten his dirty and crumpled shirt. It was obvious that he needed a shave and his hair needed brushing. His eyes had a horrible look to them, all yellowish and bloodshot.

Norah pointed back towards the camp. In a very calm voice she said, "We are nearly ready to go Dingo, so please go and clean yourself up and join us as quickly as you can."

Dingo lowered his eyes and nodded. "Yes, Miss Norah," he mumbled. He began walking off towards the camp.

At that moment, Constable Lonergan appeared from around the other side of another vehicle. He was now dressed in his work uniform of brown jodhpurs and blue shirt and wore his leather leggings with spurs and a blue broad-brimmed police hat.

"Hello Norah," he said. "Good morning girls."

The girls turned to say hello. As they did, Kylie noted that a group of TV camera men and news reporters was gathering over near the end of the line of parked vehicles. Moving to obviously speak to them was Inspector Moriarty, still dressed in his ceremonial uniform. With him were two middle-aged Aboriginal men. They were dressed in what was, even to Kylie's eyes, a very old-fashioned uniform. The Aborigines wore soft blue caps of the crumpled-at-the-front style she associated with historical photos of the American Civil War. Below that were old-style dark blue jackets with long sleeves, a high collar and a row of shiny brass buttons down the front. Off-white riding breeches stuffed into knee high black leather boots completed the outfit.

Margaret gaped and pointed. "Who are they?" she asked Constable Lonergan.

Constable Lonergan gave a wry grin and replied, "They are the Ghosts of Glenrowan."

"What do you mean?" queried Norah, her attention divided between the spectacle of the media gathering and Constable Lonergan.

"That is what they are being called, the Ghosts of Glenrowan," Constable Lonergan answered. "They are Inspector Moriarty's latest weapon in the hunt for the Kelly Gang. They are black trackers; and not just any black trackers but the direct descendants of the some of the black trackers sent from Queensland back in 1880 to help catch the original Kelly Gang."

Margaret looked at the two Aborigines with puzzled interest, then asked, "What are black trackers?"

"Black men who are skilled at following tracks. They can follow the trail left by an animal or a man in the bush," Constable Lonergan replied.

Kylie was surprised that Margaret had not known that but the very idea of men hunting down other men made her shiver. Margaret went on, "They look a bit old."

Constable Lonergan nodded. "I think they are. There aren't many real black trackers left now. Very few of the young bucks learn the skills. It is a dying art. But these blokes are ridgy-didge trackers of the old school. If they can't track the Kelly's, then nobody can."

At that moment, one of the black trackers looked down the road past the girls and pointed that way, then called out. Kylie turned to see what he was pointing at and saw Dingo hurrying back towards them.

"Here comes Dingo," she commented.

"He must know them," Margaret added.

He obviously did as the two black trackers ignored the TV people and reporters and moved to greet Dingo, the three clustering around shaking hands and greeting each other. To Kylie's astonishment, Dingo unbuttoned his shirt and pulled it up, revealing a series of welts and scars on the skin of his chest and back. It caused to her to gasp in horror.

Norah also gasped in shock. "I didn't realise Dingo had been through a tribal initiation," she said.

"Initiation?" Margaret queried.

Constable Lonergan answered her. "In traditional Aboriginal society the young men and women had to pass various tests to be initiated to various levels. The tribal secrets were only passed on to them when the elders believed they were ready for them. To show they were initiated their skin was cut in various special patterns to leave the scars."

Dingo pulled his shirt back down again and the three men spoke rapidly until a huffy and annoyed Inspector Moriarty interrupted and called the two men back to his news conference. Dingo called a last comment to the other two but as it was in an Aboriginal language Kylie had no idea what was said. In return they called to him, also in that language.

As Dingo came walking back past them, Norah called to him and he came over. "Who are they Dingo?" she asked.

"They top tracker fellas," Dingo answered proudly. "They catch them Kelly fellas for sure."

"How do you know them?" Constable Lonergan asked. "I thought you came from out near Mount Isa?"

"I do. Met 'em at the Laura Festival last year," Dingo replied.

"Who are they?" Margaret asked.

"They not using their real names for this," Dingo explained. "For this they using names like their ancestors who went to help catch the Kelly Gang. That big old guy, he is Charlie Noble, and he is calling himself Wannamulla. The bloke next to him is Jim Owens, and he is naming himself Wannarabe."

"Why don't they use their real names?" Kylie asked.

"To protect them," Dingo explained.

"You said names like their ancestors," Margaret commented. "Why not the same ones?"

Dingo nodded and looked embarrassed but did not answer. Constable Lonergan spoke for him. "I've heard that in traditional Aboriginal culture it is wrong to speak the names of the dead. So they have new names."

Kylie turned to Dingo. "They called you a name too, didn't they?"

Again Dingo looked embarrassed, but he nodded and replied, "My real name is Wirriumi."

"Are you a tracker too?" Margaret asked.

Dingo gave a shy laugh and shook his head. "Not like them fellas are. They can track a lizard across bare rock. They can even smell a man hours after he has passed a place."

Kylie did not know if she believed that but she was impressed. She wanted to ask more questions, but Norah told Dingo to hurry on and get ready to leave. Dingo nodded and hurried away. Norah then turned to Constable Lonergan and said, "Sorry Frank. We have to go."

"Heading back home, are you?" Constable Lonergan asked.

"Yes."

Constable Lonergan looked intently at her and slowly nodded. "See you again then. Take care."

Watching both faces left Kylie with the same impression as before. *He's in love with Norah for certain,* she decided. But did Norah like him? Kylie wasn't sure. Saying goodbye she turned and went with the others, only to be confronted with another unpleasant incident.

Fifty paces ahead, Dingo had been pulled to a stop by Collin. Collin had come weaving through the scattering of people and cars and called to Dingo. When Dingo ignored him, Collin grabbed his sleeve and said something Kylie didn't hear exactly what but did catch the word 'black' and was sure it was followed by a swear word or insult.

At that, Dingo swung round and wrenched his shirt free, snarling, "Leave me alone Costello, and don't call me names."

Collin placed clenched fists belligerently on his hips and glared back at him. "Remember what I said. Don't annoy Norah, or else!"

Kylie bit her lip with anxiety. It was obvious to her that Collin was both angry and drunk. He was swaying as he spoke and even had to take a short step to keep his balance. His clothes looked as though he had slept in them and were the same ones he had been wearing the night before and he was unshaven and tousle-headed. All in all he was not a very edifying spectacle and Kylie could only shake her head.

He's not making a very good impression, she thought, glancing at Norah's drawn face and tight-lipped frown.

Dingo made some reply, which Kylie did not hear. But she did see Collin's reaction Without further warning he swung a punch. Dingo tried to dodge but his reactions were slow and the blow struck him on the side of the head. That was enough. Dingo reacted by punching back.

Norah ran forward calling, "Stop it! Stop it!"

Kylie followed, dodging around people and a moving car, her heart in her mouth. As she ran, she saw Collin punch Dingo in the chest. Dingo punched back, striking Collin in the nose, enraging him more. Blood trickled. Norah reached them and grabbed at Collin's arm.

"Stop it! Stop fighting!" she wailed unhappily.

A crowd was starting to form, and Kylie was scared the fight might become a brawl. From behind Kylie came the thud of running boots and she glanced back anxiously. It was Constable Lonergan. As he passed, Kylie he shouted, "Stop that fighting you blokes!"

Kylie slowed to watch, fearing to get hurt. Collin shook Norah off, then shoved her aside. At that, Kylie shook her head. *He's lost her now,* she thought, knowing how she would feel if that was done to her.

Dingo took the opportunity to land a hard blow to Collin's face, down which a smear of blood was now trickling. Colin retaliated by a savage upper-cut to Dingo's stomach that doubled him up and sent him sprawling in the dust. Before Norah could intervene, Collin kicked at Dingo, his riding boot thudding into the fallen man's chest.

Norah tried to stop him, but Collin held her back with one hand. Then Constable Lonergan arrived on the run, grabbing him and shoving him away.

"Stop fighting or I will arrest you!" he snapped.

Collin swung to face him, his eyes blazing with fury. "The same applies to you too, Lonergan. Keep away from Norah. She's too good for the likes of you."

Constable Lonergan stopped and faced him, standing between him and Dingo, who was now trying to get up but was retching into the dust at the same time.

"Just go away Costello, or you will spend the rest of the day in the watch house," he said.

"Make me!" Collin retorted. Then he sprang forward, swinging a punch at Constable Lonergan.

Again Norah tried to intervene, but this time it was Constable Lonergan who fended her off. "Keep clear, Norah. I will deal with this, thanks," he said.

Collin landed another punch before Constable Lonergan was able to fight back. Kylie stood transfixed, hands to her mouth and watched. Norah also now stood back, her eyes anxiously following the struggle. People began to form a ring and a few excited youths began to shout the odds, most calling on Collin to 'belt the bloody copper and teach him a lesson.'

But it was all over very quickly. Constable Lonergan dodged the next two punches, then his right hand shot out and grabbed Collin's wrist. An instant later Collin had been spun round and his arm twisted up behind his back. Despite being in an arm lock he still struggled violently, making his case worse by shouting a series of foul oaths, which made Kylie blush and feel sure Norah wasn't impressed either.

Then both men were down in the dust, Constable Lonergan with his knee in the middle of Collin's back. Two more policemen came hurrying through the crowd and joined him. All three subdued Collin and handcuffed him, while the crowd called them names and urged Collin to keep fighting. But the fight had now gone out of him and as he was lifted to his feet he turned a miserable face, all streaked with blood, dust, and tears.

To Norah he cried, "Sorry Norah. I just sort of lost it."

Kylie saw Norah shake her head sadly, but she did not answer him. Instead she looked at Constable Lonergan and asked, "What are you going to do with him?"

"Take him over to the watch house to cool down. It will be up to Wirriumi here whether he is charged with assault or not," Constable Lonergan replied, gesturing towards Dingo, who now stood rather shakily to one side.

Kylie was quite surprised and impressed at Constable Lonergan calling Dingo by his Murri name. So was Dingo. He blinked then glanced at Norah before shaking his head and muttering no.

Constable Lonergan then looked at Norah and asked, "Are you alright Miss Conroy?"

"Yes thanks," Norah answered sadly. She shook her head again and Kylie saw tears glisten in the corners of her eyes. Then Norah mastered her emotions and said, "Come on, we must go." Without waiting to see if they obeyed, she started walking.

The crowd parted to let her through, and Dingo and the girls followed. As they walked Kylie glanced back and saw the policemen taking Collin away. That made her feel very sad. *He does love Norah and is really jealous,* she decided.

Then she turned to Dingo and said diffidently, "Er... Dingo. Are you alright?"

Dingo nodded and gave a lopsided grin. "Yes Miss Kylie. I bin hit plenty of times before."

"Er... do you want us to call you Wirriumi... or do you prefer Dingo?" Kylie asked.

"You call me either, Miss Kylie. They both mean the same thing, but I don't mind if you call me by my real name," he replied.

"Then Wirriumi it is," Kylie said firmly.

"Here, here!" Margaret echoed.

It was a very subdued and unhappy group that rejoined the boys and Mrs Conroy at the vehicles. Mrs Conroy had to be told the story and looked distinctly annoyed. She said nothing to Dingo at that moment other than some curt orders to get the horses ready, but Kylie sensed he was in for an unpleasant time later when she and her group were not present.

Old Neville brought the horses across to the fence where the saddles, blankets and bridles had all been laid out and the horses were quickly saddled. At Norah's insistence the safety helmets were again buckled on. As they got ready Mrs Conroy kept glancing at her watch and helping to adjust straps. "I don't want to have to push the horses and you have about twenty-five kilometres to go today," she explained.

"I could walk that easily," Graham boasted.

Old Neville snorted and said, "Oh yeah!"

Graham looked offended at not being believed so added, "We have done that in cadet hikes. We did it during our exercise against the Air Cadets last year."

"Better you than me," Old Neville replied. "A second-class ride's better'n a first-class walk anytime!"

Mrs Conroy now intervened. "Stop yapping and get mounted," she ordered.

Led by Norah the group set off. Dingo was sent on ahead to open the gate and then waited to close it after them. As he did, he sat his horse looking dejected and ashamed.

"What's wrong with Dingo?" Roger asked as they rode on down the long slope through the bush.

Kylie and Margaret both filled in some of the detail until Dingo caught them up. The boys gave him a few glances and then forgot about him and instead asked about the 'Ghosts of Glenrowan'. Kylie described them and was amused to hear Margaret explain what a black tracker was.

"Where's Glenrowan?" Roger asked.

"Roger!" Graham cried. "You should pay more attention in school. It is the place in Victoria where the Ned Kelly Gang were wiped out back in eighteen hundred and whatever."

"Eighteen eighty," Kylie put in, remembering what Constable Lonergan had said and glad for once to be able to beat her brother. As they rode down towards the Gunnawarra Road they debated whether the Kelly Gang of the 1880s had been criminals or freedom fighters. Graham held strongly to the view that they were just murderers and thieves who got their just deserts while both Peter and Stephen thought they were merely Irish rebels being oppressed by the English.

The debate kept them going across the Gunnawara Road and on till they came to Nanyeta Creek ten minutes later but none of them knew enough detail to sustain the argument and it died out as they crossed the creek. This time the creek had a shallow flow of water in its sandy bed and the horses were allowed a couple of minutes halt to drink from it.

Then it was on across the bush, following a different trail this time, one that went almost due east. The track was greasy in patches and that helped keep their minds on riding. Several times Kylie went stiff with fright when Blazer had a hoof slip, but each time the horse recovered and she patted it in appreciation.

As they rode, Kylie sniffed the fresh air. The rain clouds had all cleared away, but the grass was damp and showing some green shoots and the bush seemed cooler and nicer. In truth she barely noticed the bush she was riding through except as a backdrop to her romantic daydreams about Brian. She was now sure she was truly in love with him and kept wondering where he might be at that moment and how they might get back together.

After another ten minutes riding they came to a dirt vehicle track heading north towards Mt Garnet. They reached this at 9:25 and turned left to follow it. At 9:35 they crossed a pipeline and twenty minutes later came in sight of the town. This time they came in on the east side of the creek and did not have to cross it again, reaching the main street along a side road that came out almost opposite the hotel.

As they reached the junction with the main street, Norah halted them and swung out of the saddle. "Walk the horses across the main street," she said.

"Why?" Stephen asked.

"Safety, in case of cars," Norah explained.

Stephen looked both ways along a completely deserted main street and made a wry face. "Yes, all the traffic," he jibed. But he still obeyed.

They crossed the street in front of the shop where Kylie had met Brian. Being Sunday morning this was closed but the hotel across the street on the corner of a side street appeared to be open. There was no-one visible, but the front doors stood wide open. Norah led the way uphill for fifty paces to the vacant allotment next to the hotel. Here they walked on across the open grassy area beside the old two-story timber hotel.

"We will go around to the back," Norah said.

Again it was Stephen who queried her. "Why?"

"Because I want to go to the toilet," Norah answered, blushing as she did.

"Toilet!" Stephen sniffed with affected male superiority. "You can just go in the bush."

"I prefer a bit more civilised comfort thank you," Norah answered.

Kylie was annoyed at Stephen and agreed with Norah. "I need to go too," she said.

By then they were near the rear of the hotel in a grassy yard in which stood several outbuildings and sheds. A dozen other horses, all saddled and with saddlebags and blanket rolls strapped on to them, were tethered along the side fence. Kylie ignored them and carefully hitched Blazer to a post, took off her helmet, then followed Norah to the back door.

As she went to enter, she heard an angry man's voice snarl, "Well, where is he then?"

"I don't know," replied another man anxiously. "He went off at about seven o'clock."

By then Kylie was in a dimly lit corridor close behind Norah so she could not see the speakers. But she did see the next man who spoke. Out of a doorway stepped a big man wearing 'Ned Kelly' armour and holding a shotgun.

"Hold it right there and put your hands up!" the man growled, his voice muffled by the helmet.

Kylie stared in shock, even as her hands shot up. *Oh my God!* she thought. *The Kelly Gang!*

Chapter 17

SHOCKS AND SURPRISES

Kylie goggled at the armed figure confronting them. He was a big man and seemed to fill the hallway. It was also apparent he was angry and surprised.

He growled, "I said, who are you and how the devil did you get in here?"

After a shocked few seconds Norah managed to answer. "We just came to go to the toilet," she said, her own hands now straight up above her head.

"Toilet! How the bloody hell? Where the devil is...?" the man snarled.

From through the doorway the man had come entered by came another man's voice. "Who the bloody hell are you talking to, Pat?"

"Two girls," Pat replied. "Say they want to go to the dunny."

Another large, helmeted figure loomed in the doorframe as the second man peered at them. Kylie glimpsed hard eyes glinting at her through the narrow vision slit in the helmet and she shivered.

The second man growled, "How did you girls get in here?"

"We just rode in and tied our horses up out the back," Norah answered.

"Rode in! How in blazes did you get into town?" the second man asked.

Norah lowered an arm to point. "We came in along the back road from Newman Park," she explained.

"Not along the main road?" the man queried.

"No."

The man swore, making Kylie blush. Then he turned and called to someone else in the room behind him, "Dan, come and guard these two. Pat, go and see where the devil Mary has got to. She should have bailed this bunch up."

Mary? Kylie wondered, even as she was told to step aside. The man named Pat pushed past and made his way to the rear of the building.

Norah now pointed to the door to the ladies toilet. "Can I please go? I really need to."

The two men remaining both looked at each other and there was a moment's hesitation before the biggest one said, "Yeah. Okay. Dan, you go in and make sure they don't do anything."

Dan at once protested. "Aw! Fair go Phil! I ain't one for visiting ladies dunnies."

Phil (*Phil Kelly*, Kylie presumed) snorted, the sound peculiarly muffled in his helmet. "Baloney! Just make sure they don't escape out the back window or something. I didn't mean go into the cubicle with them."

Muttering unhappily, Dan gestured to Norah to go in. Phil turned and went back into the other room, which Kylie now saw was the public bar. She followed Norah into the toilet and Dan came in behind her. There were two cubicles so both she and Norah could go simultaneously but she felt very embarrassed. So inhibited was she that she had trouble starting to pee, hotly aware that the man was just the other side of the door and might hear her!

When she came back out, she was told to wait till Norah joined them. Both girls were then told to go through into the public bar. Once again Dan followed but he did not point his rifle at them, which was some relief to Kylie.

In the public bar were a group of eight people standing at the far wall, covered by Phil Kelly. A glance told Kylie half the story. There was a young woman who could only be the barmaid, a middle-aged man who turned out to be the publican, two men in smart casual civilian clothes and two more in jeans and work shirts with the Channel 9 logo on them. There were also two older men, both wearing worn old clothes. Remembering a comment from her sea captain father, Kylie labelled them 'barflies'. To her mind no decent person would be found frequenting a hotel bar at 9:30 on a Sunday morning.

No sooner had Kylie and Norah joined the group and faced the armed men than boots sounded in the hallway and the man named Pat came back in. He gestured towards the back and said, "Got a whole mob of them out there: five kids and a black stockman. Mary's watching them."

"Where was she?" Phil Kelly asked.

"She was looking along the back street and didn't see 'em till after they had arrived," Pat answered.

Phil Kelly turned to Norah and asked, "Who are you? What are you doing here?"

"Norah Conroy," Norah replied. "My mother and I run a trail ride business: horse-riding for tourists. We were just passing through town and stopped so that Kylie and I could go to the toilet."

Kylie felt a bit hurt by that 'tourist' label, feeling she was a local North Queenslander, born and bred, *Even if I don't come from Mt Garnet.*

Phil Kelly then asked her who she was and she gave a short explanation. Then Phil asked where they were going. Norah explained they were heading back towards Herberton via Coolgarra, an old ghost town. Phil Kelly shook his head.

"Never heard of it. Tell me about it."

Norah briefly described the planned route they were to follow and who was in the group.

Phil Kelly summed it up by saying, "Just school kids on a horse-riding holiday?"

"Yes."

Phil Kelly thought for a moment and then said to his companions, "Well, if the Inspector isn't here, we had better make the best of what we have. Pat, go and bring all those others around to the front, and our horses. Tell Mary-Kate to keep watching the back."

That got Kylie anxious lest the bushrangers planned to take her and her friends as hostages. But all she could do was obey when told to go out onto the front footpath. She did as she was told and moved through the front door along with the others. Out on the front footpath they stood in a group, guarded by Phil Kelly and Dan till Pat and the others came around the side of the hotel. To Kylie's relief, she saw that the bushrangers had only led their own horses to the front of the hotel.

While they waited she had a chance to study the bushrangers and their armour. She saw that the armour appeared to be about two centimetres thick and that surprised her. *That must be very heavy?* she thought. But it did not appear to be as the men moved easily and without obvious effort. In colour the armour was a greyish hue with a hint of silver to it. It did not look like rusty iron. *Maybe it is not real armour at all? Or is it one of those plastic armours like Kevlar?* she wondered.

What happened next both surprised and amused her. The two Channel 9 men were sent across the street with their TV camera and sound equipment and were instructed to film. Phil then directed a couple of staged events. One showed three of the Kelly Gang riding across the street to the front of the hotel, where they dismounted. The next included Kylie and her friends, all being stood under guard on the footpath.

As they did this, Graham sidled over next to her and muttered, "At least Mum will know we are alright when she sees this on TV!"

"No talking!" snapped Dan, who moved Graham away again before he could say more.

The group were then moved back into the hotel bar and told not to try anything. The three bushrangers then did an act showing them leaping on their horses and riding off across the street. While they did this Kylie kept wondering why there were no cars. "I wish the police would come," she whispered to Margaret.

Stephen glanced around. "Now's our chance to escape," he commented, gesturing towards the back.

Peter agreed. "You lead the way, Graham. Your girlfriend won't shoot you."

Girlfriend? Kylie wondered, a horrible suspicion beginning to form in her mind.

But Graham shook his head and did not move. Before they could agree Phil Kelly dismounted and came back in, followed by the two TV cameramen and the other two bushrangers.

The bushrangers lined up on one side of the room. Phil Kelly had the TV crew take more pictures and then told them to make sure they got it all on the 6 o'clock news. He then turned back to the other two better-dressed men and said, "It looks like you two are coming with us. You are better than nothing, and you should get a good story out of it, if you live to tell the tale."

One of the men began to object but Dan levelled his gun and the man's companion placed a hand on his arm and silenced him. Even as he did there was the sound of horse's hooves in the street outside. From the sound Kylie judged that the horse was being ridden at a gallop. The Kelly Gang members all looked in that direction and tensed.

Phil Kelly said, "That sounds like Brian. Go and see why he's in such a hurry Pat."

The horse came to a standstill outside and the sound of boots thudding on the veranda sounded even as Pat moved towards the front door. Kylie looked that way, her mind racing.

Brian? she wondered, then shook her head. *No, it couldn't be him.*

But it was. The moment the person came in the door Kylie was sure of it. Even though he wore a 'Ned Kelly' helmet and armour his clothes and build told her it was, even before she heard his voice. He carried a rifle and was puffing. As he came into the bar Brian pointed back along the main street towards the west, saying, "Cops have arrived Phil. Mick and Liam are fighting them now."

"Fighting them?" Phil Kelly queried, even as the faint crack of gunshots sounded in the distance.

Brian nodded and replied excitedly. "They are shooting at the police car and... and.... and. Gosh!" His voice tailed off as he caught sight of Kylie. For a few astonished seconds his eyes met hers and she was absolutely sure. It was him alright! Then he tore his eyes away and turned back to Phil Kelly. "What... what do we do now?"

Phil Kelly tapped hard at his helmet and swore, then said, "Bloody radio! It should be able to get them from here! Go out and tell them to pull back. Okay, time we were on our way too. You two come with us," he said, pointing to the two better-dressed men.

The men obviously did not want to go but the sound of gunfire and the evident earnestness of the bushrangers persuaded them. They were led out the front door by Pat.

Dan then gestured towards Kylie and the others. "What about these other people?"

Phil Kelly shook his head and said, "You TV people go outside and take a few more shots as we leave. You others stay here. Don't you people try to follow us, or else. Come on Brian, get on your horse. Dan, go and get Mary-Kate."

Brian had been staring at Kylie as though mesmerised and she was sure he was both shocked and hurt. She could only stare back as a growing sense of unhappiness mingled with anger. *He lied to me!* she thought miserably. *The man I love is a bushranger!*

She shook her head and cried, "How could you?" Tears began to form.

Brian looked back at her dumbly, only his eyes visible. Phil Kelly turned to look, obviously not sure what was going on. He glanced from one to the other and then shouted, "Get moving Brian! You can chat up the chicks later."

Brian gave Kylie one more unhappy glance, then turned and went out.

Dan hurried through to the rear, and she heard him calling to Mary-Kate. *Mary-Kate. That will be Kate, the girl Graham liked,* Kylie thought.

Then some of the odd comments and pieces of the jigsaw dropped into place and she felt both angry and annoyed. But she also could not help admiring their bravado. *Going to the races like that; and staying at the same campground as the police who were chasing them!*

Suddenly several events made sense. *It was Kate who phoned the police at Innot Hot Springs and sent the police off on that wild goose chase to the Tumoulin Woods,* she thought. That increased her admiration even more but also nettled her sense of what was right.

From outside came the sound of voices and horses hooves. These increased to a sharp clatter and she glimpsed two figures on horseback. *Phil Kelly and Dan,* she thought, as they rode across the street past the shop, then south along the side street she had come in along earlier. Then she saw the TV cameraman aiming his camera up the street and she heard the sound of horse's hooves clattering on bitumen as more horses crossed the street going uphill.

Then the TV men lowered their camera and both stood idly on the footpath, one lighting a cigarette as he did. "They've gone," he said. "You can come out."

Everyone crowded onto the footpath and looked both ways along the street. It was deserted. The TV cameraman pointed. "Two went into the bush over there and the others went out of sight up on top of the hill, heading around behind those houses towards the hill. They took the hostages with them."

"Who were the hostages?" Peter asked.

"Couple of newspaper reporters from Brisbane," the cameraman replied. Then he chuckled. "Serves 'em right! They will get the ride of their life, even if they don't get an exclusive scoop."

The man then pulled out a mobile phone and began using it. "Calling the cops," he explained. Then he and his companion readied themselves to get pictures of the police arriving.

Kylie turned to the barmaid and asked, "What did the Kelly Gang want?"

The barmaid shrugged. "Publicity, I guess. They asked where Inspector Moriarty and the two blacktrackers were, but they missed them. I said they left at seven thirty, straight after breakfast."

"Poor old Inspector Moriarty," Norah exclaimed. "That was a bit personal! The poor man has been humiliated enough already."

Stephen chuckled. "Did you see him trip on his sword at the races, then go racing around miles behind everyone else?"

"Yes, we did," Margaret answered. "And the crowd all booed and jeered. I thought it was perfectly horrible of them. He was doing his best."

Graham pointed down the street. "Well here he comes now," he commented.

Kylie looked and saw five horsemen riding out from the side road the other side of Nanyeta Creek onto the main road. Two were the black trackers and the other three were mounted police. One was Inspector Moriarty, and another was Constable Lonergan. As they crossed the bridge the police spread well out and they advanced cautiously, well spaced apart, a couple either side of the road, weapons at the ready.

On seeing that Norah walked out into the road and waved to indicate it was safe. The TV cameramen began filming and that annoyed Kylie even more. *They don't have to make the police look like complete fools,* she thought.

A red-faced and angry Inspector Moriarty reined in close to them, scowling at the camera as he did. "What is going on?" he rapped.

Norah answered. "The Kelly Gang were here," she said.

"Where are they now?"

Norah pointed. "Phil Kelly and Dan went that way, south along that side road, and Pat, Brian and Mary-Kate, plus two hostages, went off up the hill, then into the bush on the right."

Constable Lonergan called to her, "Thanks Norah."

Inspector Moriarty snapped, "You people all wait here to be questioned, and you two chaps can help by staying in off the street. We thought that was a gun you were holding." Having said that he lifted a radio from his belt and began talking into it. When he had done that, he pointed across the street and said, "Constable Lonergan, you and Wannamurra go that way. I will send Sgt Healey up after the other group."

As Constable Lonergan nodded and turned to obey the order Norah took a step forward and called to him, "Be careful Frank. They are armed."

Constable Lonergan met her eyes and grinned, but nodded. "I'll be careful. I can think of a very good reason to stay alive," he reassured her, then set his heels to his horse and cantered across the road, followed by the black tracker.

Kylie noted a blush mottling Norah's cheeks. *She does like him,* she decided. Then she had to admit she found the mounted policeman very handsome and she also hoped that he would not get hurt. A minute later he and the black tracker were lost to sight among the trees and houses on the side road.

Police sirens sounded and two police vehicles raced in from the west. They pulled up and armed police sprang out and quickly searched the hotel. A Superintendent arrived a few minutes later from the other direction and took charge. The group were told to sit in the lounge and wait and a constable stood guard to ensure they obeyed.

As Stephen sat down, he said, "Oh well, doesn't look like we will be riding anywhere much today!"

That thought depressed them all. Graham was the most put out. "But I wanted to see the ghost town," he grumbled.

"Too bad," Peter said philosophically. "At least nobody got hurt."

"Bloody Kelly Gang!" Graham muttered. "I'm getting a bit sick of them mucking things up."

At that, Stephen snorted and sarcastically replied, "That's not what you were thinking last night when you had young Kate in your clutches."

"Bite your bum!" Graham replied, glancing at Kylie and Margaret with a guilty look.

The exchange made Kylie feel both upset and uncomfortable. She was acutely aware of Margaret sitting beside her, her face a mask of apparent indifference. It was Margaret's comment which almost broke her own self-control.

She said quietly, "That was Brian, wasn't it?"

Kylie nodded and felt a wave of unhappiness. "Yes," she croaked, her throat choking up and her chest going tight.

"Sorry," Margaret went on. "Gosh! The gall of them; going to the races and to the dance like that!"

At that moment, a helicopter clattered overhead, adding to Kylie's anxieties. *The police will soon spot them from the air,* she thought.

Then she began to imagine dark scenes from movies about the 'last stand' of the original Kelly Gang. In them she pictured Brian being shot and that made her even more upset. She found she was deeply torn: by the hope that he would not be hurt, and by the despair of knowing that her love affair was over before it had fairly begun.

Even if the police don't shoot him he will end up in prison for years, she mused. She even began to hope that he might somehow escape and never get caught but those thoughts caused her waves of guilt.

Tears were very close at that moment but she was saved by the arrival of the police superintendent, a police senior sergeant and two senior constables who began calling people to another room to be questioned. When it was the time for the teenagers to be questioned Mrs Conroy, who had arrived all in a fluster, was allowed to sit in with them as the 'appropriate adult.'

That didn't help Kylie much as she found herself unwilling to say too much but also realised that Mrs Conroy knew quite a bit of the story. The questions from the superintendent placed Kylie under even more inner conflict. She found herself reluctant to answer, only telling the truth when she was asked a direct question. All she spoke about was the incident at the hotel. The fact that Brian had kissed her at the dance, and that he and his sister had been staying at the Innot Hot Springs Campground she did not mention, causing her even more mental anguish. She left the interview feeling extraordinarily guilty but relieved.

But it was all for nothing. Half an hour later the senior sergeant came to the door and called her name and beckoned. "We need to ask you a few more questions," he said.

The spasm of guilt was so strong Kylie trembled as she stood up. Feeling weak and nauseous she followed the policeman back to the interview room. This time, as she was told to sit, she thought she detected quite a different atmosphere among the police: a sort of hard silence with no sympathy.

As soon as Kylie was seated, the superintendent fixed her with a hard stare and said, "I understand that you have been meeting Brian Kelly secretly for the last few days. Would you like to explain that accusation?"

On hearing that Kylie almost fainted. *Someone has talked,* she thought, then asked herself, *How can I get out of this?*

Chapter 18

UNDER STRESS

Kylie swallowed and went red. She felt very guilty and also ashamed of her weakness at not immediately telling the full story. The superintendent kept his steely stare fixed on her eyes and seemed to glare at her.

Then he asked, "Well, what do you have to say? Are you one of the Kelly Gang? Are you helping them to avoid arrest?"

The accusation stunned Kylie. Aghast, all she could do for a while was shake her head and blush. Finally she managed to croak, "No, I'm not."

"So why didn't you tell us earlier? Why did you hide this information?"

Kylie shook her head in sick disbelief, shocked to her very core at how everything suddenly seemed to have been twisted and turned on its head. "I... I... I just... I... I didn't know that Brain was one of the Kelly Gang," she managed to say.

"Where did you first meet him?" the superintendent asked. He looked very grim and Kylie became really scared. She was vaguely aware that it was against the law to help criminals on the run and she broke into a cold sweat. Nausea and tears both became imminent. With and effort she again shook her head in denial, then gestured. "At the shop.. the one over the road."

"When?"

"Only yesterday morning," Kylie replied, thinking with amazement, *Was it really only yesterday!*

"Tell us what happened," the superintendent demanded to know.

Kylie described how Brian had waved and then spoken to her. "We, Margaret and I that is, were just standing in the shop when he came in. He was very bold, you know, fresh. He flirted with us. Then his sister Kate came in and.."

"Kate? How did you know her name was Kate?" the superintendent rasped.

In her fear-filled mind Kylie saw the black chasm of deceit open at her feet and she swallowed and tried to think what to say. The hesitation was noticed and the superintendent pressed her for an answer. Again she shook her head and then muttered, "I heard Brian call her that."

The superintendent frowned and glanced at his notes, then asked, "Had you ever seen Brian Kelly before that?"

Again Kylie hesitated, knew she should not have and blushed with anxious guilt. She shook her head but said, "Yes, but I didn't know who he was, and I didn't see his face."

"When and where was that?"

"At Herberton, when the Duke was kidnapped. I was in the crowd and saw the Kelly Gang. But Brian, I mean all of them, had their faces hidden in those helmets, so I did not see them."

"And you have never seen him before that?"

"No," Kylie insisted. She was now feeling very stressed and had to bite back the tears.

Again the superintendent studied his notes, then looked hard at her. "What about Kate Kelly, when did you first see her?"

Through Kylie's mind flashed images of the black-haired girl at Innot Hot Springs. She opened her mouth, shut it, then said, "At the Innot Hot Springs Campground two days ago," she said.

"Did you speak to her?"

"No."

Another frown crossed the superintendent's face and he snapped back, "I have a witness who says that you did."

"Oh! Oh, only to say sorry or something. I didn't know who she was," Kylie replied. She groped in her flustered mind for the exact words.

She was then stunned by the superintendent's next words. He said, "It has been suggested that you and Kate Kelly were both at the telephone at Innot Hot Springs yesterday morning when a hoax call was sent from there saying that the Kelly Gang were in the Tumoulin area."

"I... I... I was, but I didn't do that! I was only waiting to use the phone to call my mother. You can check," Kylie gasped.

She was now reeling from disbelief that things could be so misinterpreted. Unable to control her emotions any longer she burst into tears.

Mrs Conroy moved to comfort her and said to the superintendent, "I think she has had enough questions for the moment thank you."

To Kylie's relief, the superintendent nodded and she was allowed to leave. Mrs Conroy helped her up and led her to the bathroom so she could wash her face and recover her composure. As she did, she said to Mrs Conroy, "I didn't (sob) make any hoax calls Mrs (sniffle) Conroy. I had no idea who that (sob) black-haired girl was. I've never met any of the Kelly Gang before. I'd never even heard of them before that... that parade in Herber(sniffle)ton. Oh boo hoo!"

Mrs Conroy calmed her down again and then patted her till she stopped crying. "There, there dearie. Dry your eyes. It is all just a bit of a misunderstanding. I believe you."

"But the police don't. They (sniff) think I am a member of the Kelly Gang, and that I pass them information," Kylie wailed.

"It will be alright," Mrs Conroy assured her. "Now let's go out and join the others. A spot of lunch might be a good idea, if we can organise it."

As she was taken back to the lounge, Kylie's mind was in a ferment. Squirming maggots of paranoia wriggled in her emotions. *Who told the police about Brian and me, or about Kate?* she wondered.

Names of possible informants flitted through her thoughts: Stephen's first, then Peter, Dingo, Norah. To her dismay she even found herself wondering if Graham had been the one, or Margaret. That was too horrible to contemplate and she shook her head in angry denial.

Only as she gave Margaret a forced smile and settled in a chair did she consider other options. *Maybe someone from the staff at the campground saw Kate and me at the phone, but did not hear what we said,* she pondered. Then the name of Doris Peagreen slid into her thoughts and she tried to remember when she had seen Doris at the campground.

It was so unsettling that she almost burst into tears again. She was saved by Mrs Conroy saying, "Norah, take the girls out and tend to the horses. They have been standing in the sun for an hour now."

"Yes Mum," Norah replied. She stood up and gestured to Kylie and Margaret to come with her. But as they did a policeman blocked them at the door.

"Where are you going?" he queried.

"Just to see to our horses," Norah replied, annoyance clear in her voice.

"You can't. You have to stay here," the police constable answered.

Norah was obviously both amazed and annoyed. "What piffle! The animals can't be left like that."

When the constable shook his head and still blocked her path Norah exploded angrily. "This is ridiculous! Let us care for the animals or I will have you reported to the R.S.P.C.A. for cruelty."

A look of concern crossed the constable's face, but it was only when Norah began calling loudly for her mother that the man weakened. Mrs Conroy appeared at the door of the interview room, where Peter was now being questioned again, with the superintendent close behind her.

When the situation was explained the superintendent scowled, then said, "Alright, but you go with them constable. We haven't finished questioning them yet."

With that Norah pushed past into the hallway. Kylie and a mystified Margaret followed her, Kylie glancing anxiously at the policeman, who followed them outside.

"What on earth was that all about?" Norah wondered aloud as they stepped out onto the back lawn.

Kylie made a wry face and said, "The police obviously think we are going to jump on our horses and ride away."

A look of astonishment appeared on Norah's face. "What absolute rot! Why ever should they think that?"

Kylie shrugged and blushed. "They think I am one of the Kelly Gang and that I have been passing them secret information," she answered.

At that, Norah stopped and looked at her open-mouthed. "Oh what utter nonsense! Why should they think that?"

That eased one of Kylie's concerns and she mentally struck Norah off her list of suspects. Again she shrugged and then said, "Because I spoke to Kate at the Innot Hot Springs Campground and because I was dancing with Brian at the races," she explained. Images of Brain kissing her in the dark caused her to blush and she had to concede that, to an onlooker, it might have looked very suspicious.

Norah was flabbergasted. Margaret also expressed disbelief, but not quite so convincingly, leaving Kylie with a horrible niggling doubt. The girls made their way to where the horses were tethered and proceeded to take off the saddles and saddle cloths and to rub their backs, then to lead them to a wash tub which was pressed into use as a drinking trough. While they did this the constable stood close to the horse's heads, obviously intending to grab the reins if one of them tried to mount.

While they worked Kylie learned from Norah and Margaret more of what had happened that morning. Apparently, the Kelly Gang had set up roadblocks on the main road on either side of the town and then swooped on the hotel, hoping to capture Inspector Moriarty and the two blacktrackers. That having failed, through the gang having been given the wrong timings, they then acted as Kylie had seen.

"Was anyone hurt in the fighting?" Kylie asked.

Norah shook her head. "No. The Kelly Gang just stopped cars to block the road and then fired at the police cars at long range. I think they were careful not to hit anyone," she said.

The police constable looked angry but agreed with this.

"It was a very bold plan," Margaret suggested.

Norah agreed. "It has certainly made them headline news again."

"And embarrassed the police," Kylie added, giving the listening constable an angry glare as she said this. He scowled in return, and it was very obvious to her that the police were mightily humiliated at the way the Kelly Gang seemed to be running rings around them.

After the horses had been cared for, the girls returned to the lounge. Here Kylie found that all of the boys had now been questioned and Mrs Conroy was there as well. Apparently, they were now free to go. A discussion on what to do next began.

"We just continue with our ride," Kylie suggested.

Mrs Conroy very pointedly looked at her watch and said, "It is after twelve now and it is nearly twenty kilometres to Coolgarra. I don't want you pushing the horses too hard. I think you should all just phone your parents, and we will ferry the horses home in the float."

That was a real disappointment to Kylie, who had now settled down to enjoying the horse-riding and was looking forward to seeing the ghost town. Graham obviously felt the same as he at once protested, "Oh Mrs Conroy! I really wanted to see Coolgarra. It is the main reason I agreed to come, and to pay so much money."

Kylie was embarrassed at Graham's reference to money but agreed with him. They had paid a lot and she thought they should get their money's worth. It was Peter who suggested that they could compromise. "Couldn't we just trot quietly along without stressing the horses and camp at some suitable spot, then continue on tomorrow to Coolgarra?

Then we could get a lift back, or ride by some short cut to Innot Hot Springs or somewhere like that?"

Mrs Conroy thought for a few moments and then nodded, "Yes, alright, but the horses are not to be pushed."

Margaret spoke next. "But is it safe to go horse-riding?" she asked.

"Because of the Kelly Gang you mean?" Norah queried.

"Yes."

Stephen snorted and chuckled. "I don't think we are in any danger from them, except maybe Kylie if she lets young Brian have his way."

That stung! Kylie felt her eyes water, even as her resentment rose. "I.." she began.

Peter cut her off. "It is Graham who will keep us safe. He can go and sweet talk Kate. But seriously, I overheard the coppers talking and they said that the Kelly Gang have headed off southeast and we are going north."

"Where are they supposed to be?" Graham asked, taking out his map as he did.

"Somewhere along Nanyeta Creek," Peter answered, "Between the Gunnawarra Road and the Herbert River. I even heard one copper mention Blunder Creek."

At that, Stephen cried out sarcastically, "Blunder Creek! That will be the place the way these coppers are carrying on."

As he said this, Kylie saw the constable at the door glance sharply in their direction. She was not feeling very sympathetic towards the police at that moment and could only silently agree with Stephen. "I think it is safe," she said. In her heart she did not fear the Kelly Gang and she knew she still wanted to see Brian again, for all the deceit that he had shown.

Norah obviously felt the same way as she shrugged and said, "If the Kelly Gang had wanted to bother us they had us in their clutches here. I think we should go on with the trail ride. May we Mum?"

Mrs Conroy looked doubtful but then nodded and said yes.

"Oh thank you Mrs Conroy," Kylie said.

"Lunch first," Mrs Conroy insisted.

So they stayed for another half an hour. During that time the town came to life again, the people positively buzzing with pleasure and excitement at the 'Raid by the Kelly Gang'.

Seeing this Stephen made the sour observation that the event would become part of the town's local history. "They will start having annual re-enactments I suppose," he added.

"It was pretty spectacular," Peter said.

Kylie could only agree but her thoughts were away in the bush, wondering if Brian was safe. Anxiety that he might be hurt, even killed, in a shootout with the pursuing police began to gnaw at her, quite spoiling her appetite. *I hope he is safe,* she thought, managing to draw the line at consciously wishing for Brian to escape.

It was 12:30 by the time they made their way back to the horses and saddled up. For Kylie it was a relief to return to the simple tasks of adjusting girths and straps. She found the smells of polished leather and horse reassuring and friendly and was glad to mount up and ride out of town. Mrs Conroy and Old Neville drove off to take Romantic Ruby back to the homestead, arranging to meet them on the Coolgarra Road later that afternoon.

But even just trying to leave town had its irritations. On the outskirts they encountered a police roadblock: two armed constables with their car. The policemen had not been told about them and insisted they all dismount while they radioed for instructions. Only after a description of the group had been relayed to the police HQ and confirmed were they allowed to proceed.

As the group remounted and rode on, Peter looked back and commented that the police didn't seem very friendly.

Graham replied to that. "I think their pride is badly dented," he suggested.

Kylie could only agree with that but she was cheered by the thought that Brian must still be on the run if the police were still manning roadblocks. Seeing a police helicopter circling the area added to this impression. The helicopter twice circled low around them before heading off eastwards.

Watching it go Peter said, "I thought the copper said the Kelly Gang had gone off to the southeast?"

"They did," Stephen agreed.

"So why is that helicopter buzzing around this area?"

Stephen laughed. "I think that means that the Kelly Gang has given them the slip again and that they haven't got a clue where they have gone."

"Surely a helicopter would soon find people on horses in this open savannah country?" Graham commented.

"Should," Peter agreed, "especially if it has that infra-red thermal imaging stuff."

"Maybe there are so many horses in this part of the world they are having trouble sorting the false clues from the real ones," Norah said.

So, still discussing the whereabouts of the Kelly Gang, and their likely chances of evading arrest, the group rode on. Kylie soon settled into the routine of riding. After the experiences of the last few days it was all now becoming very familiar, and she could see that even the boys were becoming used to the horses. She found that, after a few stiff muscles worked loose and the odd bit of discomfort, that she was able to settle nicely into the saddle and relax a bit.

But only a bit. In her heart she was in turmoil. Falling in love with Brian had been the first real experience of romance in her life and she was still engulfed by the emotion of it all. What was chewing at her was wondering if he loved her as much as she loved him. There was also the niggling knowledge that he had not been completely honest with her, although she conceded that, in the circumstances, he could not have been.

But was he just playing with me? she worried, unsure if he saw her just as a bit of casual fun and not to be taken seriously. It was all very troubling and brought wetness to her eyes more than once, though she was careful to hide this from the others.

The road was graded gravel but quite dusty, the sun having sucked up any moisture from the recent showers. The country through which they rode was very thinly settled, just the occasional side road or house and most of the route not even fenced on both sides. Mostly it was savannah woodland and small dry creeks. They passed a few hills, but the road mostly followed the bottom of a series of small valleys.

The day was warm, but patches of cloud and a cool breeze kept things pleasant and they made good time. There was no traffic on the road at all and the only incident of any note was when the police helicopter returned and once again did a low pass over them. This caused Stephen to sneer and comment that: "The dopey coppers have lost them!"

Good! though Kylie with relief, until she realised what she was doing and felt a spasm of guilt. In spite of being lied to, she still believed she was in love with Brian.

After a few kilometres the road trended northeast away from Nanyeta Creek and up along a gentle ridge between it and Limestone Creek. The country became more and more hilly and the lie of the land much harder to distinguish, with quite a few dirt roads going off on either side, winding away into the bush. There were no more buildings and the fences ended except for a boundary fence and cattle grid. This was passed through a wire gate beside it.

The going was still easy and from the crest of the low ridges they crossed they began to get long views into the distance. These revealed a range of rugged mountains off to the north. Norah pointed to them and said that the highest one they could see was named Mt Misery.

"The little town of Irvinebank is on the other side," she added.

"Are we still going there?" Margaret queried.

Norah shook her head. "No. Not now. We have lost too much time. We will turn right before then and go back along the Silver Valley Road."

By 3:30pm they had covered 10 kilometres and were passing an area named on Graham's map as the Tully Mine, but Kylie saw no sign of that, just lots of jumbled waste ground left by the tin dredge. They dismounted and rested there for twenty minutes, watering the horses and stretching sore muscles.

From then on the road skirted large flooded areas left by the tin miners who had built long earth dams to impound the water to float their huge dredge. One lonely house was passed but they did not go in, instead turning left to ride across the top of a long earth dam lined with trees. The dam held back another large lake of murky looking water.

"The tin miners certainly made a mess," Peter observed sadly.

"That's how it was in the old days," Dingo commented.

After that the road deteriorated and wound along the side of the swampy wasteland or up on the lower slopes of increasingly large hills. After a few kilometres the road recrossed the mined area and then trended back away from the lower areas. It then wound along a gentle ridge through more open savannah country, dipping occasionally across small dry creeks.

The mining had so altered the country that Graham all but gave up his attempts at map reading in disgust. However both Norah and Dingo knew the way and quite confidently turned left at a road junction with no signposts on the edge of another mined area.

"Is it much further?" Stephen queried, shifting uncomfortably in his saddle.

"No. We are making good time," Norah answered. "Only about another hour."

That drew a groan from Stephen. "This ghost town had better be good after all this," he muttered.

"It is," Norah replied. "It is the real McCoy."

And it was. When Coolgarra finally came into sight at about 5 pm Kylie was instantly entranced.

Chapter 19

GHOST TOWN

Ghost town. The very words were enough to send a delicious little thrill through Kylie. She had read about them and even seen a couple in American movies set in the 'Wild West', but to actually see one affected her far more than she expected. To her own surprise it was more a feeling of poignancy and sadness than any sense of haunting or of fear.

To think of all that effort, all gone to rust and dust, she mused as she sat on her horse looking along the gentle valley.

The road was now only two wheel ruts in sandy soil with quite a lush growth of grass on either side. Quite a number of large eucalypts were dotted along the valley, with paperbarks and sheoaks lining the creek line off to her right. All in all it was a very pleasant scene. But what gripped her interest were the buildings. As she rode forward more and more came into view, all obviously old and all looking silvery grey in the sunlight.

She first saw the ghost town from about half a kilometre away and before the group reached it they came to an old cemetery. This was surrounded by a rusty wire fence and was marked by a couple of headstones poking up out of the long grass. At Norah's request the group dismounted, tethered their horses and then made their way into the small cemetery via a gateway half blocked by a rusty tubular steel gate which hung at an angle from one hinge.

Treading warily for fear of snakes the group began reading the headstones. Most were very old, dating back to the late 19th or early 20th Centuries. None was more recent than 1956. Old graveyards always made Kylie feel sad, especially when she read the headstones of young babies and children, and of young women.

This cemetery she found more moving than usual as she found the graves of two soldiers, both troopers and both with the surname Armanargh. One had died in the 1st World War and the other in the 2nd World War. *Oh how sad,* she thought.

"Same name," Graham observed. "I wonder how you pronounce it?"

"Foreigners from the sound of them," Stephen suggested.

Norah shook her head. "No, the Armanarghs (She pronounced it Armanarks) were Irish. There were lots of Irish pioneers around here, my family for example."

Peter agreed. "Judging by the names on the map there certainly were. Just listen to these." He then read from the map he was holding, "Whelan Creek, Condon Gully, Micky Creek, Ballyhooley Gully, Donohue Gully."

Graham looked at the map and then pointed and said with a grin, "So why is the next creek to the west the London Gully? And what about the Devon Mine, Mount Wilson, and Brownville?"

"Or even Five Mile Creek and Sandy Creek," Roger added. "They don't sound very Irish."

"Or very Australian for that matter," Dingo commented wryly.

Peter snorted. "You know what I mean. There were obviously a lot of Irishmen around here in the old days."

"Probably still are," Graham said. "The Kelly Gang are lurking somewhere in the area."

That sent a stab of worry through Kylie. "Oh Graham, don't say things like that!" she scolded, looking anxiously around at the surrounding hills.

Norah's face showed disapproval. "Stop being silly and scaring the girls," she chided. "We don't need any silly talk. Now let's get to our campsite so we have time to see the town before it gets dark."

So they glanced at a few more graves, noting more Irish names: Murphy and O'Reilly and O'Shaunessy, then made their way back out to the horses and mounted. It was after 5 o'clock by then and the sun was sinking towards the hills to the west, patterning the valley in long, soothing shadows. Once mounted they rode at a fast walk towards the ghost town, crossing a small creek on the way. This had a trickle of water in it and looked very pleasant to Kylie.

Only as they rode closer and after she had focused did she realise that her first impression of the town was inaccurate. There were in fact only seven buildings and they were widely scattered. Six were to the right of the road, between it and the main creek line. The seventh was some way off to the left across an open, grassy flat. On even closer inspection she saw that the buildings stood in their own overgrown allotments and were all about 50 metres apart, if not more. In between were the stumps, weeds, rusty water tanks and old sheets of corrugated iron that marked where other buildings had once stood.

The sound of a vehicle came to them as they reached the first house. Kylie looked back over her shoulder and saw that it was Mrs Conroy's. The group dismounted, hitched their horses to an old fence and waited. When the vehicle arrived Mrs Conroy looked out and nodded approval.

"You've done well," she said. Then she looked at Dingo and added, "Dingo, you come and help me set up the camp while the children take a look at the town. You children watch out for snakes among all this rubbish and old sheets of iron." She then let in the clutch and drove on.

Being labelled a child nettled Kylie's ego but the thought of snakes affected her more and she looked very carefully around among the long grass that even grew in what had once been the main street. When Norah led them in through another old gateway to the first house, she kept glancing anxiously near her feet for any hint of a reptile.

That old house quite saddened Kylie. Just seeing the now weed-smothered and overgrown garden in which a few roses and flowers struggled for existence made her feel sharp regret.

All that love and patient work, she thought. *All for nothing now.*

But deep down she sensed it had not been all for nothing. At the time that care and love would have helped sustain a family, have given some woman a small reward, a lift to her worn spirits.

The house, like all the buildings, was constructed of a timber frame with planks and sheets of corrugated iron nailed to it. Most signs of paint had long since been weathered off so that everything had a greyish tinge to it, if not brown rust.

The interior of the house was even more thought provoking. The house was really just a large hut with only three rooms inside. The largest had obviously once been the kitchen and living room and the front door and back door both opened into it. The side rooms were both poky little bedrooms, their walls made, to the astonishment of all the teenagers, of a sort of cardboard or paste board. This had been built up by layers of pages from women's magazines and pages from journals and books. It was all very much insect eaten now, but to Kylie it was a revelation that made her feel quite ashamed of her own nicely decorated bedroom.

The floor was made of a thin layer of concrete covered with cracked and worn linoleum. The backyard was an overgrown jumble of rubbish: a rusty water tank fallen off its rotting timber stand, the rotting remains of an outdoor dunny that had fallen over, and pieces of rusty metal.

The explorers did not venture out but only looked out through the back door or tiny windows. Even these made Kylie glad she lived now and in her own home as the windows had no glass, being closed up by hinged, sheet metal shutters instead.

Several more houses were the same and had a similar effect on her. The last building on the right was the hotel. It was larger and had an extension and a two sheds out the back. The hotel still had glass in its windows and the front veranda was roofed over. The rooms were still full of dusty junk and the permanent furniture such as the bar and the oven. It was also full of rubbish, rat and cockroach droppings and was obviously much more frequently visited. The state of the many cobwebs showed that, as did scuff marks and boot prints on the dusty timber floor.

Noting the trampled grass around the hotel Kylie assumed that it was the one building any visitor would stop and look at. Graham and Stephen both started walking towards the long building at the rear. This had the appearance of once having been stables. As they did, Norah called to them, "Don't go over there now. Have a look in the morning. We need to look after the horses before it gets dark."

Reluctantly the boys turned back but Kylie had no desire to go near the buildings. They looked dark and gloomy and had weeds and long grass all around them, to her mind the perfect home for snakes. The whole place Kylie found depressing, with its grim picture of hard work and failed efforts. She was glad to walk on across a large grassy open area to where the tents and portable toilet were now set up under a stand of large trees. Dingo already had the tents up and Mrs Conroy was cooking on the portable barbeque.

The horses were off-saddled and the saddles stored in the trailer. Then the horses were given food and water and a good rub down. Dingo and Norah went to each horse and lifted up their hooves to check that none of the horseshoes had come off or if any nails were loose.

Kylie enjoyed grooming Blazer and she happily stood and hummed as she did it, her gaze wandering across the grassy flat and surrounding hills. The evening shadows had now spread right across to the hill tops and the whole place had a feeling of peace and tranquillity that soothed her. With a feeling of relief she removed her helmet and shook out her sweaty hair, enjoying the cooling effect of the light breeze.

Mrs Conroy then pointed towards the creek line 50 metres away. "There is a good flow of fresh water in the creek. You can take the horses down and let them have another drink, and they might like a roll in the sand if you can find a good spot. You can even have a wash if you like."

Kylie thought that an excellent idea so she, Norah and Margaret collected their towels and set off walking, leading their horses behind them. The boys took longer to get organised but then followed. The creek was a delight. It was ten paces wide but with a flow of clear water that was only ankle deep in most places. Lush, soft grass grew along the banks and the trees lining it made it very pleasant.

It had been a long and sweaty day and Kylie felt quite grimy and dirty. The idea of a wash really appealed to her, but she did not want to do that with the others watching. She pointed upstream.

"You boys go that way, up around the next bend, and we girls will go downstream," she ordered.

The boys laughed and made silly comments but did as they were told, leading their horses as they walked away. Kylie then started walking downstream with Norah and Margaret. Fifty paces down they came to a small pool that was knee deep. Even so Kylie hesitated. She was shy at undressing in front of Norah and even felt inhibited by Margaret's presence. So she said, "Norah, you wash here and we will go a bit further."

Norah agreed so the two friends continued on for another fifty paces. They could still see Norah but there were a few bushes to block the view. To check if it was private enough Kylie looked back and saw Norah peel off her shirt. The sight of Norah in her bra made Kylie blush and she determined on more privacy.

"You wash here Margaret, and I will go on to the next pool," she said.

Margaret agreed and stood to let her horse drink. Kylie walked on, enjoying the quiet and the cool of the evening. As she walked, she kept glancing back but found to her annoyance that she could still see Margaret clearly and even got glimpses of Norah. She decided to walk on to the next bend in the creek a hundred paces further along. Having got there she had to think again. At that, point the vehicle track came down one bank and went steeply up the other.

I will look a bit silly if I strip off and a car comes along, she thought, giving an embarrassed giggle.

So, even though there was a nice pool there, she walked on for another fifty paces to the next bend. Here she found what she wanted, a clear pool of waist deep water. There was no sign of anyone, so she allowed Blazer to drink while she stripped off. Doing that out in the open air made her feel very self-conscious and she kept looking anxiously around.

Having undressed she waded slowly in, finding the water much colder than she had expected. Her body instantly came out in goose bumps, and she shivered. Her feet felt very tender too, having been confined to the riding boots for so long. Bit by bit she wet her skin and lowered herself to her knees. Once she was wet she found it a real lift to rinse off the dust and sweat. That got her looking critically at her body and she was dismayed to note several bad bruises and red patches where her belt had chafed her waist. Biting her lip she carefully studied the blemishes to check whether they might mar her good looks. In doing so she found several pimples and red patches from chafing.

As she washed herself, she kept looking anxiously around, mostly back along the creek, just in case. Having cleaned herself thoroughly she waded ashore and picked up her towel and began to dry herself. It was only then that she noted that the sand around where her clothes lay had been recently trampled by horses and that there was fresh horse dung nearby. Having noted this she pushed it from her mind as just being one of those things you would expect to find in the bush.

Then a sound made her freeze. Looking up, she saw that Blazer had lifted her head and pricked up her ears and was staring up the bank. Kylie had not considered being seen from that direction but now saw a well-used track leading down from the top of the bank, and walking down it was a man!

A wave of embarrassed shock swept through her, first cold, then hot. For a few seconds she froze, then she looked urgently around for a place to hide. The nearest cover was the trunk and drooping branches of one of the large paperbarks growing along the creek bed. Clutching the towel across her front she scuttled over behind it, very conscious of the cold air on her bare bum.

From behind the tree she looked up the bank, her heart hammering with anxiety. At first all she could see was the black silhouette of a man carrying two buckets, standing out black against the sunset. But as the man came down the bank and got closer, she saw with surprise that it was Brian. That drew a gasp of dismay from her, and her mind raced with a mixture of relief, speculation, shame and delight. He wore a dark blue shirt, blue jeans, and riding boots.

Brian reached the end of the track and was only ten paces from her when he saw her horse. At once he stopped and crouched behind a tree, his eyes searching fearfully in all directions. He put down one of the buckets and reached back to draw a revolver from a leather holster on his belt. Seeing the gun sent a thrill of alarm through Kylie.

Then Brian saw her clothes. He crouched lower and raised the pistol, pointing it where his eyes moved. That got Kylie scared and she called out, or rather tried to, as her throat went all dry and the sound came out as a croak. After swallowing she tried again.

"Brian, it's me, Kylie," she called.

She saw his eyes widen as he looked in her direction. "Kylie!" he cried in astonishment. "What are you doing here?"

"Having a swim," Kylie answered, now hotly aware of her nudity.

Anxiously she glanced down at her naked body and was ashamed. What bothered her the most, she realised with a shock of self-knowledge, wasn't the fear of him seeing her naked, but that her body was not perfect. *He will see all my horrible bruises and chafing,* she thought. *And those pimples!* Then she blushed with shame at her own shameless thoughts. It was a bit of a shocking revelation to find that she was not quiet the nice girl she had considered herself to be!

Brian looked around. "Are you alone?" he asked.

"Yes. The others are further up the creek," she answered.

"You can come out then," Brian replied. He stood up and walked out onto the sand, holstering the revolver as he did.

Now Kylie blushed even harder and felt her mouth go dry. "I can't. I haven't got any clothes on," she replied, then wished she hadn't told him there was no-one else around.

Brian's face broke into a grin, and he met her eyes as she peeked around the trunk of the tree. "Gee! And I haven't even asked you to take them off yet!" he quipped.

"Oh humpff!" Kylie snorted. "I was having a swim. Don't you get ideas, and don't get fresh!" she said.

Again Brian grinned and he laughed, then said, "Oh fair go! Don't be a spoilsport. Just a little look."

Kylie was ashamed to admit to herself later that she was actually tempted. But her good sense made her shake her head. "You just pass me my clothes please, and no peeking."

"And what if I don't?" he teased, picking up her shirt and holding it.

Again Kylie blushed. "Don't be cheeky," she snapped, "Just give them to me please."

"Oh, alright," Brian agreed.

He bent down and scooped up the rest of her clothes and then brought them over to her, placing them on the sand at the base of the tree. After getting him to promise he wouldn't look Kylie put down her towel and reached out to grab them, her heart beating fast with the delicious thrill.

As Kylie hurriedly tugged on her undies, snagging her wet and sandy feet in them as she did, she said, "What are you doing here?"

"I was sent to get some water for the horses," Brian answered.

That surprised Kylie, so she said, "We were told that you were hiding down along the Herbert River at a place called Blunder Creek."

"No," Brian replied, shaking his head. "We just doubled back and split up. We... er... I shouldn't be telling you that. Don't tell anyone please."

Before Kylie thought about it she said, "I won't." Then she puzzled and asked, "Who is with you?"

Brian shrugged and looked uncomfortable. "Aw... just... a couple of us," he mumbled.

"Where are you hiding?" she asked.

"In the old stables," Brian answered.

"The ones behind the old hotel?" Kylie asked, as she did up her bra.

"Yes."

That amazed her. "So you saw us ride in and go exploring?" she queried, bending to pick up her shirt and only then realising he could see her.

"That's right," Brian replied.

"You are lucky we didn't find you when we went exploring," she commented.

Brian shook his head. "No. You are the lucky ones. If you had seen us, we would have had to take you prisoner."

That was not a pleasant thought. As Kylie slid on her shirt and did it up, she pondered this, then asked, "Did you recognise us?"

"Yes," Brian replied. "I saw you."

Still doing up the last buttons Kylie stepped out towards him. Her heart was now beating fast and the sheer romance of the situation gripped her. Without thinking she hurried to him and flung her arms around his neck.

"Oh I missed you!" she murmured, tears wetting her cheeks. "I am so glad you are safe."

In reply Brian hugged her to him and kissed her. Kylie kissed him fiercely back, sure she was in love and so relieved he was safe.

Suddenly, Margaret's voice sounded from further along the creek, "Kylie! Kylie, are you finished?"

Kylie pulled her lips free from Brian's with a groan of frustration and alarm. Brian looked up the creek and reached for his gun.

Chapter 20

GUILT AND GHOSTS

Brian nervously fingered his pistol. "Who is that? Is that your friend Margaret?" he asked.

Kylie released him and stepped back, her heart hammering with alarm. "Yes, it is. Oh quick, hide!"

"Tell her not to come," Brian suggested.

Kylie licked her lips, which had become suddenly dry, and nodded. "Alright," she agreed. Turning and raising her voice she called loudly, "I'm not dressed, Margaret. Wait a minute and I will be with you."

"Okay," Margaret called back. "I was just checking that you are alright."

"I am," Kylie answered, flashing Brian a meaningful look.

Brian sighed with relief and slid the gun back into its holster. "Phew! That was close. Now, where were we?"

He grinned and moved to embrace Kylie again but she shook her head. "I'd better get back. It will be dark soon and Mrs Conroy is busy cooking tea."

Reluctantly, Brian agreed. He nodded and just gave her an affectionate squeeze of the upper arm. That got Kylie all emotional again and she asked, "Will I see you again?"

"I hope so," Brian replied. Once again, he grinned but this time it did not fool Kylie. She could see he was anxious. Then Brian took both her hands and looked intently into her eyes. "Please don't tell anyone we are here."

That really put Kylie on the spot. She knew that by agreeing she might be breaking the law ('Harbouring fugitives from justice,' she had read in some novel). But she also knew she wanted Brian to be safe. She nodded and then asked, "What are you going to do now?"

"I think we are heading off westwards as soon as it is dark," Brian replied.

"You take care then," Kylie said, her lips quavering with emotion and tears forming as she said it. Suddenly she found herself back in his arms and his lips on hers. For several minutes they kissed. Waves of emotion engulfed Kylie and she found tears streaming down her face. "Oh, I love you!" she cried.

"And I love you," Brian replied.

"You're not just saying that?" Kylie asked anxiously, wiping her tears-streaked face as she did.

Brian shook his head. "No. I think you are wonderful."

"I'll bet you say that to all the girls," Kylie said, half laughingly but actually dreading the idea that Brian might already have a girlfriend.

"Of course I do!" Brian replied with a grin. Then he squeezed her tight and kissed her nose.

"Do you want to see me again?" she asked, her anxiety still high.

Brian nodded. "Of course I do. I said so didn't I?"

"There isn't anyone else?" Kylie whispered, at last summoning up the courage to voice her fears.

Brian shook his head. Then he kissed her, holding her firmly against him. That made her sigh and feel as though she was melting with love. "Oh please don't get shot or anything," she cried, the tears starting again.

At that, Brian laughed. "Don't worry. This is the 21st Century, not the 19th. They don't hang bushrangers anymore. Beside, I have an incentive to survive; to see you again."

That caused Kylie's heart to hammer with what she thought was urgent devotion and she hugged him and gave him a fierce kiss before pulling back. "Oh please be careful. I don't want anything to happen to you."

"I will be careful," Brian said as he released her. "And I will be safer if you don't let anything slip about us being here."

That hurt a bit as it implied that he wasn't quite sure, that he did not fully trust her. *But that is only to be expected,* she thought. *He doesn't really know me.*

Once again, she nodded and said, "I won't tell."

"You'd better go then," Brian said, releasing her and stepping back. "And I'd better get this water or Michael will want to know what I have been doing."

"You won't say?" Kylie asked anxiously as she gathered Blazer's reins.

"No. You take care now," Brian said.

"You too. I... I... love you!" she gasped, blushing heatedly at her own temerity. Reluctantly she tugged on Blazer's reins and started walking back up the creek, glancing back every few paces to look at Brian.

He stood watching and raised his hand in farewell before picking up the buckets and moving to fill them. By the time Kylie reached the bend he had vanished back up the bank with them. She found she could hardly see for tears, and she had to stop and wash her face and master her emotions before rounding the bend to meet Margaret.

Dusk was setting in by then and Margaret was looking worried. "You took a long time," she commented.

"I... I undressed because I have some bad chafing," Kylie lied, then blushed, and was glad of the twilight.

As she said this, the vibration of a helicopter's rotors filled the air and a few seconds later the machine went buzzing past just above the treetops. It was the police helicopter and seeing it caused Kylie to shudder with guilt and apprehension.

Margaret watched it fly off upstream and then giggled. "Lucky for you it didn't come along a few minutes ago!" she cried.

Kylie could only grin, nod and blush. Without replying she led the way back up the creek to where they had left Norah. There was no sign of her, so the two girls went up the bank and back to camp, finding Norah and the boys there already.

By the time she and Margaret reached the camp it was just dark enough for the gas flame under the barbeque to show up brightly and soon after that Mrs Conroy lit a pressure lantern and placed it on the folding table. As the girls arrived Dingo took the horses away to neck rope them to a long rope tied between two trees.

Mrs Conroy looked up from adjusting the lantern and said, "I was wondering where you two girls had got to. We were about to send out a search party. I thought the bushrangers might have got you."

That sent a stab of anxiety through Kylie and she gasped, then shook her head, thinking of Brian and the others who were only a hundred metres away. "Oh Mrs Conroy! Don't say things like that. Besides, the Kelly Gang must be a long way away if they are down near the Herbert River."

Stephen looked up and said, "You'd know where they are."

For a few moments Kylie was so shocked, wondering if she and

Brian had been seen, that she was speechless. Then she snapped angrily, "Don't say horrible things. I didn't know that Brian was one of the Kelly Gang. And he didn't tell me where they were going. He was just being friendly."

"Very friendly!" Stephen said with a grin, to Peter.

Kylie blushed with guilt and became annoyed. She stomped her foot but Mrs Conroy now intervened and told them all to stop bickering and to have their dinner. This was steak, onions, and vegetables on bread rolls. The diversion helped Kylie to calm down, but she still felt very guilty and kept thinking of Brian and how close he was.

As Kylie sat on a folding chair munching on her steak sandwich, Margaret sat beside her and said softly, "Are you alright, Kylie?"

"Yes, why?" replied Kylie, her heart leaping with guilty alarm.

Margaret looked anxiously at her and shrugged. "You have gone all quiet and look really worried," she answered.

"Just tired, I suppose. It's been a long day, and with all that drama at Mt Garnet I suppose I am a bit worn down," Kylie replied.

Margaret accepted this and went back to eating. Darkness set in and all Kylie could see was what was in the circle of light from the lantern. Knowing what might be out in the encircling darkness made her feel very tense. Thus she was less than happy when Stephen and Graham began talking about the ghost town. She became even more concerned when Stephen suggested they explore it in the dark.

"It will be really spooky," he suggested.

Peter shook his head. "Just some old buildings. Nothing ever happened here."

"You don't know that," Stephen replied. "There might have been a horrible murder. There really might be a ghost that walks the ruins at midnight."

"Oh rot!" Margaret replied sharply, her face drawn and anxious.

"Ghosts!" sneered Peter. "What a load of old cobblers!"

"I'll bet you aren't game to walk the length of the main street on your own in the dark," Stephen challenged.

That was the last thing Kylie wanted them to do but to her dismay Graham at once rose to the challenge. "I'll bet I am!"

"Off you go then!" Stephen dared.

"Right," Graham answered. "As soon as I've had my dessert."

Knowing that Graham would do what he said Kylie tried to think of ways to stop the boys going off to explore the town in the dark. "You will just step on a big snake," she warned. "They come out at night to hunt don't forget." It was the best she could think of, knowing that Graham was very scared of snakes, having been bitten by one a few years earlier.

Graham scorned this and only saw it as more of a challenge. "We will walk slowly and they will just get out of our way, like they do on cadet night exercises," he answered.

Now Kylie hoped that Mrs Conroy would veto the idea, but she just cautioned them to use torches and to watch out for post holes and jagged bits of rusty iron. To Kylie's agitation, the boys all stood up with the declared intention of going to explore the town.

Stephen then made it worse by saying, "Come on you girls, or are you too scared?"

Kylie was, but she felt compelled to go, if only to try to head them off from going anywhere near the stables at the back of the old hotel. She made herself stand and set her jaw. "I am not," she declared as bravely as she could manage. "Come on Margaret, we will show these silly boys."

It was obvious that Margaret was not keen on the idea, but she nodded and stood up as well. Mrs Conroy smiled and said, "Norah, go with them and make sure they don't do anything silly. Dingo, you can help me wash up and then check those horses."

After collecting torches from their gear, the group assembled near the vehicle. By then Kylie was really anxious but could think of nothing to say to dissuade the boys from proceeding. So, when Graham and Peter set off along the vehicle track, she made herself follow. Margaret stepped off beside her and Stephen and Norah came behind.

Once away from the bright light of the pressure lantern, Kylie was once more able to see the dim shapes of the hill to her left and the dark shapes of the trees. However the beams of their torches, held to shine down in front of their feet, still hampered her night vision. In a desperate hope of warning Brian that they were coming she several times shone the beam of her torch in the direction of the stables.

But it was not until they were only about fifty paces from the hotel that the buildings came into sight. Graham's torch beam swept over the old building and Kylie shivered. In the shadowy light it looked even more depressing and sinister than it had in the daylight.

The group came to a stop about twenty paces from the hotel. Stephen then said, "Well, go on Graham. Walk to the far end of town on your own. When you get there shine your torch so we can see where you are."

Graham set off, his torch beam directed at the wheel ruts of the vehicle track. On seeing that Stephen called out, "Hoy! No torch. You have to give the ghosts a fair chance."

Kylie saw Graham's torch flick off and then lost sight of him. She stood with the others, nervously sweeping the beam of her own torch around. She was still hoping that the Brian or his brothers would see the light.

At that moment, the very distinctive sound of a horse snuffling came from the direction of the old stables. On hearing it Kylie felt a chill of worry, which turned to alarm when Norah said, "That sounded like a horse."

"I thought so too," Margaret agreed.

In desperation Kylie said, "It sounded like it was one of ours."

"No it didn't!" Margaret replied. "The sound came from over there in front of us."

"Maybe it is just a wild horse and he can smell our horses," Kylie suggested, now hoping that Norah would not investigate.

Norah aimed her torch beam in that direction and was about to walk that way when Margaret cried, "Oh look, there's Graham's torch."

Kylie looked along the 'street' and saw the pin-point of light which indicated where Graham now was. He seemed a very long way away and she wasn't sure she could walk that far alone and in the dark. But she knew she had to.

There is no way that brother of mine is going to tease me for being a scaredy cat! she resolved.

Peter went next and then Margaret. As they stood waiting Kylie kept praying that the Kelly Gang's horses would not make another snort. Just in case she insisted that Norah go next. That left just her, and Stephen and he began to act silly, calling loudly with noises like 'Hwoooo!' and 'Boo!' to make Norah think there might be ghosts. Then he chuckled in what he obviously imagined was a spooky way and that made Kylie think he was very immature, even though it did make her hair stand on end. Even so she was grateful for his noises, chuckles and talk about ghosts as she thought it would drown out any more horse noises.

The Kelly Gang might hear it too, and know we are here, she thought.

Then it was her turn. Gulping with anxiety she switched off her torch and began walking. She found that he could easily follow the wheel ruts in the starlight and realised she was much more afraid of stepping on a snake than about ghosts. From behind her Stephen made more ghost noises. Despite knowing it was only him trying to frighten her she found the hair prickling at the back of her neck and she came out in goose bumps. In spite of telling herself it was just a silly game she knew she was scared, and she hurried as fast as she dared, sighing with relief when the dark shapes of the others came into view.

They stood and waited for Stephen to join them. While they waited Kylie calmed down and noted that the heat of the day had dropped and that it was pleasantly cool. She felt slightly more relaxed by this time and was happy that the consensus was that they should just go back to camp and not go poking around any of the buildings.

To help reinforce this idea she said, "It is unsafe. We should just go back to camp."

In the distance she could see the bright glow of the lantern at the tents, and she just wanted everyone back there and away from the Kelly Gang. What surprised her was that she did not feel threatened by the Kelly Gang and realised that it was concern for Brian's safety that was motivating her.

There was no general agreement to this plan, but the group did start strolling back along the 'street', the discussion covering the history of the region and other ghost towns or abandoned mining settlements.

When they arrived back near the old hotel, they veered over towards it and shone their torches on it. Peter and Graham stepped up onto the veranda and shone their torches into the bar. Kylie and Margaret stepped up to join them. Margaret shone her torch onto a cobweb encrusted window, then screamed.

The scream was so sudden and unexpected that Kylie jumped with fright. Even as she did, she looked at where Margaret's torch beam was shining, and let out an involuntary scream of her own. A person was standing inside the old hotel, close up to the grimy window!

Then Kylie saw that it was Stephen. He grinned and called something, but she did not hear what it was because by then Margaret had also realised who it was and her fright dissolved into instant anger.

"Stephen Bell, you horrible boy!" Margaret cried.

Kylie stood there, her own heart palpitating with fright and her thoughts echoing Margaret's cry. She opened her own mouth, even as Stephen vanished from inside the window. She heard Graham yell to Peter, "Quick Pete, you go that way and I'll go the other and we will catch the bugger!"

"Graham!" Kylie managed to croak, not wanting the boys running around the ruins in the dark. But she was too late. Graham dashed into the nearest doorway and Kylie saw his torch beam questing the interior. Peter vanished off to the right, around the corner of the building.

Margaret grabbed Kylie's arm. "Oh the rotter!" she fumed, her hand to her bosom. "Come on Kylie, let's help Graham catch him. Maybe we can give him a fright too?"

Kylie did not want to go inside but found herself following Margaret as she followed Graham through the doorway. They went into a hallway that went straight through to the back door. On her right was a doorway leading to a dimly lit front room. To her left were the remains of the public bar. Graham went behind the counter and entered a back room over to the left. Kylie saw the flicker of his torch as its beam searched the corners.

Then Graham appeared at the side door of the back room, stepping out into the hallway. His torch swept up and down the hallway and then settled on another door, almost opposite. "Where has the bugger gone?" he muttered, moving to the door and taking hold of the handle.

Stepping carefully over litter and rubbish on the dusty floor Kylie followed Margaret towards him. Graham turned the handle, which gave a sharp screech which set her hair on end, then shoved the door open. The hinges were obviously rusty as it moved only slowly and with a spooky, groaning noise. Unable to push the door right open Graham poked his head round the door and used his torch to look.

"Not in here," he said. "He must have gone out the back."

He moved towards the back door and then kicked something metal which made him stumble. Muttering and swearing he pointed his torch down to see what it was. In its beam Kylie saw a length of rusty chain.

Graham instantly bent down and grabbed one end of the chain. "Aha!" he cried softly. "Just what we want for a haunted house, a chain to rattle." He began shaking and dragging the chain.

It did give out a spooky rattle and even though Kylie knew it was only her brother playing silly games it sent chills up her spine. Once again, she came out in goose bumps. Then she heard the sound of footsteps outside at the rear of the building. The person kicked a metal object in the long grass, cursed softly and stopped for a second, and then resumed moving towards the back door with stealthy steps.

"Back up," Graham hissed. "We will scare him."

So saying he began moving backwards along the hallway, dragging the chain behind him and rattling it as he went. As Margaret did likewise Kylie had no option but to move back as well. She swept her torch behind her to check the floor was safe and clear of obstructions and then shuffled back out of the hallway and into the bar area.

As she did, Graham hissed at her to switch off her torch and to hide in the side room. Kylie glanced that way and then took a couple of steps backwards in that direction. Then she stopped, frozen with pure fear. A large hand had gripped the back of her head. The next moment a strong male arm encircled her neck.

Unable to make her muscles move and overcome with mounting terror Kylie could only gasp with shock and stand frozen with fear, her mind racing.

Oh my God! she thought. *Who's got me?*

Of one thing she was absolutely sure, it was not one of her friends!

Chapter 21

SPLIT UP

Kylie knew instantly that the person who was holding her was not one of the boys. Not only was he much bigger and his grip very strong but he smelt different; of horse, sweat and tobacco. For several seconds she was struck speechless and did not dare move. Then it came to her that whoever he was he must be one of the Kelly Gang. At that, the first feelings of terror and panic began to recede.

Brian will make sure we aren't hurt, she thought.

From behind her, out on the front veranda, she heard a man say softly to Norah, "Just stand still Missie and you won't get hurt." Kylie heard Norah gasp and then glimpsed a torch being shone on her.

Meanwhile, Margaret and Graham continued their backward shuffle so that Margaret now bumped into Kylie. "Keep moving Ky," she hissed.

"Margg... gg..." Kylie began, only to have the man's arm tighten around her throat so that her jaw was clamped shut.

At that moment, Kylie saw the dark shape of a person step into the hallway through the back doorway. Graham sprang out, calling a loud, "Boo!" as he did. Then his torch beam lit up the person. In the light Kylie saw that it was another member of the Kelly Gang, a huge man with a massive black beard. In one hand he had a torch and in the other an old-fashioned, long barrelled revolver.

There was a strangled, "Holy shit! I... er... um!" from Graham before the new arrival snarled, "Get that torch outa my eyes, or else!"

The man's left hand came up and levelled the pistol at Graham. Then his right followed and the beam of his torch came on, half blinding Kylie.

Graham stood transfixed for a few seconds, obviously stunned by the surprise. Then he switched off his torch and muttered, "Sorry! I didn't realise who it was. We are only playing a game."

"And we aren't. Now get into that front room there," the man ordered.

While he was speaking Kylie heard more voices out the back and that told her that Peter or Stephen had been captured as well. She began to wonder where Brian was and hoped he would soon appear.

The big, bearded man now called out through the front door, "Hey Michael, how many have you got there?"

"Two Phil, a boy and a girl," Michael replied.

Phil! Kylie thought. She knew he was the big brother and was reputed to be the leader of the gang. Now she recognised his voice, although it sounded different to when she had heard it at Mt Garnet. *Because it isn't muffled by that helmet,* she decided.

Phil Kelly told Michael to bring Norah and Roger in and then called out the back, "Hey Dan, what ya got?"

Dan called back, "Two kids, two boys."

"Bring 'em in," Phil ordered.

As they were herded into the front bar, Kylie was released and shoved over to join Margaret and Graham in the corner. She heard Mrs Conroy's anxious voice calling in the distance and was tempted to call out. Then she saw Brian and the idea went straight out of her head. Phil Kelly heard Mrs Conroy too and said, "Dan, find Kate and check out why Liam hasn't got those other two. Make sure that Dingo doesn't slip away in the dark."

That dashed Kylie's hopes of immediate rescue. *They know how many of us there are,* she thought. It came as no surprise as she knew the gang had seen the group ride in that afternoon. *And Brian would have added more details. But why are they taking us prisoner?* she wondered anxiously. Horrible thoughts of being used as human shields and hostages began to crowd into her mind, even though she did not think Brian would agree to such a thing.

As she stood there, she met Brian's eyes and smiled, sure he would keep them safe. He smiled back but looked a bit anxious. To Kylie it was not really scary now, just exciting and romantic. There was her man, the armed bushranger!

And he looks so good! she thought, admiring his muscular body, handsome face, and the whole drama of the situation.

Norah and Roger were brought in from the front and an angry Stephen and calm Peter from the back. Then Kylie heard loud calls and angry voices and knew that Mrs Conroy had also been captured as she heard her demanding to know what was going on.

Phil Kelly called loudly, "Liam, did you get that Dingo bloke?"

"Yes Phil," came the reply.

"Good. Now tie his hands behind his back and then start on these kids. Brian, you start on these boys," Phil Kelly ordered.

Brian had been standing looking at Kylie, his eyes full of unhappiness mingled with meaningful glances. As he stepped forward Kylie was tempted to speak but he spoke first, asking Phil Kelly, "What about the girls?"

"'Course," Phil Kelly replied. "We don't want any slipping away to spill the beans. If you can't bring yourself to tie up your little girlfriend, then Dan will do it."

At that, Brian and Kylie exchanged glances and Kylie blushed, hotly aware that everyone else had looked at her. Mrs Conroy, who had just been ushered in through the doorway gave her a sharp glance, making Kylie feel even worse. She was glad that the light from the torches was not very good so she could hide her shame.

Mrs Conroy objected strongly to the proceedings. "How dare you!" she snapped. "Let us go! Keep your hands off me!"

"Be quiet please, Mrs Conroy," Phil Kelly said softly. "If you co-operate then nobody will get hurt and you will all be let go safely."

"What do you want?" Mrs Conroy asked as she was moved over to stand beside Norah and Kylie.

"We've got a couple of horses going lame," Phil Kelly said. "And one that's lost a shoe. We need a loan of your vehicle and horse float."

"No! I'm not helping criminals," Mrs Conroy answered.

"Then we will take it anyway," Phil Kelly replied calmly. Then his face changed, and he leant forward and snarled, "But if you won't help us then one of these pretty little girls might get hurt."

On hearing that Kylie was shocked. She looked anxiously at Brian and saw that he was looking worried as well. *He can't stop his brother,* she decided. Now fear began to seep back in, chilling her.

Phil Kelly now did a count, then turned to Brian and said, "Eight. That's the right number. Your little girlfriend was telling the truth."

At that, Kylie scorched with shame as every eye turned on her. She saw Margaret give a reproachful look and Graham looked at her with an expression of wry puzzlement.

Brian had already tied up Peter and Stephen and now moved on to Kylie. By then Liam had secured Dingo, Norah and Margaret and he now moved on to Graham. As Brian took hold of her wrists and indicated to

Kylie to put them behind her back, he looked into her eyes and whispered, "Sorry. I have to do what they say. Just do what you are told and you won't get hurt."

Kylie had been hoping that Brian would make a declaration that he would protect her no matter what, that she was safe, so it was a hurtful let down to find that he did not. Instead he bound her hands behind her back. He did not make the knots very tight, but it still made Kylie feel both angry and sad.

This was made worse when Phil Kelly said to Dan, "Just make sure that little brother has tied his girlfriend up nice and tight Dan."

At that, Brian retorted indignantly, "I tied her up tight. Leave her alone!"

Dan ignored him and moved over to check Kylie's bonds. As he did, he gave a leering grin and said, "Might be what she likes, being tied up. Some women enjoy that."

Kylie had heard a few whispers about bondage from her school friends but had not believed it. Now she felt another stab of chill. Mrs Conroy was not amused. "Stop that filthy talk in front of the girls!" she snapped.

Dan snorted. "Huh! If you don't do what we ask it won't just be talk lady," he retorted.

Kylie heard a shocked gasp from both Norah and Margaret. Graham and Peter both muttered threats but the Kelly Gang ignored them. Instead Mrs Conroy asked, "And what is it you want, apart from stealing my Four Wheel Drive?"

"We aren't going to steal it, Mrs Conroy," Phil Kelly said. "Look on it as just a loan, or, better still, just helping some needy people. I'd like you to drive it." He then turned to his gang, who had all now crowded into the room and said, "Right, you all know what to do, go and do your jobs."

Mrs Conroy was ushered out of the room by a man Kylie had never seen before, and who had the lower part of his face covered by a bandanna. To Kylie's consternation Pat and Liam then took both Graham and Peter by their arms and led them out the front door as well. Phil Kelly nodded and Dan went out the back way. Seeing Graham and Peter being led away caused Kylie a spasm of deep anxiety. She turned to Brian, who was standing close beside her.

"Please Brian, don't hurt us."

"We won't," Brian replied, but his tone was not very convincing.

"Where's Kate?"

Brian nodded towards the rear. "Minding the horses," he answered.

"What is going on? What are you doing?" she asked.

"You heard Phil. We have a couple of lame horses and one that has cast a shoe. We need transport to get out of the area quickly before the police can block off all the roads," Brian answered.

That drew a sharp comment from Phil Kelly. "No need to tell little sweetie all our plans Brian. You are supposed to pump her for information, not let her squeeze it out of you!"

"Yes Phil," Brian replied, sounding abashed.

Phil Kelly pointed out the front door. "Right, let's get these back to their camp and tie them up in a bunch while we get organised."

Kylie went out with the others, Brian holding her arm. That annoyed her and she found his touch did not comfort but instead irritated. *He used me!* she thought unhappily. But even so she yearned for him to hug her and hold her, to reassure her and to say romantic things.

All the way back to the camp Kylie wondered if that was the case, or had he just told his brother as a matter of course. She could not decide and now began to worry that perhaps he did not love her, that he was just enjoying himself at the dance *like a typical male*. It was all very saddening and upsetting to her and she found herself on the edge of tears.

These actually began to flow after they had been seated in a group at the camp when Mrs Conroy asked her, "Did you know the Kelly Gang were here Kylie?"

Shocked and embarrassed Kylie shook her head vigorously and said, "No, not when we arrived." But the accusation hurt and she did not think Mrs Conroy believed her.

Nor, apparently, did Margaret because she asked, "Did you meet Brian when you went off down the creek?"

That her best friend was also suspicious stung so much Kylie started to cry. "Yes," she admitted. "But it was not by any arrangement. I didn't know they were there. It was a surprise to both of us."

Margaret nodded and looked thoughtful. Then her face dimpled into a cheeky grin. "Did he find you swimming in the nude?"

At that, Kylie stopped sobbing and blurted angrily. "No! I'm not like you and Graham."

"Oh Kylie! Be fair! That was years ago," Margaret replied, blushing.

Norah looked interested and asked, "What was this all about?"

"Oh nothing," Margaret answered.

Seeing her friend's discomfiture helped Kylie stop crying and she replied, "Graham and Margaret used to take baths together."

"Oh! Only when we were little," Margaret defended.

They were then interrupted by the gang's preparations. Out of the darkness appeared Kate, leading to a line of horses. Kylie watched carefully to see if she looked at Graham in any particular way but as far as she could tell she did not even notice him. Instead she concentrated on securing three horses to the back of the horse trailer, then on leading the others off into the darkness, along with two horses from the Conroy's herd.

The horse trailer was hitched to the back of the vehicle by Liam and the masked man and two of the horses led inside. Then, to Kylie's alarm, both Graham and Peter were told to get into the vehicle. Up till now Kylie had not felt particularly threatened by the bushrangers as they had all handled their guns in a way that kept them from pointing at them most of the time. Now she noticed that Michael was standing at the end of the seated line of prisoners. He was holding a double barrel shotgun and was plainly their guard.

Even that sight did not intimidate her though and she cried out, "Where are you taking Graham? Stop that!"

She got no response from the bushrangers although Graham turned his head just before being pushed into the front passenger seat of the vehicle by Dan. Mrs Conroy also objected but was just told to get in and drive by the masked man, who slid into the back beside Peter, a gun in his hand. Michael Kelly joined the horses in the trailer, Liam replacing him as guard. There was nothing more Kylie could do as the vehicle was started up and drove off into the darkness. As she watched its headlights go down into the creek line she felt a horrible sense of foreboding.

For several minutes she could see and hear the vehicle as it ground its way up the hill on the other side of the creek. Then it was gone. *What is in that direction?* she wondered, wishing she could look at Graham's map. After some thought she decided it was Irvinebank. *That is on the other side of Mt Misery,* she remembered, and that was how she felt! But then she remembered that there were side roads that led off towards Innot Hot Springs and also towards Silver Valley.

Margaret now began to complain about the rope binding her wrists being too tight. Kylie was also feeling very uncomfortable but in her distress at Peter and Graham being separated from the group had not noticed. Phil Kelly told Dan and Brian to retie everyone in a line, this time by their ankles. First, they were released one at a time to get their sleeping bags and pillows to lie on. Then their hands were untied and their ankles bound. It was done in such a way as to have a short rope looped around one ankle, the rope then being tied to the long rope. This was secured between two trees. Although the loop of rope was loose enough that it did not interfere with the circulation it was still too small to slip over her foot.

Brian did this to Kylie and she saw that he looked embarrassed and uncomfortable in the light from the pressure lantern. As he worked Kylie gave him a reproachful look. Then her curiosity got the better of her and she asked, "How did you get here? When we saw you last you were heading south out of town."

"We doubled back," Brian replied. "That was our plan to fool the cops. We all headed off south after dropping the hint that Blunder Creek was our destination. As soon as we were out of sight of the houses we went down into the bed of Nanyeta Creek and rode back north along it and under the main road. It was just as the first cops were arriving and luckily they didn't see us."

At that moment, Phil Kelly, who had been conversing with Dan, looked along the line at them. He frowned and called out, "Hey Brian, I thought I told you not to give our secrets away to little sweetie?"

"Sorry Phil," Brian replied.

Kylie thought she saw a distinct look of fear cross Brian's face and that got her thinking too. *He is scared of them,* she decided.

That knowledge was of no help. Soon all six were tied up, lying side by side on their bedding on the grass. Liam settled himself on a chair at the end where he could watch them all. Brian stood and fidgeted, obviously uneasy. After a few minutes more of quiet talking Phil Kelly, Dan and Kate moved off to the horses. Kylie noted that Kate had barely glanced at them and she hoped Graham's feelings weren't too badly hurt.

A few minutes later she heard the sound of the horses moving, their hooves thudding softly on the sandy soil. For a few seconds she got a glimpse of them in the dim lantern light, noting that there were at least seven or eight and that they were heavily laden with bundles. They headed off across to the vehicle track and vanished from sight and sound into the creek line.

Going the same way as the vehicle, she decided.

Norah spoke next. "What do we do now?" she asked.

"Get some sleep while you can," Liam replied. "It could be a long day tomorrow."

"You surely don't mean we sleep out here in the open?" Norah asked.

Liam laughed and shrugged. "Why not? It's not going to rain."

"But it could get cold and there will be a heavy dew," Norah protested.

"Tough!" Liam snorted. "Stockmen and soldiers do it all the time. You won't die from sleeping under the stars in this climate. We've been doing it for a week."

"But I need to go to the toilet!" Norah added.

That presented Liam with a problem. This was added to when Margaret said the same. To annoy the bushrangers, Kylie said she also needed to go, then found that she really did. For a few minutes Liam was unsure of what to do, but in the end he said, "I will let you go one at a time. If you run away and don't come back I will do things to the other girls."

Faced with that threat the girls felt no alternative but to agree. Brian was sent to untie them and each in turn made their way out into the darkness to the portable toilet. When it was her turn Kylie was strongly tempted to try to escape, feeling that Liam was only bluffing. But then she got all concerned in case he wasn't so she walked meekly back to rejoin the group, just in case.

I couldn't live with myself if I caused them to be hurt, she told herself. Although lacking experience herself she had heard enough of the disgusting things some men did to women to make her feel revolted and afraid. Of one thing she was sure, she didn't like Liam.

And do I like Brian anymore? she wondered, then realised that the word love had not been in her head.

Her mind now turned to considering ways to escape, and what to do if she did, Kylie settled down beside the others and tried to relax and sleep. She had Norah on one side and Margaret on the other. Several times she met Margaret's eyes and gave a wry smile and tried to encourage her, but she could tell she was fretting about Graham.

Unable to get into her sleeping bag because of the rope she could only pull it half over her. Lying on the ground she found uncomfortable. She began to fidget and wriggle, trying to find a comfortable position in which to sleep.

Chapter 22

MT MISERY

After a time Kylie fell into a fitful sleep, from which she was woken by the movements of the others as they tried to get comfortable, and in doing so inadvertently pulled at the rope. Squirming into a more comfortable position and tugging part of her unzipped sleeping bag over her to ward off the growing chill, she again tried to sleep.

In this she was partially successful, the second time being jerked awake by a horrible dream. A huge, shadowy figure had loomed up out of the darkness. As he got closer, she saw he was a member of the Kelly Gang, dressed in armour and with clutching hands reaching out towards her in an evil way. She had backed off, straining to move and experiencing the ghastly sensation of being glued to the spot, when she had been seized from behind by an immensely strong, foul, smelling and hairy man. With a scream that was really a stifled groan she woke up.

She found that a member of the Kelly Gang really was looming out of the darkness, though not dressed in armour, and that the vehicle had returned. The man she had never seen before, but Mrs Conroy was with him, looking tired and dishevelled. There was no sign of Graham or Peter.

Liam was still sitting in his chair but stood up as they approached. "How'd it go, Brendan?" he asked.

"Okay. The horses are safe at the camp," Brendan replied. Kylie saw he was in his twenties and fairly chubby. "Any trouble here?"

Liam shook his head. "Nope. All sleeping like babies."

"Boss get away okay?" Brendan asked.

"About ten," Liam replied. "He should be halfway over the mountain by now."

Brendan nodded and then said to Mrs Conroy, "You get your sleeping gear and join this lot lady."

Mrs Conroy did as she was told. Kylie badly wanted to talk to her, to try to find out what had happened to Graham and Peter, but she did not want the bushrangers to know she was awake so she lay still with her eyes closed.

I might overhear their plans, she thought.

But in this she was disappointed and she drifted off to sleep again, to wake cold and stiff in the grey light of dawn. As predicted there had been a heavy dew and she found her sleeping bag damp to the touch although she had managed to snuggle in under it enough to stay fairly warm.

Now that it was light they were untied and allowed to get up. "Have breakfast and then pack up," Liam ordered. "And don't try to escape when you go to the dunny. We've got those two boys don't forget, and they will suffer if you run off."

Hearing that threat made Kylie's stomach turn over and she looked at Brian and gave him an unhappy look. He tried to return a smile but it became a guilty, lopsided grin and caused Kylie to purse her lips and look away. Feeling distinctly unhappy she made her way to the portable toilet, then came back and helped cook breakfast.

She was busy turning over fried eggs on the barbeque plate when she heard the sound of a vehicle. Glancing down the valley past the ruins of the town she saw the flicker of white in the distance. Then she noted the blue and red lights on top.

A Police car! she thought, her heart skipping a beat and starting to pound.

The bushrangers saw it too and at once became agitated. Liam swore, then bit his lip in indecision before saying, "Okay, all act naturally. Brian, you stay here with these people and pretend to be one of those boys we took. Brendan, you go over to the horses and pretend to be getting them ready. Wear one of those white safety helmets. Dingo, you come with us and start saddling the horses."

"What are you going to do?" Brendan asked him.

"Get under cover ready to use this," Liam replied. Bending down he picked up a gleaming, new, bolt action, sporting rifle with a telescopic sight on top.

The mere sight of that sent a chill of terror through Kylie. She had once looked through such a rifle sight on her uncle's farm and had then watched in horrified amazement when he had shot a wild pig half a kilometre away with the rifle.

Liam picked up the shotgun from his blankets and passed it to Brendan. "Keep it up against your body and then hide it in the grass where you can get to it easily," he instructed. Brendan finished clipping on one of the white helmets, then took the shotgun and did as he was told, calmly walking towards the horses.

Liam also held the rifle vertical against his body so that the approaching police would not see it. He then tapped the rifle with unmistakable significance and snarled, "Make them go away, Mrs Conroy. One wrong word and at least one of those coppers is going to die, and their blood will be on your hands. And you, Dingo, no tricks or you are a goner."

With that Liam turned and the two men then walked over to the horses and untied four, leading them another fifty paces upslope away from the camp. Hidden by the horses Liam slipped out of sight behind a small bush. The horses were then taken off to one side to give him a clear shot. Kylie saw the bush move once and knew that Liam was now lying down and aiming the rifle towards them.

Both Brendan and Dingo went another twenty paces. Brendan placed his shotgun down in the grass and stood with his back to the camp while pretending to groom the horses. Dingo picked up a saddle and bridle, grunting with annoyance at the dew on the leather, and moved over to another nearby horse.

Kylie now felt very anxious. She was sure that Liam was deadly serious and hoped that nothing would happen. With dry throat and beating heart she watched the police vehicle, a white Landcruiser towing a horse trailer, drive up along the 'main street' of the town, then turn off the track and head across the paddock towards them.

Brian stood with his back to the police vehicle, pretending to be cooking sausages. To help with his disguise he had also put on one of the white helmets. Several times his eyes met Kylie's, but she then avoided looking at him, only noting that he was very tense. She no longer thought the situation romantic or enjoyable and was deeply apprehensive, fearing a horrible tragedy. The police vehicle did a wide turn and came to a stop about ten metres away, left side towards them. A policeman leaned out of the window.

It was Constable Lonergan and Kylie distinctly heard Norah gasp and murmur 'Oh no!'. Constable Lonergan grinned and waved. "Hello Mrs Conroy. Hi Norah. How's it going?"

"Fine thanks," Mrs Conroy replied. "No rain and not too cold. And there is plenty of good grass from that rain over the last few days."

"No problems?" Constable Lonergan asked, his eyes roving the camp. Kylie saw him looking towards Dingo and the man at the horses but then they switched to Norah, who walked over towards him.

That got Kylie anxious until she realised that Norah had deliberately placed herself between the Liam and Constable Lonergan. *She is right in the line of fire,* she thought. She herself was now terribly tense. *Act normally,* she told herself. Glancing around, she saw that Mrs Conroy and Margaret both had very strained looks on their faces, so she forced herself to smile. *We must act normally so they will go away or Constable Lonergan could be shot dead!* she thought.

The idea made her sick, but she managed to keep working. Mrs Conroy sat with a hard smile and Kylie saw that her fingers were tapping nervously on her chair arm.

Norah walked right over to the police vehicle and leaned against the door, smiling as she did. Then said loudly, "You must have been up early."

Constable Lonergan smiled back, his eyes only on Norah. "We were. Four o'clock."

"So you haven't caught the Kelly Gang then?"

"No. But we are on their trail. They didn't go south towards Blunder Creek at all," Constable Lonergan answered.

His gaze then shifted to Kylie and his expression seemed to harden. She met his eyes and then felt very guilty and blushed. In an attempt to hide her confusion she looked down and pretended to concentrate on her cooking, before realising that probably looked even more guilty.

"How do you know that?" Norah asked.

"The black trackers. Those old fellas have picked up a good trail and are following it. Apparently one of the gang's horses has cast a shoe and is leaving really obvious tracks. We are going to get ahead of them to set up roadblocks and patrols."

Norah put her hand to her breast. "Are we in any danger?" she asked.

Constable Lonergan shook his head. "I hope not, but you should get moving and get out of this area, just in case they come this way."

"You think the Kelly Gang is coming this way?" Norah gasped.

Again he nodded. "Their tracks lead straight up this valley."

"How far away are they?"

"We aren't sure. The black trackers are working about ten kilometres south of here right now. They've been hard at it since daybreak," Constable Lonergan answered.

"Are they local Aborigines?" Norah asked.

Constable Lonergan shook his head. "No. They come from down south, Fraser Island I heard." The policeman next to him then said something and he nodded, then turned back to Norah and said, "Well, we'd better keep moving. Take care."

"You too," Norah replied.

For a moment Kylie thought Norah was going to lean forward and hug or kiss him, but she just fluttered her arms. Constable Lonergan gave her a quizzical smile before waving as the vehicle began moving. As it turned away and headed back down the paddock towards the vehicle track, Kylie gave a huge sigh of relief and realised she had been all but holding her breath. She now relaxed and stood watching as the police vehicle vanished into the creek line. It was, she noted, also heading towards Mt Misery and Irvinebank.

Liam waited till it was out of sight over the next hill before standing up. He and Brendan walked back, weapons still close against their bodies. They stood and stared towards the next hill, watching and listening. Brian stood with them watching, then described the conversation in detail. Liam nodded and said, "Phil was right. We had to get rid of 'Carbine' with her loose shoe."

"But those bloody black trackers will track her to here and they will realise something odd has happened when the tracks suddenly finish," Brian said.

"So we had better get moving and get well away before they work out that they need to investigate Mrs Conroy's Trail Ride more carefully," Liam answered. He turned to the group and snapped, "Okay, start eating and packing up. We will be moving in half an hour, no matter what. Get moving!"

They did. It was hectic and most of the camping gear was just bundled into the vehicle rather than being neatly packed, but they got it done on time. At Liam's insistence they all put on the white safety helmets. The horses were quickly saddled. Liam then gave orders on who went where. Brendan rode in the vehicle beside Mrs Conroy. He rode at the rear behind Dingo and Kylie saw that he had the rifle tucked under his left thigh in a saddle bucket. He also had a revolver tucked into a saddle bag and he showed this to Dingo.

"No tricks, or you get it first," he threatened.

The threat horrified Kylie but she was even more offended by the ugly racism. Pursing her lips with disapproval she mounted and settled in her saddle behind Brian. Norah led. Margaret came behind Kylie with Stephen behind her.

When all were mounted the group set off, walking the horses down to the vehicle track and then across the creek. The vehicle followed, catching up and then stopping for a few minutes before catching up again. By then the sun was well up and it was hot. There was almost no breeze, particularly down in the valleys, and there was no cloud.

The ride became a bit of an ordeal for Kylie. She knew she was not enjoying it at all and her whole focus now was on finding and rescuing Graham and Peter, and of escaping from the gang. But how to do it when she had no idea where the boys had been taken?

When we meet up with them, I will be able to do something, she decided. That settled her plan. *I will act scared and innocent until the opportunity presents itself,* she thought.

The road went up over several steep, rocky hills. The country was all open savannah and the vegetation varied between stands of ten metre high, black-trunked ironbarks, and four-metre-high stunted acacias and mulga type trees. On each hilltop there were long views but all they showed were a jumbled mass of seemingly endless rocky hills.

As they rode along, Kylie was appalled at how isolated and lonely she felt. They seemed to be in the middle of a vast wilderness. All she could see was the rugged ridges and mulga scrub. Apart from the rough vehicle track and an occasional side track, there were no signs of human settlement; no houses, no farms, not even a powerline.

The vehicle track was very poorly maintained and rutted. In places it was so steep, or so stony, that they had to dismount to allow the horses to pick their way slowly. Mrs Conroy's vehicle had real trouble getting up a couple of the slopes and Kylie heard its engine roaring and the rattle of loose gravel flying from under its wheels.

It was while waiting at the top of a steep hill waiting for the vehicle that she first noticed that all the bushrangers had small radios. She saw Liam talking on one and presumed it was to Brendan in the vehicle as Brian made no attempt to use his.

Ten minutes later, when cresting the next rise, she understood more clearly the bushranger's tactics. As Brian reached the top of the slope he slowed to a halt and then spoke briefly into his radio when he could see over the crest.

He is acting as scout, Kylie deduced.

That this was so became very clear an hour later when, after slogging along a rough, scrubby ridge for about 5 kilometres, she saw Brian rein in at a bend and then snatch his radio up and speak quickly into it. Glancing behind her Kylie saw Liam answer and then signal halt. Liam pulled out his rifle and after quickly hitching his horse's reins to a bush, strode forward to look.

As they sat there waiting, Kylie found her hopes and fears fluctuating wildly. She badly wanted the police to catch them, but was afraid of the possibly violent confrontation that might ensue. For some time she had been glancing back, wondering how far behind the blacktrackers were, and hoping they might overtake them, but now she realised that the bushrangers would probably be moving faster than their pursuers.

Liam came back, frowning. He called both Brian and Brendan to him and gave quick instructions, then turned and said to the group, "There is a police roadblock ahead. You will ride through it and act naturally. No tricks. No funny business. I will be watching from in the bush. If there is any trouble, there will be dead coppers and then I will start hunting you."

Having delivered that chilling threat he walked quickly into the bush on the left of the road, rifle in hand. Brendan went back to the vehicle and got in, his face a study in worry. Brian swallowed and also looked very anxious. The group then sat and waited until Liam gave a single word radio call a few minutes later.

The group moved forward. Kylie found she was sweating and very tense, so tense she found it hard to breathe and became quite dizzy. As the white police vehicles came into view she gulped several deep breaths and steeled herself for action. There were two vehicles she saw, and a horse trailer. Three armed police stood waiting.

I hope it isn't Constable Lonergan again, Kylie thought, convinced now that Norah loved him and not wanting him to be hurt.

It wasn't. She had never seen the three policemen before, but the horse trailer was the same one and she badly wanted to ask if Constable Lonergan was around. Certainly it no longer had any horses in it. But instead she sat silent on her horse while Norah spoke to the police. Kylie tried to make herself appear relaxed and forced a smile but her face felt so plastic that she was sure the police must see it was put on. Through a sort of fog she heard one of the policemen say, "Yes, we've been expecting you. Constable Lonergan said you were coming this way."

As they waited Kylie saw that they were at a road junction, another gravel road leading off downhill to the right. She saw one of the police call on their vehicle radio, presumably to report their arrival. The policeman then stood and looked at them, raising one hand to point at each person in turn.

He is counting us, Kylie thought, her anxiety going up another notch. It went up even further when the policeman walked across and said, "All of you dismount please."

They did as they were told. This put them all on the 'on side' of their mounts, with the horses between them and the three policeman, one of whom stood to one side holding a wicked looking, black automatic weapon, and obviously ready to use it. *He is the one Liam will shoot first,* Kylie thought unhappily. She was sweating now but this almost turned to trembling when she what the first policeman was now doing.

The policeman walked to the first horse in the line, Norah's, and lifted its off-side front leg and peered at the shoe, then tugged at it. With a nod and a grunt he lowered it, then walked around the horse's head to study the brand. That put Kylie into a cold sweat. *That horse Brian is riding isn't one of Mrs Conroy's*, she thought.

The possibility of imminent lethal violence started her trembling, and she broke into a cold sweat. Her stomach churned and she felt giddy, having to grip her saddle for support.

Act normally! she told herself. She watched anxiously as the policeman went around the head of Brian's horse. He then bent to examine the forward off-side leg. *He is looking for the loose horseshoe,* Kylie thought. But would he go back to check the brand?

To block him Kylie moved to stand in the gap between her horse's head and Brian's. As the policeman walked down past Brian's horse her heart hammered wildly. She swallowed to moisten her dry throat and managed to speak, asking, "Are you a mounted policeman too?"

The policeman stopped, facing her, then gestured to Brian's horse. "Don't stand behind a horse, Miss. It might kick."

Fearing her plan had failed, Kylie nodded and stepped back. The policeman did not step through the gap but bent to examine the front hoof of her horse. Once he was satisfied the shoe was not loose he lowered the leg and then looked at her before answering.

"Yes, I'm usually with the Stock Squad at Charters Towers."

He then moved to come around the head of Kylie's horse. As he did, Kylie tried to keep him engaged in conversation so that he would not remember to check the brand on Brian's horse. "What is the Stock Squad?" she asked.

"We investigate the theft of cattle, sheep and horses from properties," the policeman explained. To her great relief he turned left and went past her to reach Blazer's rump. Here he bent to study the brand, then nodded and moved on between her horse and Margaret's.

The policeman worked his way methodically back along the line. Watching him it was obvious to Kylie that he was an expert with horses and knew exactly what he was looking for.

Not once has he walked behind a horse where it could kick him, she noted.

By now he was approaching the horse Liam had been riding. He looked at Dingo and asked, "What is this horse for?"

"Spare saddle horse in case one of the others needs a rest," Dingo answered calmly.

The policeman checked the horseshoe and then moved to the brand. "This has a different brand. Whose and why?" he asked suspiciously.

Kylie went very tense, but Dingo just shrugged and said, "We have several horses on hire. We got this fella from the Atkinsons at Oak Valley."

The policeman pointed to the horse trailer. "What about that one?"

Dingo shrugged again, looking bored. "Just gone a bit lame, that's all. We givin' him a spell, eh?"

The policeman walked down past Mrs Conroy, who still sat in her vehicle, to the trailer. Kylie went all tense again as she watched the policeman open the back and go in. Luckily the horse was on the left side so he could not easily get to see the brand, but he was able to check the foreleg. To Kylie's relief, she saw him reappear and apparently not bother to check the brand. Only then, as she breathed slowly out, did she realise she had been holding her breath and was feeling dizzy as a result.

The policeman walked back past Kylie and called to Norah, "OK, you can keep going, but keep your eyes peeled in case the blasted Kelly Gang appear."

Norah frowned and nodded. "We will keep our eyes open. Thank you." She then turned to the group and told them to mount. As soon as they were all mounted, she urged her horse to start walking again.

Kylie did the same, managing to keep her forced smile on her face as she went past the policemen. Ahead of her she could see that the back of Brian's shirt was soaked in sweat, and he had his left hand down near his saddle bag.

Ready to pull out his gun, she assumed.

Then she heard the policeman ask Dingo, "Where are you going next?"

"Irvinebank, then east through Watsonville," Dingo replied.

The policeman appeared to accept this and nodded. The group rode past him and Stephen even raised a hand in a wave. But then the policeman stopped the horse float and spoke to Mrs Conroy. Once again Kylie broke into a cold seat and gripped her reins tightly. She resisted the temptation to look into the bush for any sight of Liam but she was sure he was there and the thought of that rifle aiming at her caused her skin to prickle in fear.

But it was alright. The policeman waved the vehicle through and they continued on. The last thing Kylie saw was the policeman leaning in the window of his 4WD to talk on the radio.

Once around the next bend the group came to a halt and waited till Liam re-joined them. He came puffing out of the scrub, sweating and scratched but pleased.

He called the other two bushrangers to him and they had a hurried discussion. While they talked Norah sidled over beside Kylie and Margaret. "It's just as well Frank wasn't at that roadblock back there," she said. "He would have become suspicious."

"Why?" Margaret asked.

"Because we should have turned right and gone down that other road into Silver Valley."

"Where does this road lead?" Kylie asked.

"Over Mt Misery to Irvinebank," Norah replied.

Kylie looked ahead and noted a larger than usual hill looming up a few kilometres ahead. Pointing to it she asked, "Is that Mt Misery?"

Norah looked, then nodded. "I think so. Hello, what gives now?"

The three bushrangers had separated. Liam went to his horse and swung into the saddle and Brendan went back to Mrs Conroy's vehicle. This came edging past, a very worried looking Mrs Conroy driving carefully. She gave Norah an anxious frown as she passed. The vehicle then accelerated and quickly vanished from sight ahead of them.

As Brian remounted Kylie asked, "Why did the vehicle go on ahead Brian?"

Brian just looked at her and looked unhappy. "Liam's orders," he answered shortly. Then he gestured to Norah to ride on.

The road wound on along the ridge top, or sometimes on a bench cut on the side of steeper rocky knolls. It was still very dry and rugged country and the bulk of Mt Misery looked larger all the time. Kylie saw that it was actually only one of a line of higher peaks which stretched right across their front for many kilometres and that the ridge they were on led directly up to its crest. They began passing signs of old tin mines and abandoned settlements, and passed another gravel road which went steeply down another ridge into a large valley on her right. She presumed this was Silver Valley and Norah confirmed this.

"The Dry River runs south along it," she explained. "It is the valley we rode along on the second day."

Kylie nodded and then marvelled. It was now only Day 5 but it seemed like weeks.

At Margaret's request they halted to allow a toilet break. As Kylie stiffly hobbled into the bush she was again seized by temptation to sneak away and escape. *I could go down the mountain to the Silver Valley Road,* she thought. *There is water there, and some houses. I could get help.* But then she thought of Graham and Peter and rejected the idea. *Besides, they might actually do horrible things to Norah and Margaret,* she thought unhappily.

So she rejoined the group, remounted and rode on. Ten minutes later they crested Mt Misery and she marvelled at the view. Off to the south she could see a vast expanse of country, rugged hills, then a huge, flat plain, then more distant hills. To her right she looked along the main range and now learned it was actually the Great Dividing Range; the streams on her left flowing west into the Gulf of Carpentaria. To her right she could see distant peaks which had clouds over them, and which looked black. These she was told by Brain were part of the Herberton Range and the dark colouring was rain forest.

Thinking of Herberton made Kylie feel wistful and she just wished the horrible experience would all end soon, before it turned into a nightmare. They rode on along the crest, the country ahead appearing even more rugged and jumbled than ever, line after line of hills and mountains which seemed to stretch on forever.

11 o'clock came and went as they reached an overgrown turn-off on the right. Here they went left and dropped down off the crest onto a bench cut which wound down into a steep-sided valley. By then Kylie was feeling saddle sore and tired. Glances at the others told her that Stephen was also suffering, continually shifting in his saddle, and looking very unhappy.

I wonder how far we are going? she thought.

Suddenly Brian snatched up his radio and held it to his ear. "Say again," he called into it. Kylie saw him listen, worry clouding his face. Then he turned and called to Liam, "Did you hear that Liam?"

"Bits of it," Liam called back. "What did Brendan say?"

"He is just coming into Irvinebank, and he says there are half a dozen armed coppers there and they are telling him to stop," Brian answered.

Both bushrangers now lifted their radios to their ears and strained to listen. After another anxious minute Brian asked, "Will I call Brendan and ask what is happening?"

"No fear," Liam answered. "That will only alert the coppers. We will have to go to our other plan."

Chapter 23

INTO THE HILLS

As Kylie listened, she heard the voice on Brian's radio crackle faintly the words: "Got us."

"The coppers have got them!" Brian cried, his face a mask of worry.

"Then we need to hide, and fast," Liam said. "That bloody helicopter will be here soon looking for us. Start riding!"

Liam pointed down the road and urged them all to move. Kylie's first instinct was to refuse but Liam looked so angry that her resolution melted and she used her heels to urge Blazer into a trot. Even this wasn't enough for Liam and he shouted at them to canter.

Norah objected to that. "It's not safe on this rough road," she cried. "The horses might slip and be injured."

"Bugger your horses! Ride!" Liam shouted, waving his rifle.

But Norah refused and kept her speed to a trot. Kylie found this very uncomfortable but not nearly as much as Stephen obviously did. She saw him clinging on with one hand while trying to hold his glasses on with the other. And it was dangerous. The surface of the gravel road had many washouts and rills and there were lots of loose stones. Several times horses lost their footing and nearly fell. Once it was Blazer and she stumbled so close to the edge of the road that Kylie could see over and down the steep slope below. A wave of cold shock swept over her and she found her heart hammering furiously.

Five minutes of this had them a kilometre down the mountain and close to the bottom of the valley. As Kylie looked around she noted that steep, V-shaped slopes reared up on each side and that a canopy of leaves gave some sort of cover from air observation.

Stephen glanced up at the clear blue sky and grunted. "Won't do any good if the chopper has infra-red surveillance gear on it," he commented.

At the bottom of the slope was a dry creek bed full of black stones and some patches of sand. There was no water. The road ran along close beside this. Liam kept them trotting and cantering along for about another kilometre before abruptly signalling to halt.

Dismounting, he levelled the rifle at them and shouted, "Get off! Get off and walk. And take these bloody helmets off. Brian, lead the way."

Kylie did as she was told, glad to stretch her legs and to ease the numb chafing in her buttocks. "Where are we going?" she asked Brian as he led his horse past her and down into the dry creek bed.

"Murphy's Luck Mine," Brian answered.

Liam heard that and became furiously angry. "Shut up Brian, you bloody drongo! Stop giving away all our secrets to your little girlfriend!"

Brian blushed and bit his lip, then continued walking. One by one they followed him: Kylie, Margaret, Norah, Stephen, Roger, Dingo and then Liam and the spare horse. They turned right and went up into another steep sided valley. There was no road in this, and they had to push through knee high dry grass. As she walked along Kylie licked her lips and wished she could have a drink as she was now feeling very hot and dehydrated.

"When we get there," Brian answered when she made this request.

She made a face to show she wasn't impressed, then continued on, her horse's reins in her right hand and the helmet dangling in her left. The order to remove the helmets she understood. Into her mind came images of a line of white helmets stretching back along the trail as they had ridden along.

They would be very conspicuous from the air, she decided. She also understood how effective they had been as a disguise at the police roadblock for Brian and Brendan.

For the next ten minutes they made their way slowly uphill beside another dry creek. The valley sides became steeper and steeper, and Kylie began to note signs of an old mine: piles of eroded earth, rusty corrugated iron, broken bottles, fence posts, and holes in the hillside. She noted that they were actually following a long disused track, overgrown and washed out in places. They came to a rusty, old, barbed wire fence and passed through it via a wire gate that Brian opened and closed behind them.

Another five minutes walking brought them to what was almost a gorge. Several mango trees grew there, providing shade and cover. As the group halted under them, she saw that there was a pool of water down in the creek to her right. It wasn't much of a pool, the water only knee deep and slimy with algae and moss, but water all the same. On her left, dug into the side of the hill, was the remains of an old hut, all rotted and rusted and fallen down. In the hillside beyond it was the dark entrance to a mine tunnel.

"We off-saddle here," Liam ordered.

They did as they were told. The saddles were then lugged up to the mine entrance. Liam pointed in. "Put them in there," he said. "And those white helmets."

Kylie looked in and hesitated. The tunnel was only just wide enough for a man to walk into and about as tall. It had been dug out of the mountain side but appeared to have no supports. "It doesn't look very safe," she said.

"Just don't bump the roof supports," Liam replied with a sneer.

Brian went first and placed his saddle and bridle twenty paces in. He then came back and held out his hands. "I'll take yours Kylie," he offered.

That put Kylie in a real quandary. Her initial reaction was to refuse but he looked so hurt and down that she relented and handed her things over to him. "Thanks," she mumbled.

That drew a sneer from Stephen and sympathetic looks from Margaret and Norah. Liam then indicated the others should go in. As Stephen went to enter the mine Liam stopped him.

"Where's your helmet?" he asked.

Stephen looked mystified and shrugged. "Don't know. I must have dropped it."

At that, Liam swore. "You little mongrel!" he snarled, lashing out with his left fist.

Stephen tried to duck but was too late. The blow took him on the side of the head and sent him sprawling. Kylie was horrified and would have intervened, but Brian stood in front of her and kept Norah and Margaret back as well.

Norah pushed forward. "There's no need for that!" she cried hotly.

Liam glared at her. "Yes, there is! You kids need to realise we mean business. And I don't appreciate people who drop things to make it easier for the coppers to track us. Now, you lot sit in the mine. Brian, you stand guard outside, and don't let your little girlfriends talk you into letting them escape. And you!" he smacked Stephen again, just as he struggled to his feet. "Lead me back to where you dropped the helmet."

Stephen stepped back and glared angrily at Liam, blinking behind glasses that were awry. "What if I don't?" he challenged.

"Then I will beat you to a pulp," Liam snarled. "Now get moving!"

Stephen moved. Brian stood and watched, anxiety and indecision all over his face as he was left alone with the group. "Sit inside the mine," he ordered, but he did not sound very confident.

Kylie was surprised at Stephen's plan, and at his bravery and defiance. Her admiration for him went up a distinct notch. She was also angry at how Liam had beaten him and at the ugly threats, so she was in no mood to obey.

"What if we don't?" she challenged.

Her question made Brian look quite sick. He licked his lips nervously and hefted his rifle, but that only betrayed his state of mind.

He won't shoot me, Kylie decided.

Brian again pointed into the mine. "Go in please. If you don't then Liam will bash me too."

At that, Kylie gave up and moved inside, followed by Margaret and a very reluctant Roger. But not Norah. She stood her ground. "You should help us escape," she said. "If you do that and then give yourself up, it will help you get less time in jail after you are caught."

Brian looked even sicker as he digested this. The thought of Brian going to jail appalled Kylie, but she agreed.

"Do it Brian, please!" she cried.

"I can't!" Brian cried, obviously torn.

"You can," Kylie cried back, tears starting. "Don't you love me?"

At that, Brian looked distressed. "I do!" he said, "But I can't do it."

"Why not?" Kylie challenged. "What have we done to hurt you?"

Brian looked unhappy and Norah again spoke. "We will speak up for you at your trial," she said.

But Brian shook his head and Kylie saw the argument had failed. "I can't rat on my own family," he replied. "Now sit down."

Several minutes went by. It was still and cool in the mine for which Kylie was thankful as she had been really feeling the heat out in the sun. As she waited, she wondered what to do and kept glancing at Brian and at her friends. She also peered into the blackness further in and wondered where the mine tunnel went. At the top of her mind were her conflicting emotions over Brian.

Do I love him? she wondered, *and does he love me?*

It was all very unsettling and brought the tears to her eyes again. It felt as though a wonderful picture of love and romance had been somehow fractured and she felt anxious and sad.

Liam and Stephen returned, both puffing and streaming with sweat. Liam had the offending helmet in his left hand, and he tossed it angrily into the mine, narrowly missing Kylie and Roger as he did.

"Okay, get out and get the rest of the gear," he snapped.

He was obviously now in a very bad temper and Stephen had a big bruise forming on his cheek, indicating he had been struck again. That made Kylie even angrier, but she hid her feelings and moved to obey.

Soon all the gear had been hidden except water bottles and the weapons. Norah pointed at the horses and said, "What now?"

"We walk," Liam answered, pointing up the steep slope.

"What about the horses?" Norah asked.

"They stay here," Liam replied.

"But they are ours!" Norah said, plainly concerned. "They are valuable animals."

"They've all got brands, haven't they?" Liam countered. "So you can get them back later. They will be safe enough here. There's plenty of grass and water."

Norah wasn't happy but had to give in. She insisted on a break while the girls once again went to the toilet one at a time. Kylie had a big drink, noting with concern that her water bottle was now half-empty.

"Is it far?" she asked. "I don't have much water left."

"There's water along the way," Liam answered. He opened his mouth to say more but then stopped, listening. A moment later he pointed to the mine. "Get under cover! Get back in the mine! Quick! Move!"

Reluctantly Kylie did so. She could hear the sound now and knew it was a helicopter. From inside the mine she glimpsed it pass the bottom end of the valley, flying in the direction of Irvinebank. Liam watched it go and then studied the girl's clothes.

"We need to do something about those bright colours," he said.

Kylie understood exactly what he meant. She was wearing a pale blue shirt and blue jeans, but Margaret had a yellow top and Norah wore a white, long-sleeved shirt. Roger and Stephen, in contrast, wore drab hiking shirts; Roger's dark green and Stephen's a dull grey.

"What can we do?" Norah replied. "All our other clothes are in the vehicle."

Liam pointed down to the creek. "Wash them in mud," he ordered.

Both Norah and Margaret looked shocked. "No! That will spoil my top," Margaret protested.

Liam took a pace towards her and put his face down close to hers. Kylie saw that it was mottled with anger. "Either do it yourself or I will carry you down and roll you in the mud while you are still wearing it," he snarled.

Both Margaret and Norah looked outraged, and Kylie seethed but there was no doubt that Liam meant what he said. Reluctantly both girls clambered down over the rocks to the creek bed. Once there Margaret hesitated.

"Don't look!" she called.

"Oh get on with it!" Liam spat back, but he did turn his back, muttering to Brian as he did, "Hasn't got any tits to show off anyway!"

That made Kylie even angrier, and she began to feel a deep resentment that made her determined to see Liam caught. As Brian did nothing to intervene, she gave him a reproachful look, wondering if he was really the man she thought him to be. Her feelings must have transmitted themselves to him as he gave her anxious looks and fidgeted continually.

Norah and Margaret unbuttoned their shirts and reluctantly peeled them off, hunching forward to hide themselves as they did. Looking very unhappy they rolled and sloshed the shirts in a pool of brown mud. As Margaret lifted hers out she sniffed and shook her head. "Oh yuk!" she muttered. Kylie glanced and caught her eye. Margaret returned a wry grimace and then gingerly tugged the sopping garment on.

"Hurry up!" Liam snapped at them. To Brian he commented, "We have a few minutes before that chopper returns."

"Do you think it will find us?" Brian asked.

Liam shook his head and tried to look confident. "No. They don't know which road we followed so they will have to check them all. And they will be looking for white helmets and horses. So we walk. You lead. Go straight up that re-entrant there. I will come last to make sure these kids don't try to play Hansel and Gretel and leave a trail for the coppers to follow."

Brian nodded, gave Kylie one more wistful look, and then started climbing up a steep little side valley. The bed of this was a jumble of black rocks of all sizes. A fair growth of small trees and bushes grew among these or beside the stream bed. As the small creek was dry and shut off from any wind the air was fiercely hot. Within a few minutes Kylie had sweat pouring from all her pores and was puffing hard.

"Oh! I'm not used to this!" she groaned as they plodded upwards.

None of them were and even Liam's angry urging could not keep them moving. Every hundred or so steps they all ground to a panting, gasping halt. Kylie began looking up and around, hoping to see the top. All the way along they kept passing signs of past mining activity: heaps of soil, small tunnel entrances, bench cuts, pieces of rusty iron, broken bottles and porcelain.

In ordinary circumstances Kylie would have found these interesting but now she just noted them with a sort of dull resignation. Only the threat of Liam's fist and gun kept her moving. Every time she glanced back at him, she met his eyes and she began to feel he was watching her every move. She also noted he kept continually scanning the surrounding slopes and the sky. She herself was hoping that the police helicopter would come back and find them but it did not.

Roger was also having a hard time of it. He puffed and panted and groaned. Finally he came to a gasping standstill, leaning on a rock.

Liam came up and pointed up the slope. "Get a move on, Fatty," he snarled.

That made Kylie really feel for Roger. She knew he was very sensitive about his weight and build and the comment made her dislike Liam even more. "Are you alright Roger?" she asked.

"Yes. Just getting my breath back," he replied, giving Liam a resentful glance as he did.

While they were stopped Kylie leaned on a rock beside her, an action she quickly regretted as it was hot to the touch. She was now licking dry lips and really feeling the sun on her bare head and face. *I wish I had a hat,* she thought.

Soon after that she was reminded of another lesson in bush safety in that environment. She saw Brian suddenly jump back and glimpsed a flicker of movement. Brian almost fell but managed to grab a tree.

"What is it?" Liam called.

"Bloody snake," Brian replied, staring anxiously over the top of the rock. "A yellow bellied black. He was just lying on top of the rock sunning himself."

That made Kylie feel anxious as she had been reaching up to use rocks to help her climb. She resolved to look first in future. As she stood there, she met Roger's eyes and he muttered, "Pity it didn't bite the bugger."

Kylie felt hurt at that because she was now really torn over what she felt for Brian. "It would give us a real problem getting him to a doctor," she said.

"I'd leave him," Roger replied.

As he spoke to her, he reached across and deliberately snapped off a small branch and left it hanging. Kylie at once understood what he was doing, and she glanced back to see if Liam had noticed.

"Shh!" Roger cautioned, before turning to resume the climb.

Kylie was again struck by admiration for how resourceful and brave her friends were and she resolved to also help leave a trail for the trackers to follow. She was hopeful they would be on their tracks but wasn't sure if they could track across a rocky hillside or up the rocky creek bed. Surreptitiously she broke a small twig, her heart beating with the dare.

Margaret quickly cottoned on to what they were doing and also began breaking small branches. It wasn't long before Liam saw one of these hanging down. He stopped and looked at it and Kylie, who was glancing back to watch him, felt her heart skip with anxiety.

Liam stopped and shouted angrily, "Hoy! You bloody kids, stop snapping off branches. If I see you snap one, I will break your bloody arm. Now keep moving."

Kylie met Roger's eye and he gave a sly grin before resuming the climb. "That will do for a bit," he muttered to her.

On they climbed, the valley getting smaller all the time until it became just a steep-sided fold in the hillside. By then they were near the top of the hill and Kylie began to get glimpses down the valley and across a nearby saddle to other hills beyond.

Roger came to a panting stop near her and then looked around. "Going north," he commented quietly as they paused yet again for another breather.

That meant little to Kylie but certainly increased her admiration for Roger. *If he can keep his wits about him at a time like this, he is alright!* she thought.

Roger then gestured towards Brian, who was now nearing the crest. "He's not much of a scout," Roger commented. "He should be at least a hundred paces ahead of us in this sort of country. He would never give us enough warning to avoid a trap."

As Roger was a corporal in the army cadets and did a field exercise at least once a month, Kylie listened to his opinion with respect. It made her hopeful that they might walk into the arms of waiting police. But her thoughts on rescue were focused on the mysterious blacktrackers whom she hoped were hot on their trail. To Kylie's distress and confusion, she found herself torn between wanting the bushrangers caught and not wanting Brian to be.

They came abruptly to the crest of the hill, or rather onto the crest of a ridge connecting two hills. The country was all open savannah woodland and for a minute or so Kylie had a vista of seemingly endless hills stretching out ahead of her. Seeing that gave her an awful sense of being isolated and of being lost in a vast wilderness. That sent her morale down another notch. It reinforced in her mind the vastness and emptiness of Australia.

After only the briefest of pauses they crossed the ridge, and an overgrown vehicle track which ran along it, and began descending another re-entrant into a similar steep-sided and deep valley.

Kylie kept hoping that the helicopter would return and find them but there was neither sight, nor sound, of it. Going down she found harder than going up, at least on her leg muscles. These all had to be thrown into reverse and soon began to complain and ache. She also became very thirsty and hot and said so. "I need a drink," she complained loudly.

"We all do," Stephen added, "Or we will get heat exhaustion."

"Stop moaning and walk," Liam growled. "You will get water at the bottom of this hill."

They did, twenty minutes later, but it was brackish, dirty water from a pool at the end of an old mine tunnel. The water was easy to get but Kylie was very unwilling to drink it. So were the others.

Stephen looked at it with a very dubious expression on his face. "Didn't they use chemicals like cyanide and mercury to separate the precious metals? We could get poisoned." he said.

"Just drink," Liam snapped. "We've been drinking it for weeks. It won't hurt you."

Reluctantly they did. Kylie had to force herself to suck it down and almost gagged at the gritty, stale taste. But it did make her feel better and a rinse of her face felt very refreshing. Sweat had been bringing perspiration into her eyes and the salt in that was stinging them. Washing that away was a relief.

They rested there for fifteen minutes. During that time Margaret took off her boots and examined large blisters that had developed on each heel. Kylie could also feel blisters developing and was feeling sore and stressed. The only thing that gave her a spurt of malicious satisfaction was noting that both Liam and Brian were also looking tired and footsore. Neither Roger nor Stephen seemed affected, but that did not surprise Kylie.

They do a lot of hiking with Graham, she told herself. *They are more used to this.*

Liam hoisted himself to his feet and gestured to them to get up. "Start moving," he ordered.

"Where are we going?" Margaret asked.

"You'll see," Liam replied.

Kylie now asked the question that had been bothering her since sunrise. "Will we be joining Graham and Peter?"

Liam just shrugged, then said, "You'll see. Now start walking."

Chapter 24

TORN LOYALTIES

The next stage of the journey was along the floor of a valley. The valley had been very extensively mined by open-cut methods and was mostly large areas of bare gravel and reddish clay. Steep, savannah covered hills rose up, seemingly on all sides. A maze of old vehicle tracks criss-crossed the area and the group followed one of these. The direction was still northerly. Kylie could tell that, now that she thought about it, as the afternoon sun was blazing down on the left side of her face. She knew she was getting horribly sunburnt and felt very dry and sore. The walking was easy enough but Kylie was getting tired and hungry and just wanted it all to stop.

As before Brian scouted ahead, but not far enough according to Roger, who sneered at the gang's bushcraft and fieldcraft skills. "If it wasn't for you girls being in their power I would just slip away," he commented quietly.

The criticism of Brian hurt and Kylie knew she had fallen in the estimation of her friends. That stung and made her feel even more miserable.

They must be wondering if I can be trusted, she thought ruefully.

A few minutes later Kylie saw Brian stop, then come hurrying back. "The road is just up ahead," he said to Liam.

Road? Kylie wondered, looking around.

For the last ten minutes they had been walking in a deep valley between two steep-sided hills. A dry creek bed was on their left. Ahead she now noted a line of trees and, looming above them, another, even larger hill that seemed to bar their progress.

Liam went forward to look, then came back. He stood facing them and said, "The main road is just up ahead. We are going to go fast and cross it at the run. On the other side we go straight up the hillside, and we go fast. If you hear a vehicle, then hide behind a tree or you will regret it."

"You wouldn't shoot us," Norah said defiantly.

"No, maybe not, but I might shoot the people in the vehicle, especially if they are coppers," Liam answered.

That was a sickening thought. Knowing her friends as well as she did Kylie was sure none would want to have the blood of an innocent person on their hands. But it made her dislike Liam all the more.

The group walked forward until the other road was just visible through long, dust-coated, dry grass. To Kylie's surprise it was only a gravel road. Having heard Liam call it the main road had caused her to assume it would be bitumen.

As they walked down to the road junction Stephen looked both ways along the main road, then muttered, "This is the Herberton to Irvinebank Road. Irvinebank is only a 'K' or so to the left."

Brian heard this and snapped, "Stop talking to each other and get a move on!"

Stephen turned to curl his lip at him but stopped talking. Kylie then noted that he and Roger seemed to be making a point of walking in the dustiest patches of road. *Are they making tracks deliberately?* she wondered, noting how obvious the line of footprints was. It certainly seemed to her that the two bushrangers were not aware of the tracks and did not seem to be taking any particular care to hide their trail.

Maybe they think we are far enough away and won't be tracked? she thought. But she did not give any hint to Brian and that hurt too. Now she was really feeling her loyalties torn both ways!

They crossed the road one at a time, drawing more sardonic sneers from both Stephen and Roger, who muttered, "The best way to cross this is all in extended line, side by side, and all at once."

As she crossed the graded gravel, Kylie looked both ways along it, fearing, yet hoping, to hear an approaching vehicle. None came and she reluctantly slid down into a small, steep-sided dry creek bed. Then it was up another very steep slope, this one almost devoid of grass.

She half expected the bushrangers to at least brush out their tracks where they crossed the road, but they did not. They just looked anxiously in both directions. Liam kept snapping at the friends to climb faster. Not that they could for long. All were soon puffing too much and they came to a panting standstill only a hundred paces up from the road. Even Liam and Brian were unable to keep climbing but had to pause to get their breath back.

Then it was on upwards. Until they were out of sight of the road, Liam kept harrying them and making threats. With almost no ground cover Kylie found it easy to see where she was putting her feet but she found it hard to get a grip on the stony soil because of a scattering of deadfall. This was mostly sticks and leaves from the ironbarks that dotted the hill slope.

As they struggled on up, puffing and plodding slowly, boots slipping as often as not, Kylie saw that Margaret was looking very drawn. A glance at Norah revealed that she appeared to be swaying and staggering.

I hope they are alright, she worried.

The heat was now intense, with the afternoon sun striking at them and the hills blocking the breeze. Kylie sweated and panted. She drained the last of her water from her hand-held water bottle and then licked lips that were starting to crack. It was all turning into something of an ordeal, and she hoped it would soon end.

Finally Norah came to a puffing standstill, leaning on a tree and looking very pale. "I can't go on without a rest," she panted.

"Keep moving!" Liam snapped.

At that, Kylie saw red. "Don't be stupid!" she snapped. "We will all collapse with heat exhaustion next, and where will that get you? We need a rest, and we need more water."

Reluctantly Liam assented, but only by grunting and stopping his threats. He and Brian both stood to one side and Kylie heard them muttering. "Where is the nearest water?" Brian asked.

"Have to go to Ryan's mine," Liam answered.

"Can he be trusted?" Brian asked.

Liam shrugged and then replied, "We will have to take that risk. I will warn him to keep his trap shut."

On hearing the ugly threat, Kylie felt even more dislike for Liam, but knowing that they were heading for water cheered her. She slumped down beside Margaret. For the next few minutes they rested. This was briefly interrupted by the sound of a vehicle down on the road they had crossed but it was completely hidden from view by the tree canopy. Even so Liam snarled at them to hide behind trees. Kylie reluctantly moved, her eyes questing through the gaps in the canopy, but she saw no sign of the vehicle.

A few minutes later, Liam ordered them to get up and move.

Reluctantly, for she was now feeling both exhausted and chafed, Kylie did so. Margaret and the boys stood up but Norah looked exhausted and only struggled up with Margaret's help. They then plodded slowly on up the hill.

Within a hundred paces the slope began to level out and they came to another ridge top. Yet another old vehicle track ran along this, two wheel tracks in the dry grass, and obviously disused for a long time. Liam stopped and looked around, unsure which way to go. That gave Kylie some sardonic pleasure, but she could understand his doubts: whichever way she looked there seemed to be deep valleys and steep, rugged hills.

Liam finally chose to go right, and they trudged along a gently rising ridge top for several hundred metres before the track angled left down across a very distinct saddle. On the other side they came to a track junction and once again Liam appeared to be unsure. At length he chose left and they set off that way.

This track began to descend steeply down a ridge with a very steep-sided re-entrant on the left and a huge valley opening out ahead. After a couple of hundred paces Liam stopped them and shook his head.

"Sorry, must be the other way," he muttered.

"Bloody drongo!" Roger muttered, but took care that neither bushranger overheard him.

Kylie understood. *If it was Graham or any of the boys, they would have their maps out and be using a compass,* she thought.

So they sweated back up the steep ridge, exposed to the full glare of the afternoon sun on their backs. It took two stops before they arrived back at the track junction. By now Kylie just wanted to flop down and rest and she insisted they have a break while she went to the toilet.

To do so Liam took all three girls. They went back down the track for fifty paces until out of sight of the others. He allowed the girls to crouch behind bushes where he could see their heads. As before Kylie was strongly tempted to try to slip away but fear of retribution on her friends made her stay.

Brian had also been off to the toilet with the boys. On his return Kylie studied him, noting again his ruggedly handsome profile and sparkling eyes. But now he seemed drained and down and he did not smile when she met his eyes.

Do I still like him? Kylie wondered.

For a minute or so memories of those wonderful moments of pure romance engulfed her and her emotions rose until she was near to tears.

She felt a deep need to talk to him, to find out what he really felt for her, but that was not possible with the angry Liam and her friends all sitting close by. What she was sure of was that she really wanted to find true love, to live the romance. So she clung to the memories of those glorious minutes, and of his loving words.

He said he loves me and wants to see me again, she told herself by way of comfort.

Then it was on along the track. For the next kilometre it wasn't too bad. They plodded along a bench cut to another saddle, then around the lower slopes of a distinct hill to yet another track junction. This time it was left with no hesitation and on northwards along a ridge so narrow and steep sided she understood the term 'razorback' when Stephen used it.

While plodding along the ridge Roger nodded to the right and whispered, "I think that is the Herberton Road down there."

Kylie looked when Liam was not watching her. Hundreds of metres below and about half a kilometre away she saw a wide gravel road winding along the bottom of the valley. The road went past a distant cluster of buildings beside a large area of bare ground and on eastwards over rolling, bush covered hills towards distant mountains.

"That looks like a mine," Kylie muttered to Margaret and Stephen.

"I think it is on the Herberton Road," Stephen replied. "I remember seeing something like that last time my oldies drove out here on one of their weekend history trips."

"If we could get there, they should have a phone," Margaret suggested hopefully.

But it wasn't to be. Liam noted them looking and gave them a snarl and a warning glance. He hefted his rifle to indicate he meant business and Kylie felt even sicker and more depressed. Once again, she felt her loyalties being torn. Half of her wanted to help her friends but the other half wanted most desperately for Brian to escape and be safe. But seeing the distant building really hurt.

To be so close to possible help! she thought unhappily.

On the next knoll they turned left and followed yet another old, overgrown road. This also ran along a ridge top, gently descending and travelling northwest. By this time Kylie was sure she would not be able to walk much further as her tongue seemed to be swollen and her throat dry. But Norah was visibly worse, stumbling and puffing and looking very pale.

Stephen gave Norah the last of his water and then said accusingly to Liam, "You had better find us water fast or Norah is going to collapse from heat stroke. That could be fatal in these conditions."

Liam glared at him but looked both baffled and guilty. Obviously, this had not been factored into the bushranger's plan. They had another rest, slumped into the pitiful shade of an ironbark and enjoying the faint breeze that was stirring.

"Half past four," Stephen announced, after checking his watch. "Only a couple of hours to sunset."

That annoyed Liam too but stung him to making them get up and move. Reluctantly Kylie hoisted herself up, her aching muscles and blistered feet sharply complaining. They continued on, still downwards and almost directly into the setting sun.

The track along the ridge dipped ever steeper and became difficult to walk safely along without continually slipping on loose stones. The track was eroded and overgrown and had obviously not been used in years. They came to yet another track junction and Liam opted to go straight ahead. Two hundred metres further on he took a left turn at still another junction. Then the track went even steeper down the spine of a spur which ran west.

All along the way they kept passing old mines. Some were half-filled tunnel entrances which led directly off the track while others were marked by heaps of old spoil. There seemed to be an old mine every fifty paces or so, along with the usual scattering of rusty sheet iron and iron objects and broken glass. Several times they stopped without orders to peer into one of the mines and both Roger and Stephen muttered about exploring.

"Might still be a few old bottles around here," Stephen added, his eyes looking hopefully around. Kylie knew that Stephen's parents, both schoolteachers and keen amateur historians, had quite a collection of such artefacts. For a few minutes it made their ordeal seem almost ordinary, until she looked at Brian and felt the sharp tugging of her heart. But she was also very aware that this was real drama and that the ones she loved was in great danger.

Abruptly Liam halted them and pointed left. "That way," he ordered.

Kylie had been too intent on watching where she was putting her feet to look around, but she now saw that a much better vehicle track came up the slope to where they stood, and then went left. This side track ran across the side of a hill on a bench cut and ended in a small fold in the hillside. Below the fold the re-entrant was half filled by the tailings of a mine. Most of the stones and soil looked very old but there was some new soil spread down the slope.

Parked at the end of the bench cut was a battered old grey Land Rover. Just beyond it was the mine entrance. Liam ordered them to sit and told Brian to guard them while he looked for Ryan. Kylie thankfully lowered herself down, noting that Norah and Margaret just flopped down. Not so the boys. Stephen and Roger both peered at the mine entrance with great interest and began muttering about similar mines they had seen the previous year at Stannary Hills. The entrance was only about a metre wide and two high, a mere slit in the side of the hill and it appeared to have no supports or shoring that Kylie could see.

"That doesn't look very safe," she commented. "I wouldn't like to work in there."

"Me neither," Stephen agreed. "Roger might though. He's the real underground expert."

Roger snorted and said, "Pig's bum!" so vehemently that it raised a tired smile.

Five minutes went by before Liam re-appeared. With him was a chubby man in his twenties with a friendly but anxious, round face. He wore filthy jeans and a yellow pullover that was almost exactly the same colour of the soil being dug from the mine. The man was not introduced but Kylie assumed he was Ryan.

It was also obvious he was not keen on doing what Liam asked. "I could get into real trouble," he complained. "If the coppers find out I could go to jail."

"So tell them we forced you," Liam retorted, "Now drive us to our camp."

Still muttering Ryan climbed into the cab. Liam pointed into the open tray back of the Land Rover and snapped at the friends, "Get in!"

That took Kylie some doing as her muscles had begun to cramp and the climb was just too high to be easy. As she struggled to get up Brian swung aboard and then held out his hand. For a few seconds Kylie stared at it, her mind racing.

Do I snub him and reject the offer? she wondered. What she was now torn over was worry about what her friends would think.

In the end she took the offered hand, but when she saw the anxious little smile that Brian gave her in return she experienced a wave of emotion and felt even more unsure of which side she wanted to win. A sour look from Stephen and a slight shake of the head by Margaret upset her even more so she looked away, giving Brian a defiant little smile.

Once they were all in, seated on the litter of dirt, tools, lengths of rope and pieces of chain and steel wire, Ryan started the engine and slowly reversed the vehicle back along the bench cut. That was not an experience that Kylie enjoyed as she could see right down the steep side of the re-entrant. She comforted herself by the thought that Ryan must do the same thing every day.

Once out at the main track the Land Rover was turned and headed down the hill. The track was so rough that each jolt bounced Kylie and the others so that they cried out and had to clutch at each other and the sides to stop being thrown around. In doing so Kylie found Brian tossed hard against her. He apologised, sensing her mood, and tried to move away but another bump threw him back again. This time she stayed pressed against him, still clinging to her hopes and comforted by his presence.

In this manner the vehicle made a slow, low gear descent of the hill. Kylie was scared and bruised but still glad as it was easier than walking. *I don't think I could have walked much further,* she thought, ruefully aware of her blisters and chafing. She was also feeling very sick from the sunburn and dehydration so that the beginnings of a severe headache were starting.

Ten minutes of this had them at the bottom of the ridge, on another dirt road that wound its way along the bed of yet another steep-sided valley. Stephen's watch said 5:30 and for that Kylie was relieved as it meant the sun would soon be gone. In fact, as they drove slowly along, they passed into the shadow of yet another big hill. The relief was immediate. This was helped by the faint breeze from the vehicle's forward motion.

After another few minutes, however, they came back out into the sun, the road leaving the larger hills and winding along beside quite a large creek bed. This even had a couple of shallow, scummy looking pools in it and in places had stretches of white sand in its tree-lined bed. Roger suggested they were now heading almost west and the sun bore this out.

After a few minutes, the Land Rover was turned to the right onto a track that was just two wheel ruts in the long grass. It followed this for perhaps a hundred metres before the track turned abruptly left and dipped down across the bed of the creek. This was just near a largish pool. Up under the big paperbarks on the other bank Kylie saw horses and a small tent.

The vehicle ground up the bank, the incline so steep that everyone in the tray had to cling on or fall in a heap against the tailboard. Again Kylie found Brian pressed hard against her and she wasn't sure if she wanted that. Once up on the level the Land Rover stopped. As it did Kylie looked around but all she could see were four or five horses tethered under the trees and the small tent. There was no-one in sight.

Then, from behind a tree, stepped one of the Kelly Gang in full armour and pointing a rifle at them. *It is the bushranger's camp,* Kylie thought, not sure if she was glad or anxious.

When the Kelly Gang member saw who it was he lowered his rifle and took off his helmet. Kylie saw that it was the man named Dan. From behind another tree stepped another bushranger, the one named Pat. Liam climbed out to talk to them.

Dan frowned and asked, "What happened Liam? Where are the horses?"

Liam told him, causing Dan to frown even more. He looked thoughtful, then said, "I dunno what Phil wants. You'd better go over to Mont... er... to his camp in Ryan's truck here and ask him." With that he turned to the back of the vehicle and snarled, "You lot all get out, and no funny business. Brian, sit 'em over under that tree and tie them up."

Brian nodded, then turned to help Kylie down. She accepted gratefully as all her muscles had now stiffened up and she felt very weak and sore. Sighing with relief she hobbled over to the indicated tree and sat down. Then she looked around, hoping to see Graham or Peter. But there was no sign of them, and her hopes went down again.

Norah remained clinging to the vehicle after climbing down. "Drink and toilet," she insisted.

"One at a time," Dan replied. "Pat, you and Brian, guard them. Make sure they don't slip away."

Norah went first, hobbling slowly down the creek bank out of sight, with Pat following as guard. The others joined Kylie under the tree. Brain brought them water bags and cups and then went to collect rope. While the water was shared around Dan, Liam and Ryan had an argument. This was settled by Dan, who snarled and tapped his rifle, "If you know what is good for you, you will just do what we want."

With obvious reluctance Ryan nodded and climbed back into his vehicle. Liam climbed into the passenger seat. The vehicle's engine roared into life and it drove on along the track. Dan then moved to look at the prisoners and to quizzing Brian about the details of their trek.

Norah returned and was tied up by one leg. Margaret was next to go to the toilet. On her return Kylie struggled painfully to her feet and limped down the bank and into the bushes. She was hotly aware that Pat was only ten paces behind. She hobbled down into the creek bed and along it, looking for a suitable bush to hide behind.

When she saw one up ahead, she turned and said, "Wait there please."

Pat also blushed and nodded. He replied, "Don't fret little girlie, I ain't a pervert." With that he turned his back and walked a few paces further away. He was gentleman enough to stay back just out of sight when she actually pulled down her trousers. Even so Kylie found it very embarrassing and she had trouble making herself start.

As she was relieving herself she heard the sound of horse's hooves up on the flat. *More of the gang?* she wondered. She stood up and did up her trousers, blushing because Pat was still standing only twenty paces away.

Getting back up the steep bank through the belt of trees was almost beyond her, so stiff and cramped were her leg muscles, but she managed it, watched by an amused Pat. As she struggled to the top of the bank Kylie heard a girl's voice cry "Brian!"

There was the sound of running feet and a loud sigh. Curious to know who was there, Kylie looked through the screen of trees and bushes, and stopped in her tracks. Her heart also seemed to stop as her eyes took in the scene.

Brian had run to meet the girl, a big, fair-haired girl, and he was holding her tightly and kissing her!

Chapter 25

In a sort of dazed shock, Kylie stared at Brian and the girl he was kissing so passionately. Horrible suspicions and jealousies swirled to the surface of her mind. Needing urgently to know she turned to Pat, who had followed her up the bank and was standing just behind her.

In a voice that was little more than a croaking whisper she asked, "Who is that girl Brian is kissing? Is she his sister?"

At that, Pat broke into a broad grin and shook his head. "Sister! Nah. His sister's at the other camp. That's Maureen, his girlfriend."

"Girlfriend!" Kylie echoed, her throat choking up as ghastly emotions welled up in her. "Maureen?"

"Yeah, Maureen O'Grady. She lives on a property near here," Pat answered.

Kylie barely heard him as she stared in miserable horror at Brian as he kissed the girl. There had been something about the way the two were kissing that had made her instantly suspect she wasn't his sister. Now the truth dawned on her like a stunning, humiliating blow.

"Girlfriend!" she gasped. "He lied to me!"

Pat nodded and replied, "Yeah well, some blokes do that."

But Kylie barely heard him. Now she was experiencing waves of heat and cold in surges so strong she was only dimly aware of her condition. Anger, jealousy, hurt, shame, all swirled in her. Now she could hardly focus on the kissing couple as her eyes had misted with tears.

Oh, what a fool I've been! she thought bitterly.

Images of how her friend's would sneer when they found out made her flame with humiliation. She pictured the scorn she would have to endure, and her emotions rose to make bitter bile in her throat.

Despite her distress, Kylie could tell that Brian and Maureen were so taken up with each other that they had not noticed her. Nor were any of her friends in sight. For a few seconds she was gripped by a jealous rage so strong she wanted to rush forward and claw his, her, his eyes out. But then the shame overwhelmed her.

Margaret will be all sympathy, but Stephen will sneer and Norah will think I am just a stupid little girl, she thought.

Stung beyond reason, she turned and fled back down the bank, stumbling and pushing Pat aside as she did. At that moment, she just could not face her friends. Pat protested but made no move to restrain her. Instead, he turned and came running after her.

"Hey! You can't run off!" he called.

"Yes, I can. Shoot me if you want to!" Kylie wailed.

At that moment, everything seemed black and as the pain and despair grew she did not care if she was killed. Never in her life had she been so hurt, and so potentially humiliated. Just thinking about the mocking, sneering, told-you-so looks, and the behind-the-hand sniggers to come, made her burn in anticipation. Tears came and almost blinded her.

She stumbled on rocks and blundered through bushes, then came to the far bank. Here Pat caught her up and grabbed her arm.

"Hey! Stop! It's not the bloody end of the world," he said. "You can't leave."

"It is! He told me he loved me!" Kylie wailed, breaking out into sobs that brought her to a standstill, gasping for breath. "He lied to me!"

"Aw, he's only a kid," Pat said. "And so are you. You'll get over it."

That stung too! Kylie turned and snarled at him. "Being young is still no reason to lie!"

Pat stepped back, holding his hands up in a placating gesture. "Yeah, well, you are right. Now calm down. We have to go back camp."

"In a minute," Kylie sobbed.

Turning her back on him, she slumped down on the sand of the creek bed, crying her eyes out. She just knew her heart was broken, and that it would never be repaired!

But after a few minutes she cried herself dry and calmed down a bit. Reluctantly she stood up and turned to face Pat. As she did, her mind was hard at work with a churning mixture of plans to win Brian's affection, and to get revenge for her humiliation. As she started walking back towards the camp, she resolved to escape at the first opportunity.

I will get the police, she thought. In her heart she did not believe that the bushrangers would actually take revenge on any of her friends. *Well, maybe Liam might,* she conceded.

Feeling sick at heart and burning with shame, she made her way up the creek bank and through the belt of trees to the camp. She half expected to find Brian and Maureen still kissing, or at least holding hands but To her relief, she found them well apart and busy unstrapping saddle bags from two pack horses.

As she joined the others, Kylie noted Margaret flash an anxious look at her. *She is wondering if I know,* Kylie deduced. She decided to pretend ignorance and hope that it might help her escape. So she sat quietly down and looked towards Maureen.

"Who is she?" Kylie asked. "I didn't see her when we arrived."

"Don't know," Margaret replied, her eyes flicking with curious and sympathetic anxiety. "She just rode in with those two pack horses."

At that moment, Brian looked over his shoulder and his eyes met Kylie's. What Kylie took to be a look of guilty concern crossed his face. He was certainly frowning as he turned back to his task. A wave of hurt swept through Kylie and she had to keep a tight grip on her seething emotions lest she act too soon. What she felt like doing was running over and hitting at him and calling him hurtful names.

She certainly thought them. Words like cheat, liar, cad, scoundrel, beast, all flashed across her mind, mingled with tormenting images of him kissing her at the dance while sending her into raptures of romance and desire. Oh, how it hurt!

For the next ten minutes Kylie sat quietly and pretended not to be interested. In reality she noted every little thing and her mind kept bringing up plans and examining them. As she looked around it suddenly dawned on her that all of her friends were securely tied up, both their ankles and wrists. A strong rope was also tied around each one at the ankles to hold them together as a group.

Dan has forgotten to tie me up! Kylie thought excitedly, her heart beating faster with anxiety.

Very cautiously she looked around to see if anyone was watching, then slowly put into execution the plan that had instantly formed. She carefully slid her legs in under the long rope and then gently twisted it around her ankles so that, to a cursory inspection, it would appear that she was tied up like the others. Both Margaret and Roger kept meeting her eyes, fully aware of what she was doing.

During this time the three bushrangers talked and Maureen fed and watered her horses. Kylie gave Margaret a secret little smile and a nod but did not dare discuss her next move as she had no idea what it might be.

Perhaps I can sneak over and get one of those horses? she wondered.

During all this she slowly calmed down and was even able to get some sardonic amusement out of watching Brian as he spoke to his girlfriend. It occurred to Kylie that he must be more than a little anxious about Kylie letting Maureen know what had gone on at the races.

That would cook his goose, the two-timing, lying rat! she thought.

But then tears welled up again as she thought she still loved him and wondered if she could lure him away from the other girl. But a study of Maureen quickly depressed Kylie. Maureen was several years older, and with all the advantages that brought, a shapelier figure and greater confidence.

She is very pretty, Kylie had to reluctantly admit, noting the nice oval face framed by glossy, shoulder length black hair. Maureen's eyes were hazel and sparkled and she had very white teeth in what Kylie was sure all the boys would think was a very kissable mouth. She also had spirit. Just by the way she spoke Kylie could tell she was a strong character. *Lots of fire and passion there,* she decided. That depressed her more and she saw her chances of competing successfully slipping further. *Unless I make it known to her that he has been kissing me,* she decided.

But how? Short of just walking up and telling Maureen Kylie could not think of a plan. *It would be more effective if she learnt from someone else,* she decided. But who? And when? *Margaret would do it, if I asked,* Kylie thought.

As she watched Maureen tell Brian where to place the stores he had unloaded, Kylie had to smile. *She is the one who wears the pants,* she thought. Then she saw Brian casting her anxious little looks. *He is worrying she will find out alright,* Kylie decided. Then she concluded, *Maureen is too good for him, the sneaky beast!*

But still no clear plan came to mind so Kylie sat back in silent misery and brooded over her lost love. From the little looks and gestures that Maureen gave to Brian it was obvious that she loved him and that she had no idea he had been 'two-timing'. That made Kylie even sadder.

I thought I had found the love-of-my-life! she mused miserably.

It was twilight by then and a gas cooker was set up and the preparation for a meal began. The prisoners were all provided with water and only then did Kylie appreciate just how dehydrated and sick she felt. The sunburn and lack of fluids now combined to give her a splitting headache, which, along with her crushed romantic hopes, made her very snappy and irritable.

A meal was provided: stew with mixed vegetables and tinned meat. There was bread as well. Kylie found it delicious and realised she was now very hungry. She ate everything she was given, her mind diverted off escape plans by the food.

While they were eating, they heard the sound of a vehicle approaching. The bushrangers all picked up their guns and moved out of sight behind trees and bushes. Before he hid Dan warned the group not to do anything silly. All this time Kylie had remained untied, and she now wondered if her chance had come. Without appearing to she looked carefully in all directions in the twilight and tried to decide if she had any chance of slipping away in the gathering darkness. Reluctantly she concluded she did not.

Dan is just behind me and Brian and Maureen are just over there behind those trees, she thought.

To her annoyance they also blocked any chance of sneaking over to take a horse. As the headlights of the approaching vehicle came into view through the trees, she became quite tense, hoping it might be the police but anxious lest people get hurt in any ensuing fight.

But it was only Liam and Ryan returning. Liam climbed out of the vehicle and told Ryan to keep going. Ryan was obviously only too pleased to do so. He quickly drove on across the creek and within a couple of minutes the sound of the vehicle engine could not be heard. By then the other bushrangers had come out of hiding.

"Any problems?" Liam asked, shining a torch along the group of prisoners.

"Nope," Dan replied. "What does Phil want us to do?"

"Stay here," Liam answered. "He will tell us what to do next. Hey! Why is that one not tied up?"

Liam's torch had settled on Kylie and she experienced a wave of anxiety and disappointment. *Drat! He noticed,* she thought.

"Aw, she just went to the dunny," Dan answered.

"Tie her up, and don't take any chances," Liam snarled. He was obviously tired and in a bad mood and that cheered Kylie a little.

Dan came over and knelt to loop a rope around Kylie's wrists. While he did this, he glanced at her ankles but in the gloom must have decided they were actually tied up as he made no move to secure them. He did not tie the knots very tight. It seemed to Kylie that he was annoyed at being spoken to like that by Liam.

Maureen now came along and handed each a blanket and told them to rest. As she reached Kylie, she could not help looking intently at her and it took all Kylie's willpower not to speak about Brian. Maureen appeared not to notice as it was now almost fully dark. Liam ordered the prisoners to lie down and then organised the bushrangers to be guards on a roster.

That led to another argument. Maureen shook her head. "I gotta get home or my dad will get suspicious. As it is he will want to know where I've been," she said.

Reluctantly Liam agreed. "Okay then, get goin'. We will see you in the morning?"

"I'll bring more bread," Maureen answered. Then she turned to Brian and said, "See me off please."

That really stabbed at Kylie's heart and watching the pair walk off into the darkness to where the horses were tethered brought another attack of jealousy and misery. She just knew they would be kissing. The thought caused her to grind her teeth in frustrated misery.

A few minutes later, Kylie saw the three horses move off along the vehicle track, heading westwards. That got Kylie thinking. *If she lives on a property nearby then that track might lead to it, or to a road that I could follow,* she reasoned. But first she had to escape!

To complicate the possibility of escape, Dan now seated himself on a box at the end of the line of prisoners where he could watch them all at once. Kylie noted that he had a big torch but that he leant his rifle against a tree. That made Roger shake his head.

"Bad practice that," he muttered.

"What is?" Margaret asked.

"Leaning a rifle against a tree," Roger replied. "We are taught never to do it at cadets."

"Why not?" Margaret queried.

"A piece of bark could fall down the barrel," Roger explained. "Then, if the rifle is fired the bullet can be slowed down, or jammed, and the barrel or breech can burst."

For a few seconds Kylie tried to imagine the bullet spinning down the barrel, pushed by the rapidly expanding gasses. Then she pictured the steel splinters slashing into the firer's face and eyes and she winced in horror.

Oh, how ghastly! Should I tell Dan? she wondered.

But she didn't. *He won't be shooting anyone,* she thought confidently, remembering how he had chased after her that afternoon.

When Roger and Margaret kept talking Dan turned the torch on and shone it at them. "Stop talking and go to sleep," he ordered. "And no funny business!"

Seeing that both Liam and Brian had unrolled bedding nearby, but between her and the horses, Kylie lay back and tried to relax. She was almost at once assailed by cramps and stiffness and the pain was so severe she cried out.

"What is it?" Dan asked, shining his torch towards her.

"Just a cramp," Kylie replied.

The pain was intense but she gritted her teeth and stifled more cries. *I don't want him to come and look in case he discovers my legs aren't tied up,* she thought.

She wasn't the only one who was sore and she heard quite a few groans and stifled muttering. Several times she met Margaret's anxious gaze and returned what she hoped was a cheerful smile. *Margaret is still wondering if I saw Maureen and Brian kissing,* she thought.

"It will be alright Marg.," she whispered.

"Stop whispering," Dan called. "You need all the rest you can get. We might have to walk even further tomorrow."

That brought groans and muttered protests from most of the group but then they settled. After squirming to get her hip as comfortable as she could on the hard ground Kylie tried to relax. Only then did she fully realise just how sore and worn out she was. She closed eyes that felt hot and gritty and felt her senses swim and spin. Before she realised what was happening exhaustion claimed her and she fell into a deep sleep.

* * *

Movement woke Kylie. She was so tired that it took an effort to drag her eyelids open but when she had she saw it was Liam taking Norah and Margaret to the toilet. He had obviously untied them from the main rope. Norah was protesting that her hands were numb and that he must loosen them or he would regret it. She also objected to Liam being nearby when she actually went to the toilet. But Liam obviously did not pay heed as he later led both girls back and then knelt to retie them.

The thought of doing a pee made Kylie want to go but she did not dare mention it. *Liam will discover my legs aren't tied,* she thought. For the whole time he worked next to her with his torch shining on Margaret's legs Kylie lay still and pretended to be asleep. As she did, she silently prayed that Liam would not notice.

To her relief, he did not, but that did not seem to help as the bushranger seated himself on guard and Kylie could not think of any way to sneak away without him seeing. Lying on her back she was able to note that there was no moon but that the stars still gave so much light that any attempt to escape would be immediately seen.

If only he would drop off to sleep, she thought exasperatedly.

But it was she who dropped off to sleep, her sore limbs still aching.

* * *

Kylie woke some time later, and for a few minutes was so groggy that she had no idea where she was. Seemingly aching in every part of her body she lay on her side and felt the numbness in her arms and legs. Only when she tried to rub her eyes and found her wrists tied together did memory return. To make herself more comfortable she rolled on her back and straightened out. This was so painful that she gave a low groan, then remembered the bushrangers. Anxiously she lifted her head and looked.

A person was sitting on the box. But Kylie's eyes were so sleep-gummed and gritty and it was so dark that for a few seconds she could not identify who it was. Then she saw that it was Brian. Next she noted that he was slumped sideways, leaning against a tree.

He is asleep! Kylie thought. *This might be my chance!*

But that thought instantly caused her a dilemma: to wake the others and all try to escape? There was also the glimmering of doubt about what her escape might do to her relationship with Brian. *He won't like me if I make him look like a fool,* she mused. But then, did he like her anyway? *Was he just using me for a bit of cheating pleasure?* she wondered. Her unhappiness decided her. *It will serve him right,* she thought, the image of Brian suffering Liam's wrath giving her some jealous pleasure. *Maybe revenge is sweet?* she considered, suddenly aware that she was perhaps not as nice a person as she had always thought.

For a few more minutes Kylie lay still while she observed and made a plan. Reluctantly, she decided to sneak away without waking any of the others. It would obviously involve them in a lot of movement and whispering and might wake the bushrangers. Kylie could not see herself trying to hit Brian over the head if he woke up, and the picture of her snatching up his gun to use against him, or against Liam and Dan did not form very well either. In her heart of hearts she knew she could never pull the trigger, not to save herself anyway.

I will just go, and hope they don't notice I am missing until too late, she decided.

Now that she was resolved to go, she became very tense and anxious, fearful lest Brian wake up. After glancing at both Margaret and Roger to check if they were awake, she began to move. Both seemed to be sound asleep. So Kylie began her attempt. Slowly, bit by bit, she began to ease the rope from around her legs.

But her efforts were unsuccessful, so she pushed herself into a sitting position and used her bound hands to slowly unwrap the rope from around her ankles. This took several minutes and twice Brian gave a loud snuffle and shifted position. Each time Kylie's heart leapt into her mouth, and she froze, her eyes fixed on Brian. Only when it was clear that he was still asleep did she resume her attempt.

One of the reasons that she took so long was the utter silence of the sleeping bush. There was no breeze and there were none of the usual bush noises to be heard. Everything seemed to be still and silent. The almost total absence of sound was, to Kylie's city bred ears, somewhat frightening. It was so quiet she could hear her own breathing and heartbeat and even the soft rustle of her clothes.

Once she had freed her legs Kylie sat for a minute listening and watching, steeling herself to make the attempt. Now that the moment had arrived, she was very excited and found that the thumping of her heart was impeding her hearing. The result was a sort of rhythmic swashing noise in her ears.

Come on, get moving! she told herself.

She had no idea what time it was but was afraid that the night might be over before she could reach help. So she went to get up, and all but failed! Her stiff muscles protested so much that she gasped in pain and had to pause while her body and mind adjusted to the shock of finding that her muscles did not want to obey.

Then, biting her lip to stifle any groans, she gingerly rolled into a kneeling position and stood up. As she did, she kept her eyes on Brian.

What will I do if he wakes up? she wondered.

As he had not moved, she cautiously began to walk towards him.

Chapter 26

NIGHT MARCH

As Kylie began moving, she began to have doubts about her ability to make it. Her muscles were so stiff and her body so sore that she could barely move. On top of that stabs of sharp pain instantly assailed her from blisters and chafing.

Oh my God! she thought. *Am I too weak to do this?*

She certainly knew she could not hope to outrun Brian if he woke up. Gritting her teeth she carefully took one slow step after another, her eyes mostly fixed on Brian's sleeping form. Because he was seated beside the track, she had to move towards him. The alternative was to try to detour through the bush and she thought that would be too noisy and possibly wake him, or worse still, wake Liam.

With five painful steps she gained the dusty wheel rut closest to her. After another anxious glance at Brian she set off slowly along it. A faint noise beside her made her freeze and look that way. It was Dingo. Kylie saw his eyes glinting in the starlight. Then she saw his head nod with what she thought was approval of her plan. He then lifted his bound hands and made a curious turning motion. At first she thought he was asking to be untied but when he did it again she saw he was actually pointing to the left.

He is saying turn left when I get to the road, she thought.

As that coincided with what she had already reasoned, she nodded. As quietly as she could, she padded over to him and held out her bound wrists. Dingo went to work to untie them, but it was difficult. The best he could do was to loosen one knot. Then Brian snuffled and moved.

Both froze and looked. Dingo shook his head. "You get going in case he wakes up," he whispered. "Go left on the road."

"I was going to," Kylie replied. He nodded in reply and then lay back. Kylie turned and started walking slowly. As she did, Brian grunted and moved again.

By then Kylie was almost within arm's reach of Brian and she froze. But he mumbled and settled again. She tried not to breathe or make a sound as she started walking again. Luckily the dust muffled her footfalls, and she was able to pad silently past with slow steps. Once she was past, she began to speed up and relax. While he was in sight, she kept looking back over her shoulder to check that he was still asleep. Only when she rounded the first bend in the track did she concentrate more on what was ahead of her.

Made it! she thought exultantly.

Feeling very excited she began to walk faster, ignoring the stiff muscles and the sharp pains from chafing and blisters. It was a revelation to her just how much such apparently trivial injuries could hurt. Shaking her head and gritting her teeth she kept pushing herself to walk faster. As she walked, she used her teeth to work at the knots holding her wrists. Dingo's efforts now paid off and after ten minutes she was able to pull the ropes loose and slip her hands free. That was an immense relief and she found it easier to keep her balance in the darkness.

The going was easy, and it was only as the immediate fear of the bushrangers receded that thoughts of other possible dangers began to squirm their way to the surface of Kylie's consciousness. Top of this list were snakes, and she began to strain her eyes as she anxiously scanned the dusty track. As the wheel ruts had a line of grass between them, she was not able to relax, fearing that one of the poisonous reptiles might be lurking in every tuft of grass she had to pass.

After a few minutes walking, Kylie found her muscles easing, the stiffness going as they warmed up. But not the pain from chafing and blisters. If anything this increased until at last it became a sort of burning misery. She was also very thirsty and needed badly to go to the toilet. That was fairly easy to do, except she did not like the idea of pulling her pants down so close to the bushranger's camp.

But finally she had to. It was either that or wet herself. Having thought about peeing she found she was assailed by a sharp and painful urge. Reluctantly she stopped, found a fairly open area of bare clay where no snakes were visible and then as quickly as she could she relieved herself, hauled her trousers up again and resumed her march.

A dry creek, smaller than the one near the bushranger's camp, angled in from her left. The track went down across it. Going down the slope Kylie nearly stumbled on the rough ground but managed to keep her feet. Climbing up the other side she found harder, her tired muscles protesting.

The effort soon had her perspiring, despite the apparent cool of the night. Thirst began to bother her, and her headache became worse.

After another ten- or twenty-minutes walking she came down over a low rocky hill to flat ground. A grey smudge in the darkness ahead caused her to stop and stare. The hazy change of light went from right to left across her front and it was only after moving cautiously closer that she realised what it was.

"A road!" she muttered with relief.

It was a graded gravel road which indicated to her that it was probably a public road, not a farm track.

Keeping in mind Dingo's gestures, she stepped out onto the road and turned left. Now she felt safer and more confident. There was no grass overhanging the edge and she could walk in the middle, well away from the possible hiding places of snakes. Instead she began to worry about other possible dangers that might lurk in the silent bush.

"I wonder if there are wild pigs in this dry country?" she asked herself.

She knew she did not stand a chance against such a creature. *I would never be able to outrun it to climb a tree,* she thought ruefully, very conscious of how weak she felt.

As she plodded along the road she looked hopefully around. What she was hoping to see was a house but there was no sign of any habitation. All she could see was dark bush with no sign even of fences, fields or gates. Then she made a wry face.

If Maureen lives on a property somewhere around here it might not be a good idea just to waltz up to a house and ask for help!

That also got her worrying about what to do if a vehicle came along. At first she had been hoping that one would so she could flag it down and get a lift. Now she began to worry that any vehicle might be driven by the bushrangers, or by one of their friends or supporters. It was now apparent to her that the Kelly Gang was managing to avoid the police because of such help, either freely given, or, as in the case of Ryan, coerced.

Then another thought crossed her mind, and she stopped in dismay and slapped her forehead. *Oh, you idiot!* she told herself.

While thinking about cars she had considered that, if her escape was discovered and the bushrangers came after her, then they would not know which way to turn. It had just occurred to her that she had been leaving a clear trail of boot prints in the dust. Bitterly she reproached herself and for a minute or so debated going back, at least to the track junction, to try to brush out any tracks. Then she shook her head.

Take too long, and the brushing would be just as obvious as the boot prints, she decided.

Having decided that she resumed her march. *If any cars come from behind me, I have to hide as soon as I see their headlights,* she thought. But what about cars coming from the front?

Undecided about them she plodded on. She noted that hills were appearing ahead on both sides of the road. This was what she expected so it heartened her. *Irvinebank is in among hills,* she reminded herself. She also noted a dark line of trees on her right. This was apparently angling closer to the road. *A creek line,* she decided.

It was. A few minutes later she came to a dip, and as she went down it she saw a wide strip of blackness across the pale shadow of the road. Only as she got closer did she realise that the blackness was water. The faint gurgle of water trickling over stones came to her. Then she stepped onto concrete and knew it was a floodway. These are typical features on the secondary roads in the dry inland. As the creeks only flooded for a few hours or days in the 'wet' season, the local councils saved the expense of building bridges by laying a short length of concrete to prevent bogging.

But how deep was the water? When she reached it Kylie stopped and bent to peer hard at it. She saw stars reflected in it but was quite unable to determine its depth. *Can't be more than knee deep,* she reasoned, thinking of cars driving through it.

Then she shrugged. Wet socks and feet seemed of small importance now. Slowly she waded in, discovering To her relief, that the water was only a few centimetres deep and did not even reach as high as the tops of her riding boots.

Still dry shod she reached the other side, a matter of only about twenty paces. Here she again paused. She was feeling very thirsty. *I wonder if it is safe to drink?* she thought.

In her mind she had a short debate, confused by the conflicting things she had heard. Some people had told her that running water was safe, but others had said it just carried any disease and so on down with it. She had once heard Graham and Peter discussing how creeks in old mining areas might be contaminated by toxic material.

They used cyanide or something to help extract the gold I think they said, she debated anxiously. But she was very thirsty, and she decided it was a tin mining area, not a gold mining area. *Anyway, it shouldn't make me sick for a while and by then I should have reached Irvinebank and contacted the police,* she told herself.

Now determined to get the police she knelt at the side of the causeway and scooped up water in her hand. It tasted cool and fresh so she drank as much as she could. Then she rinsed her face. Feeling considerably refreshed she continued walking.

By this time her aches and pains had melded into a mass of dull misery, and she was more worried about her overall weakness. She felt so tired that she began to experience periods of blurred vision and had depth perception problems. As a result she stumbled on numerous small potholes and protruding stones and found she was staggering. She began silently praying for her ordeal to end.

"It can't be much further," she muttered.

Fear of collapsing and thereby failing in her task caused her to grimly grit her teeth and force herself on. Ignoring the hot agony of the blisters and chafing she took one dogged step after another.

Fifteen minutes of determined marching brought her to another floodway. She knew it was the same creek, the road recrossing it. Once again, she drank and washed her tired and grimy face. That lifted her for a few minutes, but it was all she could do to straighten up and force her aching legs back into motion.

The nature of the road changed too. It began to run along a bench cut with a steep drop down into the creek on her right and with steep cuttings or hillslopes up on her left.

I might have trouble getting off to hide if a vehicle comes along, she worried.

Wondering about the lack of traffic got her guessing at the time. There was still no sign of any moon and it seemed as dark as ever. She concluded it must still be well before daylight. Shrugging at her inability she trudged on.

Half an hour of this, with more stumbles and near falls, brought her to a sudden bend to the left. Now the hills were high on both sides, and she felt sure she must be close to Irvinebank. That got her mind focused on what to do when she got there. Having visited the place on day trips with the family she had a rough idea of the layout. What she could remember was a park with a toilet at a T junction, and also a hotel. The adults had gone into the bar and the children had drunk soft drinks on the veranda.

There is a telephone booth out the front of the hotel I think, she remembered.

She decided that was to be her objective. Even if there were houses before then she resolved to by-pass them in case the inhabitants were friends of the Kelly Gang.

Soon after that the road again curved to the left. Kylie now found herself walking along a section of road which had quite a dense growth of large trees overhanging it from both sides. As a result it was very dark, and she had to slow down to limit her stumbles. Her progress became little more than a painful shuffle and that made her even more anxious as she was very aware that time was passing.

"The bushrangers must have discovered my escape by now," she muttered.

For some time she had been expecting to hear sounds of pursuit and she stopped from time to time to listen. She guessed they would follow by horse because they did not have a vehicle immediately available.

I need to be alert so that I have time to hide before they catch up, she told herself.

Still thinking this she trudged on. Suddenly a sound beside her made her heart leap in alarm and she froze, then began to move.

But too late!

Before she realised her peril, footsteps thudded across from a large tree close on her right and a man's arms reached out and grabbed her. Kylie tried to dodge, then to scream but even as she did the man's hand closed over her mouth! Fear almost paralysed her but then it galvanised her to move. Desperately she struggled to escape, squirming and kicking at the man. But to no avail. He was much bigger than her and very strong. She tried to bite but that drew a warning growl from the man and a clip over the ear.

To save his hand from being bitten the man took it away from her mouth. Instantly Kylie took her chance and sucked in her breath to scream. The man however tightened his grip on her throat with his other arm, choking her off.

"Scream all you like little girl," he growled. "There ain't nobody to hear you."

Phil Kelly, Kylie recognised.

Now that she thought about it she was able to identify the smell of horse and stale, sweaty clothes and feel the prickle of his beard. Despite his warning she did try to scream but that only made his grip tighter.

Once again he held her in a grip so strong she felt quite powerless. Then he said, "Stop your bloody wriggling before you get hurt."

Kylie did. She knew she could not break free. *I will have to wait for another opportunity,* she thought. Bitter tears of defeat prickled her eyes. To be so close to succeeding!

Phil Kelly proceeded to pull her hands behind her back and then to tie them tightly with a short length of rope. Then he added to her discomfort and distress by tying a smelly handkerchief around her face so that it went between her teeth as a sort of gag.

That done he held her from behind and said, "Ok Liam, I got her."

At that, Kylie's mind raced. *Liam! Where is he?*

She guessed instantly that her escape had been discovered. But there was no sign of Liam in the darkness. Phil went on to say, "Alright. First, I'll get to my meeting with Jerry. Then I'll come to your camp, okay?"

Then Kylie realised that Phil was talking on his small radio. That surprised her as she did not think they could transmit that distance, especially among big hills. The puzzle was answered for her when Phil said, presumably to Liam, "Just as well you called when you did. I was just about to leave for the meeting. Now stop yakking in case the coppers are monitoring the radio. I'll see you in about two hours."

Phil then took a strong grip and turned Kylie to face the trees. "Start walking girlie, and watch out for the slope. It's pretty steep."

So saying he propelled her forward into the darkness. As soon as they reached the edge of the road, Kylie felt the ground drop away and had to feel for where to put her feet. Phil held her from behind and but for that she knew she would have fallen. Slithering and shuffling the pair slid and clambered down the steep bank of the creek to its rocky bed. Here Phil again held her up while pushing her forward. Kylie had no choice but try to walk. In the darkness she had so much trouble seeing she could only stumble and slip across the rock-strewn bed of the creek. Once again it was only Phil's tight grip that stopped her falling over and hurting herself. As it was, she suffered several sharp knocks and bruises to her legs and knees.

After fifty paces of this they reached the far bank of the creek and Kylie was pushed upwards. “Climb!” Phil hissed, pushing her from behind.

Reluctantly she went up, her feet scrabbling on loose sand and rocks for a firm foothold. It was steep but only five metres up and she soon found herself on a gravel road.

That disoriented her. *Is this the same road?* she wondered. As Phil shoved her to get her walking along the road to her right she looked around in the starlight. What she saw made her think that it was not the same road. *That big hill in front of us is the one that was on my right before,* she thought.

The dirt road turned sharply to the left and Kylie saw that a second creek ran beside it on her right, entering the main creek at a bend. The road now proceeded up a narrow valley on a bench cut. After a hundred paces they came to a wider area where the road was dusty and rutted. Just beyond that they came to a fence. As they paused for Phil to open a small steel gate, Kylie saw with something of a shock that the whitish objects she could see on the other side of the fence were tombstones.

A cemetery! she thought with growing fear.

Up till now she had expected to get a bit of rough handling and perhaps a tongue lashing, at worst a bit of inappropriate touching. Now she experienced a stab of pure fear.

Maybe he is going to murder me? she thought.

Chapter 27

THE CEMETERY

As Kylie was pushed through the gate waves of growing terror almost paralysed her.

Surely he won't kill me? she thought.

The idea of death made her feel nauseous and she broke into a sweat, all the worse for being chilled by both fear and the cool night air.

Phil Kelly kept shoving her, so she had only the choice of falling or walking. She walked, but with legs that were on the verge of collapse. Once in among the headstones Phil stopped her and then pushed her roughly down onto a concrete slab. Once again Kylie was swamped by terror and she cringed, expecting to be murdered at any moment. Her mind swirled with horrible options: strangling, stabbing, her throat being cut. The only thing she was sure of was that she would not be shot.

This is the Irvinebank Cemetery, she remembered, having briefly visited it once. *It is too close to town to use a gun. People would hear.*

Unable to resist she found herself rolled on her side. Then Phil knelt with one knee on her left thigh to hold her down while he quickly bound her legs together. By now she was so scared she was praying and wanted to beg for mercy, but the gag reduced this to a stifled whimper. Having tied her legs securely, then knotted the end of the rope so that she could not draw her ankles up near her hands Phil Kelly did a last check, then grunted with satisfaction and stood up.

Kylie braced herself for the end. Through her mind raced images of her life and fleeting pictures of her dreams and hopes. Misery and despair flooded her thoughts, the worst being that it was so unfair.

I haven't even lived yet, I'm too young to die! she told herself, picturing all those things she dreamed of doing, or being: dancer, lover, wife, mother, worker.

Then she deliberately calmed herself and began to pray. *Dear God, please make it quick, and please take me to Heaven. And please make it easier for Mummy, and for Graham and Alex and...*

Her terrified prayers tailed off as Phil Kelly abruptly turned on his heel and strode away. For a few seconds all Kylie could do was lie and tremble with relief. Then shock and fear gripped her so that tears and shaking overcame her.

Slowly she calmed down. After a few minutes, once she was sure she was not to be immediately put to death, she craned her head to look around. *Where did Phil Kelly go?* she wondered.

But the fear of death did not leave her. The gravestones all around her saw to that. Never in her whole life had she been alone in a cemetery, let alone in the middle of the night! As she looked around it all seemed to take on an eerie, spooky glow. She now saw that the concrete she was lying on was actually the slab over someone's grave. Next to her head was the tombstone. The thought that there was a dead body, or at least a mouldering skeleton, underneath her made her shudder with revulsion.

"Sorry person. I don't mean to desecrate your grave," she tried to say through her gag. In the back of her mind was the concept of the dead person objecting and somehow coming up to haunt her.

Then a flicker of white movement caught her eye and the word 'ghost' instantly rose to the top of her consciousness. Immediately her heart rate shot up, her skin came out in goose bumps and all the hairs on her neck and head 'stood up'.

The moving white thing came closer, and she saw it was heading towards her through the cemetery. Fear again froze her, and she lay gripped by icy chills at the base of her skull. Her breathing almost stopped as she went tense with fright.

Then she heard the crunch of boots on sand and deadfall and that puzzled her. *Ghosts shouldn't make a sound,* she thought.

From all the stories she had read, seen or heard they floated along. But this white thing was obviously walking, and dodging between the gravestones. Then she saw it was a person with a white sheet draped over them. Even as she realised this the person walked past her, not even glancing in her direction.

Definitely a man, Kylie thought, some relief easing her tight chest.

But then it occurred to her that he might be the executioner and that the sheet was his disguise. She knew it wasn't Phil Kelly as the 'ghost' was shorter and had come from the other side of the cemetery, down the slope. The 'ghost' vanished from view towards the gate.

Kylie shuddered with relief, then strained to hear. The footsteps stopped and she heard the mutter of voices. *Meeting Phil Kelly,* she decided. From that she could only conclude that the ghost outfit was a disguise in case the man was seen by someone.

Minutes began to drag past. Still the two men talked quietly. Kylie became very uncomfortable and cramped. Her fear subsided slightly but she was so tense she had trouble breathing. The gag didn't help. In an attempt to ease her sore body she tried to change position but this was unsuccessful. The best she could do was roll onto her back.

Lying there, trembling from fear and overexertion, she thought she was starting to hallucinate. Then she realised that the light was changing. *Daylight?* she wondered hopefully.

But it wasn't. A few minutes later she realised that the glow silvering the top of the mountain above her was the rising moon. Then the moon slid slowly into view, a half-moon but still welcome for the light it gave. It made it possible for Kylie to distinguish details around her.

Then she heard boots crunching on the sandy ground again and she stiffened up with anxiety. It was the 'ghost' coming back and this time Phil Kelly was with him. *Oh no! I hope they aren't coming to kill me,* she thought, her heart rate shooting right up again.

The two men came to a stop beside Kylie. She stared up them, her eyes wide with fear and her whole being chilled by dread. Perspiration prickled on her cold skin but perversely she felt hot and dry in the throat and her stomach churned.

Then the 'ghost' pointed to the headstone beside Kylie and grunted. "Good spot to put her," he said with a chuckle.

Hearing that sent new waves of terror through Kylie and she shuddered in apprehension. Then curiosity made her glance at the tombstone. In the light of the rising moon she was just able to make out the inscription.

It read: 'Of your charity pray for the soul of Constable Edward Lanigan. Died 6 Sept 1894'

Lanigan! Kylie thought in shock. But then, *No, Frank's name is Lonergan.* Then she began to worry; was it some sort of ghastly omen?

Phil Kelly bent to read it, and muttered, "A good copper, eh?"

"If you mean a dead one, then yeah," replied the other. Kylie noted that he sounded older and had a faint Irish accent. "Sad story it is," he added.

"Oh yeah? What happened?" Phil Kelly asked.

"I don't remember all the details," the 'ghost' answered. "I only read it once. Apparently, this fella and another copper were chasing an Aboriginal named Jacky. Jacky had run away from the Native Mounted Police and was making a nuisance of himself thieving and so on. Anyway, the two coppers caught up with him and the first one tried to grab him. Apparently, the other copper drew his revolver and in the struggle it went off, hitting this Constable Lanigan fella in the lung, killing him."

Phil Kelly grunted, "Bad luck," he said.

"So it was," agreed the 'ghost'. "Apparently this Lanigan fella was engaged to a girl over at Coolgarra. She took his death real hard, and so did his mate, who felt responsible."

"Did the blackfella get away?" Phil asked.

"Nope. They caught him and he was sent to jail."

"Yeah well, I'll be more careful," Phil Kelly replied.

"You do that," the 'ghost' answered. "And you'll need to be. As I said, the place is now crawling with coppers, and they are pretty angry."

"I'd better get going," Phil Kelly said. "It will be daylight in a few hours and those blasted helicopters will be up and about."

"I'd better make tracks too," the 'ghost' answered. "Take care, and good luck."

"Yeah, be seeing ya," Phil Kelly answered as the 'ghost' started walking.

The 'ghost' was quickly lost to sight, heading uphill into the bush. Phil bent down at Kylie's legs and she again tensed, bracing herself for the worst. But all he did was untie her ankles.

"Up you get," he ordered, hauling her up by her arms.

Kylie tried to stand but found that her legs would not function. She tried to say so but was muffled by the gag. To her dismay, she toppled over and would have cashed to the ground if Phil Kelly had not grabbed her.

"Hey! What's the go?" he snarled.

"Crampff," Kylie managed to gasp as he held her up.

She felt like a sack of potatoes but was also now burning with shame as his arm was tight under her armpits and across her front. To add to her distress, her legs began to shake uncontrollably and she felt as though she wanted to faint. Phil Kelly grunted in annoyance and then bent down and hoisted her off the ground with his arms under her back and legs. With no apparent effort he set off walking, heading back towards the front gate of the cemetery.

Being carried was both a relief and an embarrassment to Kylie. It did ease her mind a bit because he was so gentle that she felt sure he did not intend to kill her. But the trembling would not stop and when he halted at the gate and stood her on her feet she would have fallen if he had not kept a tight grip.

Phil Kelly bent down and picked up a pack and swung it over his left shoulder. Then he lifted Kylie up again and set off back along the gravel road they had arrived along. Kylie felt the pack as it swung against her shoulder. *Cans?* she wondered. Not having seen the pack earlier she decided that the 'ghost' had brought it and handed it over.

Helping the Kellys with food? she wondered.

A minute's walk had them at the sharp bend in the road where the two creeks joined. To Kylie's surprise Phil Kelly turned left and made his way down the steep bank of the side creek. There was a faint trail through the grass and rocks and they were quickly at the bottom. The side creek was only a couple of paces wide so almost at once they were on the upslope. Phil Kelly found this hard going. Kylie could tell that from his laboured breathing and pounding heart, but she also decided that his male pride would not allow him to admit he could not do it.

On the other side they set off along a flat trail which led in against the steep slope of the mountain. This puzzled Kylie as she saw it was obviously man made. *It looks like a bench cut,* she thought, remembering a term she had heard her brother use. But it looked too narrow to be a road. The cut was almost vertical up on the left and the drop on the right was almost as steep.

After about fifty metres of this they came to some horses. A person holding a rifle stepped out of the shadows and a girl's voice said, "What ya got there, Phil?"

It was Kate. Kylie could tell that at once. Phil Kelly lowered Kylie to the ground with a sigh of relief and answered, "Little girl who got away."

Kate bent to look and then gave a grin. "Kylie, Brian's little bit of fun from the races," she said.

Oh that burned! Kylie felt a surge of anger and would have told Kate what she thought of her two-timing brother if she had been able. Little bit of fun!

And I thought it was true love! she thought bitterly.

Phil began untying her legs. As he did, he snarled, "Yeah, well, young Brian's gunna get a good blast over letting her get away. She could have wrecked the whole show if she'd reached the coppers."

He quickly untied her legs, then rolled her roughly on her face and undid her hands. "Get up girlie," he growled.

Kylie tried to but she was still trembling and suffering muscular spasms. She struggled to sit up and shook her head. Without further words Phil Kelly just hoisted her up, then half carried, half dragged her to a horse.

"Get on," he commanded. But she couldn't do that either, so he lifted her. "Help me Kate, damn and blast!" he snapped.

"Watch out the little troublemaker doesn't try to bolt," Kate warned as she moved to assist.

That very idea had just flashed into Kylie's mind but was now squashed as quickly as it was born by Phil Kelly ordering Kate to hold the reins. With much grunting and soft cursing he managed to hoist Kylie up onto the saddle. She found it uncomfortable and undignified to be manhandled like that but consoled herself that at least the horse stood still.

He seems a nice quiet horse, she thought, catching the animal's eye as it turned its head to look at her.

That reassured her more than anything, feeling sure she would be alright on that particular horse. By then Phil Kelly had settled Kylie in the saddle and placed her left boot in the stirrup. Next, he walked around to the other side and did the same for her right foot.

All the while Kylie had been experiencing waves of pain and numbness in her wrists and hands and she tried flexing her fingers and massaging them to restore the circulation. To her annoyance and distress Phil Kelly now said, "Hold your hands down on the saddle girlie."

Having no option Kylie did as she was told. He then proceeded to retie her wrists, this time lashing them to buckles on the saddle. To her further annoyance the reins were looped up and tied in a knot. Then a long neck rope was secured to the horse and led forward to another horse. Phil Kelly went to this and transferred the contents of the pack to saddle bags on that horse.

Tins of food, Kylie noted as he did, pleased that her guess was right.

Phil Kelly then swung into the saddle and told Kate to do the same. Kate mounted another horse and swung into line behind Kylie. Last in line came a pack horse loaded with large bundles.

With Phil Kelly leading the horses walked in single file along the narrow bench cut. This was an experience Kylie did not enjoy. The moonlight seemed to affect her depth perception and she had the feeling that the steep drop close on her right was a long way down. It was lined with trees growing below her in the bed of the large creek and she was sure that a fall could have very nasty consequences. All she could do was trust to the horse.

The bench cut was not only narrow. In places it had fallen logs across it or was partially blocked by landslips. The horses managed to negotiate these without trouble, but each time Kylie broke into a cold sweat of fear. Being lashed to the horse added to her sense of anxiety.

If it slips over, I can't even jump off, she thought unhappily.

But it was a relief to be riding instead of walking. Bit by bit the trembling and cramping of her muscles eased and she began to relax. Now she was sure she would not be hurt by the bushrangers. Even though she did not like Kate she was certain she would not allow her to be ill-treated.

After about ten minutes riding Kate called to Phil Kelly, "Hey Phil, are we going to follow this old railway all the way?"

"Yeah, it's safer. Jerry reckoned the coppers are out looking and are really alert."

Old railway! Kylie thought. That made sense. She remembered that Graham and his friends had a thing about hiking along old railways. *They probably hiked along this one when they did that trip to Stannary Hills last year,* she thought. Into her mind came images of the huge HO Scale model railway the boys had constructed under Roger's house. It had a mountain railway section which was set in the dry mining country. *Part of the track runs along in a gorge just like this,* she remembered, picturing the tiny silver rails on the layout.

She knew they were going back the way she had come. *The road I walked along must be on the other side of the creek,* she thought.

A couple of minutes after that the flicker of lights through the trees ahead confirmed her theory. *A car,* she decided, *and heading for Irvinebank. Oh, why didn't it come along an hour ago!*

She knew that was an unreasonable idea as she had decided to hide from any cars coming from that direction, but it was frustrating all the same. It was even more galling to see that the vehicle, when it went past only 50 metres away, was a police car! Boiling with the desire to escape she watched the flicker of the headlights as it vanished behind them.

Kate again called to Phil Kelly. "You were right, big brother. That was a cop car."

"Told you so, now stop talking and ride. It will be daylight in two hours, and we've got a lot of ground to cover before then," Phil Kelly replied.

So they increased their pace. Kylie now began to worry about the reception she would receive when they returned to the bushranger's camp.

Brian will be really angry, she thought. *He won't like me much after this!*

Chapter 28

SERVES YOU RIGHT!

After half an hour of riding, Kylie was feeling exhausted and sick. The worst thing was the gag in her mouth as it stifled her air flow and cruelly hurt her cheeks. Several times she almost vomited and she began hoping that Phil Kelly or Kate would notice her distress. But her chance did not come till they detoured off the old railway to make their way down a steep-sided embankment into the bed of a side creek. Kylie did not enjoy that at all because she could not control the horse, nor lean back enough to counter the steep angle. All her weight slid forward and she had to push hard at her stirrups. It was an unpleasant and frightening experience, but the horse managed it safely, despite her unbalanced seat.

At the bottom Kylie saw that there had once been a culvert, but floods had washed it away. Once the riders were all safely in the creek bed Phil Kelly reined in and dismounted. He then moved to check the horses and have a drink.

As he drank, Kylie looked hard at him and let out muffled pleas. By now she was in genuine distress and not too proud to beg. It was Kate who heard her and supported her.

"She must be thirsty, Phil. You'd better give her a drink," she said as she took out her own water bottle.

Phil Kelly nodded and came over to Kylie. Looking hard at her he said, "You start yelling and screaming and the gag goes straight back on."

In answer Kylie nodded. To allow him to reach the gag she had to lean right over, an uncomfortable proceeding as the saddle dug into her stomach and ribs. But it was such a relief to have it removed that she sighed and panted. Then he could not reach her mouth with the water bottle.

"Untie me please," she croaked. "I won't try to ride off on you."

Phil Kelly looked doubtful but finally untied one of her hands. That still did not work as her hand was so numb and sore she could not hold the water bottle. Only after a couple of minutes flexing and massaging was she able to grasp it. Then she lifted it to her lips and drank greedily, sucking in the warm liquid in gulps. Some splashed down her chin and onto her shirt, but she ignored that.

Feeling much relieved, Kylie handed the water bottle back. Phil Kelly screwed on the cap and returned it to a saddle bag. Then he remounted and said, "Don't touch those reins, or you'll regret it."

With that he put his heels to his horse and the journey was resumed. They made their way back up onto the old railway on the other side of the gap and continued on along it. They followed it for another kilometre or so before again detouring down across another washed out embankment. But instead of going back up onto it Phil Kelly turned right and led the way across the bed of the main creek. This was rocky and uneven, and the horses had to pick their way slowly across. Once again Kylie was glad her horse seemed to be so quiet and sure footed.

On the other side they climbed up the bank onto a grassy flat. Kylie now saw that they were coming out of the big hills and a couple of minutes later they reached the gravel road she had walked along earlier. They crossed this and then halted while Kate dismounted and brushed out their tracks. Then she remounted and they rode straight into the bush up a low, stony hill among a stand of ironbarks.

No sooner had they done this than Kylie heard a vehicle coming. It was from the direction of Irvinebank. Phil Kelly heard it too and said, "Ride faster. We need to get over the crestline before it arrives."

Kylie wanted to go slow but Phil Kelly had her horse's lead rope, so she had no choice but to follow at an uncomfortable trot. They did make it over the top of the hill before the headlights became visible in the distance. The vehicle went past, heading fast to the north. Kylie did not see it, only the flicker of headlights on the trees, so she had no idea if it was a police vehicle or not.

They continued on down the far side of the hill and then across a wide grassy flat beyond. The country was a mixture of savannah woodland and thickets of prickly little bushes and small, gnarled trees that were just high enough to scrape the face and arms. Apart from having to dodge them it was fairly easy riding as the moon now gave plenty of light. After about ten minutes riding they came to a sandy track that led to the left beside another large creek. Kylie suspected this was the creek that the bushrangers were camped beside.

She was right. After another fifteen minutes or so they reached the camp. On arrival she even discovered the time when Liam met Phil Kelly and said, "Bloody four thirty! You took your time."

"Had a lot to do," Phil Kelly answered as he swung out of the saddle. Then he stretched and said, "Where's that useless little brother of mine?"

Liam jerked his thumb towards where the group of prisoners sat watching. Kylie could clearly see them in the moonlight and could only shake her head by way of apologizing for her failure. A figure stood up and walked towards them and Kylie saw it was Brian.

As Brian reached him, Phil Kelly snapped, "Well, how did your little girlfriend get away? Did you let her go?"

"No I did not!" Brian cried.

He was plainly embarrassed and that gave Kylie a spurt of malicious satisfaction. *Good!* she thought. *Serves him right! His little bit of fun at the races am I! I'll show him, and that Phil Kelly. He's a bully.*

Phil Kelly was obviously very angry. He strode over to Brian and stood over him. "Well, how did she get away then?" he demanded to know.

Brian glared back at him. "Pat forgot to tie her up, so she was able to sneak away," he replied.

At that, Pat stood up and cried angrily, "Oh good on you, you dobber! It was you that went to sleep on guard!"

Phil Kelly turned from one to the other and then said with obvious disgust, "Went to sleep on guard! You silly little drongo! That could have wrecked all our plans."

"Yeah, well it didn't. You caught her," Brian answered in a sulky voice.

"No thanks to you!" Phil Kelly snapped. "If Liam here hadn't woken up and gone to the farm to phone me, she would have made it to the coppers in Irvinebank. As it was, I only got there a couple of minutes before she did."

Hearing that made Kylie feel awful. *If only I'd walked faster!* she berated herself.

Phil Kelly went on, "Anyway, no time for this. It will be daylight in an hour or so and we can't take the risk that this place is known to the coppers. So get packed up and move to your next campsite. Make sure there is nothing left here. Now start packing and move!"

Pat and Liam at once set to work rolling up swags and buckling saddlebags and bedrolls onto horses. Brian was left to guard the prisoners. This included Kylie, who was untied and hauled down from the horse.

She ignored Brian and hobbled stiffly over to her friends. "Sorry," she muttered as she rejoined them.

"Never mind," Margaret said, patting her. "You had a good try."

Brian scowled and snapped, "Stop talking," but Kylie ignored him and proceeded to tell the others what had happened. Brian scowled some more but made no further attempt to stop her talking.

Weakling! she thought scornfully.

Within 15 minutes the camp had been packed up and the horses loaded and saddled. Phil Kelly then got the bushrangers to search carefully using torches.

"Make sure there isn't a single thing left here that can be linked to us," he instructed.

That done he and Kate moved to their horses and mounted, leaving the spare horse but taking the pack horse. Liam called to them. "Where are you and Kate going?"

"To our other camp. We will stick to the original plan as much as we can and will meet you at the Ivan....er... at the… the er... the next hideout tomorrow morning. And make sure none of these bloody kids gets away, or that Dingo fella."

"What about those new maps you promised?" Liam asked.

"I'll send Maureen over with one as soon as I get back to camp," Phil Kelly answered. "Now get moving. It will be daylight in half an hour."

With that he and Kate set off along the same track Kylie had followed earlier. Liam now took charge. "Okay, mount up," he said to the other two bushrangers, then to the prisoners, "Start walking."

Oh no! Kylie thought in dismay. "I can't!" she cried. "I'm exhausted. I can't do it. I've been walking half the night, and I need a rest and a drink."

For a few seconds Kylie thought that Liam might try to force her but then he scowled and said, "Give her your horse, Brian."

"Oh, why should I?" Brian objected.

"Because you let her escape, so you walk," Liam retorted. "And make sure you keep hold of the reins. Tie her on like she was before," he added.

On hearing that Kylie experienced a sweep of emotions: satisfaction at seeing Brian ordered to walk; relief at being allowed to ride, worry that her friends might resent her riding while they walked.

Anyway, serves him right! she told herself again.

A grumbling and annoyed Brian called on Pat to help him while he assisted Kylie to mount, then to tie her hands. He was in a foul mood, so he tied them tightly, despite her protest. Several times he met her eyes, and she could tell he was angry and humiliated.

I think the love affair is over, she told herself wryly.

Now what she wanted was an opportunity to break free. *On the horse I might have a better chance of getting away,* she reasoned.

But Brian held the reins and added a neck rope which was secured around his waist. The group then set off across the creek. Liam led, followed by Brain and Kylie, then Norah, Dingo, Margaret, Stephen, and Roger. Pat on his horse, leading the packhorse, brought up the rear.

On the other side of the creek Liam turned left and headed cross country through the bush. It was mostly easy going, undulating and with fairly open savannah. An occasional gully or thicket caused the group to make small detours. To begin with, Kylie found it very hard going as all her muscles had stiffened up again but after a while she warmed up and was able to relax and let the horse do the work. Now she thanked her lucky stars for all the riding lessons and practice over the last few days.

As she recovered, she began to take note of what was going on and where they were going. *Heading northwards,* she reasoned, using the still rising moon as a guide.

To confirm this, she noted that the big hills where Irvinebank lay were now behind her. Off to the right she got frequent glimpses of more hills but did not pay them much attention as they were travelling parallel to them. What lay to the north she had no idea.

She also began to speculate on where they were going and who they might meet there. *I wonder if Graham and Peter are there?* she thought. Their possible location and wellbeing were frequently on her mind.

For the next half hour they moved steadily through the bush. The walking prisoners were obviously suffering and seeing that made Kylie feel guilty and sympathise. She now knew just what bad chafing and blisters felt like. Even though she was on the horse she was still suffering from these herself. She could see that Margaret and Norah were limping badly and wondered if she should not offer them turns on the horse.

The group came to an even larger creek. This had steep banks and a rocky bed with a flow of shallow water in it. The group stopped for five minutes to drink, and Kylie was offered a cup by Pat. He could only shrug and indicate her bound wrists. The best that Pat could manage was to get her to lean down while he held the cup to her lips.

Brian wasn't pleased at that and muttered, "She doesn't deserve it, not after the trouble she has caused us."

Pat ignored that and asked Kylie if she wanted more. She did but the water tasted mucky, and she was afraid it might make her sick so she shook her head and said, "Someone else might like a turn on the horse, Margaret or Norah maybe?"

Pat turned to the girls and asked them. Both said no but Kylie was sure they were suffering and were just being self-sacrificing. But they insisted they could still walk so Kylie remained on the horse.

The group climbed up the far bank and then threaded their way across a large area that had been mined. There were old vehicle tracks running in all directions and heaps of gravel and red earth all partly overgrown. It did not look very nice to Kylie, even in the moonlight. Beyond that they entered the bush again, going down a long gentle slope through a stand of ironbarks.

Another dry creek was crossed and then the group came out onto an obvious cleared line in the bush. They turned to follow this, still heading north. At first Kylie did not pay much attention, but when they detoured off the clearing to skirt around a washout at a small creek she noted an obvious earth embankment beside her.

"This is the old railway," she said to Margaret.

"What old railway?" Margaret queried.

"The one that goes to Irvinebank," Kylie said. "We rode along it earlier."

At that, Brian turned and snapped, "Stop talking or I will gag you."

Kylie fell silent but she kept turning to look around and noted Roger giving Stephen significant looks. When they halted twenty minutes later for a short rest Roger confirmed what she had been thinking. "This is the old railway to Stannary Hills," he whispered.

Stephen nodded. That sent a thrill of hope through Kylie. "Have you been here before? Do you know where we are?"

"We didn't walk this bit," Roger replied quietly, "But we both know roughly where we are and where this track goes."

Liam finished drinking from a water bottle and scowled at them. "Stop yer whispering," he snarled. "Now get moving."

Reluctantly the group started moving again. As they did, Kylie noted that it was definitely getting lighter. The hills to the east were now sharply silhouetted by a pale grey light. *Be daylight soon,* she reasoned. That cheered her up, thinking of police helicopters and patrols.

As it grew slowly lighter Kylie noted the grey smudge of a road off to her left. Liam saw it too and turned right off the old railway to move away from the road. He took a line parallel to the old railway and about a hundred metres to the right of it. A dirt vehicle track was crossed and several small creeks and Kylie noted that the bush was thicker, with large trees. She also saw that they had changed direction and were now moving in a more easterly direction. They began angling towards the northern end of the line of hills.

Daylight came and still the group did not stop moving. But the bushrangers became obviously very wary and kept looking anxiously in all directions. Liam and Pat both rode with their rifles in their hands and Brian carried his as he walked along, or rather limped along. Seeing him hobbling gave Kylie another malicious spurt of satisfaction.

Serves you right! she thought. Seeing the looks of grim determination and obvious pain on her friend's faces made Kylie call for a few minutes rest. *They are all too stubborn to admit they are hurting or to give in,* she reasoned. Liam was all for pushing on.

"Only another hour and we will be there," he said.

"You will be carrying a couple of us by then," Kylie retorted, "and you'll probably be calling for an ambulance."

Pat supported her. "Another ten minutes won't matter," he said. "We can hide here as well as anywhere."

Liam gestured upwards. "It's that bloody helicopter I'm worried about," he answered.

"So?" said Pat with a shrug. "We can hide here while we rest. Some of these kids look all in."

"They are," Kylie interrupted. "Give Margaret a go on the horse." At the front of her mind was the thought that Margaret was the best on a horse and if anyone had a chance of escaping that way it was her.

Margaret protested she was alright, but Pat agreed. Liam said nothing so Pat came and untied Kylie and then helped her to dismount.

She was so stiff and cramped up that she was quite unable to get down without assistance. Pat had to call on Norah and Roger to help him and they lowered Kylie to the ground. For the next few minutes Norah and Margaret pummelled and massaged Kylie's limbs while she lay groaning on the ground.

While they did this Kylie noted Liam studying a map and discussing it with Pat. Brian sat down on a log to guard them. Stephen and Roger both knelt beside Kylie and asked anxiously if she was alright. She nodded and said, "Just a bit stiff. How far have we come do you think?"

"Only four or five kilometres I reckon," Stephen replied.

"We are going east, aren't we?" Kylie asked.

Stephen nodded. "Yes, we are."

"Isn't that back towards Herberton?" Kylie asked.

Again Stephen nodded. "Yes, it is. I think the road over there on our left is the one that leads to Hales Siding and Bakerville and then on to Herberton."[4]

"We seem to be going in a big circle," Margaret suggested.

Stephen shook his head, then glanced towards Brian before replying softly, "Might be, but I think it is more of a zig zag."

"Is it far to Herberton?" Kylie asked.

Both Norah and Stephen answered at once, both saying it was. Norah suggested 20 kilometres and Stephen 30. These sounded daunting distances to Kylie. "What about those places you just named, are there people living at them?" she asked.

Both Roger and Stephen shook their heads. Stephen answered, "Not at Hales Siding anymore but there are still people at Bakerville."

Roger now added, "That is where Graham walked to when he went to get help last year when we were in trouble at Stannary Hills."

"I'll bet this gang don't know we have this sort of local knowledge," Margaret suggested.

Stephen nodded. "No, and we must make sure they don't find out," he said.

All this cheered Kylie enormously. "One of us must try to get away and get to Bakerville," she whispered.

As the others nodded Liam gave them a sour look and called, "Stop plotting how to get away. Now get up."

---

[4] Refer to END MAP, pg. 285

Margaret was mounted on the horse and her hands tied. She still protested that Kylie should stay on the horse, but Kylie could see that she was actually relieved not to have to walk for a while. The group began moving and Kylie immediately regretted her decision. Her blisters and chafing hurt so much the pain brought tears to her eyes. But she bit her lip and hobbled on, hoping that the others would not notice.

The route they followed led them parallel to the old railway, between it and the northern end of the hills. The bush was fairly open and easy to move through, more savannah woodland with an undergrowth of knee-high grass, prickly bushes, and young trees. There were several small dry creeks but otherwise the going was almost flat. If it had not been for her aches, pains and exhaustion Kylie knew she would have found it easy going. That the others were finding it hard going, including Brian, was obvious. They looked tired and most were hobbling or limping. Norah looked drawn and grey with fatigue and only Stephen and Dingo appeared fit and well.

After half an hour of walking Kylie felt she was ready to drop. Her feet and thighs hurt so much it felt like one huge sharp pain and she felt dry and drained.

I hope it isn't much further, she thought, not wanting to give up in front of the others.

Gritting her teeth with determination she forced herself to keep putting one foot in front of another. To help take her mind of her misery she closely observed the country and the bushrangers.

She noted that they had come to a side valley that led off to the south through the hills. A quite large creek made its way northwards along the valley floor. The creek twisted and turned and had a small flow of water in it. To Kylie's surprise they turned right and began following the creek.

We are now going south, she thought, thinking that this would take them back towards Irvinebank or the hills around Mt Misery. *Maybe we are going in circles?* she wondered.

Following the creek was hard work as they had to cross several tributaries and small gullies that came in from the side. This meant a steep slither down and then a difficult and tiring climb to get back up on the level of the floodplain.

I can't take much more of this! Kylie thought in dismay as she arrived gasping up on the level ground again.

Five more minutes of painful trudging followed, then Liam led them down into the creek bed again. *Oh no!* Kylie silently moaned, *another blasted gully to cross!*

But as she reached the lip and looked down, she at once changed her mind. Stretched across the gully was a large camouflage net. This was tied to the trees on either side. Down underneath it were five horses and four people. One of them was Graham. Standing next to him was Peter. When Kylie saw them, she experienced a wave of intense relief.

They are alright! she told herself. *Now we can try to get away.*

Chapter 29

GREEN-EYED MONSTER

As quickly she could hobble, Kylie hurried down the steep bank. She ran to Graham and threw herself into his arms.

"Oh thank God! I've been so worried," she cried.

"We are alright," Graham answered. "We've been worried about you lot."

As Kylie calmed down, she saw that the other two men were bushrangers: Michael Kelly and a solidly built man with dark hair she had never seen before. His name she learned when Pat called to him.

"How are you, Sean? Things going okay?"

Liam interrupted the greetings as he dismounted. "Never mind the 'how-do-you-dos'. Tie this lot up again. We don't want any of them getting away again."

"Getting away?" Graham asked as he released Kylie from his embrace. "Who got away?"

"Me," Kylie replied. "But they caught me again."

"Bad luck," Graham answered.

"They won't catch me next time," Kylie replied in a fierce whisper. She now had the glimmerings of a plan and was determined to try it at the first opportunity.

"Good for you!" Graham replied, giving her a pat of approval.

Liam now organised the prisoners to sit in a line and ropes were produced from saddle bags. Once again, their legs were tied up and then secured to a long rope tied to a tree. Brian was then seated at the end as guard. Being cautioned to stay awake by Liam caused a sulky look to cross his face and Kylie had to hide a smirk.

I need to lull him into a false sense of security, she thought.

As soon as they were all seated, Roger called out to Liam, "Hey! What about some breakfast? I'm starving."

It was obvious to Kylie that Liam resented being spoken to but, after scowling, he did reply, "You'll get fed, though from the look of you, you could miss a few meals and it would do you good," he replied.

Kylie felt for Roger, knowing he was very sensitive about his chubbiness. But Roger's request did work. After the bushrangers cared for their horses, they began preparing breakfast. Pat and Michael prepared the food. It was cold ('No fires in case the helicopters have infra-red detection equipment', Peter suggested): sandwiches with either ham and pickles or asparagus, both out of a tin. Kylie didn't mind. She was very hungry by now and managed to eat one of each type. She then had a big drink of water and sat back feeling much better. Her chafing, muscles and blisters still hurt but at least she was with Graham and could relax. She sat and whispered to Graham, asking if he knew where they were.

Graham had some idea and once he was given more information by the others became quite excited, a condition he struggled to conceal. "If only one of us can escape we have a good chance of reaching a phone and calling the police," he said.

Kylie nodded in agreement. She was still puzzling over how to set up the situation she wanted but she had at least the outline of a plan. She now lay back to try to think out in detail how to implement it. To help her visualise it and to shield her tired eyes from the glare of the sun she closed them, and promptly fell asleep.

When she awoke, she was at first so muzzy and sore that it took her some minutes to wake up properly and to remember her situation. Her whole body felt stiff and sore, and she felt worse than when she had gone to sleep. The worst thing was the horrible taste in her mouth, but she also had a headache. She stretched warily, not wanting to risk a cramp, then looked around. Seeing Peter was awake she asked what time it was.

Peter checked his watch and replied, "Just after midday."

"Roger should ask for lunch," she joked, finding she again felt hungry.

"I will," Peter answered.

He sat up and called to Sean, who was the guard at that moment and asked if they could have a drink and something to eat. While Peter did this Kylie rubbed eyes that felt sore and gritty and carefully looked around. She saw that most of the others, including Liam, Pat and Brian, were all lying on the ground asleep. The other thing that she noted, and which fitted in with her embryonic plan, was that the bushrangers had left their horses saddled, presumably for a quick getaway. But the horses were twenty metres away under another camouflage net.

How can I get to them and get away on one? she wondered.

She was still puzzling over this when all the others were woken up to eat. The food was the same: tinned meat on bread, plus some tinned vegetables. To her surprise, Kylie enjoyed it and ate hungrily.

While they ate, she heard Graham mutter to the boys, "They are a slack mob, these bushrangers."

Peter nodded. "You can say that again! No sentry on guard, gear all over the place," he agreed.

"If it was me, I'd have a sentry up on top of the bank where he could see out over the flat in both directions," Graham added.

"Sssh! Not so loud," Stephen warned. "We don't want to teach them new tricks."

Having eaten and had a big drink Norah now asked if she could go to the toilet. Liam scowled but nodded. "Michael, you take her up the gully a bit," he ordered.

Michael did so, leading Norah away on a path that took them right past the horses. That gave Kylie an idea. *If I push him over, I might be able to get on a horse and get away before he can get up,* she thought. She began planning this, trying to visualise every movement required.

When Norah came back with Michael Kylie put her plan into action. "I need to go too," she said.

"Aw bloody hell!" Michael muttered. But he did untie her.

As she went to stand up, Liam called, "Don't trust that one, Michael. Keep her tied up while she does it. The little witch is the one who got away from Brian last night."

Michael made a face. "Then Brian should be doing this."

"You do it!" Liam ordered.

To Kylie's annoyance, she had a long rope tied around her left ankle. To further frustrate her plan Michael walked behind her holding the end of the rope. Thus, even though they went close enough to the horses to touch them, she had no chance to push him over or to get away. Irritated and peeved, she went on with going to the toilet. Now that she had said she wanted to go, she found she really needed to. But it was embarrassing. They went far enough up the gully to be around the bend but there was no way Kylie was going to drop her trousers with Michael able to see her.

"Don't watch," she said.

Michael made a wry face and blushed deep red. "I won't, but I gotta tie you to that tree first, and I gotta be able to see your head," he said.

So that was how it was done. *Oh drat!* Kylie thought as she dressed afterwards. Her plan had failed. She allowed herself to be led back to rejoin the others. Back with the others and again tied to the long rope, she sat and brooded. *Poor Mum and Dad,* she thought unhappily. *They will be beside themselves with worry.*

Graham was thinking along the same lines too, but he was also wondering where the Duke was. "He must be with the others at their other camp," he surmised.

"Probably," Peter agreed.

Stephen looked around to check where the bushrangers were. "How many of these blokes are there, do you reckon?" he asked.

Making sure that Michael could not hear they held a whispered conference. This was assisted by Margaret telling Michael she needed to go to the toilet as well.

"Bloody hell!" Michael cried. "Is there anyone else?"

"Yes me," Roger indicated.

So did Peter and Stephen. Michael grumbled and shook his head. "I will take all you blokes in a group when I bring this one back," he said. He then led Margaret away.

As the other bushrangers were sitting a bit further away, the group took the opportunity to discuss their chances of escape, and also to consider what they knew about the Kelly Gang.

"There were six of them in their armour at Herberton," Roger said.

Graham began listing them; "They would have been Phil Kelly, young Michael here, the lovely Kate, your boyfriend Brian…"

"He's not my boyfriend!" Kylie cut in, hurt pride giving a sharp edge to her lowered voice.

"Sorry Sis. It just looked that way," Graham answered. He then went on: "There is also Liam here, Pat. Patrick Mulligan I heard his name is; and that horrible fellow named Dan..."

"Yeah, Dan. Where is he?" Stephen asked. "He was with us at that other camp last night."

Nobody knew. "He must have left at some time last night," Roger said.

Kylie now added her bit. "There is Sean here, and I heard them talk about a bloke named Shaemus when we were at Mt Garnet."

"And that Brendan fellow who drove the vehicle with Mum in it," Norah said.

"I think the coppers caught him at Irvinebank," Stephen said.

Norah nodded. "I hope so. Oh! I hope my Mum is alright!"

That upset Kylie who again thought of the worry all their parents must now be going through. She said, "There was also that Ryan fellow who drove us to the camp."

"I don't think he is a member of the gang," Stephen said. "He looked like he was being forced to do that."

Roger nodded. "I agree. So is that all?"

Kylie shook her head. "There is Maureen O'Grady," she said, unable to keep the bitterness out of her voice.

"Who is she?" Graham asked. He looked at Kylie but she found she was unable to speak. Instead she sat there burning with embarrassment and jealousy.

Norah answered. "She is Brian's girlfriend."

Graham and Peter gave Kylie surprised looks, which made her burn even more. To change the subject Peter asked, "Well, is that the lot?"

Kylie now found her tongue. "There was the man at the Irvinebank cemetery last night; Jerry or something like that, the one who gave them the food."

"Is he a member of the gang, or just as sympathiser?" Peter asked.

"Just a supporter I'd say," Kylie answered. "I think the gang has a lot of friends, which is why they have been able to avoid capture so far."

Peter agreed. "They give them information, food and hiding places."

Dingo had been sitting listening to this and he now gave the total. "That is ten of them; eight males and two girls, plus a few supporters."

"And there are five here, so where are the other five?" Stephen asked.

"At their other secret camp with the Duke," Roger replied.

Further conversation on the subject was made difficult by the return of Michael with Margaret. As soon as Margaret had been retied Michael took the boys away. Kylie sat and talked quietly with Margaret, trying to concoct a plan that would work. She told Margaret about her idea of grabbing a horse and Margaret nodded.

"I thought of that," she said. "I reckon I could outride these guys."

The boys came back and Pat took over as guard. Michael moved away and lay down to sleep. Pat was stricter and would not allow talking so the friends lay down again. It was nearly 2:00pm by then and the air in the gully was quite hot and still. The effect of this was to induce drowsiness and Kylie fidgeted for a few minutes to get as comfortable as she could on the ground, then closed her eyes to rest.

I might need all the energy I can find if I get a chance to get away, she thought.

She dozed fitfully for the next hour. Just after 3:00 she opened her eyes and stared up at the clear blue sky, visible through the trees and netting. The air was hot and still. She heard voices and looking down the gully saw Pat nudging Brian with his boot.

"Your turn on guard," he said.

Grumbling and obviously not happy Brian got up and picked up his rifle. Next, he had a drink, then checked that all the prisoners were still tied up. While doing this he made a particular point of testing Kylie's bonds. During this she kept her eyes closed and pretended to be asleep, not wanting to make eye contact with him. He then moved to sit on the ground up the gully between the prisoners and the horses.

That did not suit Kylie's escape plans at all so she lay there simmering with annoyance and resentment. *His little bit of fun at the races, eh?* she told herself, feeding the resentment. Then she felt very unhappy and knew with a certainty that she was not just hurt at being lied to and used; she knew she was jealous.

Dingo now sat up and asked Brian if he could go to the toilet. Grumbling even more Brian untied Dingo and followed him warily up the gully. As he did, Kylie noted through half-closed lids that he kept well clear of Dingo and kept his rifle aimed at him.

He's scared of Dingo, she noted. Then she wondered, *Can I get away while he is gone?*

She looked towards the others, who were all lying down. As she did, she heard one of the small radios crackle. Liam rolled over and picked it up.

He said, "Yes, over." Then he listened and replied, "Just follow the creek upstream Maureen. You can't miss us." After again listening he added, "Okay, see you in ten minutes, over."

Suddenly an idea came to Kylie. As it formed in her mind her heart rate shot up and she felt quite breathless. For a few seconds she turned the idea over, but she had no chance to polish it, or to explain to the others because she knew it had to be done at once. By then Brian and Dingo were visible coming back along the gully.

As Brian knelt to refasten Dingo's legs, Kylie sat up, pretending to wake up. She looked at Brian and forced a smile.

"Brian, can I go to the toilet please," she asked.

"Oh alright!" he grumbled.

Having retied Dingo, he moved to Kylie's legs and untied them. She wanted to ask him to also untie her hands but knew that might make him suspicious so she just hoped he would not leg rope her like Pat had done. To her relief, he did not. Groaning at the stiff and sore muscles she levered herself up, then stood for a moment to rub her muscles. Then she started walking the other way, down towards the creek.

"Hey, why that way?" Brian asked suspiciously.

"Because... because..." Kylie stammered, blushing red. Her plan involved some deceit and she was ashamed of herself, but it also involved concepts of feminine hygiene and that did embarrass her. "Because it… it's... it's that time of month and I need to wash myself after, you know," she stammered.

Brian frowned and then went red as he grasped what she was hinting at. "Oh, er, er. alright," he said.

Kylie nodded. She then walked stiffly down the gully past the other bushrangers, who all lay stretched out dozing or asleep on their bedrolls. At the creek she hesitated. Right, or left? *He told Maureen to follow the creek upstream*, she thought. Her eyes noted the gentle trickle of the current and that told her which way to go. She turned left and walked down the bed of the creek.

After about 25 metres and one bend, Brian called out from behind her, "That's far enough."

"I don't want anyone to see me," Kylie answered. "I'm embarrassed."

"So am I, but I don't want you running away. I've got to be able to see you," Brian replied.

Kylie now began her act. She was now very excited and was having trouble hiding it. "Oh Brian, I'm sorry for last night," she said. So saying she turned to face him, noting as she did that they were out of sight of all the other bushrangers. "I didn't mean to get you into trouble," she added.

Brian made a face. Kylie saw that he was holding his rifle but not pointing it at her. Knowing that time was running out fast she made herself keep acting. She allowed her eyes to screw up and made her face crumple.

She let out a couple of sobs and wailed, "Oh Brian! I love you! I don't want to hurt you!"

With that she stepped closer to him. She saw his face soften and he went red. Their eyes met and locked. She stepped closer again, breathless with anticipation.

"Please," she whispered. "I truly do love you. I think you are the most wonderful man I have ever met. You are so handsome, and so brave. I think of you almost every minute. Oh please hold me!"

By then she was within arm's reach. Brian moved back a step and Kylie saw a mix of emotions flit across his face, noting that he really was very handsome. Desperate to make her plan work, and blushing with shame at the lies, she said, "Please hold me! Please kiss me again!"

This time Brian did not step back. He looked both pleased and puzzled. He actually let go of his rifle with his left hand and then placed his left arm around her shoulders. Playing her part to the full Kylie sighed and snuggled into his embrace, resting her head on his chest and shoulder, to hide her face. Then, once she had regained control of her face she looked up, lips parted, eyes beaming adoration.

"Oh please kiss me!" she whispered in what she hoped was a sexy, sultry voice.

Brain swallowed, then nodded and bent to do so. Kylie allowed him to kiss her,-even though it caused her a wave of revulsion, and another bad attack of jealousy.

He really is very handsome, and he is a nice kisser, she thought.

She felt her resolve weaken as her emotions swirled in torment. For a few seconds she hoped she could actually win him back, before memories of that burning humiliation of being cheated on stiffened her resolve. To keep the act going she pressed her body hard against his in a way she knew was shameless and which set her burning with both shame and desire. To add to it she lifted her bound wrists and placed them around his neck. Then she returned his kisses with all the pretend fire and passion she could muster, breathing fast, sighing and rubbing herself against him.

She then put her head on his shoulder and held him tight, looking over his shoulder down the creek. Movement caught her eye, a person on a horse, Maureen!

A shiver of triumph ran through her and she resumed kissing him. "Oh Brian! This is wonderful," she murmured, nibbling at his ear.

She could tell he was enjoying the experience. As they kissed, she looked over his shoulder with one eye and was gratified to see that Maureen had now seen them and was staring open-mouthed.

To make sure that Maureen identified Brian, Kylie lifted her arms from around his neck and snuggled against him. She felt his arms stoke up her back, and then suddenly stiffen.

He's seen her! she deduced.

Maureen's voice suddenly sounded, "Brian! What are you doing?"

Brian jerked around and pushed Kylie away from him. Guilt showed plainly on his face. "I... I... er, I was..."

"I can see what you were doing, you cheating bastard!" Maureen shouted. She put her heels to her horse and the animal sprang forward. Both Kylie and Brian scrambled to get out of the way, but Maureen reined in and vaulted out of the saddle. She flashed furious eyes at Kylie. "Who are you?"

"I'm Kylie," Kylie replied. "I'm Brian's girl, but now I'm sorry I ever met him because he has me tied up and he was trying to do horrible things to me against my will," she added.

"Brian's girl!" Maureen shrieked. She turned on Brian who was staring at Kylie in horror at her words, and who then tried to deny it.

"I've never seen her before she was taken prisoner," he cried.

Kylie really became angry at that. "Oh yes you did!" she spat. "You met me at Mt Garnet and we went to the races together. We danced all night, well, not all night, we…"

She never got any further because Maureen's face went deep red, and she turned on Brian in jealous fury. "You bastard! You told me you only went to the races with Kate."

"She's lying!" Brian cried, flicking a venomous glance in Kylie's direction.

"I don't think so!" Maureen snapped angrily, her eyes blazing and her hands on her hips as she confronted him.

Kylie saw that this was the only chance she would get. She had hoped to grab the horse, but it was now on the other side of Brian and Maureen. As the two began to argue she turned and began walking away down the creek. She did not run, although it took all of her willpower not to do so.

Running will alarm them and attract their attention, she told herself. So she kept it to a steady walk.

Chapter 30

RUN!

As Kylie walked away, Brian turned and called to her, "Hey! Where are you going? Stop!"

Kylie half-turned, noting that Maureen was angrily focused on Brian, rather than on her. "I am just going to the toilet," she snapped back.

"Don't go out of sight," Brian warned.

On hearing that, Maureen drew in her breath sharply. She shouted at Brian, "Oh, you pervert!" Then she slapped him hard on his left cheek.

Brian jumped back, almost stumbling into the creek. Clutching his face he shouted in return, "Oooh! You bitch! I wasn't going to watch her doing it. I just have to keep an eye on her."

"Don't call me a bitch, you sneak!" Maureen screamed.

She tried to hit him again and continued to call him names like 'two-timer', 'cheat' and so on. While Maureen did this Kylie continued walking down the creek. By now her heart was hammering wildly with both excitement and hope. She reached he next bend in the creek and glanced back. Seeing that Brian was now arguing furiously with Maureen and apparently trying to stop her scratching his face or eyes she hurried on around the bend. Another glance back showed her that she was out of sight.

Run! Kylie told herself.

She at once set off down the creek, hoping that neither Brian nor Maureen would notice for a few more minutes. She knew it was a slim chance, but it was all she had, and she took it. It was the thought of Maureen's horse that bothered her most.

She will catch up in seconds on that, she thought.

The obvious solution was to try to escape across ground that did not suit horse-riding. Close on her left was a small gully. She turned up it and scrambled up to the level of the plain. As she arrived on top, she cast a hasty glance to the left. Fifty metres away she could just make out the top of the camouflage nets where the others were but, to her relief, no heads were showing above the lip of that gully.

She started running across the flat but her first impression got her thinking hard. It was at least a hundred metres of flat, fairly open ground before the bottom of a small hill. There were logs, bushes, and termite mounds, but not enough to really hide behind.

Not from a search by four or five people, she reasoned. The hill was not very steep and looked open and easy to ride up. *That doesn't look like the best way to go either,* she thought.

Away to her right was the more thickly vegetated ground they had ridden in across but even it looked flat. *I need to trick them*, she decided.

Another quick look back over her shoulder showed no sign of pursuit yet so she instantly changed direction and ran to her right. This took her across the flat ground beside the creek. Twenty metres ahead was another of the side gullies that had so annoyed and exhausted her as they had travelled to the camp. Now she saw it as her salvation.

Can I reach it before anyone comes up onto the bank and sees me? she wondered, her heart in her mouth with anxiety.

She did. A few seconds later she was slithering down into the gully. It was steep sided and in places washed out and she had to slow down or risk a bad fall. As it was, she slipped a couple of times and felt a sharp pain in the muscles on the inside of her thigh. By now she was gasping for breath so needed to slow down anyway.

A quick scramble down the gully brought her back to the main creek. Here she paused and peeked around the corner. As she did, she saw Brian go dashing out of sight up the gully she had first followed. Then she got a fleeting glimpse of Maureen, now mounted on her horse, as she urged it up onto the flat.

I must move! Must get away from here! Kylie told herself.

The best route seemed to be down the creek, so she went that way, remembering not to tread on any bare sand as she did. Now she was worried that other bushrangers might come along the creek from their camp and see her, so she only ran as far as the next bend. This went to the right and she thankfully dashed around it and out of sight. Twenty paces around the bend was another curve to the left, and at this point yet another side gully came in, this time from the other side of the creek. Immediately she changed her plan and took it, clambering up over some eroded washouts.

This was hard to do because of her bound wrists. That made it difficult for her to keep her balance or to get a grip. For a few seconds she paused, both to get her breath back and to see if she could untie her hands. Deciding she could not easily do it she resumed her flight.

The gully snaked its way into the flat on the other bank. Its sides were steep, being eroded bare clay in many places. It was also very narrow and difficult to move along, and she saw that she was leaving boot prints in the sandy bed. Again she paused, wondering how to brush them out. Then she shrugged and hurried on, deciding it would waste too much time.

More important to get right out of the area, she told herself.

But the next section of gully almost defeated her. With her hands tied she found it very difficult to get a good handhold to climb up a steep washout. To try to get free she paused and worked her wrists to and fro. That did not seem to work so she tried using her teeth to undo the knots but that didn't work either.

From behind her to her right she now heard voices, men yelling. Hearing that brought a sardonic smile to her lips. *Brian will be in double trouble now,* she thought, though not without a twinge of regret at the 'might-have-been' romance.

After about fifty metres the gully narrowed and became noticeably shallower. A number of even smaller gullies fed into it. Kylie realised she was coming up to the level of the plain, so she slowed and cautiously peeked over the top. At first she could not see the area she had left so she raised herself higher behind a tree and then was able to see out over the creek onto the plain on the other side. Movement caught her eyes, and she noted several men hurrying away from her through the bush. At the base of the hill beyond the bushranger's camp she glimpsed Maureen on her horse.

She is the most dangerous, Kylie decided. *Not only is Maureen mounted she might see me as a rival for Brian,* she thought.

She now turned her head the other way to look for the best route to follow. To her dismay she saw it was just more flat bush and that the nearest hill was at least half a kilometre away and apparently beyond another creek line. For a few more seconds she hesitated, wondering if she should just hide where she was.

Then she shook her head. *No. If they search each gully they will find me,* she reasoned. *I must get further away.*

To do that without risking being seen meant crawling in the grass across the flat and on realising that Kylie cursed her light-coloured shirt. *It will be very visible,* she thought, wondering how to darken it.

Not having any method immediately available she decided to keep low and push on. With that in mind she slid over the lip of the gully onto the flat ground and began squirming forward on her tummy.

This immediately became an ordeal. Not only was it hard to do but there wasn't nearly enough grass for her plan. She found she could turn her head and get glimpses of the bushrangers as they searched the other bank.

If I can see them then they can see me, she reasoned.

But there did not seem to be any other option but to go on. So she resumed crawling, dragging herself along as low to the ground as she could manage. That brought with it the fear of encountering a snake and that almost paralysed her. To get her breath back and to summon up her courage she lay panting, stretched out flat for half a minute. Then she continued on.

Several times shouts made her think she had been spotted and she lay flat and froze but each time her anxious looks told her that the search was still on the other bank and now at least 150 metres away. Satisfied she was escaping she forced herself to wriggle on, thrusting thoughts of snakes to the back of her mind.

After about 50 metres Kylie suddenly found herself beside a dirt vehicle track. It was only two wheel ruts in the grass but it still gave her pause. She slid forward and looked both ways along it, noting both recent tyre tracks and also hoof prints.

I had better not leave any tracks as I cross this, she told herself.

Very carefully she crawled across, then turned and brushed out any signs and straightened some bent stalks of grass. Then she crawled on another 50 metres to get away from the track.

The bushrangers might use it, she thought, knowing that a person seated high up on a horse would have a much better view down into the grass.

The road also got her thinking about which way to go next. *It runs north,* she reasoned. *So it must join that gravel road that goes to Bakerville. If I go that way, I can then follow the main road to get help, at least, not follow the road but move parallel to it and use it as a navigation aid.*

Having worked that out Kylie turned left and continued crawling. By this time she was at least 200 metres from the bushranger's camp and felt reasonably confident she had escaped the initial search. Even so she moved further away from the camp, heading across the crest of a very gentle ridge. As she did, she began to consider getting up on her hands and knees. The crawling she found exhausting and painful. The front of her clothes was now dirty and covered in grass and she noted she had lost a button.

She contemplated this, noting that it allowed the front of her shirt to gape slightly, giving glimpses of her bra. *Oh dear! That will give Brian ideas if he sees it,* she thought, colouring with embarrassment.

Of more concern was that her knees, elbows and hands hurt, and that she had almost scraped her knuckles raw. For a couple of minutes she lay in the grass behind a bush and sucked her bleeding knuckles.

She then resumed her slow movement, this time crawling on hands and knees. As she moved, she cast frequent glances over her left shoulder. No sooner had she moved out from the bush she had used as cover than she heard voices. She froze and tried to focus her eyes. To her annoyance her vision seemed to blur, and her eyes felt sore. She had trouble focusing but then into view seemed to leap Brian on a horse.

To her dismay, she saw he was riding towards her, apparently searching the grass on her side of the vehicle track. To his left, following what Kylie thought must be the line of the vehicle track, was Maureen. Fifty paces to her left, between her and the creek, rode Liam. Just visible beyond him and near the bank of the creek, was Pat.

They are searching in extended line, Kylie thought.

In her mind's eye she pictured them combing the country in a long line side by side. By this time she was lying as low and flat as she could in the grass, in what now seemed to be very short, sparse grass! Squinting through the tuft in front of her face she studied the approaching riders, her heart beating faster and sweat breaking out all over her body. The only comforting thing she could see was that only Liam seemed to have a rifle in his hands.

As the riders got closer, Kylie's fear increased. Her muscles tensed and she cringed in anticipation. It seemed to her that Brian could not help seeing her, so close would he pass.

Oh blast! she thought. *To get so close to escaping and then to be caught like this!* Lying there on the flat ground she felt like a fly on a white ceiling. *He must see me soon,* she thought, her anxiety increasing till she was tensed and quivering.

By then Brian was close enough to hear. Kylie had deduced that he would pass only ten paces or so to her left, between her and the vehicle track. She heard him say, “This is bloody hopeless. She is long gone. We will never find her now.”

“Keep searching,” Liam called back. “There is still a chance.”

Yes, still a chance! Kylie thought bitterly as Brian rode ever closer.

Liam pointed and called, “We will search as far as the road on this sweep, then work out what to do next.”

“Get on with the next part of our plan while we can,” Brian suggested.

As he spoke, he kept turning towards Liam, for which Kylie was grateful. But by now he was only 50 metres away and she could not see how discovery could possibly be avoided.

Maureen now spoke. “If you had been more careful none of this would have happened.”

Brian looked at her, obviously upset. “I was being careful,” he replied.

Maureen curled her lip. “Careful about what, not being seen by the others while you snuck off for a little bit of a pash?”

“Oh Maur! It wasn’t like that. I was just taking her to the toilet. She was the one who threw herself at me and kissed me.”

“Crap!” Maureen snorted. “It didn’t look like that to me. So why did she say she was your girlfriend; that you took her to the races?”

Brian was now only 25 metres from Kylie and she lay perspiring with tension. Ants crawled on her, but she did not dare move. To her intense relief, she saw Brian blush and then turn his horse towards Maureen. Lowering his voice, presumably so that Liam could not hear him, he said, “Maureen, I love you. It was all some sort of a trick on her part.”

“Well it worked!” Maureen retorted with a sneering laugh. “You fell for it, hook, line, and sinker. But I’m still not convinced. What did happen at the races?”

Brain went even redder, glanced towards Liam and urged his horse even closer to Maureen. This took him past Kylie at a distance of about 20 metres and she saw that he was so busy trying to convince Maureen that he was focused on her and not searching the ground.

And then he was past.

As soon as Kylie could see his back she got ready to move. She slowly wriggled round, her eyes now on Maureen, who was turning her head to talk to Brian. By now Kylie could not hear the words distinctly but it was obvious from her angry tone that Brian had a lot of making up to do.

Serves the cheating rat right! Kylie thought.

She then began crawling away to her right, all the while glancing back over her left shoulder to check on the locations of the riders. To her relief, they continued on until they were at least a hundred metres away. They then stopped and grouped together.

That road must be just there, Kylie thought as she slithered in behind a small spiky bush.

The bushrangers sat on their horses in conversation for some minutes. Kylie even heard raised voices and it was obvious they were not a happy band and that there was a lot of acrimonious blaming and fault finding. That cheered her up too, being balm to her injured pride.

Suddenly the bushrangers stopped talking and split up. For a second Kylie feared they were about to resume the search but then she saw that Maureen was riding off almost directly away from her while the others were heading back along the vehicle track in single file. As they went past at a trot it was clear that they had reached some decision and were acting on it. It was also plain to her that Brian was very unhappy.

Maureen was soon lost to sight, heading off down slope to the northwest at a canter, while the others vanished from sight back down into the creek line. That left Kylie wondering what to do. After a few minutes she decided she had better keep moving.

I need to get help, she reasoned.

Having decided that she set off crawling on hands and knees, angling off to her right, away from the direction the bushrangers had gone in. This took her down a long gentle slope into an area with quite a thick scattering of grasstrees. There were also numerous large termite mounds and large trees. All these provided cover. By then her knees and hands were stinging and bruised. After a careful look in all directions she cautiously rose to her feet and began walking.

A couple of minutes' walk had her at another creek line. This one had steep banks among a thick stand of timber. In its bed was a trickle of clear water. That cheered Kylie some more because she was now feeling very thirsty. She slid down to the bed and knelt to drink, cupping the water with difficulty in her hands. While doing this she was careful to avoid standing on any sand except in the flowing water.

The bindings on her wrists made drinking awkward and she was concerned to note that both hands had taken on a sort of greyish tinge. *The blood is not circulating properly,* she thought, remembering

First Aid lessons at Guides which stressed the dangers of the tourniquet. She resolved to free her hands as soon as she could. Her first attempts were to no avail. Her teeth were quite unable to grip the knots to tease them loose.

Frustrated and worried with memories of horror stories about gangrene setting in and limbs having to be amputated she resumed walking, climbing up through a thicket of gnarled and twisted little trees to the flatter ground above. As she walked along, she noted with some alarm that she was actually very close to the gravel road. She was about to swerve further away from it when she noticed that there was a barbed wire fence paralleling the road on the other side.

The barbs might be able to cut these knots, or snag them, she thought.

With that in mind she crept closer to the road, continually looking in both directions. In this way she reached a bush close beside the road. Once again, she checked both ways and tensed ready to cross. Then, just as she stood up to take the first step, she glimpsed movement to her left.

In a second she was back down in the grass, her heart pounding with alarm. *Did they see me?* she wondered.

To check she edged forward to a small bush and peeked through it back along the road. The movement, she now saw, was a lone horseman riding fast in her direction, a rifle resting across his saddle. Kylie realised he was coming her way at a canter.

Anxiously she glanced behind, seeking a covered withdrawal route and a place to hide. Then she took another look, just to be sure. As the horseman went down into the dip where the road crossed the creek Kylie saw that the rider was Brian.

Where is he going on his own? she wondered, still thinking he had seen her and was hurrying to recapture her.

Then, just as she began backing away, she glimpsed more movement back to her left. Even though Brian was now only a hundred metres away she paused to look. Back on the crest of the ridge she had hidden on she saw a horseman cross the road, followed by a line of walking people.

They are leaving the area, Kylie thought in dismay. She was instantly sure of that. *They think their camp is no longer a safe place to be and are moving to a new hideout before I can get the police,* she reasoned. But where were they going to? *And where is Brian off to in such a hurry?* she worried.

From behind a bush she watched the group cross the road in the distance, counting them as they did. She counted all of her friends and was sure they were tied together. When only one more horseman and three pack horses followed the walking figures across she was puzzled.

That isn't all of them. I think that was Michael leading and Liam at the rear. So where are Pat and Sean?

By then she had left it too late to crawl away without risking being seen. All she could do was huddle in behind a log and a termite nest in the grass. Somehow, she felt that Brian had not seen her, thinking that if he had then more of the bushrangers would have come to make sure she was caught. Even so she was very anxious. She broke into a sweat and all her muscles tensed up. They tightened up so much that she experienced an agonising cramp in her left calf muscle. The agony made her gasp in pain. She had to bite on her knuckles so as not to cry out.

As she did, Brian went cantering past. Kylie watched him, wide-eyed with anxiety, through the small bush. As he went past her suspicions were confirmed. He obviously did not know she was there and was staring ahead, not scanning the bush. He looked so downcast that Kylie felt a momentary twinge of sympathy for him (and then an even bigger surge of self-pity for herself).

Watching his back as he moved quickly away from her got her mind working quickly. Where was he going, and why?

He is going the way I want to go, towards Bakerville, she thought. Was his intention to get ahead of her and somehow trap her or cut her off from reaching help? It seemed highly likely to her. *And Pat might have been sent south along that other vehicle track in case I went that way, and Sean could have gone west along this road*, she speculated.

Then another problem rose to bother her. *What is the point of me going to get help if I don't know where to lead the police to?* she worried. That got her all in a dither of indecision: *Do I go to the police and hope that the black trackers can follow the trail; or do I follow Graham and the others to see where the next hideout is, then try to get help?*

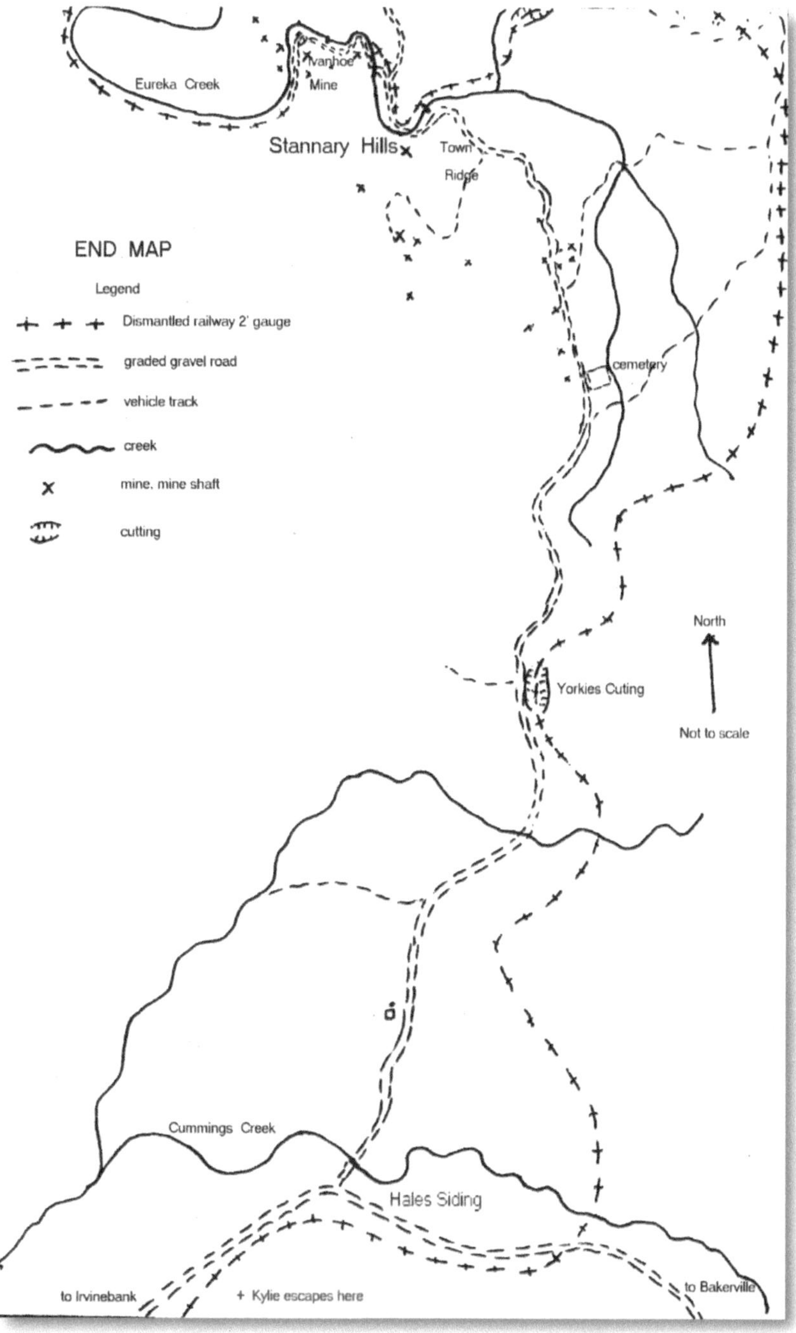
Eureka Creek
Ivanhoe
Mine
Stannary Hills
Town
Ridge
END MAP
Legend
Dismantled railway 2' gauge
graded gravel road
vehicle track
creek
mine, mine shaft
cutting
cemetery
North
Yorkies Cuting
Not to scale
Cummings Creek
Hales Siding
to Irvinebank
+ Kylie escapes here
to Bakerville

Chapter 31

WHICH WAY?

Kylie lay in the grass, ignoring the ants and prickling, until Brian vanished from view around the next bend. As soon as his back was no longer visible, she looked to her left to check there was no-one there, then she quickly rose to her feet. This part of her plan almost failed because the cramp returned. All she could do was whimper softly and punch at the knotted muscle. In doing so she sank back to one knee. After a minute or so the cramp eased but it left her trembling and afraid. It had hurt so much she was in fear of moving lest she induce another.

I can't stay here, she told herself. *Get up and move, you big baby!*

So she gritted her teeth and tried again. This time it was her other muscles that bothered her. They had all stiffened up and she groaned at the pain of forcing them into action. The result was that she hobbled across the road, moaning softly and worrying that she might be seen.

Oh, I couldn't have run away! I hope I am up to this, she thought.

Now she returned to her original plan. She limped over to the barbed wire fence and then along it till she found a place where there were plenty of bushes and logs close handy to provide a hiding place should she need one. Carefully she crawled under the fence. Then she set to work on the knots. This time she was more successful. The barbs hooked into the rope and she was soon able to loosen part of the knot. The barb also frayed the rope, giving her the idea that, if she could not undo the knot, then she could eventually cut the rope. To her enormous relief, she soon worked one of the strands loose enough for her to grip it with her teeth. After that it was only the work of seconds to undo it.

As soon as the rope was untied, she moved to cover and sat down. For several minutes she massaged and rubbed, whimpering in pain as the circulation returned. While she did this her mind was busy on trying to work out which way to go.

Do I make for this Bakerville place and contact the police; or do I follow my friends to find out where the bushrangers have their next secret camp? she wondered.

In favour of going to Bakerville was the fact that it was only fifteen kilometres or so. Against it was the fact that Brian had gone in that direction, and she was sure he would be in hiding to try to catch her as she went past.

I will have to walk cross-country well away from the road to avoid him, she thought.

That bothered her greatly as she lacked confidence in her ability to navigate through the bush, particularly as she had no map or compass. As it was, she knew it could take her five or six hours to get to Bakerville.

And getting lost in the bush could mean waiting till tomorrow, she considered. There was also the problem of not knowing where the bushrangers had gone once she had contacted the police. *I will look a bit of a goose if I take the police to an empty camp and they can't follow the tracks to the next one,* she worried.

That got her contemplating just how good the so-called 'Ghosts of Glenrowan' might be. *Can they really follow tracks through the bush with that much certainty?* she wondered.

Her ignorance on the subject made her ashamed because she had read about black trackers at school, and she had an idea the traditional tribal Aborigines had been unrivalled at the skill. But were these men as skilled?

But when she made her mind up it was not on such logic that she made the decision; it was on the more emotional grounds of not wanting to lose her friends and of the hope that she might be able to help them escape too. She knew it was possibly the wrong decision, but she rationalised it on the grounds that she had to be able to take the police somewhere.

I will follow the group, she decided.

Having decided that, she set off down the slope through the bush, her eyes now searching for some sign of them. That became her next anxiety, knowing she was wasting valuable time if she lost the trail and then had to backtrack.

I'd better not get lost, she thought, looking back to try to memorize the route she was following.

At least the going was easy: a long, gentle downslope through sparsely grassed savannah woodland to a fair-sized creek lined with paperbarks. That was just as well, because she was in so much pain she was having trouble walking. Her chafing and blisters all added to the misery of stiff muscles.

How on earth do those silly boys get any pleasure out of hiking as a hobby! she marvelled.

She reached the creek and saw that it had a sandy bed ten metres wide along which was flowing an ankle deep run of greyish looking water. The water eased another of her fears, that she might regret her decision as she became hungry and thirsty.

At least there should be plenty to drink, she reasoned.

That made her thankful it was April and not later in the year, when she knew that creeks like this were just dry sand.

After drinking her fill she splashed across, then saw that her boot prints were very obvious in the sand. *I had better brush them out in case someone comes along,* she thought.

She used a branch with dead leaves on it to do this. While she was doing so it occurred to her that the group must have left a very obvious trail if they crossed the same creek.

They should be somewhere down to my left, she told herself.

That was also downstream. She set off that way, walking on the top of the bank so she could also see into the flat bush. This made for awkward going because of the curves in the creek and the small side gullies that came in, each of which necessitated a tiring climb down and up.

But she persevered as she knew she was now twenty or thirty minutes behind the group. Once she had overheard Graham and Peter discussing how fast they could march and it had been a kilometre in ten minutes on flat ground.

They could be two or three kilometres away by now, she thought anxiously, well aware she could only see a few hundred metres through the bush.

She reasoned she had to be sure of finding the crossing, or waste more time. So she kept on walking west, keeping close to the creek.

Five minutes later Kylie found the place where the group had crossed. Seeing it quite amazed her. The line of boot prints and hoof prints was very clear. It led off northwards. She was also surprised to note that the tracks were quite easy to follow through the grass. Partly this was because the soil was sandy and in the bare patches the imprints were plain to see, but in the grassy areas a very clear trail of flattened grass showed.

They don't seem to be making any attempt to hide their tracks, she thought.

That puzzled her and got her wondering, even as she set off following. Was it because they were confident the police were not looking in this area? That made her realise she had not seen the police helicopter at all that day. She considered whether it was because the bushrangers or their friends had spread more false rumours and trails. Or was it because the police still thought they were back in the hills south of Irvinebank?

"They also seem to keep splitting up a lot, either into small groups or going off individually. Maybe that also makes them hard to track," she muttered. Then a more worrying thought came to her about the clear trail she was currently walking along: were the bushrangers doing it to try to recapture her, hoping she would do exactly what she was doing? That got Kylie all anxious, but she could not see what else she could do.

If I don't walk along the track I will lose it, she reasoned.

Anxious scanning of the bush ahead made her very conscious that she would easily be caught if one of the bushrangers just waited on his horse. The country was so flat and open she could not possibly outrun them or even hide effectively. But then she shrugged. Having decided to follow all she could do was press on and keep a sharp lookout.

The 'pressing on' soon dominated her mind. The sheer effort and pain of walking got her gritting her teeth in determination. Only as her muscles warmed up did she find it easier. All the various aches and pains then seemed to meld into one overall feeling of physical misery. Even the chafing went from sharp agony to dull ache.

So she limped on. The ground stayed easy to walk over, a long, very gentle upslope with short grass on sandy soil and almost no undergrowth in under the forest of large gum trees. The trail kept on northwards. After fifteen minutes walking she came to a vehicle track; the usual two wheel ruts in the grass. The group had turned right to follow it so she did the same.

Apart from her pains and weakness the walking was easy. But Kylie felt very lonely and isolated. There was no sign of any human settlement: no houses, huts, fences, or clearings, just bush. More worrying was the glimpses she began getting of a range of hills ahead. As she plodded on up to a wide, flat crest, she saw that the hills were very extensive and seemed to curve across her front for half her horizon. She doubted if she was up to many hills.

I need food, and a good rest, she told herself, well aware that physical exhaustion was slowing her down. But she did not rest. *I must catch them up,* she told herself.

She was also thirsty again. The afternoon sun was blazing in on her left, the heat making her sweat continually. She also knew she was badly sunburnt and wished she had a hat.

But there seemed to be nothing for it but to press on, so she did. Then she noted that there was a road junction ahead. It was near a clump of rocks. She limped to it and stood looking both ways along the graded gravel road she had reached. Then she berated herself, "Oh, you silly girl! Don't walk out into the open where anyone can see you!"

Quickly Kylie moved back among the trees and resumed her study. What was bothering her was whether this was the same road as the one she had been following earlier.

I have been walking more north than anything else, she reasoned, aware of the sun sinking lower on her left, the west. *I thought Herberton and Bakerville were to the east?*

Biting her lip she tried to remember the conversations back at the last camp. She noted that the gravel road curved to the northeast and went down a long slope before curving left around the end of a hill a kilometre or so away.

There is a barbed wire fence on the other side of the road, she noted. *A brand new one,* she added, noting the shiny wire.

But which way did the group go? She peered carefully at the dust, and got a shock. There were no tracks visible! That got her heart beating with anxiety. For a couple of minutes she cast back and forth before she was convinced that there were indeed no tracks at the road junction, or on the gravel road.

"They must have turned off somewhere!" she muttered, dismay and annoyance at her own mistake lowering her morale.

She realised she had been so taken up with just walking that she had not been paying attention. Suddenly she just felt like giving up; of just sitting beside the gravel road till a vehicle came along.

But then she smiled wryly and thought, *And the first vehicle to come along will be the bushrangers!*

After a couple of minutes sitting on one of the rocks, she pushed herself upright. *Come on weakie! Get moving. The others are depending on you!*

Painfully she began walking again. She went back along the two wheel tracks, carefully studying the ground.

Within a hundred paces she found the place where the group had turned off. They had gone left, northeast. To Kylie's relief, their tracks were still plain to see, a flattened path in the knee-high grass. Almost sobbing with exhaustion she set off to follow them. Her anxiety was now being fuelled by an awareness that the sun was sinking fast, was so low in the west it could only be an hour or so to nightfall.

It was quickly apparent that the trail was running roughly parallel to the gravel road as she kept getting glimpses of it off to her right. The trail wound around several clumps of rocks as it went downslope. Even in her tired state Kylie noted that there had been an abrupt change in both the vegetation and soil type. On the down slope there were no more large eucalypts with white trunks. Instead there were thickets of small, spindly paperbarks. These were easy enough to move through and gave better cover, for which she was thankful as she was now approaching the first of the hills and the trail appeared to be heading directly for it.

That thought stopped her to scan the scrub-covered slope ahead. It was as well she did because she saw the flicker of movement through the trees just up on the next hill. Quickly she hid behind a tree and watched.

Yes! It is them, she thought, the relief coursing through her body.

They were, she estimated, only four or five hundred metres ahead. They all seemed to be walking, the bushrangers leading their horses as they threaded their way up the slope around clumps of rocks and thickets of small trees.

Kylie waited till they vanished from view over the distant crest line, then set off as quickly as she could limp down the slope. Within five minutes she was at a small creek. This flowed over sharp rocks, running to her left. The creek was so small she could step across, but the water looked alright, only slightly greyish in appearance. Needing the drink and not sure when she might get another she paused to do so. Then she felt the urge to go to the toilet and that delayed her a few more minutes while she squatted anxiously in the grass with her trousers around her ankles.

The short break refreshed her a lot and she really wished she had time to have a proper wash. Painfully aware of the effort it would cost she set herself at the slope beyond. This was steeper, but not really a steep slope. Even so she soon found she was puffing and perspiring as she plodded up. The trail through the grass was still easy to follow but changed direction frequently to avoid rocky areas and thickets of low trees. As she got higher up the slope, she noted that the gravel road was still off to her right a couple of hundred metres away.

It took Kylie ten minutes of gasping effort to reach the crest of the ridge. As she approached it she slowed down and looked carefully for any sign of an ambush. There was none and she arrived safely on top. To her disappointment, the trail went down the other side into a small valley. Ahead another line of hills, even larger, stretched right across her front. That depressed her as it was obvious the bushrangers had gone that way. By now she felt she was close to the end of her strength. Off to her right she saw the gravel road curving around to the left and getting closer. It crossed the next line of hills at a low saddle in front of her.

This looked to be close to where the bushrangers were heading but she could see no sign of them among the trees. As she could think of no sensible alternative to following, she resumed walking. Going downhill she found hard, all her muscles being thrown into reverse and her knees complaining with hot little pains. As she walked, she kept a wary eye on the country ahead, hoping to avoid blundering into the bushrangers.

It was as well she did because, as she approached the next crest, she heard a horse snuffle quite close to her. Instantly she froze, her heat rate shooting up. She sank down into the grass, her eyes flicking around to try to locate the source of the sound. Then the murmur of voices came to her straining ears.

They are just up ahead, she thought.

But why had they stopped? Was it just for a short rest, or were they camping for the night? Kylie glanced around, noted that the sun was still just above the hilltop to her left and decided that there was still about an hour of daylight, ample time to set up a camp.

For the next five minutes she lay in the grass, listening and scanning the bush. Twice more she heard the sound of a horse fidgeting and several times she heard the low murmur of voices. But there was no sign of anyone, so she began to carefully crawl forward to try to see what was going on. Luckily there were plenty of small trees and the grass was reasonably lush and waist high, so she had plenty of cover. Also the curve of the ground favoured her.

It was a horse's head she spotted first. It was only about 25 metres directly in front of her and that, she thought, was a bit too close for comfort. *It might smell me,* she worried.

So she carefully backed off and slithered through the grass away to her left, looking for a position that was upwind and from which she could look over the ridge she was now on.

Ten minutes of slow (and painful) crawling brought her to a small bush beside a large tree about 50 metres further up the gentle ridge line from where the horses were. That put her with the sun at her back, a factor she had considered when choosing to go that way. Very cautiously she raised herself above the tops of the grass and looked down the ridge.

The ridge, she now observed, ran on down for about a hundred metres to an obvious saddle. At that, point the gravel road came up over the ridge before curving away to the right along the top of a long, flattish spurline covered with ironbarks. At the point where the road crossed the saddle was a clearing and a rough vehicle track turned off to come up the ridge past where she was hidden. Just beyond this road junction was some sort of big ditch or cut across the spine of the saddle. She puzzled over this till she realised that the earthworks of the old railway came out of it and went off to her left, curving away from her into the bush around the side of the re-entrant on the north side of the saddle.

It is a cutting for the old railway, she reasoned.

But it was not the now overgrown and long abandoned railway that held her attention but the group of people and horses 50 metres from her. The scene was more or less what she had expected to see, although not so close to a road. Seated in a group among a thicket of small trees were her friends. Standing guard over them was Pat. Down beside the road stood Liam.

Kylie studied the layout and the people, hoping to find a way to release her friends. Pat she wasn't so worried about, but she knew Liam was the dangerous one.

He is just standing there looking back along the gravel road, she thought. *He looks like he is waiting. Who is he waiting for?*

Chapter 32

MUCH HARDER

I wonder who they are waiting for? Kylie thought as she watched Liam standing out beside the road. *Must be more of the gang, or some friends,* she decided.

So she lay in the grass and watched, ignoring the discomfort, ants, and growing thirst. As she watched, Kylie began looking for some way to help her friends. But it was quickly apparent that the bushrangers had tightened up their security. Her friends were all bound hand and foot and then tied to a rope which was tied to a tree.

Even when Pat set to work to unload and unsaddle all the horses he did not use them to assist. They stayed seated and under his watchful eye. That at least meant that he had no time for looking around, so Kylie felt much safer. It even made her smile.

They are riding around the other roads looking for me and I am here where they don't suspect!

But then her plans were thrown into disarray. First she saw Liam answer a call on one of the little radios. He was obviously not happy, but finally growled, "Oh, alright! Wait ten minutes."

He then stalked up the track to where the others were and spoke to Pat. Pat also looked annoyed but nodded. All this puzzled rather than worried Kylie but her emotions turned to something like dismay when she saw Liam and Pat untie her friend's ankles and then order them to their feet. They were left tied to the long rope by their wrists. When they were ordered to start walking Kylie felt sharp stabs of worry.

Where are they going now? she wondered. *And what should I do?*

For the second question the immediate answer was lie low and watch because the group, guarded by Pat, was walking across her front only 25 metres away, heading north down the side of the ridge. What really puzzled her, and threw her into indecision, was that Liam did not walk with them and the horses remained tethered under the trees.

Quite naturally Kylie wanted to follow her friends, but for the time being she could only lie low. Then she saw that it would be wise to wait as the group re-appeared lower down, walking in single file along a low spurline parallel to the road.

If I move now and Pat glances back he will spot me coming down the slope, she reasoned.

Worse still, once she got out onto the same low ridge, she knew she would be visible to Liam, who had now walked back to the side of the road. All Kylie could do was lie in the grass and fret, acutely conscious that with every minute her friends were getting further away and that the sun was sinking fast; had now dipped below the hill top behind her. When the walkers vanished from view among the ironbarks on the ridge she became quite upset. So anxious and worn out was she that she feared she was going to be sick. Only with an effort did she prevent herself retching. But it left her lying in the grass shaking and feeling drained.

Too much sun and not enough water, she told herself.

Then Liam lifted his radio and spoke into it. A couple of minutes later the sound of a vehicle reached Kylie's ears. She tensed ready and saw Liam peer down the road from behind a tree and then walk out into the middle of the road. Into view rattled a dirty, old, brown painted Toyota Landcruiser with an open tray back. The back was piled high with bags and boxes. In the cab sat two men. One of them was a stranger to Kylie: middle-aged, dark-haired, unshaven, looking most unhappy. The other was Michael Kelly.

The vehicle clattered to a dusty stop and the engine was switched off. Both men got out and began a conversation with Liam. Even from hundred paces away Kylie could tell it was not a happy discussion. The middle-aged man shook his head a number of times and appeared to be disagreeing. Then he shook his head and walked up to the horses. Michael drove the truck up close to them and Liam joined them.

The middle-aged man lifted a saddle and bridle from the back of the vehicle and set to work saddling one of the horses. While he did this Liam and Michael loaded their own saddles and gear into the back of the truck.

Now is my chance to crawl away, Kylie reasoned, noting that the men were fully engaged in their tasks.

She began moving back and to her left, keeping flat in the grass and edging along. It was slow and hurt but she did not want to take any risks with Liam so close.

She had only gone about 15 metres when the middle-aged man swung into the saddle. From behind a dead log Kylie saw that he had neck-roped all the other horses to a lead rope, and he now tapped with his heels and set off down the track leading them.

As he did, Liam snarled, "You keep your mouth shut, Molloy, or else."

The middle-aged man, Molloy, snapped back over his shoulder, "And when you are caught, don't dob on me for helping you!"

"And don't forget to phone Devlin," Liam added.

"I won't!" retorted Molloy. "He will leave home as soon as it is dark and should be at the RV by eight."

The Kelly Gang have people helping them alright, Kylie mused, *But most don't seem too keen about it.*

She decided that the horses belonged to Molloy and had been on unwilling loan. For a few more seconds she watched until she saw Molloy turn right when he reached the road. He vanished from view back the way he had come. For a few moments Kylie contemplated trying to catch him up and asking him for help but she saw that to do that she would have to crawl back across the ridge and then would have to try to catch up with the horses.

I can't do it, she decided, taking stock of her weakened condition and aching body. So she continued moving in the direction her friends had gone. Then another idea came to her: Pat was alone with the prisoners. *Can I somehow catch up and get them to overpower him or something?* she wondered.

It was a good idea and got her moving faster. But by the time she reached the small dip at the bottom of the slope she knew that plan was doomed to failure. She heard the truck start up and a minute later it appeared below her on the road, heading in the same direction as the group. As it went past Kylie lay flat in the grass but she did note that both Liam and Michael were seated in the cab. Within another minute the vehicle had vanished around the next bend along the road.

Kylie stood up and dusted herself, then set off after it. *I hope they aren't going far,* she reasoned.

But even so she wondered if she was up to the task. The wait had allowed her muscles all to cool and stiffen up and now the chafing and blisters returned with stinging pain. This made every step one of gasping agony.

Determination kept her going. Doggedly she put one foot in front of the other, anxiously aware that the shadows were lengthening and that the sun was now only shining on the treetops and on the hill away to her right.

I need to catch up before dark, she told herself.

The thought of trying to locate the group after dark, and of possibly blundering into the bushrangers, got her all anxious and helped speed her progress.

But it was all pain. Tears came and also many doubts. *Maybe I should have gone to the police,* she thought. But then she shook her head. *No. Now the bushrangers have covered their tracks even more. The horses are gone and they are using a vehicle. That will be hard to track.* Then an even more dismaying thought came to her: what if the bushrangers loaded their prisoners into the vehicle and drove away? *They could be hundreds of kilometres away by tomorrow!*

But that just made it even more imperative to catch up, if only to know what happened. So she forced herself to ignore the pain and trembling and to walk faster. Luckily the going was easy. The wide flat ridge line had almost no rough patches and very little grass. The country was noticeably drier and the ground almost bare in places.

For about half a kilometre, the ridge curved very slowly to the left, the gravel road twenty metres to her right. Then it began to curve back to the right and she stopped behind a tree to study the ground. Half a kilometre away, parked beside the road at the next bend, was the truck. People were visible moving near it. That left her no option but to back up and then go left through the bush to get down into the top of a small valley. Once there she was able to advance under cover to a low hill that was aligned in the desired direction.

By then Kylie was limping and was so ill she felt dizzy, but she gritted her teeth and plodded on, stumbling over small stones and logs in the short grass. Her chosen route led her around behind the crest of the low ridge. From time to time she angled back to the right to cautiously peep over the crest. This route had her in the last reddish glow of the sunset and she really began to fret that darkness would set in before she could get close enough to see the layout.

When she did come back to a position from which she could observe she was annoyed to find that the hill had split. The spur she was on was now separated from the lower, flatter one where the group were visible sitting in the grass near the vehicle. To reach them she had to either risk being seen walking down a bare hillside, or detour another couple of hundred paces down to her left to sneak down a small re-entrant, then back up the gully dividing the two ridges. She opted for this as the safest and hurried on.

In the process she stumbled into an embarrassing situation. As she came back up the other re-entrant, she spotted movement and went down behind a bush. From that poor cover she saw that Michael was heading directly toward her.

Has he seen me? she worried, tensing for flight. But then, when he stopped and unzipped his fly, she knew he hadn't. *Oh no!* she thought, burning with embarrassment. Not that seeing boys pee was any novelty really, not with two brothers. But she was still embarrassed and tried not to look.

When Michael vanished back up the slope, she angled left and up, keeping low and moving from bush to bush, or from tree to log. There was even a large termite's nest that she hid behind. Finally she reached a position behind some rocks and small bushes about 75 metres from the group. By then twilight was setting in and the last of the sunlight vanished from the distant hill tops out to the east. Behind her a reddish sunset allowed enough light for her to see clearly.

But her sense of satisfaction and relief at catching up was short lived. What she saw happening dismayed her even more. Chains! Michael came walking across from the vehicle carrying chains!

Oh no! That makes it a lot harder! she thought.

She heard Liam snort in derision and say, "Bloody dog chains! Why couldn't you get something better?"

"It was all we could find in a hurry," Michael replied defensively. "Anyway, we tested 'em. They are too strong to break with your bare hands and the padlocks will be better than knots."

Kylie now watched as the bushrangers untied her friends and then passed the dog chains around their waists and locked them on with a padlock to each person. The chain was then padlocked around a tree.

That is going to make it much harder to set them free, she thought.

So what to do next?

All Kylie could do was lie and watch. She could see no immediate solution to the problem. Only fleetingly did she consider leaving and trying to walk to Bakerville to get help. But she was painfully aware that she was now further away and much less likely to make it. Her frustration was then given an added twist when Pat began feeding the prisoners. Kylie could see it was only tins of small sausages, plus bread and jam, but even that set her mouth watering and her tummy grumbling.

Darkness slowly set in. By then Kylie had a good idea of the layout. The prisoners were about 50 metres from the road, secured to a tree on top of an almost flat rise among a stand of ironbarks. The vehicle was parked beside the road. The three bushrangers seemed to either sit on a log between the vehicle and the prisoners, or move to the vehicle and back.

Why are the bushrangers waiting here? she wondered. She remembered Molloy saying that Devlin would be there at about 8 o'clock so she assumed the meeting place was here. *But why beside a road?* she wondered, thinking that a bit risky.

What did give her some hope was that there were no lights. Both prisoners and bushrangers sat in darkness, apart from an occasional torch light when one of the bushrangers went to the vehicle. She also noted that both groups did a lot of talking. It seemed that the bushrangers were making no attempt to stop the prisoners conversing.

They must be confident that the police have no idea they are here, and that there is no-one else around, she decided.

That all helped her to make her next decision. *I will creep over and let the others know I am here,* she thought. *Maybe they can come up with some ideas?*

So she began to inch her way towards them, sliding and crawling slowly along on her stomach. It was easier than she expected as she kept the group between her and where she could just detect the bushrangers. She could not actually see them but could hear the murmur of their voices and from time to time saw the glow of a cigarette she thought was being smoked by Liam.

As she got closer to her friends, Kylie detected a sudden, tense change in their speech pattern. She did not actually hear them say anything like 'What is that?' but she was sure they whispered that to each other. Not wanting them to raise the alarm, thinking she was some feral animal, she risked calling softly, "Sssh! Don't be alarmed. It's me."

Back came Graham's soft answer, "We worked that out. What are you doing here? Why haven't you gone to get the coppers?"

Peter then said, "You others keep talking to drown out Kylie's voice."

Immediately Stephen and Norah began a conversation about cattle raising in the hill country. Kylie crept even closer but stopped about five metres away behind another big termite nest. She had been wondering how to answer Graham's accusing questions.

To do so she replied, "I wasn't sure where I was, or which way I could safely go. They were watching all the roads. And I needed to know where you had been taken to. Do you know where we are?"

"Too right!" Graham replied. "We know exactly where we are, and we don't think these bloody bushrangers have a clue that we do."

"Where are we?" Kylie asked.

"Stannary Hills," Graham replied.

"The place you came to last year?"

"That's right. We are about two hundred metres from a road junction of an old road to Mutchilba. You can see it from here, just down the hill. The old cemetery is just the other side of it," Graham answered.

"Then this is the road you walked along to get help?" Kylie said.

She knew the story well, from Peter and Stephen, both of whose lives he had saved. It had been an epic march of about 15 kilometres in the dark, alone and with a broken bone in his ankle.

Graham grunted and said, "That's right. And if I can do it once, I can do it again, if only I could get free."

"They've chained you up, haven't they?" Kylie asked.

"Yes," Peter answered. "Padlocked the chain around our waist and then around that tree."

"Where are the keys to the padlocks?" Kylie asked.

Stephen answered that. "No chance of getting them. They are in Michael's left pocket."

That stumped Kylie. She bit her lip and thought hard, wondering what to do next. Suddenly a torch beam came on and she flinched and ducked back behind the ant hill. Her heart, already beating fast, began to hammer and her mouth went dry with fear. She watched anxiously as the torch beam slowly moved along the line of her friends. Margaret's anxious face showed very clearly for a moment.

Then Pat's voice called, "What are you lot all whispering about?"

Stephen answered at once, his voice dripping with sarcasm. "We are trying to work out how to escape of course. What else would we talk about?"

"Oh very funny!" Liam called back. "Just don't try it. I might shoot this time."

"Shoot what, shoot your mouth off?" Stephen sneered.

On hearing that Kylie sucked in her breath and worried that Liam might walk over to hit Stephen. However he just replied, "Don't get cheeky, you little smart aleck! Any more of that and I'll belt you. Now keep quiet you lot."

The torch went out. There was silence for a minute and then the bushrangers began talking again. Stephen ignored the order to be quiet and Margaret answered him. They began chatting about tin mining. When Liam ignored this the others began talking quietly again.

Kylie risked whispering again. "Why did the bushrangers camp here, do you know?"

"No idea," Peter answered. "They just told us to stop and chained us to this tree."

"I think I know," Kylie said. "I heard them talking to the man who took the horses away. He said they are to meet someone called Devlin at eight o'clock."

"What man took the horses?" Norah asked.

"Someone called Molloy," Kylie answered. "He didn't seem very happy and I don't think he loaned them willingly."

Norah agreed. "I wondered what happened to the horses. I hope mine are alright."

A pang of concern for Norah's horses bothered Kylie for a few seconds until Peter asked, "Where are they meeting this Devlin, and why?"

"Here I suppose," Kylie answered. "I do know that Molloy would not arrive until you had all been moved away. I suppose that is why you are hidden here in the bush, so that Devlin can't see you."

"Or so that we can't see him more likely," Peter suggested.

"Both, I think," Kylie replied.

Norah leaned closer, then asked, "Do you think this Devlin character might be bringing them more horses?"

At that, Kylie could only shrug. "Don't know," she replied. "It might be just food or information, like back at Irvinebank Cemetery."

"You seem to know a lot about them," Stephen commented. "Have you been squeezing information out of young Brian?"

It took a moment for the meaning to sink in but then Kylie felt deeply shocked and hurt. "No! I overheard them when I was lying in the grass back at that place where you were a couple of hours ago."

"Yorkies Cutting," Graham put in.

Still feeling a bit bruised emotionally Kylie whispered, "What do you think I should do?"

"Go and get help," Graham answered.

"I don't think I can walk that far," Kylie answered, "and I don't know which way to go."

"Easy," Graham answered. "Just follow this road back to Hales Siding and turn left. There's a sign there to tell you which way to go, and another at the junction with the Irvinebank Road."

"I'd rather help you escape," Kylie replied.

"So would I, but how?" Graham answered.

Dingo now spoke, "If we had an axe, we could probably cut the chain. It ain't very thick. Or maybe we could cut down the tree and we could all get away as a group."

"Where can we get an axe?" Kylie queried.

"They got one in the back of that truck," Dingo replied. "I seen 'em put it there, on the other side, just behind the cab."

Hearing that instantly got Kylie's hopes up. "I will go and get it, then come back; and if we get a chance you might be able to get free," she said.

Margaret spoke, saying, "But how could we, with these men just there?"

"I could decoy them away somehow," Kylie suggested.

"But how?" Margaret asked.

"I don't know," Kylie answered, "But I will think of something. But first we need the axe. I'll go and get it."

"I still think you should go and get the cops," Graham answered.

Kylie now got stubborn. "I'll get the axe first," she insisted.

"Don't you get caught," Graham cautioned, his concern clear in his voice.

"I'll be careful," Kylie answered. With that she turned around and began crawling away from them.

For the next twenty minutes she moved slowly and carefully in a wide semi-circle. Many times she froze as she stepped or knelt on a dry twig or found dead leaves crackling under her feet but she was far enough away from the bushrangers for them not to hear her. Her route took her down the hill to her left. In the dark she became disoriented several times and she was also gripped by fear of snakes in the grass.

After a while she stopped and looked fearfully around, aware that she was off course, if not actually lost. *Which way is the road?* she wondered. Then she had a vivid image of her mother and of her bedroom. *Oh, I just want to go home!* she thought.

Misery welled up, fuelled by exhaustion and homesickness and she was unable to control it. Tears began and her lip trembled.

Then a loud sound startled her, and in the process saved her from breaking down completely. *That was someone slamming one of the doors on the vehicle,* she told herself. Now she was able to work out where she was. *Keep the uphill on my right,* she told herself.

Once again, she began moving slowly through the bush. After what seemed like an eternity, but was actually only five minutes and a hundred paces, she at last saw the pale gleam of the gravel road ahead of her. Sighing with relief, she hurried forward, and promptly fell into the grass-covered drain. The drop was so unexpected that she went down hard, crashing into the grass and snapping several dead sticks in the process. The fall winded her and she lay for a minute or so, scared that she had broken something.

Careful examination by trembling fingers revealed nothing more than few scratches and bruises so she cautiously struggled to her knees and peered over the grass. In the starlight she could not see any sign of the men. Nor could she hear them. Being only a teenage girl she was very afraid of them, but she had told her brother she was going to get the axe, so she summoned up what resolve she still had and stood up.

Cautiously she moved out onto the road. She then crossed over and crept uphill just in the edge of the grass. It seemed to be further than she thought but at last she made out the shape of the vehicle ahead. From then on she crawled along the other side of the road until she was directly across it from the parked vehicle.

Once there she paused, listening. Satisfied that the bushrangers were still seated on the log 25 metres away she crossed the road at a crouch, keeping the vehicle between her and them, and moving with all the stealth she could manage. Even so she was afraid they would hear the crunch of stones under her boots. To her that sounded very loud.

On reaching the vehicle she again paused and allowed her heart to slow down. She found her hands were sweaty and her heart was pounding so loud it sounded like a thudding washing machine in her ears. Having calmed herself she stood up and groped in the back of the vehicle.

Where is that axe? she asked herself.

Suddenly she went cold all over and began to quiver. The men were walking through the bush directly towards her!

Chapter 33

THE AXE

For a moment Kylie froze. Fear flooded through her and she began to quiver.

They must have heard me! she thought.

Panic began to swirl in her mind. By then the men were only a few metres away on the other side of the vehicle. She could tell because they were talking and she could hear their progress through the long grass.

I must run! she told herself.

She turned and began to tiptoe away, crouching low and still hoping that she was unseen. Her haste was almost her undoing. Her boot came down on a loose stone the size of a tennis ball and she stumbled. It was so unexpected that she was unable to keep her balance. As she fell, she put down her hands to break her fall but still landed heavily on the gravel on her hands and knees. A sharp pain shot through her right ankle.

It all hurt but she continued moving, scrambling to her feet. As she did, she heard the men speak again. It was lucky she did because she was just about to bolt into the long grass to try to make a run for it, twisted ankle of no twisted ankle.

Michael said, "Come on, Liam. I don't feel like going to a cemetery on my own."

From further away Liam replied, a sneer sounding clear in his voice. "What, ya scared of ghosts, eh? Ya big sook!"

Michael answered, his voice quavering with hurt. "It's just that you know Devlin better than me and he might help us if you ask him."

"Oh, alright. But I still reckon it's just because you are afraid of the dark," Liam taunted.

By then Kylie had understood that the men did not know she was there. Despite her fears, she regained control of herself and she was able to slow down. She sank to a crawl and slowly made her way into the long grass beside the road. Five paces into the grass she got another shock. The ground fell steeply away and was studded with football sized rocks with sharp edges.

Ouch! Lucky I didn't run, she thought, picturing the nasty fall that would almost certainly have resulted.

As the men slid down the low bank to the road, she lay motionless in the grass. From there she could not see them, but she could hear them plainly. One man opened the passenger door and climbed in and another walked around the rear of the vehicle to her side, then opened the driver's door and climbed in. As that door was slammed, Kylie heard Pat call out from back up where her friends were.

"Are you blokes liable to be long?" Pat asked.

"Don't know," Liam answered, telling Kylie that he was the passenger. Liam then added, "Don't fret. We are only going to the cemetery and it's just down the road a bit."

The vehicle's engine was started and the headlights flicked on. Kylie lay as flat as she could, feeling very exposed. Now she could see the cab and lights out of her right eye. To her relief, the vehicle began moving. A few seconds later it was well past her and heading down the slope around the slight curve in the road.

As it went out of sight Kylie felt a surge of dismay. *The axe!*

Without the axe, how could she hope to set her friends free? She was so downcast by this unexpected turn of events that her lip again trembled, and it was all she could do to stop herself blubbing. As it was a few tears squeezed out.

What can I do now? she wondered.

The answer came to her almost at once. In the distance she heard the sound of the vehicle's engine change. Lifting her head above the grass she glimpsed the flicker of headlights through the trees.

The vehicle is being turned around, she reasoned. Then she began to worry that it was coming straight back. But it didn't. For a few seconds she saw the two headlights glowing and then they went out. Next came the faint, but unmistakable, sound of the vehicle's doors being slammed. *They have stopped and got out,* she told herself. For a minute or so she lay there, turning over in her mind the comments that the cemetery was just down the road, that it was only a few hundred metres. *That's what Graham said too,* she reminded herself. *But can I walk there? And is that a sensible thing to try to do?*

She knew the men were going to a meeting. But would both men leave the vehicle? And what if she was heard?

But I want that axe, she told herself. *I need it!*

With that she made up her mind. *I will follow them,* she decided.

Slowly and painfully she stood up, her eyes scanning the dark bush for any sign of Pat. She could just hear her friends talking and hoped he was with them. Stealthily she stepped out onto the road, and stopped, sucking in air as a sharp stab of pain lanced through her ankle.

Twisted it alright, she told herself.

But that just made her grit her teeth with stubborn determination. Hobbling painfully under the multiple assaults of chafing, blisters, and sprained ankle, she began moving down the road. She had no real desire to go near another cemetery in the dark. Nor did she want to risk being caught by the men, but she did want that axe.

It was that thought that carried her down the 300 metres of road. It even kept her going after she again twisted her ankle again in a rut on the rough road surface. She passed a turn-off to the right and then slowed down. Now the road ran in under trees. It was not a real forest, just savannah woodland of ironbarks, their black trunks visible even in the starlight, but the road was narrower and here the trees overhung it. The effect was to make it quite dark and gloomy.

Unable to see very well in the darkness Kylie slowed to a crawl and got down on her hands and knees. That hurt as the road surface was gravel with numerous small, sharp stones. It was also dry and dusty. To make it harder for her to be seen she kept right over against the edge of the grass but when she made to enter that it rustled so loudly (or so it seemed to her) that she stayed just on the edge.

After about fifty metres of slow crawling she noted two gateposts close on her right. A silver-painted, wrought iron gate hung between them. Raising herself to see over the grass beside her Kylie stared hard in the night. Then she felt a shiver and broke out in goose bumps. Her hunch had been right. She was just outside the cemetery. Just visible in the starlight were the tops of tombstones poking out of the long grass.

Again she shivered as irrational fear gripped her. *Don't be silly,* she tried to tell herself, *There are no such things as ghosts.* But that wasn't very convincing, and she had to acknowledge that maybe there were. *After all, they talk about the Holy Spirit in church every Sunday.*

It took her a minute or so to regain her composure, to fight down the urge to flee. Then she resumed her stealthy crawl. Ten paces past the gate she stopped and sank against the grass. Dimly ahead of her she could make out the vague shape of the vehicle. Seeing it sent her heart rate shooting up again. Her rational mind had worked out that it had been turned around and was facing back towards her so now she was held by the worry that the men were sitting in it watching her. She thought she had heard doors slam but was not sure.

Anxiously she lay in the edge of the grass and strained her eyes to try to detect if there were people in the cab or not. But all she could see was the dark oblong of the windshield. To her it took on sinister dimensions but gave no clue. In her tired state her vision began to blur, and she had the un-nerving suspicion she was hallucinating.

For several minutes she lay there, edging slowly into the grass. Then the murmur of voices reached her and she breathed out. The two men were standing at the back of the vehicle. That was a relief and for another couple of minutes she just lay and recovered. Only then did she realise her chest hurt from holding her breath.

But what to do next? The axe was in the back of the vehicle, close to where the men stood. That thought held Kylie in cover. She reasoned it would be a silly risk to try to get the axe while they were so close. So she waited.

How long she waited she wasn't sure, although at the time it seemed like hours. Later she decided it was only about fifteen minutes. The tension was broken at last by the sound of a vehicle. It was coming from the north, from beyond the parked vehicle. Then Kylie saw the flicker of headlights on the trees. That got her anxious about being seen so she wriggled further into the grass, hoping that the sounds made by the approaching vehicle were masking the noises she was making.

A few seconds later, the vehicle came over a low crest and its headlights lit up the area. Kylie looked, then remembered that her eyes might reflect the light the way animal's eyes do, or that her white face might show up. Shutting her eyes to slits she lay face down and peered through her fingers.

The vehicle shuddered to a stop five metres from Michael's vehicle and a swirl of dust swept over it. This set Liam and Michael coughing and cursing but Kylie was glad of it as it hid her until the new arrival's headlights went out. As soon as they did she opened her eyes and lifted her head to watch. There was the sound of a door opening and closing and then the crunch of boots on gravel, followed by the murmur of men's voices.

Is this the moment? Kylie wondered. She decided it was. *The men will be talking, not looking around, and the longer I leave it the more likely they are to drive off.*

That decided, she started to move. As she did, she was very conscious of having difficulty hearing as the swashing thud of her heart sounded loud in her ears. Her throat was dry and she trembled with excitement as the adrenaline kicked in. But she did it. Very carefully she stood up and began walking slowly forward at a crouch.

Step by step she made her stealthy advance, keeping the vehicle between her and the men. When she reached the front of it she crouched and had to stifle a fit of shaking. Gulping for air she gripped the cold, dusty metal.

Come on! Get on with it! she told herself. Forcing herself to act she moved to the driver's side and peeked around.

As she did, she distinctly heard Liam say, "Did you bring us any supplies?"

"Yeah, I did. They're in the back," replied a man's voice. He then continued, "There's a fair bit, but it will be the last I get you."

"Why is that?" Liam asked.

As he asked this, Kylie heard the men's boots crunching on gravel as they walked away from her to the second vehicle.

"Because it's too damn risky, that's why!" replied the man. "The cops are everywhere and have already questioned me once. They are talking to every person who ever knew any of you. You should get out of the area as quick as you can."

"We would, but we gotta wait for Phil and the others," Michael said.

"Don't wait long," the man said. "I heard they got them black tracker fellas on yer tail."

"We won't," Michael answered. "We join up tomorrow morning at…"

He got not further as Liam cut in. "No need to say too much Michael. The fewer people who know our plans the better. No offence Devlin. Now, do you know where those blacktrackers are?"

Devlin grunted and then said, "They are..."

Kylie could not make out the next bit as it was drowned by the rattle of metal objects being moved in the tray of the second vehicle. Dimly in the starlight she saw a person standing at the side of the second vehicle, leaning in to shift things.

Now is my chance, she thought.

Sucking in her breath she stepped around the side of the vehicle and tip-toed along to the rear of the cab. As she did, she was very aware that if she could see the man at the second vehicle then he would probably see her if he looked in her direction. Shaking with excitement and fear she reached the tray and again groped inside, her eyes flicking from there to the second vehicle.

Her questing fingers felt dirt and rope and then cold steel. No good, a shovel. She felt quickly around among the litter of tools and odd items. As she did, she heard Michael ask, "How is the road to Mutchilba? Is there a police roadblock on it?"

"Not yet," the man replied. "The cops are concentrating their search around Irvinebank, or so Connor told me. And I tell you what, your chances of gettin' away ain't all that good. They reckon they've got five hundred coppers looking for youse. They've called them in from all over the state. They are as thick as fleas on a dingo down around Herberton."

That was both good news and bad to Kylie, but she had no time to ponder it as at that moment her fingers touched more steel and she recognised the feel of an axe head. Her hand closed on the wooden handle and she felt quickly along it to make sure it wasn't stuck or tied in. It wasn't so she quickly lifted it out. As she did, she quivered with excitement and a feeling of exultation.

A few seconds later she crouched at the front of the vehicle, shaking and sweating. *Now, how do I get away?* she wondered.

One option was to sneak off into the bush and later creep back to the place where the others were and try to free them. But there were two objections to that.

There will then be three bushrangers to deal with, not one, she reasoned. *And what if they drive back, load Graham and the others into this vehicle and drive off?*

The thought of just being left behind in the dark bush caused a wave of dismay to sweep through Kylie. It also helped her make up her mind. *I must hurry and try to set the others free before these two return,* she told herself.

She also knew that crouching directly in front of the vehicle was not a smart place to be, as the men would walk towards her to get in and when the headlights came on she would be in front of them.

That got her moving. After a hurried peek back around the side, which showed her that the men were lugging bags and boxes from one vehicle to the other, she set off at a crouching walk. As she did, she kept the vehicle between her and the men, anxiously aware that as they walked forwards each time they might see her. All she could do was hope it was dark enough to hide her.

Five paces, ten. There was the cemetery gate on her left. Tombstones were visible on the starlight. A white shape in the grass caught Kylie's gaze. Shivers swept through her. *Only a stone monument, not a ghost,* she told herself. She hurried on, her ankle hurting and boots padding in the dust. *Will they spot my boot prints?* she worried.

But there was no time to brush them out. Gripping the axe head tightly in her sweaty right hand in the way Guides had taught her to safely do it, handle up her side, she went as fast as she dared.

Several times she kicked stones and caused them to chink and rattle. Three times she stepped into ruts or potholes and twisted her sore ankle. Each time a stab of hot pain shot up her leg, causing her to gasp. Despite the evening chill beads of perspiration broke out on her forehead. After two minutes of such progress she passed the grassy triangle where the side road came in. By then she was sure the men could no longer see her, so she straightened up and hurried on.

Made it! she told herself, holding the axe up and gripping it with both hands. But now the even more tricky bit, how to free the others with Pat still on guard?

As she walked up the road past the road junction Kylie bit her lip and puzzled over how to do that. She decided that the best thing would be to creep back and talk to the others. *They will come up with a plan,* she told herself, having enormous regard for the resourcefulness of Graham and his friends.

With that in mind she turned off the road to her right. Pushing thoughts of snakes aside she made her way into the grass.

"Remember the ditch! Remember the ditch!" she muttered.

Just in time she detected the eroded drain in the long grass. As carefully as she could she stepped down into it, sucking in her breath at the resulting pain in her ankle. Then she clambered up the other side, the sharp spear grass pricking near her eyes. On the uphill side she set off up the long gentle slope as fast as she dared. All the while she kept glancing back and straining her ears for the sound of the vehicle coming back.

Keeping direction became her next concern. She did not want to miss her friends. Nor did she want to just blunder into Pat. After stumbling over some rocks in the grass she slowed down. Her eyes made out what she thought was the top of the flat ridge, but she did not have enough experience to be sure. As she walked slowly forward, her trousers swishing in the long grass and her boots bumping stones, ant hills and sticks, she again began to sweat, sure that Pat must hear her and be waiting.

And there he was! Kylie froze. A dark shape moved across her front about fifty paces away. Then it crouched down. *Is he kneeling to aim his rifle better?* she wondered as stabs of terror splintered through her.

Slowly she sank down to a crouch, her heart hammering and mouth dry. But then the man stood up; it had to be Pat, couldn't be anyone else. He walked back across the slope ten paces and bent down, then began to rummage in a bag or pack.

No, he hasn't seen me! Kylie thought, relief coursing through her.

Over to her right ten paces away was a large termite nest. Moving slowly, step by step at a crouch, she made her way to it. As she reached it, Pat stood up and again walked across to her left. Here he squatted and she heard metal on metal and a bluish glow lit up his face and front.

He is cooking on a small gas stove, she decided.

That was good news. But where were her friends? Kylie peeked around the termite nest and listened. Almost at once she detected the murmur of their voices. They were twenty metres away to her right front.

I have come too far to the left, she reasoned.

So she began crawling on hands and knees towards them, keeping a wary eye on Pat as she did. Carrying the axe was the difficult bit. Now she had to use one hand to feel for sticks and shift them so she did not step on them and make a noise. She reasoned that Pat would be unlikely to see her because his night vision would have been degraded by the glow of the flames.

As she crept towards her friends, Kylie saw that a large log lay on the ground ten paces to her left. She recognised it as the one that the bushrangers had been sitting on earlier. This was confirmed when Pat stood up and again walked back to it. As he did, Kylie lay flat in the grass, ignoring the sharp prickles which poked through her shirt and trousers. Once again Pat rummaged in a bag or pack, muttering with annoyance as he did.

Then, to Kylie's dismay, he switched on a torch. She froze and lay flat, tensed and ready to run. But he wasn't looking anywhere but into the bag. The beam of the torch was directed into it and Kylie could clearly see his face, his mouth working as he mumbled with irritation. But she could also see something else too. Leaning on the log was Pat's rifle.

Instantly a plan formed in Kylie's mind. *If I can only get that rifle,* she thought.

She bit her lip and screwed up her resolve, then waited. As soon as Pat stood up and walked back to his cooking she acted. Slowly she moved, using a stealthy crawl, trying to get across behind him. As she moved, she kept glancing at Pat. To begin with he was side on but within ten metres she was behind him, between him and her friends. By then her heart was pounding so hard she felt her head was going to burst.

And there was the gun! It was only about ten paces away. Again she nerved herself to act. By this time she was trembling, her hands sweaty, and her heart full of fear. In her mind she began to rehearse what to do with the gun. But Kylie knew it was going to be all bluff. She had only ever fired a gun a couple of times in her life, at her grandfather's farm. Not only did she have no real idea how to work this one but she knew in her heart she would not be able to pull the trigger. But there, only ten paces away, were people who she knew were trained to use firearms.

Graham will know how, she thought. *He is an army cadet with three years' experience.*

Now she looked towards her friends and realised they must all be watching as they sat in a silent line. After a quick glance over her shoulder, which showed Pat still crouched over his cooking, she lay flat and began crawling towards the log, inching along so as not to make any noises in the dry grass. As she did, she heard the distant sound of a vehicle door slamming and then the noise she had been dreading, a vehicle's engine starting up.

Oh no! Here they come. I must act fast! she thought.

Her first thought was to spring up and rush across to grab the gun but then she saw Pat lift his head and look towards the vehicle. Knowing he would probably see her and that would make it a deadly race she decided on another plan.

I will give the axe to Graham and they can cut themselves free while I keep Pat from using the gun.

She knew it would be a terrible risk but in her heart she believed that Pat was too nice a person to shoot.

So she stood up and began walking towards her friends.

Chapter 34

TRAINING TELLS

As she heard the vehicle start accelerating, Kylie almost went into a fluster of panic. But by then she had reached the others. In the starlight she could just recognise them. Nearest to her, at the end of the line, were Peter and Dingo. Next were Stephen, Norah, and Margaret. Graham and Roger were at the other end.

"Is that you Kylie?" hissed Peter.

"Yes, and I've got the axe," Kylie whispered urgently back.

Dingo reached out. "Give me the axe."

"What will you do?" Kylie asked as she handed it to him. "You can't cut the chains with it."

"Chop down the tree," Dingo replied.

Stephen then hissed, "What about Pat? He's got a rifle."

"He won't use it," Kylie answered.

"You hope!" Stephen replied.

"We've got to risk it. Oh hurry! The other two are coming back," Kylie cried, gesturing towards where the glow of headlights was now visible through the trees.

"Keep down Peter," Dingo ordered as he rose to his feet.

Peter did so but Dingo had trouble getting into the position he desired because of the chain.

"Oh quickly!" Kylie squeaked. She saw Peter crouch low so that Dingo would not hit him as he swung the axe.

Dingo hefted the axe in both hands, feet braced wide apart. Then he measured his stroke and swung the axe back, then forwards.

Thunk!

The axe blade bit into the bark of the tree. Kylie had no real idea how long it might take to chop down such a tree. It was, she saw, only as thick as both her hands might reach around. Dingo at once wrenched the blade free and swung it back for a second blow.

But by then the scene had dramatically changed. At the sound of that first axe blow Pat had sprung up and swung round. Now he directed his torch beam on Dingo. "Hey! What the hell! What are you doing? Stop that!" he yelled.

Dingo ignored him and drove the blade in with all his force. Kylie saw chips fly and the lighter colour of the wood inside. Pat hurried over to the log and shone his torch along it, obviously looking for his rifle. That was what Kylie was dreading. She saw him snatch it up and felt her stomach turn over with dread. The terrible moment had arrived!

Pat swung the torch beam onto the group, then steadied it on Dingo. "Stop that, or I'll shoot," he called.

Kylie felt nausea swirl in her stomach but she forced herself to act. *The moment of truth!* she told herself.

Was her reading of Pat's character right? Lives now depended on it she knew. She stepped into the torch beam, standing between Dingo and Pat.

"You will have to shoot me first," she said, aware that her voice was quavering.

"Kylie! Where did you spring from?" Pat cried, his voice sounding very agitated. "Step aside. Get out of my line of fire."

"No," Kylie heard herself say.

It was as though another person was speaking for her through a wooden dummy. Cold terror now gripped her, and her every instinct was to run, but she stood her ground and steeled herself for what might now happen. Her skin came out in goosebumps, and she felt herself cringing and flinching in anticipation of the bullet smashing into her body. Behind her she heard the axe thud into the tree.

Pat hopped from one foot to the other, plainly uncertain. "Please, Kylie. Get out of the way," he cried. "I don't want to have to shoot you."

From behind Kyle came Dingo's voice, hard and menacing. "You shoot her and I will kill you with this bloody axe."

Peter added to this, snarling, "And if Dingo doesn't get you then I will. You will have to kill us all."

Kylie saw that Pat was looking very unhappy. He was also having trouble holding the rifle in one hand and the torch in the other. Swallowing to moisten her dry throat she croaked, "Pat, put down the gun. If you shoot you will go to jail for murder."

"I... I... I can't let you go!" Pat wailed, glancing over his shoulder towards the approaching headlights as he did.

"Forget Liam," Kylie replied. "You can't shoot any of us. You are too nice a person. This whole business has got out of hand, and it isn't worth having murder on your conscience. Now go and tell Liam what is happening."

"And take your finger off that trigger before there is a nasty accident," Graham added.

"But I can't!" Pat cried.

"Then shoot," Kylie snapped in reply, her fear fuelling her anger.

Pat again shifted his feet and fidgeted with the rifle. Dingo kept chopping at the tree. Suddenly Pat let out a sob and then turned. A moment later he was hurrying away from them down through the dark bush towards the road. For a few seconds Kylie just stood, her mind not taking in what she was seeing. Then she sighed with relief and almost fainted as she relaxed.

But that was only for a moment because the glow of the approaching headlights reminded Kylie of a far more dangerous person. *Liam! He will shoot,* she thought.

By then Pat was visible at the edge of the road, waving his arms in the beam of the headlights. As she saw this, Kylie gulped and held her hand to her heaving breast, very apprehensive lest she had precipitated a tragedy.

During all this, Dingo had been wielding the axe like a man possessed. Kylie glanced towards the tree and was astonished. She saw that he had made a very clean cut halfway through on the side away from them. He moved around to their side and paused; axe held ready in both hands.

"Peter, you push as I cut. Push away from us," he ordered.

Peter stood up, chain chinking, and leaned on the tree well above the cut and to one side. Dingo grunted with approval and then swung the axe in a short, fast stroke in under Peter's arms. The blade bit into the bark about ten centimetres below the existing cut. Peter pushed half a metre above that. Kylie instantly understood what they were doing.

They are making sure that the tree doesn't fall on us, she reasoned.

By then she could hear Pat shouting out on the road and saw that the headlights of the vehicle were more than halfway up the hill.

"Oh hurry, hurry!" she cried, waving her arms in her anxiety.

Chop! Chop! Chop!

Even in the dark Kylie could tell that Dingo was an experienced axeman who knew exactly what he was doing. Suddenly there was a sharp cracking sound.

"Push!" commanded Dingo.

He let go of the axe with one hand and sprang in to help Peter. The tree began to totter and then went crashing down, the branches breaking and leaves and dust swirling into the air.

"Now step aside and duck," Dingo said.

Peter went flat and Dingo swung the axe again and again. The blade chopped down into the splintered remains of the trunk at the point where it had snapped over. Kylie saw that because one cut had been above the other the butt had not sprung back towards her and her friends but had helped the tree to fall away from them. Now Dingo severed the remaining strands of timber with a few sharp blows. The butt of the trunk fell clear. Instantly Dingo dropped the axe and bent down. A second later he straightened up, the chain in his hands. He lifted it over the stump and held it up.

"Got it!" he said. "Let's go."

Bending down he scooped up the axe in his other hand. As he did, the others rose to their feet. Graham led off, heading away from the road into the dark bush. By then the vehicle had come to a shuddering stop out on the road and Kylie could hear the bushrangers shouting angrily.

"Oh quickly!" she cried, her anxiety making her hyperventilate. "They will catch us."

They began to run, Graham leading. Kylie wanted to yell to him to warn him which way to go but held her tongue when she saw that he was angling away from the road towards the top of the re-entrant she had come up.

He can read the ground like a soldier, she understood.

The idea of trying to run up an open slope away from the bushrangers and exposed to the full glare of the vehicle's lights made her terrified.

Suddenly the group running beside her all went down in a crying, cursing, scuffling heap. It took Kylie a moment to realise what had happened, but Stephen enlightened her by crying, "Ouch! Sorry. I bloody tripped."

She realised that if one went down all the others had to stop or fall as well because they were all chained together. Yelling excitedly to get up and to run she danced beside them in anxious impatience. The others understood the need for speed and hastily scrambled to their feet, then set off running again.

"Stay behind the person in front of you and don't go the wrong side of a tree," Peter cautioned.

The image of them all tangling around a tree caused Kylie another bout of anxiety. Behind her she glimpsed torch lights and dark figures and then heard the roar of the vehicle's engine and saw the glow of its headlights pointing straight towards them. As the vehicle was down on the road they were in shadow so she thought they were safe, but when the engine note roared even louder and she saw the headlight beams swing up to point at the treetops, she felt another chill of fear.

They are trying to drive the vehicle up into the bush! she thought in terrified amazement.

When she saw the headlights suddenly appear on top of the bank, bouncing and pointing directly at them she felt such a spasm of fear that she nearly wet herself. The bushrangers had succeeded!

Once again, the thought that they should give up before someone got hurt flashed through her mind but the others kept running so she did too. Then she understood Graham's reasoning: they were now over the crest and heading downslope into the re-entrant. Within a couple of paces they passed from the direct light into shadow. Behind them she heard the vehicle roaring and noted the beam of the headlights flicker and jump up in the trees.

They are trying to cross that little drain, she decided.

She forced herself to keep running, ignoring the sharp, stabbing agony on her ankle and the less obvious pains of chafing and sore muscles.

Suddenly the line came to another standstill, people crying out in pain. This time only Margaret went down but she was at once dragged up by Roger.

"What the? What happened?" Norah called.

Roger replied, "My fault. I went the wrong side of the tree." There were mutters and grumbles but also a couple of chuckles.

"Like two dogs on a walk," Peter said.

The group sorted itself out and hurried on down into the re-entrant. As they did, Kylie kept glancing back, expecting at every step to see Liam silhouetted against the glow of the headlights. She could tell by the glow that the bushrangers had finally gotten the vehicle over the drain but by the way the headlights kept swinging from side to side she decided that it was slow going driving it around the logs, rocks, and trees.

The group reached the bottom of the gully. This was rocky and steep-sided and gave good cover but also meant it was slow going. Graham obviously thought so too.

"Liam will easily catch us here," he said. "We need to break the chain."

"But how?" Margaret wailed.

"Stop!" commanded Dingo.

They did. All looked at him, the reflected glow from the headlights giving enough light to make out faces and even expressions. Dingo pointed to a large rock in the side of the gully.

"Hold the chain against that rock," he ordered Peter.

Peter did so. Dingo hefted the axe and measured his stroke, then swung.

Ching!

Sparks flew as the steel struck both chain and rock but the chain fell apart. It was still padlocked around their waists, but Dingo was now free.

"Move along," he ordered, gesturing impatiently.

They did so. The axe swung again and then again and Peter was free. Again the line shuffled along and Stephen and Norah held the chain up between them. The thought crossed Kylie's mind that chopping steel on a rock must be making horrible nicks in the axe blade but then she gave a short giggle as the absurdity of such a concern came to her.

Chang! Whang!

More sparks and Norah was free. Then Margaret. She stumbled forward and Kylie caught her. Margaret hugged her fiercely and cried, "Oh Kylie, you were wonderful!"

"I was very scared," Kylie admitted.

"You were very brave," Margaret added.

Graham grunted and said, "And foolish. You could have been shot."

While they talked Roger moved into position. Kylie released Margaret and then realised she was shaking so much she had trouble standing. So afraid of Liam was she that she kept looking back for signs of the bushrangers. She noted that the vehicle had stopped moving, its headlights able to shine into most of the re-entrant. Where they were was still in shadow, but she was sure Liam would be moving down or watching.

Clang!

The axe bounced and the flat of the blade struck Roger but he barely flinched, just re-adjusted the chain ready for Dingo to strike again. Thang! Kylie saw the silver steel snap and a link fall out. It was done. They were all free!

Without another word Graham set off down the gully. The others crowded behind, almost pushing each other over in their anxiety to get away. Kylie slipped into line ahead of Dingo, who came last. Fifty metres were covered and there was still no sign of Liam, only the glow of the headlights and voices calling angrily. Kylie noted that they had moved out of the direct line of the headlights and that cheered her up too.

Then she heard Liam yelling and, looking back over her shoulder, glimpsed him. He was walking along on top of the bank above the re-entrant. A bend in the gully hid him from sight but sheer fear pulsed through Kylie and she hurried on, twisting her ankle again and barely noticing the lancing pains.

Graham came to the junction of the re-entrant coming down from the left. This was the one Kylie had crept down at sunset but before she could say so Graham turned and went scrambling up it, crouching low to keep hidden. The others followed. As they did, Kylie noted the headlights swing over her head and then start moving down the spurline behind them.

By this time Kylie was gasping for breath and her heart was pounding fit to burst. She was perspiring and the many pains made her wonder if she could push herself to run much further. But by a teeth-gritting effort of will she managed to keep scrambling up, stumbling on rocks, banging her knee on something, falling headlong in the grass. She was hauled up by Dingo and pushed on upwards. Glancing back as she got higher up the gully, she clearly saw the vehicle. To her surprise it was now lower than her and heading down the other spur at right angles behind her. Of Liam there was no sign.

But now they had reached the upper end of the re-entrant and it petered out into a shallow dip and then to a bare, grassy hillside. There was nothing for it but to run, the distance to the crest of the saddle being about fifty paces.

Suddenly a beam of brilliant white light swept out and transfixed them. A glance over her shoulder told Kylie what its source was. *A spotlight, the sort that hunters use to shoot animals at night,* she told herself. It was on the vehicle.

Now new fears gripped Kylie, of people being shot. Horrible images of gasping people lying on the grassy hillside while dark blood pulsed out of the bullet holes in their bodies made her feel sick. The thought that she would be partly responsible by organizing the escape added to her sense of horror.

Liam's voice boomed out, loud and echoing around the hills. "Stop or I shoot!"

"Down!" Graham cried.

They all fell flat. As she hit the grass and dirt Kylie heard a vicious *crack!* close overhead, followed by a thumping noise behind her. Graham told her what it was by swearing and snarling, "The bastard! He nearly hit me then."

Liam is shooting! Kylie thought in horror.

She now understood that the crack had been the sound of the bullet passing. "We had better give up," she gasped.

"Not yet," Graham snarled. "That was only a warning shot. If he'd wanted to hit one of us he could have. Start crawling, fast!"

Kylie accepted that Graham knew what he was talking about but now thought it stupid and dangerous beyond belief to go on. But when the others began scurrying forward on hands and knees she went with them.

Crack!

Again the rifle fired. This time Dingo let out a sharp exclamation of pain. "Aargh! Bastard's winged me!" he gasped.

They all went flat and Kylie felt sick. Peter called, "Is it bad? Can you run?"

"I can run, I think," Dingo replied through gritted teeth.

Graham lifted his head behind a tree trunk, his face white in the bright light. "Run and scatter. Go to the left," he ordered.

Then he was up and running, angling off across the slope to the left. Kylie cried out in dismay at the fearful risk he was taking. She heard Liam yell, then another shot. Kylie's heart stood still with dread but then began to hammer again as she saw Graham keep going.

Missed! she thought.

Graham dodged around several trees and now changed direction and went upslope. The beam of light moved to track him.

"Now!" Peter hissed. "Now's our chance. Get up and run!"

In spite of her fear Kylie found herself up and sprinting, gasping for breath and sobbing at the pain. Fear such as she had never known swept through her and she cringed in fear of a bullet striking her body. Her terror was reinforced when she heard another shot. She flinched but had no idea who it was aimed at.

As she ran, Kylie heard a voice yelling, "Liam, stop it! Stop shooting you mad bugger! We are in enough trouble already, without killing anyone."

Kylie thought it was Pat's voice, but it might have been Brian's. But then she was over the crest and in shadow. At once she threw herself flat but Peter stopped and grabbed her arm.

"Get up! Keep running! We are in dead ground."

"Dead ground?" Kylie croaked as she heaved herself to her feet.

"Military term," Peter gasped. "Means ground you can't be seen in, or you can't see the enemy in. Go right."

"Graham!" Kylie gasped.

"Here he is," Peter replied, again grabbing her arm and swinging her to change direction. Kylie saw Graham come running back towards her. He dashed on past, pointing and calling to keep running. It puzzled her but she obeyed.

"Why this way?" she asked.

"Decoy," Graham called. "He saw us go left over the crest so now we will go right."

Kylie nodded and followed, glad to have Graham's fieldcraft skill in the lead. Others were running with her, and she was able to glance around and see that all the others were safely over the crest as well. A glance over her shoulder showed them strung out in a line behind, some puzzled and others just running. Ten paces ahead of her was Graham, scampering along the hillside, apparently without effort.

"Gra... Graham... Sl... slow... down!" Kylie gasped.

She saw his face look back, then he nodded and slowed. He needed to because Roger had taken a tumble and then Dingo fell. Norah helped him up. Graham pointed on along the hillside and said, "Keep going. Liam will be up on top in a minute, and we need to be out of sight."

Driven by that fear they pushed on, hurrying at a fast walk. Even so Kylie slipped and stumbled several times, as did most of the others.

Graham hissed to be quiet and then that he was doing a quick recce. With that he ran on again, soon vanishing around the curve of the hillside. Kylie kept glancing back, noting that the glow of the spotlight beam was wandering along the crest in both directions but that it was falling quickly behind. She was quite confident that the vehicle could not follow them across the gully so she began to feel some hope that they might escape. As they rounded the curve of the hillside this hope increased.

Liam won't know which way we went, she reasoned. That got her worrying whether he would be able to see their tracks trampled in the short grass but, looking back, she found them difficult to detect. *We might do it,* she reasoned.

And there was Graham again. He was waiting at another low saddle. He waited till the group had closed up, then pointed over the saddle and said, "We will go back over that way and down across the road. They won't suspect that."

Peter and Roger both nodded in agreement. Stephen adjusted his glasses and then asked, "What do we do then?"

"We will talk about that when we are sure we have made a clean break," Graham answered. Then he turned to Dingo. "You okay, Wirriumi?"

Dingo nodded but Kylie could see a dark stain on his shirt. He was gripping his upper right arm and was plainly in some pain. Seeing that made her bite her lip with anxiety. She was also impressed that at such a moment, her brother could be so sensitive. Only later did it dawn on her that no-one questioned Graham's leadership.

"We should come down to the road near the old cemetery," Graham explained. Then he added, "No talking."

Signalling with his hand to move he turned and led the way over the crest at a crouching trot.

Chapter 35

WHAT NEXT?

As the group made their way back across the crest of the ridge, Kylie felt ready to collapse. She was gasping for breath, trembling from emotion and limping badly. Pains seemed to engulf her and she realised she was sobbing. But she was also feeling a sense of fierce elation.

I did it! We are free! she thought.

The wonderful, but inconsequential, thought crossed her mind that her big brother would never be able to tease her again for dancing and being 'sooky'. That added to the glow of satisfaction and helped her to grit her teeth and keep on stumbling along.

Graham led them down into another re-entrant. This was smaller and more confusing to Kylie than the one they had just left. There were a number of small side gullies which she found hard to negotiate in the dark with her sore ankle. This time Graham did not follow the bed of it; rather he chose a route that kept them just on the left of a low spur line that led down beside it. This was easier walking, being just grass and trees and the odd rock or log. To begin with there was plenty of light because the headlights of the vehicle were shining in their direction, even though it was at least a hundred metres away. Also the powerful beam of the spotlight swept several times along the crest beside them.

But then the glow of the headlights shifted. Graham signalled them to stop and hurried up to the crest and peeked over, being very careful to do so from behind a bush next to a tree trunk. A few seconds later he was back.

"The vehicle has turned around and is driving back up the ridge. They are shining the spotlight on the rise to the south of where we were camped."

"That's good news, isn't it?" Margaret asked.

Graham nodded. "Yes it is. It means they think we went that way. But, just in case they come this way, we need to get down off this ridge fast and across the road."

"Where is the road?" Margaret asked.

Graham pointed down the slope. "Just down there," he replied, his voice indicating surprise that she did not know.

That made Kylie blush too because she had been somewhat disoriented herself. Now she glimpsed the grey ribbon through the trees and felt slightly foolish.

Led by Graham they hurried on down. The ridge was quite steep in places and several times she slipped or twisted her ankle again, each time gasping with pain. Tears came to her eyes, but she gritted her teeth and continued, not wanting to make a fuss lest it delay them. A minute later they reached the road. They had to scramble down a bank to reach it but Graham led the way straight across.

"Cemetery," he said softly as he padded out onto the gravel.

Kylie followed his pointing arm with her eyes and was just able to make out the gate and tops of the tombstones in the starlight twenty metres to her right.

This is where I came to, she thought.

Graham then called softly back, "Wirriumi, cover our tracks man."

"Will do," Dingo replied.

By then Kylie was across. As she stepped into the long grass between the cemetery fence and the steep sided gully close beside her on her left, she glanced along to her right and glimpsed the faint glow of lights through the trees. The bushrangers now seemed a long way away and she thought they were searching away from them. That made her feel much safer.

Graham pushed past and began leading them along the top of the gully. As he did, Kylie heard Margaret say, "What are those things there?"

"Headstones," Kylie answered. "Graves. It is the cemetery. This is where I came to get the axe."

"Graves!" Margaret answered, her voice having a noticeable quaver.

Stephen chuckled then added, "Dead centre of town."

"People are dying to get in there," Peter commented.

"But it's dead boring," Stephen added more.

"At least the neighbours are quiet," Peter replied.

The boys chuckled but Kylie could tell Margaret was scared. She wasn't amused herself and was annoyed that, even with all her friends with her, the hair on the back of her neck was standing up and she was coming out in goosebumps.

"Stop it you silly boys!" she snapped.

The group moved on, finding its route sandwiched between the fence of the cemetery and what looked to be a very steep sided gully. Several times Graham halted and she heard him muttering and looking around as though looking for a better way but then he continued slowly on. Kylie felt quite anxious lest she slip so she kept gripping the wires, several times snagging her hands on barbs. Once past the cemetery they made their way down into the valley of a larger creek.

By this time Kylie was almost groaning with every step. She had to force herself to keep going, pushing the sharp pains to the side of her mind. That she was not the only one having trouble walking was then brought home to her very forcibly when she heard Norah ask, "Dingo, are you alright?"

Dingo replied in a voice tight with pain, "I can go a bit further Miss Norah."

Norah called ahead, "Graham, find a place where we can hide for a few minutes. Dingo is wounded."

"Righto," Graham called softly back. "Down in the creek line. There should be water there."

How clever Graham is, Kylie thought, admiring how he could think of such things at such a time.

The group continued on for another fifty metres or so until they came to the creek. It wasn't much of a stream, only two paces wide and with steep little clay banks a metre high, but there were a few trees and bushes to hide amongst. Graham scouted for a minute and then led them in among some small bushes to a stretch of rocky creek bed with water flowing past it. In the starlight the water looked black, but Kylie guessed it was only ankle deep.

Graham pointed back up the slope. "Roger, sentry, facing back the way we came," he ordered.

Roger stopped and faced back, crouching beside a tree trunk. The others crowded down into the area between the bushes and the creek and slumped down. Margaret started to talk but Graham shushed her. "Sssh! We will just listen for a minute," he said.

Kylie knew that Margaret would be blushing at that but agreed. Thankfully she eased her sore legs and then sat listening. In the far distance she heard men's voices and once she heard the vehicle's engine but saw no sign of it. She reasoned that they were now three or four hundred metres from the campsite at least.

Graham nodded and then said, "I don't think they have any idea where we are. And I doubt if they can track us in the dark."

"If they had dogs they would find us in five minutes," Stephen said.

"They would," Graham agreed. He then turned to Dingo. "Now, Wirriumi, how bad is your wound? Let's have a look."

Kylie had all but forgotten Dingo crying out but now she saw in the starlight how the side of his shirt and trousers looked black in the starlight. Guessing that was blood, she sucked her breath and felt a horrible sense of apprehension. Norah and Peter both moved to help Graham. They undid Dingo's shirt and trousers and eased them away from the wound. Several times Dingo cried out, but each time he stifled his cries.

"Just grazed me," he grumbled, trying to sound calm and tough.

"Some graze!" Norah retorted.

"The bullet isn't lodged in you," Peter commented. "That's good."

Even though it made her feel sick to do so Kylie found she had to look. In the dark she saw Norah bathing blood away using a handkerchief. This revealed a long weal that ran from Dingo's lower right buttock up across his hip and across the side of his ribs to a knick under his armpit that was dripping blood.

"Bloody lucky that wasn't a bit higher," Graham said as he gripped Dingo's arm tightly. "Another centimetre up and it would have hit the artery under your arm."

"Or shattered the bone," Peter commented.

Thinking about that made Kylie feel nauseous and a little desperate. *We are a long way from a doctor,* she thought.

The others worked quickly and efficiently, between them having sufficient First Aid training to staunch the flow of blood. Both Norah and Peter tore strips from the hem of their shirts to make bandages. When the bandaging was done as well as it could be in the circumstances the First Aid party washed their hands.

Graham bent to drink. "Tastes okay," he commented.

That reminded Kylie how thirsty she was, so she made her way down to the water and drank from her cupped hands. The others did likewise. Dingo lowered himself with several painful grunts and lay flat, to lap at the water.

Once that was done Margaret asked, “Well, what do we do now?”

“Get medical help for Dingo,” Norah at once replied.

“And get the cops,” Stephen added.

That much was self-evident. Margaret asked, “How do we do that?”

From out of the darkness Roger said quietly, “Get Old Zeke to help.”

“Of course!” Graham cried. “Well done Roger.”

“Who is Old Zeke?” Norah asked.

Stephen answered that. “He is the old tin miner who saved our lives last year.”

“I fell down his mine,” Roger added.

“Where does he live?” Norah asked.

Graham pointed down the creek. “That way, about a kilometre.”

“Then let’s go!” Norah cried.

“Not so fast,” Peter cautioned. “He may not be there anymore. Last time we saw him he said he wasn’t finding enough tin to pay the cost of mining.”

“We still have to check,” Graham answered. “Let’s go.”

“We don’t all have to go,” Peter replied. “You and Roger go and we will wait here.”

“Okay. That alright Roger?”

“Yes,” Roger answered, but Kylie detected a distinct moan in his voice.

“Wait here,” Graham said. “We will be half an hour or so.” He stood up and pushed his way through the bushes to where Roger sat. After a whispered consultation the two boys set off. They went across the side gully and then angled up the gentle slope in a north westerly direction.

Kylie felt a surge of relief. *Won’t be long!* she told herself.

As the sound of the boy’s progress died away she shifted to a more comfortable position and carefully lay flat. She did not really want to lay her head on the grass, thinking of ticks and other wee beasties, but she was so sick and tired she really did not care. With a sigh that was as much a moan she stretched out and tried to relax.

The others also settled down, Margaret beside her on one side and Peter and Stephen on the other. There was some quiet conversation but mostly they just lay and listened. Time then crept in the way it always does when waiting for something important. Several times spasms of cramp shook Kylie and she found her tired muscles trembling continually. Her eyes felt hot and gritty, and she had to get up to drink some more. Then she had to go to the toilet. That meant walking off into the long grass, a very unpleasant experience, with images of snakes tormenting her. But it had to be done so she did it.

About three quarters of an hour later, she heard a stick snap up towards the road. Then she heard the sound of grass rustling and then another stick break. For a few seconds she froze, fearing that it was the bushrangers, though how they could have found them lying out in the dark bush she could not imagine. Carefully she lifted her head. She saw that both Peter and Stephen were alert and looking towards the sounds.

Then she heard Roger's voice and was able to relax. *Not long now,* she thought. But a minute later, when Graham and Roger came walking in out of the night her hopes were dashed.

"Not there," Graham said as he sat down. "The whole camp site is bare. The sheds and machinery are all gone. The place is deserted."

Hearing that caused Kylie's spirits to drop enormously. She almost burst into tears. As she bit her trembling bottom lip she realised she was nearly at the end of her strength and that she had been placing great hopes on Old Zeke and instant deliverance.

"So we have to go further for help," Stephen commented.

Graham nodded. "Yes."

Peter now asked the hard question. "So, who goes? And which way?"

"What are the choices?" Norah asked.

Graham pointed up and down the creek. "Back that way about fifteen kilometres is Bakerville. Mutchilba is about thirty the other way. Bakerville is our best bet. I can make that in a few hours."

"In the dark?" Norah asked.

"Done it before," Graham answered.

And with a broken ankle, Kylie thought. However she said, "But you can't walk along the road this time. The bushrangers are back that way."

"Only those three," Graham replied.

Kylie shook her head. "No. I saw Brian ride off that way this afternoon and I thought he was going to lie in wait to catch me as I came past. There are also Rory and Sean somewhere."

"You seem to know the gang pretty well," Stephen jibed.

Graham chuckled. "Honorary member since Brian kissed her."

Both comments hurt and tears misted in Kylie's eyes for a second.

But they also stung. "You would know them better too, if you bothered to pay attention!" she snapped back. "You were with them long enough."

"Sorry Sis," Graham replied. "But it doesn't change what I said. We just go a bit slower and go cross-country."

"In the dark?" Margaret queried.

"We've just done a kilometre cross-country in the dark," Graham said.

"We do it all the time on cadet exercises," Peter explained. "In this open savannah country it is no real problem."

Having just done a fair bit of walking and crawling cross-country Kylie could see that what the boys were saying was not unreasonable. "So who goes?" she asked.

"We should all go," Norah said.

Dingo shook his head. "I don't know if I am up to that Miss Norah," he said. "My wound is starting to stiffen up. I would only slow you down. Better that you leave me here."

"Not on your own," Norah insisted.

"So, who goes, and who stays?" Graham asked.

That put Kylie on a real spot. She was so sore and worn out that she did not think she could possibly walk 15 kilometres, let alone cross-country and in the dark. "I will stay," she said. "I've sprained my ankle and I am badly chafed from all that walking we have done."

Margaret at once spoke up. "I will stay with Kylie," she said.

"And me," Roger added.

Peter knelt low and used the light in his watch to check the time. "Just coming up to ten," he said. "So, if we manage two kilometres an hour we should be at Bakerville in about seven or eight hours, say by five or six in the morning. That would get the coppers here by just after daylight."

"So the sooner we get moving the better," Stephen suggested.

Kylie now spoke up, voicing a worry that had been niggling at her. "While we are here, we can watch which way the bushrangers go."

"Good idea," Graham agreed. "They will be long gone by daylight."

Stephen nodded. "They could be a couple of hundred kilometres away in that truck," he agreed.

"I don't think so," Kylie said. "I think they will still be in the area."

"Mugs if they are," Stephen commented.

"Why do you say that Kylie?" Peter asked.

"Something I overheard them say when I was getting the axe," Kylie answered.

"That was very well done, brilliant!" Roger said.

Kylie glowed at that praise and was not put out when Graham added, "And bloody stupid, the way you defied Pat. He could have shot you."

Kylie shook her head. "I was sure he wouldn't. He is much too nice."

"Very brave anyway," Norah added.

"What exactly did they say Kylie?" Peter asked. "We need to give the coppers all the information we can."

Kylie tried to remember all the snippets of information she had overheard. In doing so she recounted her actions that afternoon and evening, gaining more praise from the others. "So I think they are waiting to meet up with Phil Kelly and the others at their hideout," she concluded.

"If we knew where their hideout was we could watch that too," Graham said.

"It is somewhere with a Russian name," Kylie replied, thinking hard to try to remember exact details.

"Russian?" Peter asked. "What name was it?"

Kylie bit her lip and thought hard, then said, "I think it was Ivan, or something like that. When one of them saw me listening he stopped himself from saying the whole name."

"Ivan?" Peter repeated.

Kylie nodded. There were a few seconds of silence while the boys thought hard. "I wish we had a map," Graham commented.

Suddenly Stephen clicked his fingers. "Ivanhoe! Not Russian. Old English. You know, Sir Walter Scott's novel, *Ivanhoe*. There is an Ivanhoe Mine at Stannary Hills. We went into it, remember?"

"Yes!" Peter cried. "It is the one just near the old battery site, where the railway runs through the cutting on that sharp loop of Eureka Creek."

Graham nodded. "Where the big concrete slab for the huge pulley wheels is," he added.

"That's it." Peter agreed.

"That's the place then. The bushrangers are using the old mine tunnels to hide in!" Graham cried, excitement sounding in his voice.

"To hide their loot in," Roger added.

"Not loot," Kylie put in. "The Duke."

"The Duke! I'd forgotten about him," Graham said.

Peter spoke next. "So, the people who stay can watch which way the bushrangers go and then tell the police as they go past," he said. "Now, let's get moving. We've got a long way to go and the sooner we get there the better."

"We can't watch the road from down here," Graham said.

"So someone stays to do that as well," Peter replied.

"I will," Graham answered.

"You don't want to walk to Bakerville again?" Peter queried.

Graham shook his head. "You can be the hero this time. You and Steve. I would rather keep an eye on the bushrangers."

Norah then surprised Kylie by saying, "I will stay too. I don't think I can walk that far. I will only slow you down."

Peter looked doubtful but agreed. "Just you and me then Steve. Is that okay?"

Stephen nodded. "Fine by me. Let's get moving. I'm getting stiff and cold just sitting here."

Anxiety now gripped Kylie. "How will you find your way in the dark?" she queried.

Peter grunted and she sensed he was annoyed. "I've seen the map often enough! We know the general lay of the land," he replied.

Margaret spoke next. "Good luck then," she said.

At that, Peter gave another grunt then said, "We depend on skill but thanks."

Graham gave a chuckle and Roger made a quiet 'raspberry'. "Skill!" he muttered. "Headquarters Platoon!"

Stephen gave a muttered response and stood up.

Kylie was amazed that the boys could tease and joke at a time like this. She knew that Peter was the Headquarters Platoon sergeant in the cadet unit but thought he was very capable. "Be careful then," she said as Peter also stood up.

"We will be. See you in the morning," Peter replied.

Peter then crossed the creek, stepping from rock to rock. Stephen followed and the two boys made their way east up the hill side beyond. As they vanished into the night, Kylie understood. *They are going across the valley to get well away from the road before they turn south.*

She had every faith that Peter could navigate cross-country, even without a map. Within a minute they were lost to sight in the dark bush.

There was a pause then. Kylie lay flat and shuddered as the tension eased out of her. Now things would be alright. People had gone for help and they had escaped. The only real worry was whether Dingo's wounds might not be more serious than they thought.

He might bleed to death, she worried.

For a while the friends talked quietly, discussing the problems of navigating to Bakerville, then speculating on where the other members of the gang might be. Graham organised a sentry roster. He wanted them to do two hours on but Roger objected and Norah supported him. So it was arranged for one hour on, changing every half hour.

Dingo insisted he would do his share. "I won't sleep much anyway with the pain," he said. "And my ears still work okay."

Graham now got them to lie in a line, side by side, in the order in which they were to do the duty. "That's how they do it on small patrols," he explained, "And you don't have to try to remember who is next, or have a written roster. It is just the next person in line."

Kylie saw the logic in that but grumbled when she had to move as she had just made herself as comfortable as she could. Now she had to wriggle and dig to make a new bedspace in the grass. That done she stretched out and tried to relax. This was easier said than done as she found her aching body kept her aware of it. Also her mind kept turning over the events of the last few days. Anxiety over Dingo, and over Peter and Stephen, allied to a nagging worry that somehow the bushrangers might find them, all kept her on the edge of wakefulness.

At 2330hrs she took over from Dingo as sentry. For the first half hour she was on with Roger. When she tried to talk, he shushed her and said that good soldiers did not talk on sentry duty. Kylie felt a bit miffed by that but saw the logic of it. Even so, when Margaret took over from Roger at midnight she did have a whispered conversation with her, until Graham growled at them to be quite and to listen.

So she sat there, slowly getting chilled and stiff. But she was not bored. Her mind kept thinking about the Kelly Gang. What she found herself wondering, over and over, was what their plans were. *Where are they going to go next?* she thought. *And how can they possibly hope to evade capture much longer?*

It was obvious to her, from what she had overheard, that the gang's friends were all distancing themselves. That seemed quite reasonable to

Kylie as she did not think the Kelly's cause was good enough to risk years of prison for.

Not if you are just a friend, she thought. In fact she did not think a true friend would ask friends to help in that case.

Where is their hideout? she puzzled. *And is the Duke with them? Or is he with Phil Kelly and that horrible Dan Murphy?*

After a time she gave a wry smile, *And what about Brian and Maureen?* she thought. She had a suspicion that their romance might be over. *And so is mine!* she told herself sadly. That got her all depressed and a single tear trickled out. *Oh! But it was wonderful while it lasted!* she thought, sighing at the pleasant memories of those golden moments at the dance.

When she was relieved at 0030hrs by Norah she voiced another thought that had been worrying her off and on for two days. "I hope your horses are alright Norah."

"I think they will be," Norah whispered back. "There was plenty of water and good grass."

"I hope you make these Kellies pay for any that get hurt, and for lost business," Kylie added.

Norah just snuffled at that but agreed. "Go to sleep now," she said.

But Kylie couldn't. She lay back and closed her eyes but her mind was too active. Images of the Kelly Gang, and thoughts about where they might be and what they might be doing, kept swirling through her mind. It was over an hour later that she drifted off to sleep, her head still swarming with ideas.

* * *

Kylie sat up and found she was shivering. She had snuggled up against Margaret and had her arm around her. Margaret was obviously cold too and was on the edge of being awake as she opened her eyes with a start and said, "Kylie, what's wrong?"

"Cold," Kylie said.

Then she shook her head. It was not the cold that had woken her up. It had been an idea, expressed in a vivid dream. She looked around and saw that Dingo and Roger were sitting up on guard.

To them she said, "We should go and find the Kelly Gang's hideout."

Chapter 36

ROGER REMEMBERS

Roger snorted softly and replied, "I don't think so. We should just hide here and wait for the police. They can do the looking."

"But they may not know where to look, or they might be too late," Kylie replied. The more she thought about it the more she wanted to do it.

"We have taken too many risks already," Roger replied. "We should keep away from the Kelly Gang. That Liam might not miss next time."

Kylie felt anxious when she considered that, but she still held to her idea. "How far is it to this Ivanhoe Mine place?" she asked.

"From memory about two or three kilometres," Roger answered.

"How long would it take us to walk that?" Kylie asked.

Roger shook his head but said, "If we just walked along the road then only half an hour to three quarters of an hour. But that might not be a good idea. They might have a guard watching the road and we could blunder straight into them."

"So we sneak through the bush," Kylie answered.

In her mind were images of how she had followed the gang the previous afternoon and how she had snuck up on them. To her that did not seem all that risky.

Again Roger shook his head. "We could," he said, "But it would be slow going. The country gets a lot rougher from here on in. The hills are a lot bigger. It would be no joke in the dark."

At that moment, Graham spoke. "Stop talking you lot. You are too loud."

"Sorry," Kylie whispered. She went to lie down but Roger reached over and shook her. "Don't lie down Kylie. It is nearly time for you to go on watch again."

"What time is it?" Kylie asked.

"Two twenty," Roger answered.

"Ten minutes yet," Kylie answered.

"Doesn't matter. Dingo isn't feeling very well and you are awake anyway," Roger said.

That got Kylie worried. She knelt and reached across to Dingo. "How are you Dingo?" she asked. Somehow, she did not feel it was right for her to use his tribal name.

Dingo shook his head. "Not too good. I feel a bit hot."

Kylie placed her hand on his brow and at once felt anxious. Dingo's skin was hot and dry and he was trembling. "Does it hurt?" she asked.

"A lot," Dingo answered. "It all stings and tingles."

"Are you bleeding?"

Dingo shook his head. "Don't think so, but every time I move I tear the scab off the dried blood."

"Then you lie down and rest," Kylie insisted.

Dingo did as he was told and Kylie stretched and sat up. She was cold now, so she stood and did some exercises with her arms. When she felt warmer, she looked around, staring into the darkness. Everything was still. There was no breeze and no clouds. The sky was a million bright stars and the starlight gave the dark bush an eerie feel. This was increased when a curlew gave its mournful cry further down the creek. There was no sound of the bushrangers and she could not imagine them blundering around the bush in the dark in the faint hope of actually stumbling over them.

They will think we are a long way away by now, she reasoned. Which only reinforced her wish to try to locate the bushrangers hideout. *They won't be expecting that,* she thought. *They will think we are just trying to get to safety.*

As Roger would not talk all she could do was sit and think. Her thoughts ranged from worry about how her parents must be feeling, to concern for the horses, to anxiety about Peter and Stephen. She pictured them stumbling through the dark bush and then had awful thoughts about one or the other tripping and injuring themselves.

A broken leg, she thought, *or a broken back!*

Thinking about that got her all sick with apprehension but as there was nothing she could do about it she went back to reliving the last few days.

Wistful romantic memories of those first golden moments of her crush on Brian led to hot and guilty thoughts about kissing and caressing outside at the dance. These thoughts were replaced by hot spurts of jealousy and anger when she remembered seeing Brian kissing Maureen.

There was at least the satisfaction of having tricked him so that Maureen knew he was a two-timer. That got her feeling hurt and vengeful. She was ashamed of that but still felt a strong desire to make sure Brian knew he had hurt her.

That rekindled the wish to seek out the bushranger's hideout. *I want to see his face when he is caught,* she thought.

0300hrs came around and Roger woke Margaret. Margaret shivered and also stood to warm herself by rapid movement. Then she settled beside Kylie and the two girls began to whisper, until first Roger, and then Graham, told them to be quiet. That did not help Kylie's bad mood. The boys acting so superior and thinking they were always right made her feel annoyed.

For the next half hour she sat there brooding. In her mind's eye she pictured herself sneaking up to watch the bushranger's camp; saw them relaxed around their campfire, unaware that SHE was watching, ready to bring the police.

I am going to do it, she decided.

But did she have the strength? That got her testing her stiff muscles and feeling her chafing and blisters. These certainly hurt but she decided she was good for a few kilometres yet. The few hours rest had helped.

Then something else helped stiffen her resolve. At first she could not work out what she was looking at but then she realised that the light had changed. A check of the watch showed her it was just coming up to 0330hrs and the end of her sentry duty. Then she looked up and saw the silver rimming to the trees across the valley and realised she could see the dark silhouette of the opposite ridgeline.

The moon, she told herself. And then it dawned on her. *That will make it easier to move through the bush.*

She had already decided she needed to be hiding near the bushranger's camp by sunrise. Now she turned to Margaret and said, "I am going to find the Kelly Gang's hideout."

"Oh Kylie, don't be silly!" Margaret replied, plainly horrified.

"I am," Kylie answered, "I don't care what you say."

She was being stubborn and knew it but that just fuelled her anger and determination. *I can do it,* she told herself.

"Not on your own," Margaret insisted.

"I will if nobody else will come with me," Kylie replied.

Graham now sat up. He was plainly grumpy. "I told you girls to stop talking on sentry duty," he growled.

"I know you did," Kylie hissed back, "But I'm not one of your cadets, so ask nicely!"

Graham muttered something, then looked around and said, "What's the time?"

"Three forty-five. And the moon is up, and I am going to find the bushranger's camp."

"Don't be silly, Kylie!" Graham snapped.

"I'm not being silly. It's a good idea. I can help the police. And you can't stop me."

"I will if I have to," Graham answered.

"You'll have to tie me up," Kylie retorted.

"I've done that before," Graham answered. But he was looking around. He shivered and then stood to warm himself. After a minute or so he said, "Stop talking please. You will wake the others."

At that, Norah answered, "I was awake anyway. I'm too cold to sleep."

"Me too," added Roger.

Kylie looked and saw Dingo's eyes gleam in the moonlight. Knowing that she had woken everyone made her feel a bit guilty. But it also made her want to go. She said, "I'd like to go and find the bushranger's camp. It would be much easier and safer if some of you came with me. I don't know the way, but you do."

"I still think it is silly," Roger answered.

"It might be, but you can remember the way, can't you?" Kylie asked.

"Yes, of course I can," Roger replied. He sat up and groaned.

Kylie was now feeling frustrated. She did not really want to go off on her own, did agree that was silly, but she could not think what argument to use.

Suddenly Graham said, "It will be easy with this moon." Then he added, "I'd like to find the bushranger's camp too."

"You can lead me then," Kylie said, her hopes shooting up, along with her fears and doubts.

"Not you girls. It is too dangerous," Graham told her.

"Oh you sexist pig! It is not," Kylie snapped. "If anything it is safer for us. None of the bushrangers would hurt a girl."

"Liam might, or that Dan," Margaret said.

"Maybe. But I think it is a fair risk," Kylie replied. "They are not real bushrangers. They aren't murderers or robbers or anything like that. They are doing this as a stunt to get publicity."

"You just want to see Brian again," Graham teased.

"And you just want to see Kate!" Kylie retorted.

"I do too!" Graham replied with a grin. "So, who would like to come and who is staying here with Dingo?"

To Kylie's surprise no-body offered to stay, not even Norah. She said, "I'd like to help catch those bug... er, those crooks. They have caused me a lot of worry."

"But somebody's got to stay with Dingo," Kylie said.

Dingo shook his head. "I'll be alright on my own. I will just move up closer to the road where I can see better who goes past."

That idea horrified Kylie but Dingo was adamant. "You kids go. I will be safer on my own. I can hide more easily. Them fellas won't find me."

"But what about your wound?" Margaret asked.

Dingo shrugged. "It ain't bleeding. If I just lie still, it should be okay. Anyway, it's only a coupl'a hours to sunrise. If you guys want to find them bushrangers by then you'd better get a move on."

Kylie still did not feel good about it and still thought someone should stay. She was surprised that Norah didn't offer but could understand why Margaret didn't. *She will want to be with Graham,* she told herself. She looked at Roger but he shook his head.

The decision was then taken out of her hands by Graham standing up and saying, "Alright, it's four o'clock. Let's move. Wirriumi, just tell the coppers we are at the old battery site, near the Ivanhoe Mine. It's about three kilometres."

With that he led the way into the long grass, heading across the end of the gully which came down past the cemetery. This was the way he and Roger had gone earlier so she didn't question that. Indeed it took all her attention to force her tired and sore body into motion. The first few steps were very painful, and more aches and pains returned at every other step. That she was not the only one feeling it was obvious when she heard both Margaret and Roger give a few mumbled groans as they set off behind her.

Looking back she saw Dingo painfully get to his feet and then start hobbling off through the grass, dragging his right leg in a painful limp. Seeing that made her feel bad but she could not think of what to say, other than offering to stay with him herself, and that was something she did not want to do. Her desire to find the bushranger's camp was fierce.

Seven minutes later the friends, minus Dingo who had gone off to the left, were up at the side of the road. They reached it about a hundred paces to the north of the cemetery. Graham instructed Roger to brush out their tracks and then led the way straight across. On the other side were a flat area and a low saddle on the left. On the right was the end of a hill. Graham headed straight for the high ground.

Seeing they were heading away from the road Kylie asked where they were going. Graham pointed up the ridge. "This ridge runs all the way to the Ivanhoe Mine," he explained.

"Have you been this way?" Kylie asked.

Graham shook his head. "No."

"What if we get lost?"

"I remember seeing it on the map. Trust me. If we get lost, we just go right until we come down to the road. Then we follow it, but this will be a lot easier, and will also avoid anyone watching the road," he said.

Kylie had to be content with that. She actually had enormous faith that Graham could find his way around the bush in the dark. So she set herself to follow, focusing instead on her tender ankle and on the other pains in her body. After a few more minutes walking, she found that her sore muscles bothered her less once they were warmed up but the chafing was savage and the ankle very tender. At every second step she winced and sucked in her breath till she worked out how to put pressure on that foot without too much pain. Of more concern was the effort of walking uphill.

After a few minutes she had to call out to Graham to stop. He was drawing quickly ahead, and she saw that all of those behind her were gasping for breath.

"You are forgetting we aren't fit," she said to him. It peeved her to notice that he had been strolling up the hill without any apparent effort.

Graham grumbled about this but did slow down. The march then became a steady upwards plod, stopping every hundred paces or so to let them get their breath back. The ridge wasn't steep, but it went on and on.

At least there is almost no grass or undergrowth, Kylie noted.

The ground appeared almost bare. Only a few spindly tufts of grass grew on the sandy soil, which was covered by a matt of leaf litter and dead twigs. That made it easier to avoid logs and rocks in the moonlight.

They came to a level hilltop and that was a relief. Suddenly Graham stopped. Kylie peered past him at the dark bush. "What is it?" she hissed, thinking of bushrangers or snakes.

"Bloody great hole," Graham replied. "Roger, come and a look at this bastard."

Only then did Kylie see what Graham was pointing at. Close beside the animal pad they had been following she saw a dark patch. She had thought it was just dead leaves or something and was shocked to realise it was actually a large hole in the ground. Beyond it was a mullock heap.

"Is it a mine shaft?" Margaret asked.

"Yes," Graham answered. He bent and picked up a stone and tossed it in. "One... two... three... four!" he counted. Kylie heard a soft thud. Graham said, "That's about thirty metres deep. That's a lot deeper than the one you fell down Roger."

"It is," Roger agreed, with feeling. "You wouldn't be climbing out of that."

Now the enormity of the danger broke upon Kylie and she shuddered. *Thirty metres!* she thought in dismay, imagining herself or one of her friends falling down such a shaft. She saw it was about three metres square but quite hard to see, even in the moonlight.

Graham resumed walking, saying casually, "You'd better watch where you are putting your feet this time Roger."

"I will!" Roger said, giving the forbidding looking hole a wide berth.

Kylie now wondered if she should persuade them to call off the whole plan, but Graham just pressed on. Passing another mine shaft a few minutes later did nothing but add to her sense of dread. Then Graham had to backtrack, the main ridge of the spur being over on their right fifty metres away.

"We have to keep exactly on the crest all the way or we could end up miles off course," he explained.

He found a rough vehicle track coming up from the right and apparently following the ridge line. When he commented on this Kylie strained her eyes to see what he was talking about. Only with difficulty could she make out the wheel ruts, but Graham seemed to just stroll along it. This track dipped across a saddle and then went on upwards. Slowly Kylie's body adjusted to the effort. The aches and pains all melded into a general dull ache and her ankle stiffened up. Her breath came in smaller gasps as she got her second wind and found she was perspiring, despite the early morning chill.

After a few hundred metres Graham lost the track again. The ground seemed to become very confusing to Kylie, but Graham stopped them and wandered around for a few minutes. Then he came back and said, "Sorry. I should have taken the left track back there."

Left track? Kylie wondered, having lost sight of any sort of track.

As they made their way back around the top of a re-entrant Margaret asked the question that was now puzzling Kylie. "Graham, how do you know we are going the right way?"

They were just dipping down into what looked like a jumble of steep gullies and re-entrants, so it seemed a very fair question to Kylie. Graham stopped and pointed. "See that hilltop to our left front? We have to get to that. And I am keeping those even bigger hills on my right front. They are over beyond the Stannary Hills town site."

He now led the way down across a narrow saddle with a big re-entrant on the right and a very obvious little valley going off to the left. Kylie saw that they were again following an animal pad. Even so it was slow going and she kept calling on Graham to slow down or to halt to let her rest. An hour went by and Graham began to mutter about it soon being daylight.

They next followed a fairly easy ridge line, along which there were more of the dangerous mine shafts. Then it was up an old road that was all washed out and overgrown. The grass gave way to numerous small grass trees. What did surprise her was how big the hill was. The group seemed to rise steadily up and up until they were above the level of nearly all the surrounding hills except those in front. That gave her a view out over miles of hills, the trees all silver in the moonlight.

Rather pretty really, Kylie decided.

But she was also struck by how isolated she felt. Lines of hills stretched off on both sides into the far distance. There was no sign of human habitation in any direction.

Not a light to be seen, she thought. *We are a long way from any help,* she worried.

The thought made her shiver with apprehension. Now she wondered if she should not try to talk them out of the expedition. The closer they got to their objective the more scared and anxious she became.

Oh! I wish I hadn't talked people into this, she thought, worried that one or more might get hurt because of her jealous anger.

She finally plucked up courage to suggest that maybe this wasn't a good idea, but unfortunately she did so just after they had reached the top of the hill and had begun to walk down a long down slope. Graham shook his head emphatically and said, "Not now. We are almost there. See that big open ridge down to the right? That was the old town site. The railway station was in the valley closer in on our right front, right in the bottom of the valley, and the Ivanhoe Mine is straight ahead, this side of those big hills."

Knowing that made Kylie feel both glad and also excited. *We are getting close,* she thought.

At her suggestion they had a good rest to get their breath back. While they sat there, she noticed a distinct greying of the sky away on her right. That got her worried again.

"What time is it?" she asked.

Graham checked his watch, then said, "Ten past five. Only half an hour or so to daylight. You can see it starting to get light away to the east already."

"You don't think we should turn back? I'd hate anyone to get hurt," Kylie said, in a last attempt to ease her conscience.

Graham shook his head and Roger said, "No. I don't think the bushrangers will hurt us, even if they catch us again. As you said, they aren't real bushrangers."

"They didn't hurt us before, did they?" Norah added.

"If they see us, we can just split up and scatter. They won't be able to catch us all and one of us will be able to tell the police where to go," Graham said.

"We will stay well back and keep out of sight," Norah said firmly.

"I agree," Graham said. With that he ended the argument by standing up and starting down the ridge. Luckily, they found another old vehicle track. This was easy to follow and appeared to be following the crest of the ridge down.

The next twenty minutes was just a slow plod. The slope got steeper, and Kylie slipped several times on the loose soil and dead leaves. The vegetation remained the same: a forest of black trunked ironbarks and almost no undergrowth except that they began passing small outcrops of rocks and a few clumps of bushes.

As they descended the ridge, Roger became more and more excited. He kept looking from side to side and then pointed down to the right and said, "See that bend in the big creek? See that overgrown vehicle track? That leads to Old Zeke's mine. It is just in that next ridge over."

Graham stopped and looked back. "Where did you fall in Roger?"

Roger frowned and pointed further down the ridge on their left. "Somewhere down there. Among one of these clumps of bushes."

"Don't fall into it again," Margaret cautioned.

"No fear!" Roger agreed.

They continued on down, the ridge widening out as they went. They began to encounter thickets of small trees and then mullock heaps and more old mine shafts. The ground became rocky and rough with small washouts hidden in the grass. This slowed them to a crawl and caused Kylie quite a few more twinges in her sore ankle. Ahead of them a large hill loomed ever higher, and Graham grunted with satisfaction. That reassured Kylie that his navigation had been accurate.

Suddenly Roger hissed and pointed. "Check this," he said, indicating a clump of bushes a few paces over to their right front.

By then it was starting to get light, the grey of dawn combining with the moonlight to make visibility quite good. He went that way so the group detoured and followed over to the bushes. As they got closer, Kylie saw that the bushes were growing in a litter of stones. At first, she assumed these were a natural outcrop but when they reached them she saw they were a circle of stones dug up from the mine shaft.

Graham went right to the edge and looked down. "Is this like the one you fell down Roger?" he asked.

Very gingerly Roger edged forward and looked down. "Yes. The one I fell down is just like this, all hidden in bushes," he replied. Then he visibly shuddered and backed away.

Having heard the story of Roger's underground adventure several times Kylie could not resist a peek, but kept hold of a small tree, lest she slip on the loose gravel. She found it both thrilling and disappointing. The mine shaft was still in darkness, but she could just make out the bottom. It did not look very deep, but she was able to make out the black opening of a tunnel.

"Keep back!" Roger cautioned as Norah and Margaret both made their way forward to look in.

Graham grinned. "What if the Kelly Gang are hiding in a mine tunnel Roger? Will you go in?"

"No fear!" Roger cried softly, obviously horrified at the thought.

"Not even to escape?" Graham teased.

"Not even to rescue a princess!" Roger affirmed.

Kylie had to smile at that because she was sure Roger actually would, if it was required of him. Graham now turned and led the way on down the ridge towards where a steep drop could be seen a hundred metres on. Kylie saw that this was the main creek, the same one that had been on their right for the last half kilometre. It now did a sharp curve to the left on her right front, curling around the end of a small spur which extended out from the right-hand end of the main ridge. This spur was covered with what looked like mullock heaps and rotting timber beams.

Another old mine, she deduced.

The creek then bent to the right and went across her front for a hundred metres or so before curving sharp left again and going back southwards on her left. Beyond the creek was a line of steep bluffs and even small cliffs. Large hills stood behind the bluffs. These hills towered over the area on three sides. The hills were also clothed in savannah woodland, rocks, and bushes. To Kylie it looked to be very rough country.

Graham signalled for silence and slowed down to a cautious creep from tree to tree. He led the way to a clump of bushes growing right on the edge of a steep drop above the creek line. Kylie and the others crept forward to join him. Once she was safely hidden among the bushes Kylie looked down.

Graham pointed down. "Eureka Creek," he whispered. "That is the line of the old Boonmoo Railway below us, the railway that went to Irvinebank. See where it comes around the end of that little spur on our right? The old railway station was over in the next part of the valley. To our left, where that heap of grey stones is, was the old battery. You can see where the railway had a spur line running into it and where the main line went left through a cutting to follow along beside the creek."

Kylie nodded. She now saw that the steep drop in front of her was actually mostly an artificial cutting, with the bench cut along which the railway had once run being very clear as a roadway five metres below her. The rails and sleepers were gone but the earthworks were very obvious. She also noted that the big hills across the creek forced the creek to turn the way it did.

"Is that a dam?" she asked, pointing to a small concrete wall built across the bed of the creek twenty metres below where they hid.

"Yes," Graham replied. "There is another one further upstream, but it is full of sand."

This one had a small pool of water in it but the rough concrete was cracked and broken. Kylie noted that the creek was about 25 metres wide and its bed was very rocky, with only a few patches of sand. There was plenty of water in pools, with a trickle flowing between them. *At least we won't get thirsty,* she thought.

"Where is the Ivanhoe Mine?" Margaret whispered.

Graham and Roger both pointed along the top of the wide flat ridge to their left. "There," Graham said, indicating old timber beams and piles of rocks about a hundred metres away above the point where the railway and creek both curved abruptly to the left.

"And there is a great little mine tunnel down in the creek bed directly across from it. Look down near the grey gravel, near that big pool. You will... Oh! Ssh! Look!"

Kylie had been following Graham's directions carefully so immediately saw what he was pointing at. As her eyes focused on the creek bed in the growing light she noted movement and felt a thrill of excitement and fear course through her. It was a man! And not just any man, but an armed man wearing Ned Kelly armour!

Chapter 37

KYLIE'S REVENGE

Kylie stared at the distant figure in horror. The bushranger swivelled his helmeted head from side to side, apparently looking around.

"Has he seen us?" she whispered, her heart hammering urgently.

Graham pressed his hand on her shoulder. "Sssh! No, I don't think so. Keep still."

Kylie froze, anxiously hoping that the bushes gave enough cover. To her they seemed very few for a proper hiding place. Beside her Roger slowly lowered himself to lie flat on the ground while Margaret crouched wide-eyed. Having looked in all directions the bushranger stepped across the creek from one rock to another and then began clambering up the steep side of the creek bank towards the bench cut of the old railway. As he climbed up he went out of sight, to reappear a few seconds later up on the overgrown road that now ran along the bench cut.

To Kylie's concern the bushranger again halted and looked around, rifle held ready. Then he began walking along the old railway towards them. As he did, she tried to keep still. She also tried to identify him.

It is Brian, I think, she decided, noting his build and height.

Beside her Margaret whispered, "Where did he come from?"

Graham answered. "Out of the old mine tunnel I was telling you about. It runs straight into the base of the cliff from the creek bed. Now, be quiet."

As the bushranger got closer, Kylie eased herself flat. The sharp little rocks and twigs hurt but she ignored that. By now she was sure it was Brian but as he got closer the old railway curved slightly and he went out of sight in the cutting below her. Twenty seconds later he re-appeared to her right, still walking along the old railway and apparently unaware they were watching.

"There is no top in the helmet," Roger whispered.

Kylie had noticed that. Graham had too and he chuckled and whispered, "We could toss a grenade down into it, like blowing up a tank, if we had a grenade that is."

"We could drop a big rock," Roger suggested.

Kylie was not amused at the boy's silly chuckles and horrible ideas. But she was now absolutely certain it was Brian. She had seen his hair and hands close up. "Where is he going?" she asked, keeping her voice as low as she could.

"Don't know, but he looks ready for action," Roger replied.

"He is talking to himself," Margaret added.

Graham shook his head. "No. The helmets have radios in them. He is talking to someone else."

That was a worrying thought. Kylie looked anxiously around, even glancing over her shoulder. "To Liam and Pat perhaps?" she suggested.

Again Graham shook his head "No. The radio waves wouldn't carry that far, not in these hills. The person is close, and in line-of-sight."

That got them all looking anxiously around but Kylie could not see another person anywhere. By this time Brian was fifty paces away to their right, still following the old railway as it curved to the left below the remains of the old mine on the little spur.

Graham gestured behind them. "We had better move back to better cover. Start crawling away and keep low. I want to watch where he goes."

Kylie carefully turned herself around. Then, with continual anxious glances over her left shoulder, she followed her brother's lead. The five friends crept away on hands and knees, heading back up the wide ridge. Within a few paces they could no longer see the old railway and Graham stood up and began walking quickly, moving diagonally to his left. Kylie and the others followed his lead.

It was easy going but she worried that their boots might be making too much noise as they crunched on the deadfall. As Graham apparently did not think so, she kept following his example. But they had only covered about fifty paces before Graham let out a hiss and indicated they should go down. The nearest cover was only a dead log, but they all slid in behind it. As she went down Kylie saw why Graham had done this. Brian had come into view again, but he was not walking along the old railway. Instead he had turned off it, going up to his right near the end of the little spur and was climbing up onto that among the mullock heaps of the old mine!

Did he hear us? she wondered, her heart hammering anxiously.

But Brian vanished from sight up a small gully near the lower end of the spur. The friends lay watching and waiting for several minutes but he did not reappear.

"Where did he go?" Roger whispered.

Graham frowned and replied, "I don't know, but we need to find out." He stood up and cautiously began walking east across the ridge, his eyes quartering the ground ahead and along the small spur. Kylie did not know if Graham wanted them to stay hidden or not, but when the others stood up and began following she did the same. As she walked slowly forward, she saw that the ridge was not as flat as she had at first thought. Between her and the lip of the 'Railway Station' valley she noted two gullies, both running down the ridge across her front. The first was small, only a metre or so deep. It joined the creek to the left of the mullock heaps. The second was larger and was the one Brian had vanished into.

As they got closer to the mullock heaps near this second gully, Graham crouched, signalled and then went down on his belly in the short grass. He then wriggled forward to hide behind another dead log. Kylie and the others did likewise. The log wasn't very large and she could still see over it as she lay flat, so she was able to see Brian. She saw that he had stopped on the narrow crest of the ridge which ran down between the gully and the Railway Station valley. When she first saw him he was standing, looking intently into and along the Railway Station valley but then he selected a spot among a small clump of rocks and sat down. After a look in all directions, which made Kylie freeze with anxiety, he laid his rifle on the rocks, its barrel pointing over the top of the rocks into the next part of the valley. Then he took off his helmet and seemed to relax.

Yes, it is Brian, she thought. To Graham she said, "What is he doing?"

Graham made a wry face. "It looks very much like he is on guard. That might be their sentry post. From there he should be able to see all the way along the stretch of the valley where the old railway station was."

"What do we do?" Norah asked.

"Nothing. Just lie still," Graham answered. "If we move and he looks around he will see us."

A glance showed Kylie this was likely. There was very little cover and she could see that Brian would be able to see right up the ridge they were on for hundreds of metres.

Graham made a very careful scrutiny of the whole spur, then said to Roger, "Can you see anyone else?"

Roger, who had done likewise, shook his head. Graham then said, "If he is a sentry, he didn't relieve anyone. So there can't be many of them."

"Might be their day sentry post," Roger suggested.

"Where is the person he was talking to then?" Margaret asked.

Graham pointed back to their left rear into the creek bed. "Back at the mine tunnel in the creek bed most likely."

By then it was full light and Kylie saw that the sunlight was lighting up the trees up on top of the hills across the creek. She squirmed to make herself more comfortable and then tried to relax. As she did, she puzzled over what was going on and what to do next. Ants then began to crawl on her and flies arrived to bother. She tried to ignore these.

Minutes crept by. Brian remained sitting, mostly staring over into the next valley, but occasionally looking around. He fidgeted as well and toyed with his rifle. Graham was then sure he was a sentry. After twenty minutes he was obviously a bored sentry, even to Kylie's inexperienced eyes. The sun rose higher, the first rays angling in through the trees where they were. This at least provided better cover by giving a dapple of light and shadow, but Kylie still felt horribly exposed.

Margaret fidgeted and then whispered, "What are we going to do? We can't just lie here."

"Yes, we can," Graham replied. "Peter and Steve should have reached Bakerville by now and the cops should be on their way. We can just wait for them."

"But Brian will see them coming," Kylie said.

"He might ambush them," Roger suggested.

That was a horrible thought and made Kylie feel quite sick and helpless. In her heart she did not think Brian was capable of cold-bloodedly shooting another person, but she wasn't sure.

"We need to be able to warn the police that Brian is there," she said.

"Bit risky," Graham said. "We would have to creep right across to the side of the ridge where we can see down into the Railway Station valley."

That did look risky to Kylie. From where they lay to the top of the bank was about fifty metres of fairly bare, open ground. Just going down into the gully in front of them would be risky. She saw there were plenty of trees, but they were all ironbarks with thin trunks. Even so she felt the risk had to be taken. "We must try," she hissed, a sense of dread gripping her.

Graham looked reluctant and studied the ground. "Only one of us... Hello! What's he doing now?"

They all looked, and Kylie saw that Brian had stood up. For the next minute he fumbled at the side of the body armour, then undid it. He struggled out of it, lifting it up over his head. The body armour was placed on the ground beside the helmet. Next Brian picked up his rifle and then vanished from view over the crest.

"Now where's he going?" Roger muttered.

"Don't know, but now's our chance. Come on!" Graham said. He at once stood up and began walking quickly towards the east side of the ridge, aiming for some rocks and bushes about 50 metres up the ridge from where Brian had been sitting. Kylie sprang up and followed, her eyes finding it hard to focus on the details she was so excited. She found her heart was really hammering and that her mouth had gone dry. As she walked quickly forward at a crouch, she wiped perspiration from around her mouth.

The first bit was easy, that was 25 metres down and across the small gully. As she hurried across it Kylie felt very exposed, knowing that if Brian came back up to the rocks, he must see them. Then they had to cross another 25 metres of flat, ground. However the friends reached the bushes without being seen and crept in among them. As she settled beside Graham Kylie saw Brian again. He was down in what Graham had named the Railway Station valley. Down to her left a hundred metres away she could just make out where the road came into view after doing a tight curve around the bottom end of the small spur. The road then ran along to almost below where she was before bending away from her to go across the bed of the creek. The creek crossing was just stones amid a trickle of water, the road passing through a stand of large She-oaks. Up on the other bank was an area of bare ground.

"That's where we camped last year," Graham explained, "And the railway station once stood where that mango tree is."

Kylie looked and saw that on the other side of the creek the road then went to her right, joining another that angled down from the big hills to her left before running along the flat for half a kilometre back to another bend, this time curving to the left away from her. She found it hard to make out the actual road because of the trees which grew in the valley. Having surveyed the general layout she shifted her focus back to Brian.

He had gone down the slope to the road near the bend on her left and was busy taking off his shirt. His rifle was placed against a rock.

"What is he doing?" Margaret asked as she joined them.

"Don't know. I think he... Uh oh! Don't look you girls," Graham replied.

Kylie did look. To her embarrassment she saw Brian unbutton his shirt and shrug it off. He then walked down through the long grass to a nice pool of water in the creek bed. Then he tugged off his riding boots and socks and began unbuckling his belt.

He's undressing, she decided.

He was. As she watched in embarrassed but fascinated interest, she saw him peel off his trousers and then his underpants.

"Lucky he is standing facing away from us," Roger muttered..

"Stop looking, Margaret," Graham hissed. Kylie saw he was scarlet with embarrassment.

Roger chuckled and whispered, "Why is that, Graham? It's nothing she hasn't seen before. I heard that you and Margaret have often been skinny dipping together."

"Oh don't keep bringing that up!" Margaret hissed, also flaming red. "That was years ago, when we were little."

Brian, now naked, stepped gingerly down over the rocks to the pool and began washing himself. For a few seconds Kylie watched with interest and even regret. Suddenly an idea came to her and she stiffened.

"Now's our chance," she hissed. "We can disarm him and take him prisoner."

"How?" Graham asked.

"I will walk down and tell him, while one of you sneaks down and gets his rifle. He will be too embarrassed to get out of the water."

"You hope!" Margaret answered with a giggle. "What if he does?"

Roger chuckled and said, "Then she will see what Brian is really like."

"Roger! Don't be crude!" Norah snapped, her face also crimson with embarrassment. By this time Brian was gingerly wading into the pool.

Kylie sniffed and poked her tongue at Roger, then said, "It won't be anything I haven't seen before, not with brothers like Graham and Alex. Anyway, let's not waste time talking. That water looks cold and he won't stay in long. Who is coming to get the gun?"

"I will," Graham replied. He at once stood up and began moving back through the bushes. "This way, Kylie," he ordered, pointing back over the crest into the gully on the western side.

Kylie saw the sense of that and quickly followed him. Graham went back over to the gully at a fast walk. Kylie followed, glancing down to her right as she did. Now she was very excited. Just before Brian vanished from view she saw he still had his back to her and was ducking his head to wash it.

Brother and sister hurried down the gully between the ridge and the remains of the old mine. Kylie was surprised at how fast Graham moved but she forced herself to do the same. As she did, she had to detour around several large holes and heaps of stones. Rotted timbers which had once been the supports for the mining machinery lay broken on the ground. As she reached the road at the end of the gully Kylie was aware that she could see all the way along the 'battery' stretch of the creek. That made her anxious lest they be seen by anyone there.

That her anxiety was justified was confirmed when Graham suddenly stopped and motioned her to hide. Kylie crouched behind a tree and stared along the creek in the direction Graham was looking. Through a tiny gap in the trees growing in the creek bed movement caught her eyes and she stiffened with fear. Then, very clearly, as though with a camera coming into focus, she saw a man moving at the place where the mine tunnel was. The man suddenly bent down and she saw he had a billy or cook pot in his hand. He filled this with water and then turned and vanished from view.

They are hiding in that old mine alright, she thought.

But there was no time for any discussion as Graham was already moving again. He ran to his right along the old railway, gesturing urgently to her to follow. Twenty-five metres on he stopped at the bend where the old railway curved sharply to the right around the end of the small ridge. Edging slowly forward he looked cautiously around.

As Kylie joined him at the bend he said, "Be quick. Brian might be out of the water already. Just follow me around and then keep him talking."

It was all happening a bit too quickly for Kylie's liking, but she understood that speed was vital. Graham turned and went crawling quickly around the bend on his hands and knees, keeping below the level of the grass. Kylie followed, heart hammering wildly. Then, as she walked around the bend onto the Railway Station straight, she was able to see down into the creek on her left. To her relief, she saw that Brian was still in the water. He was standing with his back to her in waist deep water, splashing himself and rubbing his arms and back.

Seeing that Graham had almost reached Brian's rifle Kylie swallowed and turned left to make her way down the steep bank. This was rocks and long grass and she remembered to look for snakes as she did. As she got closer, she suddenly felt both calm and angry.

Ooh! Revenge is sweet! she thought, aware that her plan had succeeded and that Brian had still not seen them.

She reached the edge of the water and stood with hands on her hips looking at Brian. There was a twinge of admiration and regret when she noted his well-muscled back and shoulders. Then she remembered Maureen.

"Brian!"

The effect was comical. Brian spun round, dashing water from his face. His mouth sagged open and, as realisation that she was a girl sank in, he subsided into the water to hide his nakedness.

"K... K... Kylie! Where did you spring from?" he gasped.

"Just up there. Now, just stay where you are for a minute and don't do anything foolish like calling out. We've got you covered."

She pointed up the bank behind her and saw Brian's eyes go wide as he saw Graham. Kylie glanced that way and noted that Graham was now standing up, holding Brian's rifle and aiming it at him. Astonishment, fear, and then anger, all flitted across Brian's face. His anger and embarrassment grew when Graham called out to Roger to come down and help tie Brian up. Brian rose, forgetting to cover himself but then saw Norah and Margaret. He went even redder and hastily covered himself, but not before Kylie had glimpsed his now shrivelled manhood.

He is a nice-looking boy, she thought sadly.

He was also a very angry and humiliated one, but he made no resistance when ordered out of the water. Covering himself with his hands he waded ashore, and then tried to climb the rocky bank. In doing so he stubbed his toe and Kylie could not help a malicious smirk.

As Roger slid down the slope to join him, Graham gestured and said, "Go away Kylie. Go back up to where he was on guard and keep watch in case the fellow at the mine comes this way."

Kylie did as she was told, shamefully aware that she wanted to see more of Brian naked. She scrambled up the bank and then climbed ten metres up the steep, grassy slope to the little ridge. Here she found a spot among the rocks and bushes where she could see along the battery stretch of the creek. Nearby lay Brian's helmet and body armour.

Remembering her duty she looked carefully in all directions. There was no sign of anyone, so she peeked back over the crest to see what was happening. She saw that Brian now had his trousers on and that his underpants had been wrapped around his neck and in his mouth to gag him. Roger was busy ripping up Brian's shirt to get material to tie his hands with.

Three minutes later, Brian had his hands securely trussed behind his back. Graham then stopped aiming the rifle at him and examined the weapon. That done he moved to toss Brian's boots and socks into the long grass. Then he turned and looked up.

Seeing Kylie, he called softly, "You keep watch the other way, Kylie. You shouldn't have been looking."

Kylie blushed and said, "Margaret was."

Margaret gasped, and even from 25 metres away Kylie saw her face mottle crimson. She and Norah then both turned to look out along the Railway Station valley. Kylie turned to watch west along the creek while Graham and Roger shoved and pushed Brian up the slope. Brian resisted and protested and obviously had trouble walking on the sharp little stones in his bare feet, but he got no sympathy from either of the boys. He was taken up to the bushes where Norah and Margaret waited.

Graham next made his way back down towards Kylie. As he did, an idea formed in Kylie's mind. She knew it was very risky, but the idea seemed to be a good one. Even so she tried to push the temptation out of her mind, knowing it could have fatal consequences. But by the time Graham had reached her it had become a full-blown plan. She paused and watched while Graham picked up the helmet and examined it.

Kylie watched him as he inspected it. As she waited she wrestled with her conscience. Then she shrugged. *I think we should do it,* she told herself.

She knew it was a calculated risk, but also thought it would be worth it. As Graham put the helmet down and reached for the body armour she asked, "What are we going to do now?"

"Wait for the police. I thought I might pretend to be the sentry and listen to their radio," Graham answered, then added, "You go up and join the others."

Kylie met his eyes and said, "We should go to the mine and rescue the Duke."

Graham looked surprised but then glanced along the creek and nodded. "He might not be there," he replied.

"So why else are two of the bushrangers guarding this place?" she replied.

"Be risky," Graham went on. That told Kylie that he thought it was a good idea, so she pressed her advantage and explained her plan. As he listened a slow grin spread across Graham's face and he nodded. "Good idea," he complimented, "But you won't get to see this other bloke with no clothes on."

"Oh poo! That's not why!" Kylie retorted, blushing as she did.

Graham grinned but then nodded. "Let's do it. But we will go around to the other end, not go straight along the creek bed. Come on, we will tell the others."

Placing the body armour down Graham set off up the slope. Feeling very pleased with herself Kylie limped along behind him. When they joined the others in the clump of bushes Graham did not even ask them if they agreed. He just told them they were going to rescue the Duke.

"Roger, you come with me and lead the way across to the Ivanhoe Mine. Kylie, you come with us. Norah and Margaret, you stay here with lover boy and keep him quiet."

Kylie blushed at that 'lover boy' and she saw Brian scowl, but she was still glad her plan was accepted. Roger said, "When?"

"Right now," Graham replied, glancing at his watch. "It is seven twenty and the longer we wait the more likely it is that those other bushrangers will arrive. Margaret, you and Norah keep a good lookout for them and yell out if you see them coming."

Margaret and Norah nodded and Brian scowled again. He gave Kylie a resentful glare, but she ignored that and stood up, her heart hammering rapidly.

Chapter 38

CALCULATED RISKS

Roger now led, followed by Graham and Kylie. As she started limping after them Kylie experienced a rush of pure fear.

Oh no! Maybe this is not a good idea after all, she thought.

But she said nothing and kept walking. They crossed the gully and then walked diagonally up across the flat ridge, angling away from the railway. That took them out of sight of anyone in the creek bed or on the railway. Once they were well clear Roger changed direction and walked west. Even though she was suffering badly from her chafing, blisters and sore ankle Kylie gritted her teeth and kept herself moving at the same speed.

Five minutes' walk brought them to the far side of the ridge. The ruins and mullock heaps of the Ivanhoe Mine were now visible on their right. As they passed a pile of rocks and soil Roger pointed to it.

"Keep well clear," he warned. "There are a few vertical shafts that have a long drop down them. The sides are all crumbly and you could slip in."

Kylie had no intention of going near any of the several mullock heaps she could see and felt distinctly uneasy at the thought of falling down one. Roger continued on until he reached the edge of the ridge. From there they could see down into the next reach of Eureka Creek. The slope below them was very steep so they turned left and walked along, looking for a safe way down. Kylie saw that there was an almost vertical drop of about ten metres to the old railway, here even more overgrown, and then another steep drop to the creek bed.

Fifty paces along to the left the slope was less steep and they were able to safely descend. They quickly clambered down. As they did, Kylie noted that the old railway continued off away to her left for hundreds of metres, curving slowly westwards. The creek had large pools in its bed and a thick belt of large, dark green sheoaks. Across the creek was another very steep sided ridge which led up to the big hills overlooking the battery site. As she turned right to follow the boys back along the overgrown railway Kylie noted that the hillside across the creek was pitted and scarred by more old mine tunnels.

Graham pointed back across the creek and said, "That's where the crook's mine is."

"And the entrance to Old Zeke's mine is back up to our right," Roger added.

Graham pointed up the side of the cutting they had just descended. "And I climbed up just here when I was trying to get away. That's where I blacked out."

The three walked back towards the bend Graham pointed down to the left. "See all that light grey sand and stuff on the slope? They are the tailings from the battery. It was just there, on that bend."

Kylie studied the area with interest. She noted that the old railway came through a steep sided cutting. The remnant of the ridge beyond the cutting extended to a small flat area inside a very sharp curve in the gorge. On this flat area were the remains of another mine. Beyond that was the slope of crushed rock. There was also a concrete slab that had obviously once been the base for some machinery.

Just before they reached the cutting, they came to the collapsed entrance to a mine tunnel. This opened right onto the old railway. Both Graham and Roger stopped, and Graham pointed and commented.

"This has been deliberately collapsed since we were here last," he said, a note of regret in his voice. "Last year we were able to walk inside. It was a good tunnel."

"Be part of that program of making old mines safe, I suppose," Roger replied.

"Pity, it was a good old mine that was fun to explore," Graham answered.

From what Kylie had heard of the risks the boys had run exploring the old mines she did not agree but said nothing. Going into any tunnel that might suddenly collapse did not appeal to her.

By now the three had reached the point where a vehicle track deviated around the end of the spur between a wired-off mineshaft and the concrete slab, and where the old railway cut through in a deep cutting. The cutting was now partially blocked by fallen rocks and a dead tree. Graham indicated she and Roger should get under cover.

"Wait here for a minute while I do a bit of a recce," he instructed.

Then, rifle at the ready, he made his way around along the vehicle track, continually peeking over into the creek bed. For Kylie there followed more than five minutes of anxious waiting. When Graham returned, he did so through the cutting. Crouching down he drew a quick map in the sand. While he explained his plan Kylie had to smile, noting how alive with the adventure of it all he was.

He is loving every second of this, she thought.

Satisfied they each understood their part Graham led them forward through the cutting. This was easy enough. On the other side they emerged onto a bare, flat area about five metres across where, Graham explained in whispers, there had once been a set of points and a spur of the railway which led to the left along to the battery in the bend of the creek.

Now Graham made them crawl on hands and knees across to the edge. From there they could look down into the creek above the bushranger's mine. Lying flat on what was now hot sand Kylie was able to easily pick out the places of importance. Despite being partially concealed by a small tree the entrance to the mine was very easy to pick out, once she knew where to look. Graham slithered back away from the edge and then led the way to the right for twenty metres to where a small swelling of ground in the slope down to the creek offered a covered route down to the jumbled rocks and bushes of the creek bed.

To Kylie's dismay Graham went straight over the edge of the bank, sliding down what looked to be a very steep slope. The slope was composed of a mixture of sand, stones and fine grey grit, which Kylie supposed were deposits from the rock crushing battery. For a few seconds she hesitated. Then she reminded herself that it was her plan and that time was important. With some trepidation she followed. It was easy enough but several times she slid out of control and feared she would overbalance and roll to the rocks five metres down. The effort of keeping her balance wrenched her sore ankle, bringing tears of pain to her eyes, but she bit her lip and managed not to cry out.

When he reached the bottom Graham did not even look back. He began clambering over the rocks in the creek bed, the rifle held in one hand at its point of balance. It was so obvious he was enjoying the adventure, and that he was capable of doing such things, that Kylie again smiled and felt proud of him. Personally she felt sick with apprehension lest her plan turn to a ghastly tragedy, but she felt powerless to stop what she had begun. What had seemed like a good idea in the first flush of capturing Brian now appeared foolish in the extreme and she regretted having thought of it.

"We should just have waited for the police," she muttered to herself.

But there was no going back. Graham and Roger both quickly but carefully made their way from rock to rock to the other side of the creek bed. Graham then looked back at Kylie and pointed to where she was to hide behind a clump of rocks on her side of the creek. All she could do was nod, swallow, and start creeping forward. As she did, she found her heart hammering and her eyes seemed to have trouble focusing. She had to wipe sweat from her forehead and then made an effort to get her eyes to see properly through the trees and bushes in the creek bed for glimpses of the mine entrance, ready to duck down if the bushranger appeared.

At the same time Graham and Roger crept forward along the other side of the creek until they were crouched behind big rocks just to the right of the mine entrance. Kylie had about fifty paces to go and she took it slowly, partly to sneak from rock to rock and partly to be sure she did not twist her sore ankle again on the uneven rocks. But the closer she got the more horribly aware she became that she could see the entrance to the mine.

If that bushranger comes out now he must see me, she reasoned, her heart pounding with anxiety.

But she made it. Gasping, she crouched down behind the rocks and bushes. As she settled into her hiding place almost directly opposite the mine entrance Kylie looked back over her shoulder along the creek bed to the spur at the far end but could not see any sign of Margaret or Norah, although she was sure they were watching.

Peeking around the right of the big rock she saw Graham. He met her eyes and gave her a grin and a 'thumbs up'. Both he and Roger were crouched in position so as to be behind and to the left of anyone coming out of the mine shaft and going down to the water's edge. From there Graham could fire his rifle with no danger of hitting her. That thought got Kylie sweating with anxiety. Her instructions were, if the bushranger did not obey and surrender, to duck down and hide while Graham and Roger 'dealt' with him.

Oh dear! Kylie thought anxiously, not wanting Graham to do anything violent or illegal, *I hope this plan works!*

After crouching down, heart hammering, she peeked through a small bush to again check that she was where Graham wanted her to be. Her hiding place was not quite in line with the mine tunnel but from it she could very clearly see it and the gentle rock slope which led down from it to the pool. The mine entrance was only about ten metres away across the creek.

Now we wait, she thought. That was the weakest part of her plan. *If that bushranger doesn't come out for some reason, we might get caught here by the others turning up*, she told herself. Then it would be hiding and hoping, waiting for a chance to slip away.

And there he was!

With no warning at all the bushranger appeared at the entrance to the tunnel. He wore riding boots, dirty jeans, and a khaki long-sleeved shirt. In one hand he had a torch and in the other a bucket loaded with dirty plates. He had no rifle but wore a pistol holster on his belt. It was Sean. He obviously had no inkling that they were there as he strolled down to the water and knelt down.

Kylie couldn't believe their luck. Shaking her head she thought, *He's doing the washing up!*

Then, at Graham's nod, she stood up. For a moment she hesitated, aware she was trembling. Knowing she must act she sucked in her breath and called out, "Hello Sean."

Sean looked up and goggled. Then he stood up and his hand reached for the pistol. From close behind him Graham called softly, "Don't touch the gun. Put your hands up."

Sean froze in shock, then slowly looked over his shoulder. When he saw Graham aiming the rifle at him his eyes went wide and he quickly raised his hands.

"Good boy!" Graham said, then called, "Face the water, undo your belt and take it off."

"And if I don't?" Sean snarled back.

"Then you get badly hurt," Graham answered.

Very reluctantly, and with obvious bad grace, Sean did as he was told. Resentfully, he tugged the belt loose and tossed it and the holster to one side. As he did, Kylie noted that it had a small radio clipped to it.

Graham then said, "Good! Now undo your trousers and lie face down."

Even more reluctantly Sean obeyed, his eyes flicking to Kylie as he did. He made no attempt to pull his trousers down, just undid them, then lay flat. As Sean lay down Kylie let out her breath and sighed with relief. As soon as Sean was spreadeagled face down on the rocky beach, Graham moved down over the rocks to his left, then said, "Roger, go and disarm him."

Roger moved out from behind cover and clambered over the rocks to a position between Sean and the mine entrance. Only then did the horrible thought come to Kylie that there might be more bushrangers in the mine. But it was too late to do anything about that. First Roger glanced to check he wasn't in Graham's line of fire, then he glanced into the mine before stepping forward to drag the belt and holster to one side. Next, he moved to stand between Sean's legs, his right boot near Sean's crutch. Roger then bent forward to pat him down, checking for hidden weapons. A pocketknife was extracted and placed in Roger's own pocket, then a wallet.

It was obvious to Kylie that both Graham and Roger were a team who knew what to do. Roger quickly pulled Sean's wrists behind his back and then buttoned the cuffs of the two sleeves to each other. Next, he pulled Sean's trousers down around his ankles. Having done that he unclipped the radio off Sean's belt and hooked it to his own. Then he slid the holster off Sean's belt and used the belt to tie his ankles together.

While doing so, Roger found a bunch of keys dangling on a key ring. Unclipping them and holding them where Sean could see, he asked, "What do these unlock?"

Sean just muttered and scowled. Roger moved away and picked up the holster. From it he extracted a pistol. Kylie saw that it was a small, old-fashioned looking revolver. Roger checked the revolver for safety and then stuffed it into his pocket.

Graham now called to Kylie to join them. "Find something better to tie him up with," he instructed.

Kylie clambered nimbly down over the rocks, grateful for all the dancing lessons that gave her excellent balance. Being careful not to further twist her sore ankle she jumped lightly across the creek, here only a metre wide. What she really wanted to know was whether the Duke was in the mine or not. So she nodded to Graham and picked up the torch from beside the dirty dishes.

"Is there anyone else in there, Sean?" she asked.

Sean refused to answer but Graham said, "Have a peek without going in, Kylie. It isn't a long tunnel, only about thirty or forty metres, and there are no side tunnels."

When he heard that Sean looked at Graham in surprise and then scowled. Kylie nodded and nervously made her way forward to the entrance, trying to keep to one side. This was difficult because a small tree grew half across it, very effectively hiding it, but she reached the entrance and then shone the torch inside, pressing her body to the rocks as she did.

There was no need for the torch. At the far end of the tunnel she saw that a pressure lantern was burning brightly, lighting up most of the tunnel. In its glow she saw a man seated on one side amid a litter of blankets, bags and boxes. The man had his hands in his lap and was looking towards her.

"Hello," Kylie called, then she paused, startled by the echoes. "Are you the Duke of... of..." She tailed off, ashamed that she had forgotten his correct title.

"Yes, I am," came the echoing reply. "Who are you?"

"Kylie," she replied. "Wait a moment and we will get you out." She turned and told Roger to follow. "Bring those keys," she instructed.

Roger made a face to show what he thought of going into old mine tunnels, but he did as she asked. Kylie switched on the torch and made her way carefully into the mine. She found that the roof was so low she had to stoop. The walls were very rough, just bare rock. As she moved the beam of the torch around, checking the roof and sides for safety, Roger said from behind her, "It's alright. This mine was blasted out of solid granite."

Re-assured, Kylie moved forward at a crouch, using the torch to see where she was putting her feet. It was easy enough, but she still found it scary and the further she got from the entrance the more anxious she became. Within half a minute she had reached the Duke. He sat watching, his face calm. In the light from the lantern Kylie saw that he looked tired and drawn and that he was older than she had supposed, in his thirties rather than his twenties. His lower face was covered with a thick stubble of beard.

"Hello," he said as she arrived. "You aren't bushrangers, are you?"

"No!" Kylie replied. "We have come to rescue you." She did not know quite why she said that, but it caused the Duke to smile.

He said, "You are too young to be the police. Who are you?"

Roger answered that before Kylie could think of what to say. "Army cadets," he said.

"Ah! Army cadets eh? That's good. I was an army cadet. That explains why you were so expert at dealing with that fellow out there." He nodded his head towards Sean as he did.

Kylie now saw that the Duke had handcuffs on and that these were joined to leg irons by a chain. "Keys, Roger," she said. She wanted to deny being an army cadet but let it go to save time.

Roger moved into the light and began checking the keys. The Duke pointed to one and said, "That one for the hands, and the bigger, silver one for the feet."

Roger quickly inserted the key in the handcuffs and unlocked them. As soon as they were removed the Duke sighed and began to rub his wrists while Roger bent to the leg irons. For something to say Kylie asked if he had been in the cave long. Suddenly she felt very shy.

It's the first time I have ever spoken to a real Duke, she told herself.

"Four days," the Duke replied. "Tell me, how did you know who I was and where to find me?"

"We were at Herberton when you were kidnapped. Roger and Graham were in the cadet Guard of Honour," Kylie explained.

"Graham?"

"My brother. That's him outside," Kylie said.

"He's our company sergeant major," Roger added.

"Sergeant major, eh? Good show. And what rank are you, Roger?"

"Only a corporal sir," Roger replied. He grunted with effort and then the lock on the manacles clicked and they fell loose. He at once scooped them up. "If you'll excuse me, sir, I will just go and secure that fellow properly."

"Good idea," the Duke replied.

As Roger hurried away, Kylie said, "Are you alright, sir?"

"Yes. Can we get out of here please? I haven't really enjoyed my stay."

Kylie at once turned and made her way out, shining the torch on the floor so the Duke could see where to put his feet. Half a minute later they stood in the bright sunshine. The Duke blinked and looked around him, sniffing the fresh morning air with evident pleasure.

"Ah! That's better. Thanks chaps," he said.

"That's alright sir... er... sir," Graham answered, going red at the praise.

Kylie felt embarrassed too, but she said, "Sorry sir, but we know there is a correct way to address a duke but we don't often meet one so we can't remember."

At that, the Duke smiled, quite winning Kylie's devotion. "And when did you last speak to a duke then?" he asked.

Kylie went red and giggled. "Never," she admitted. "I've only seen it done on TV or at the movies."

Again the Duke smiled. Then he said, "My full name is Cuthbert Montague Charles Dudley de Beaufort and I am, among other things, the seventeenth Duke of Fitzwater. But I would prefer it if you called me Bert, at least in private. The correct salutation is 'My Lord', but I don't think that is appropriate among friends. May I count you youngsters as my friends?"

"Why y... yes, sir," Kylie stammered, blushing.

She tried not to stare but knew she was. She saw that the Duke still wore his full-dress, navy blue uniform with its crusting of gold lace and braid. In the sunlight the silver chain shoulder straps and gold badges of rank and buttons glittered but she saw that the cloth was soiled and worn and threads of gold lace were hanging loose.

The Duke looked tired, dirty and unshaven, and his hair was untidy. He smiled at them and asked, "So, whom do I have the pleasure of counting as my rescuers?" Looking at Kylie he said, "You are Kylie, and this is your brother Graham, the sergeant major. Hello CSM."

"Sir!" was all Graham could reply, almost snapping to attention as he did.

"And this handy chap is Corporal Roger. Roger who?" he asked.

Roger straightened up from securing the handcuffs around Sean's wrists and said, "Roger Dunning sir, and this," he nudged Sean with his boot, "is Sean, junior member of the Kelly Gang."

"Yeees," drawled the Duke. "I have met the bad-mannered, unhelpful and surly Sean. Now, what happens next?"

"We get out of here before the rest of the gang turn up," Graham said.

Roger gestured to Sean. "What do we do with grumpy here?"

Graham pointed into the tunnel. "Make sure he is well secured and leave him in there. His mates will find him, if the police don't arrive first."

That got Kylie anxious. "What if they don't arrive? He might die of hunger and thirst."

"Thirst Kylie," Graham answered. "It takes weeks to die from starvation. He will be found before then."

The Duke now said, "I overheard the guards say the rest of the gang are due here today, and that they are then moving to another location."

"That would be sensible," Graham commented. "This place is more of a trap than a hideout. It's also often visited by tourists and by locals fossicking."

The Duke pointed up the creek. "The bushrangers have put up a sign back along that road saying it is a mining area where explosives are being used and for trespassers to stay out or be prosecuted."

"But why come here at all?" Roger asked.

"To hide in the mine from helicopters, for their cooking and so on," the Duke replied.

That made sense to Kylie. She stood with the Duke and watched while Graham and Roger lugged the unhappy Sean inside the mine. Roger then tossed the bucket of dirty dishes in after him, saying, "Here, lick these if you get hungry."

Graham now led the way back across the creek and up the steep slope to the old railway. A minute later they had all scrambled to the top. Without hesitation Graham turned left and started walking quickly along the old railway back towards the spur where the others waited. As they got closer Kylie saw both Norah and Margaret watching from up near the mullock heaps.

On reaching the bend to the left just below the mine Graham said, "You others go up the gully to join Norah and Margaret."

"What are you going to do?" Kylie asked.

"Collect that armour," Graham answered, turning up the gully and starting up the slope.

Kylie followed him. "I will help," she said, gesturing for Roger to continue on up the gully with the Duke. They did this while Kylie and Graham climbed to the crest of the narrow ridge where Brian had left his armour.

As she arrived puffing on top, Kylie heard Norah call a warning. Looking along the ridge to where Norah sat among the rocks and bushes, she saw her cup her hand to her ear.

"A vehicle!" she cried softly.

Kylie heard it a few seconds later, coming from the direction of the cemetery. "It might be the police," she said to Graham.

Graham looked along the valley, then glanced down at the helmet beside him and shook his head. "Might be," he replied, "But someone is calling Brian on this radio, and I think it is Liam."

He called to Roger and pointed up the slope. "Quick Roger, get the Duke up there and out of sight. If Brian gives any trouble belt him with a rock or something."

Roger and the Duke at once increased their pace, hurrying up towards Norah and Margaret. Graham bent and scooped up the body armour. Kylie watched, heart in mouth. At every second the sound of the vehicle grew louder and then, through a gap in the trees, she saw it. It rounded the far end of the railway valley and began heading towards them.

It was the truck that the bushrangers had been using the night before!

"It's them! Oh quick Graham, quick!" she squeaked.

Graham turned from watching the approaching vehicle and said to Kylie. "Quick Sis, help me put this armour on."

Kylie helped hold the armour, noting with surprise how light it was, even though it was about two centimetres thick. *Plastic of some sort,* she decided.

There were a few flustered seconds of all fingers and thumbs before they worked out how it went on. Then it was easy. It just slipped over the head and two shoulder pieces held it in place. Velcro strips then closed the open right-hand side, the left being already secured by leather thongs. As the vehicle came into view down on the creek crossing between the sheoaks Graham snatched the helmet up and placed it over his head.

He then stepped up onto the top of the slope, the rifle in one hand and the other held up in friendly greeting. As he did, this Kylie heard him talking. So struck with admiration for his cool action was she that it was only at the last moment she remembered to duck down into a hole.

As she did so, she got a glimpse of the vehicle's cab and saw three men in it: Liam, Michael and Pat. The sight of them sent her already rapidly beating heart into a fury of pounding. Anxiety dried her mouth and she began to pray. To her relief, the vehicle did not slow but drove past below her and then around the end of the spur.

Going to the bushranger's mine, she decided.

But then she heard the squeal of brakes behind her where the road curved back around the western side of the spur. So anxious was she that she knew she had to look. Noting Graham moving to do the same she slid up behind a bush and peeked down at the road. What she saw sent her heart rate shooting even higher. The vehicle had stopped at the end of the gully and both Liam and Michael were scrambling out, obviously in a hurry and looking up to where she was hiding.

And both carried rifles!

Chapter 39

NORAH

Kylie stared at the bushrangers in horror.

Oh no! They must have seen us! she thought.

Desperation filled her and she began to fluster, wondering what to do to avert a tragedy. Beside her she saw Graham fingering the rifle.

But then it dawned on her that the two were not pointing rifles or making threatening moves. Instead both began scrabbling in the back of the truck. A tarpaulin was hastily dragged aside and the two bushrangers began grabbing at more armour. As the pair began helping each other to put the armour on Kylie found herself confused.

They don't know we are here at all, she reasoned. With that she lowered herself back into what little cover she could find.

The situation became slightly clearer when Liam, now wearing the body armour but minus his helmet, walked to the cab and spoke to Pat, who was still seated in the driver's seat, and said, "Those troopers will be here in a few minutes. We will hold them up. You go to the mine and get Sean and that bloody Pommy Duke and get moving to the next camp. Make sure you don't leave any gear in the mine."

Kylie did not hear Pat's reply but a few seconds later the vehicle began moving. Liam and Michael both stood clear, then picked their rifles up and began making their way up the gully. On seeing this, Kylie nearly panicked, sure she was about to be discovered.

But they took a slightly different route, angling up the slope past where Graham still stood. As Liam went past, he said, "What's wrong, Brian?"

From inside Graham's helmet came the muffled words 'radio' and 'transmitting'. She saw Graham tap the side of the helmet with his hand.

"Are you receiving okay?" Liam asked.

Graham nodded. Liam then pointed along the Railway Station valley. "The bloody troopers are just along there. They nearly got us. We will hold them up for a while, to give the others time. Brian, you get down under cover where you are. Mick, go another ten paces up to that next clump of rocks. I will go further along."

To Kylie's mingled relief and dismay, Liam turned and began walking up the ridge towards where Norah, Margaret and the others were hiding. Through the grass she was just able to see him. To her relief, he stopped when about 25 metres short of the place where they were hiding and crouched down behind a small clump of rocks. He then placed his helmet on and settled into a fire position, aiming his rifle over the crest and down into the Railway Station valley.

Michael moved to the rocks between him and Graham and did likewise. Graham followed their example, crouching down very close to Kylie. That left Kylie lying in her sparse cover, wondering what to do. Her first thought was to sneak away but a careful glance around showed her that any attempt to do so would be very risky. Regardless which way she went she would be liable to be seen if one of the bushrangers looked around.

The police are coming, she told herself. But that also got her almost hyperventilating with anxiety. *The bushrangers are going to ambush them. How can I warn them?* she wondered.

Then the sound of a vehicle door slamming behind her gave her more reason for worry. Glancing sideways she was just able to glimpse movement through the trees. She saw Pat go sliding down into the creek bed, heading towards the bushranger's mine.

Oh no! He will find Sean and then the cat will be out of the bag! she thought.

Once again, she broke into an anxious sweat. Worry about a possible fatal shoot-out began to swamp her emotions.

She looked back up along the ridge and saw Liam adjust his position and cradle his rifle into his shoulder. Almost holding her breath with fear Kylie glanced down to her left into the Railway Station valley and saw movement among the trees near the mango tree; blue shirts on horses, mounted police.

I must not let the police get ambushed, she told herself.

There seemed to be only one option open to her, even though it meant revealing her presence and risking capture or being shot. *I must call out,* she reasoned. With that she began getting to her feet. As she did, she saw the first horses appear down at the creek crossing among the sheoaks. Now she wished that Pat would call out but there was no sign of him, nor any sound from back down the creek.

Kylie saw Liam aim his rifle. Gulping in air to yell and shaking like a leaf she stood up. As she opened her mouth to yell, Norah beat her to it.

"Frank! Look out!" Norah screamed.

In a sort of blurred slow-motion, Kylie saw Norah spring out of the rocks, waving her arms and yelling. At the same moment, Liam's head swivelled to look toward her, then swung back to his rifle sights. Down on the road Kylie glimpsed three mounted police. Two wore dark blue, old-fashioned uniforms and were Aborigines.

Police trackers, her mind registered, even as she recognised the third mounted trooper as Constable Lonergan. All three were staring up the slope and reining their horses in.

Oh too late! Kylie's mind screamed, even as the terrible prophecy she had overheard at the Irvinebank Cemetery flashed through her mind.

Liam's rifle cracked. In a sort of ghastly slow-motion Kylie saw Constable Lonergan's horse rear and fall and its rider go down with it. But by then Kylie was running. She dashed up the ridge past Graham, her eyes on Michael and the drama further along.

As she did, she called, "Graham, stop Michael!"

Now everything became a frantic blur. Kylie saw Michael's helmet begin to swivel in her direction but by then she was very close. There seemed to be only one simple option so she took it. She jumped on his back and head, kicking the helmet down. In the process she stumbled and fell heavily on her hands and knees. Ignoring the pain from bruises and skinned knuckles she sprang to her feet and dashed on up the rocky slope, twisting her ankle again and nearly falling, but barely aware of that. Her whole mind was filled by images of Norah running towards Liam, who was now half standing and swinging his rifle towards her as he reloaded it. Beyond Norah was more movement: Margaret, Roger, and the Duke.

Seeing Liam's rifle coming up to aim at Norah Kylie took instant action, aided by another stumble. There under her hand was a rock. In a flash she picked it up and hurled it with all her strength. The rock, the size of a large mango, flew straight. Just as Liam aimed his rifle it thudded into the back of his helmet. He lurched forward and at the same time pulled the trigger.

Bang!

Kylie screamed, although she wasn't aware of doing so. She saw that Liam had missed. He stumbled, swore, then re-cocked the bolt action rifle and tried to bring it up again. But Norah had reached him. Screaming in fury Norah grabbed the rifle and hung on, literally for grim death. Liam swore and shouted and then let go with one hand to punch at Norah. She took several savage blows to her face but clung on with grim determination.

Kylie now saw red. *Liam is bashing Norah!* her mind screamed.

Boys hitting girls was one of her pet hates. Her temper boiled over and she raced up the ridge and sprang on Liam's back, cannoning into him so hard that they all lost their balance and fell. Rocks battered at Kylie's arms, head and back but she ignored the pain. She felt stones digging painfully into her hips and buttocks and then she became aware she was being kicked in her shins by a furiously struggling Liam.

Kylie found she was gripping his helmet, so she twisted it. This elicited screams of pain and anger from Liam but also gave her an idea. Locking her legs around his body she deliberately pulled the helmet hard so that it slid around his head. When she could see the eye slit was at the back, she stopped turning it and began to pound at it with the heel of her fists. Liam went into a desperate paroxysm of struggling and heaving to try to shake Norah and Kylie off.

To her dismay, Kylie found that she wasn't strong enough to hang on with her hands. She was flung off, hitting the stones hard with her back and shoulder and bruising her right elbow. But she became aware that other people were there. She saw Roger and the Duke both grapple with Liam. They began trying to drag the rifle out of his hands, but Liam clung on tightly. That gave Kylie an idea. Something her big brother Alex had painfully taught her sprang to mind. Acting on it she reached forward, seized Liam's little finger, and yanked as hard as she could. Liam screamed in pain and rage, but his hand jerked convulsively open. The rifle was snatched clear.

Margaret appeared and she wrenched the helmet off Liam's head, banged it down hard on his crown, then tossed it down the slope. She then grabbed his other arm. Suddenly, a big man in a blue shirt grabbed Liam's other arm out of Kylie's weakening grip and twisted it back up.

"Let go Kylie and get out of the way," the man commanded.

It was Constable Lonergan. Kylie at once let go and rolled clear, then helped hold down a wildly thrashing leg. She saw that Roger had the other one. Constable Lonergan called to Norah, and she helped twist

Liam's other arm around to behind his back. Then Constable Lonergan knelt on Liam's back and used one hand to snap handcuffs on. While he was doing this a second trooper joined him.

"Okay kids, get away from him," Constable Lonergan ordered.

Thankfully Kylie let go and rolled away. Shaking violently she staggered to her feet, aware that her eye felt numb and that her lips was split and bleeding. She felt battered all over. After shaking her head to clear it she looked around. Margaret, Roger, and Norah stood near her, all gasping and excited. Holding the rifle and aiming it at Liam was the Duke. Constable Lonergan and the other policeman both stood, chests heaving, looking down at a still furiously struggling Liam.

Kylie then became aware of other police scrambling up the side of the ridge, some on horses and some on foot. She glanced around and saw Graham standing over Michael. Michael lay on the ground without his helmet. There was blood was trickling out of his nose. Even as Kylie looked two more police pounced on him and began handcuffing and searching.

A red-faced and panting Inspector Moriarty arrived, pistol in one hand and a radio in the other. He looked at the Duke and said, with obvious surprise and relief, "My Lord, you are safe!"

"Yes," the Duke replied. "These young cadets rescued me."

Inspector Moriarty looked astonished, and glanced at Kylie and Roger. Then to the Duke, "Are you alright with that rifle, My Lord?"

A pained look crossed the Duke's face and he gave a wry smile. "My dear Inspector," he said in a casual drawl, "I am one of the landed aristocracy, the huntin', fishin' and shootin' folk! I was born with a gun in my hand. Besides, I am a major in the Grenadier Guards. I do know how to use a rifle."

Kylie saw Inspector Moriarty's face mottle even redder with embarrassment. "Yes... er... yes, well, anyway, My Lord, I would prefer it if you gave it to one of my men and allowed us to take you to safety."

"If you wish, but I am safe enough here with my young friends," the Duke replied, giving Kylie a friendly grin.

Kylie blushed and felt very pleased. She pointed down the creek. "There are two more bushranger's down there. One is Pat and I don't think he will give much trouble, if he hasn't already run away. The other is Sean and he is chained up in the mine."

"Thank you, Miss," Inspector Moriarty said, giving her a quizzical appraisal. He ordered one of his men to take the rifle off Graham and then said, "Sgt Healey, take Mulvaney and go and secure those two men."

"There are more of them lurking somewhere," Kylie warned as Sgt Healey, the sergeant with the mutton chop whiskers, went scrambling down into the gully followed by another constable. As the two policemen made their way out onto the old railway, Kylie added, "There are eight in the gang."

"Yes, we know," Inspector Moriarty commented. "And you are Miss Kylie Kirk, is that right?"

He didn't sound very friendly to Kylie and she had a vivid flashback to when he had interviewed her at Mt Garnet. *He probably still thinks I am one of the gang,* she thought. But she could only nod. Then her attention was taken by Norah. Norah flung her arms around Constable Lonergan's neck and hugged him, kissing him fiercely.

"Oh Frank!" she cried when she stopped kissing. "I was so afraid. I thought he had shot you."

"No, he got my horse though," Constable Lonergan replied. He then hugged Norah to him and kissed her. "Oh thank you, Norah. You saved my life. Oh God I am glad you are safe! I've been so worried. Oh, I love you! Will you marry me?"

"Oh yes!" Norah cried, kissing him again.

Kylie's heart felt as though it had suddenly swelled up and wanted to burst. Tears of happiness sprang to her eyes and she could only feel glad. She saw that Margaret was crying too, while smiling at the same time. Even the Duke was smiling.

But not Inspector Moriarty. "Yes, well. That's all very nice," he commented, "But you have a job to do, Constable Lonergan. You can do all that later. Now get on with your duties."

"Yes sir," Constable Lonergan replied. But then he grinned and kissed Norah again before gently releasing her.

Kylie turned back to Inspector Moriarty. "Did Peter and Stephen warn you? Are they safe?" she asked.

"Yes, we got their message about an hour ago," Inspector Moriarty replied. "Luckily, we were already in this area. My Ghosts of Glenrowan were hot on the trail."

"What about Dingo?" Norah asked.

"We met young Wirriumi," Inspector Moriarty answered, adding, "He is probably already in hospital by now."

"And my mother, Mrs Conroy?" Norah queried.

"Safe at home. She has your horses there too. We rescued her at Irvinebank two days ago," Inspector Moriarty replied.

Hearing all that allowed Kylie to relax. She said, "You should see the bushranger's cave Inspector, where they had the Duke prisoner."

"Yes, I'd be interested to see where they have been hiding, seeing how we have searched so hard to find the blasted place," Inspector Moriarty said. "But we'll just make sure those other fellows are secured first." He then called on his radio, "Sgt Healey, have you got Mulligan yet? Over."

Kylie clearly heard Sgt Grogan's reply. "Not yet sir, but he is standing beside his truck with his hands in the air."

"Right. Okay, let's go and have a look at this bandit's lair. Grogan, you look after this lot," Inspector Moriarty ordered.

Leaving three of the troopers to guard Brian, Liam and Michael; and the trackers to mind the horses, the group made its way down onto the old railway. Kylie found it painful to walk but she was still so excited she really wanted to show the inspector. As they walked along the old railway towards the bushranger's mine Kylie and Inspector Moriarty led, followed by Graham and Margaret, then Roger and the Duke, with Norah and Constable Lonergan bringing up the rear.

As the group rounded the bend onto the battery straight Kylie saw that Sgt Healey and the other trooper had reached Pat, who was immediately handcuffed and then searched. He made no attempt to run or resist and looked very unhappy. Seeing that made Kylie feel sad.

The Kelly Gang have hurt a lot of people in their quest for justice, she mused. Then she thought, *I wonder where the other members of the gang are?* Even as she did she saw Sgt Healey and the trooper with him look over their shoulders then put their hands up. *That's odd?* Kylie thought. *Why are they doing that?*

The answer came almost immediately. From out of the same cutting that she and Graham had snuck emerged a group of people. Leading them was a big man in Kelly Gang armour, pointing a shotgun at the two policemen.

Oh no! The Kelly Gang! Kylie thought, her heart leaping into her mouth with anxiety.

Chapter 40

KYLIE DISOBEYS

Kylie felt her heart hammer with a thrill of fear. "The Kelly Gang!" she gasped as more people in armour came into view.

The group came to a standstill about 50 paces from the cutting. Directly opposite the end of the cutting was the bushranger's truck. Standing next to it were Sgt Healey and a trooper, both now with their hands in the air, and Pat, with his handcuffed behind his back. All looked astonished and afraid. Facing them with a levelled shotgun was the tall man in Kelly armour.

Dan Murphy, Kylie decided, hearing his voice booming from within the helmet.

From the cutting advanced five more people, two in Kelly armour. One of these Kylie immediately recognised as Kate by her build and legs. *So the other big one, the one holding the revolver to that girl's head, must be Phil Kelly himself,* she deduced. That left only Rory unaccounted for. *Where is he?* she wondered, glancing up at the top of the creek bank. But there was no sign of Rory so Kylie transferred her attention back to the drama.

To Kylie's surprise, one of the group, a man in his thirties dressed in denim and jeans, had a TV camera and was using it. Another man was dressed in civilian slacks and a very crumpled and dirty white shirt. Kate had a rifle held to his back. After a moment's thought Kylie realised the two men were the two newsmen taken hostage at Mt Garnet.

Well, they are getting their story now! she thought.

But the person who really got her interest was the girl held by Phil Kelly. She was a pretty blonde with a stocky but shapely build. The girl wore a pale green, long-sleeved shirt, jeans and riding boots. Phil held her by one arm and menaced her with a very big, old looking revolver.

From behind Kylie Graham said softly, "Oooh, a 44 Navy Colt."

"The six gun?" Roger queried.

"Yes, except I think it only has a chamber for five rounds," Graham replied.

Further discussion by the boys was ended by Phil Kelly shouting at them, his voice echoing and booming from inside the helmet. "Stand still, you people! Any false move and these people get shot."

Inspector Moriarty lowered his pistol and said calmly, "We won't take any action until we have talked. What do you want?"

"I do the talking Mister Policeman," Phil Kelly boomed. He waved the huge revolver and said, "First tell those coppers to drop their guns and you drop yours."

Inspector Moriarty shook his head. "Sorry, no. We will negotiate but we are not going to hand over any more hostages to you."

After that he raised the radio and spoke to the policemen behind them. Kylie now stood very still, almost frozen by fear as the horrible reality of the situation sank in.

If anyone shoots it will be a bloodbath! she thought.

Inspector Moriarty now raised his pistol slowly and just as slowly stepped across in front of Kylie. As he did, he called out of the corner of his mouth, "You people move back. Constable Lonergan, join me."

"Stand still!" barked Phil Kelly. "Move and we will shoot one of these hostages. There are three so I can afford to shoot a couple just to prove I mean business." He again waved the huge revolver near the girl's head. The sight of it made Kylie feel sick with dread and she did not know what to do. Phil Kelly then turned and snapped at the TV cameraman, "Go on you! Keep taking pictures. Move wherever you need to, to do it. We need the publicity and you ain't gunna get shot by us."

The TV cameraman licked his lips and nodded, then moved right out to the edge of the old railway between the two groups, his camera in almost continual use. Phil Kelly also moved over to the edge of the steep bank, dragging the girl with him by her sleeve. Once there he turned and looked over the edge into the creek.

"Pat, where the hell are Sean and that bloody Pommy duke?" Phil Kelly snarled.

Pat tried to speak, then had to clear his throat before answering. "Sean's down in the cave all chained up and the Duke is that dude standing at the back of this bunch."

"Chained up! What the bloody hell! What happened?" Phil Kelly demanded to know. Then he shouted angrily, "You coppers, let Pat go."

"Don't!" bellowed Inspector Moriarty.

There was a moment's tense stand-off before Phil Kelly swore loudly and aimed his revolver at Inspector Moriarty. "Listen you dumb copper, don't push your luck or you will be responsible for a lot of deaths."

"No, you will be," Inspector Moriarty answered coolly. "Now be sensible and put down your weapons."

As this went on Kylie saw the girl held by Phil Kelly turn and give him an anxious look. *That's odd,* Kylie thought. *That is the first time that girl has looked scared. If it was me I'd be terrified. Who is she anyway?*

Phil Kelly again called to Pat. "Pat, where are the others?"

"The coppers have got 'em. They are on that ridge in front of you Phil," Pat replied.

Phil swore and then spoke to Inspector Moriarty again. "OK Mister Police Chief, what say we trade? You give us Brian and Michael and we give you these two coppers, then we both back off?"

Before Inspector Moriarty could answer, Pat interjected, "Liam's up there too, Phil."

"Stuff Liam!" Phil yelled angrily. "They can have the useless, disobedient bastard. It's Brian and Michael we want. What do you say copper?"

"No," Inspector Moriarty replied.

Hearing Phil Kelly swear annoyed Kylie. *I'm getting mighty tired of being treated badly by this Kelly Gang,* she thought.

So she called loudly, "Don't swear please. There are girls here."

Phil Kelly turned to point the gun at her, causing her bowels to feel like liquid ice. Then he snarled, "Girls! You, you little bitch! You are the one who has been giving us trouble all week. Don't you tell me what to bloody do!"

"I asked you not to swear," Kylie retorted, fear fuelling anger. "You won't win much sympathy by being a foul-mouthed bully." With that she pointed to the cameraman, who was still filming.

The girl held by Phil Kelly now frowned and said something to him. This was too soft for Kylie to hear but it confirmed her thoughts that something wasn't right.

Phil Kelly muttered something in his helmet, then said, "Dan, go and get our stuff out of that cave. Kate, you keep those two coppers covered."

Dan, who was now behind the others, moved around the rear of the parked truck and vanished down the bank. As there were so many people in the way Inspector Moriarty made no attempt to stop him. Instead he gestured and said, "All keep moving slowly back please. Lonergan, you stand your ground."

This last drew a gasp from Norah and a calm "Yes sir," from Constable Lonergan. *Oh, lucky Norah, to have such a good, brave man fall in love with her,* Kylie thought. But then her jealous admiration turned to apprehension. *But he could be shot dead in the next few seconds. Oh this is awful!*

Suddenly she resolved to act.

Instead of edging backwards Kylie stepped around Inspector Moriarty and walked forwards. Inspector Moriarty gasped and then cried out, "Kylie stop! Come back here."

Kylie deliberately disobeyed him. As she walked towards Phil Kelly, her whole being became focused on him, her body just a numb adjunct to her brain.

As she did so, she heard Sgt Healey say, "I told you she was one of the gang."

That hurt but Kylie ignored it. She also ignored the revolver that Phil Kelly was now pointing directly at her chest from five paces away. Stopping, hands on hips, she looked him straight in the eyes. "Stop this nonsense before somebody really gets hurt," she snapped.

"Don't tell me what to do, you little troublemaker! You are now my prisoner. Tracey, grab her," Phil Kelly ordered.

Tracey? Kylie wondered. Her eyes moved to meet Tracey's and she noted Tracey shake her head and remain where she was.

"Tracey!" Phil Kelly snapped angrily. "I said grab her. Move, you dopey bitch!"

Still Tracey did not move, except to give Phil Kelly an angry glare. Kylie watched the by-play and then shook her head. Turning to Kate, she cried, "Kate, this is stupid! If shooting starts you will lose all the sympathy you might have won. I know this is just a publicity stunt, but it is getting out of hand and is about to all go horribly wrong. Tell Phil to give it up before anyone gets hurt, please!"

Kate stood looking at Kylie, her eyes flicking from her to Phil Kelly and then to the newsman and policemen she was guarding. Kylie could only see her eyes, but she was sure that Kate was half convinced. Getting no answer Kylie tried again.

"Please Kate. Look, there's Graham. Do you want him shot down just because your brother is being stubborn?"

Kate's eyes flicked to where Graham stood and then back to Kylie. Kylie saw real pain in them. *She is torn, the poor girl. She wants to be loyal to her family, but she can also see how stupid it is.*

Once again Inspector Moriarty called to Kylie, telling her to move back. She ignored him and shook her head angrily. "Oh Phil Kelly, don't be silly! You have made your point! The whole of Australia knows about your case now. Don't undo all your good work by pushing it too far."

Phil Kelly swore in reply, but Kylie could tell he was wavering. Kate then turned to him and said, "She's right Phil. We should give up."

"Shut up, little sister!" Phil Kelly shouted. "I give the orders here!"

"Yes but..."

"Shut up, I said!"

At that moment, the sound of horse's hooves came from behind Kylie and she turned to look. It also silenced Phil Kelly. To Kylie's astonishment, two women came riding at a fast canter along the old railway from the bend below the Ivanhoe Mine. Both had long blonde air and both rode very well. They wore jeans and shirts. As they reached the group, the women reined in and sprang off their mounts in a way that told Kylie they were expert riders.

Inspector Moriarty moved to stop them, saying, "Who are you? What are you doing here?" The two women pushed their way forward through the group. When they ignored him, he stepped over in front of them and said, "Stop! You can't go there."

"Oh can't I just!" cried the first of the two women in a shrill angry voice.

Kylie now recognised the second woman as Maureen O'Grady. *Brian's girlfriend!* she thought in astonishment. *And the older girl looks like her sister.*

This was confirmed a second later when, in reply to Inspector Moriarty's repeated demand to be told who she was and what she was doing there she said, "I'm Bessie O'Grady, and I've come to speak to Phil Kelly."

By then Bessie O'Grady had passed Inspector Moriarty, sidestepping his outstretched hand. He called angrily. "Stop! Why should you speak to Phil Kelly? This is a hostage situation. I am in charge here."

Bessie O'Grady stopped beside Kylie, her hands on her hips and an angry glint in her eye. She glared at Phil Kelly, and then at Tracey. "So it is true!" she snapped. "Phil Kelly, stop this stupid nonsense at once and give yourself up to the police."

Phil Kelly made no reply. To Kylie he appeared to shrink, to wilt. Tracey, equally puzzled asked, "Who are you?"

Bessie O'Grady looked hard at her and then said, "I told you. I'm Bessie O'Grady and I am Phil Kelly's fiancé."

"Fiancé!" gasped Tracey, her colour draining from her face. "I... I don't believe you."

"Well, I am!" retorted Bessie O'Grady. To prove it she thrust out her left hand. "Look, here's the engagement ring," she said. "He is not only my fiancé, he is the father of my child and I want him alive so that little Ned has a dad."

"Fiancé! Father of my child!" croaked Tracey. Before Kylie's eyes she underwent a sudden transformation. Blood darkened her neck and then her lower face. Fury glinted in her narrowed eyes. "Phil, is it true?" she asked.Phil Kelly hung his head and muttered something.

This obviously really stung Tracey as she suddenly shouted, "Why... Phil Kelly, you lying bastard! You told me there was no-one else! You told me you loved only me!"

Phil Kelly stood, pistol lowered, his arms flapping ineffectually at his side. "I... er... I." he mumbled.

Tracey suddenly flung herself at Phil Kelly, hammering the heels of her fists on his armour. "You rotten, lying cheat!" she screamed.

Phil Kelly stepped backwards and made a feeble attempt to hold her off. That just seemed to sting her to even greater fury and he took another backward step away from her blazing anger. Then, before he realised his peril, he stumbled backwards over the edge of the steep slope. For a second his arms clawed at the air and he struggled to regain his balance, but Tracey kept hitting at him. Down he went.

As Phil Kelly vanished from sight, Kylie rushed over to the edge of the steep bank to look, along with Bessie O'Grady and almost everyone else, including Kate. She was just in time to see Phil Kelly rolling sideways over and over down the slope. He hit the rocks at the bottom with a sickening thud. His helmet whacked against a big rock and he lay still. The revolver flew out of his hand and clattered on the rocks.

Tracey stood, appalled at what she had done. Bessie O'Grady let out a sob and started sliding down the slope towards him, again ignoring Inspector Moriarty's call to stay where she was. He turned and called, "Mulvaney, get down there and secure him."

Kylie turned and saw that Kate was standing beside her, her whole body drooping with defeat. The rifle she had been holding was now in the hands of Sgt Healey.

"Sorry Kate," she said, "But it is over."

But it wasn't.

From out of the bushranger's cave appeared Dan. He held a small steel box under his left arm and carried his shotgun in his right hand. When he saw everyone standing along the top of the bank and Bessie O'Grady kneeling over Phil Kelly's unconscious form he stopped and then hefted the gun to hold it one handed ready to use.

Inspector Moriarty yelled down at him, "Daniel Murphy, throw down the gun! You are under arrest."

"Not yet I ain't," Dan snarled back, his voice echoing in the helmet and rocky gorge. "I ain't goin' back to jail without a fight!" He raised the barrel of the gun.

"Get down!" Constable Lonergan shouted, pushing Norah flat.

Inspector Moriarty tried again. "Give it up man. You can't possibly escape!"

"I can try! Now back off or somebody gets hurt," Dan shouted, aiming the gun at the inspector.

Kylie saw that Inspector Moriarty was still standing and her emotions boiled with apprehension. But the threat of extreme violence had her diving for the ground, heedless of prickles and burs.

Inspector Moriarty shook his head but kept his pistol levelled. "Don't kill him men," he shouted over his shoulder. "We want him alive. Shoot only in self-defence or to save someone else. If you have to shoot, remember how we dealt with Ned Kelly!"

Through eyes that were all blurred with excitement Kylie noted the kneeling or lying troopers aiming their rifles and feared she was about to see a person killed. For a moment Kylie was puzzled and then it came to here.

They will try to hit him in the legs, she decided, as she remembered how the police caught the original Ned Kelly.

After a few tense seconds, Dan half turned and began clambering back along the rocky creek bed. As he did, he tried to keep the shotgun aiming at the inspector.

"Stop!" Inspector Moriarty yelled, "Stop in the name of the law! Drop that weapon! If you do not stop we will have to shoot!"

Then, as Dan jumped from one rock to another, his boot slipped. To save himself from a bad fall he let go of the steel box, which clattered on the rocks. The box burst open on the rocks, scattering hundreds of bank notes. It then vanished down a crevice. Dan regained his balance on top of the rock, swearing as he did. His eyes flicked from the money to Inspector Moriarty and back. This looked so comical Kylie felt an urge to laugh, except she was dreading a real tragedy.

Inspector Moriarty snorted with exasperation. "Oh give it up man! It's over. Put that gun down before you hurt someone," he called.

Dan's response was to raise the shotgun again. Kylie flinched and ducked, then stuck her head up to see what happened next. She saw that Inspector Moriarty had stood his ground but still he did not shoot. Then Dan wobbled as he tried to balance on top of the rock. He let go of the gun with his left hand and used it to try to keep his balance. The next moment his right boot slipped and he fell heavily, landing right astride the pointy rock. His helmet fell off and he let out a sharp gasp of pain. His face contorted with obvious agony. As he did, the gun went off but luckily it was pointing up the creek.

Boom!

Kylie saw the smoke blossom from the barrel of the shotgun in Dan's hand. Sheer terror coursed through her as she heard the pellets zinging and ricocheting around the rocks. She ducked down, her mind telling her that was way too late. So she lifted her head again. Through eyes that were all blurred with excitement she saw that Dan was curled up in pain and clutching at himself with his left hand while trying to keep hold of the gun with his right. Having seen her brothers hurt like that, Kylie winced in sympathy and shook her head.

But despite his obvious agony Dan broke the shotgun and ejected the fired cartridge. Then he began to fumble in his pockets and, to Kylie's dismay, extracted another shotgun cartridge. As he did, Inspector Moriarty kept calling on him to surrender, while warning everyone to keep down.

It was Bessie O'Grady who reacted. Leaving Phil Kelly she dashed over and snatched the gun from Dan's hand. "Stop that, you silly man!" she shouted. "Ye've done enough harm already. Now give yerself up!"

Inspector Moriarty shouted orders not to fire and then told his men what to do. Sgt Healey and Constable Lonergan went scrambling down into the creek bed, weapons at the ready. In seconds they had the whimpering Dan handcuffed. That was enough for Kylie. She heaved a sigh of relief as she got to her feet. She was just glad it was over with no-one killed or seriously hurt. She saw that Margaret was looking as ill as she felt so she hurried to her friend and hugged her. As she did, she passed Graham and Roger, both of whom were watching the drama with evident interest.

Silly boys! she thought. But she loved them!

After that it was just tidying up. The person Kylie felt most sorry for was poor Tracey. *To be lied to like that!* she thought, remembering her own burning humiliation and hurt when she found that Brian had not told her about Maureen. *Oh, if only!* she sighed. *He is such a good-looking boy, and I do so much want to find love!*

It hurt to watch Brian being placed in a police car. It also hurt to see the carcass of Constable Lonergan's once magnificent black horse lying beside the road. Liam's bullet had broken its leg so it had been 'put down'.

How sad! Kylie thought, hugging Margaret, who was even more upset by the spectacle.

"But all of us are safe," Margaret said as she lifted a tear-streaked face to Kylie's.

"And Norah has found her true love," Kylie added.

"So have I, if only he would realise it!" Margaret wailed, glancing towards Graham.

"Oh he will, Margaret, he will," Kylie said, patting her friend's shoulder.

And I hope I do too! she thought wistfully.

AUTHOR'S NOTE

This story is a work of fiction but is set in real places. Readers are asked to kindly keep in mind that the descriptions of these places may not be accurate when they read this book as many things are always changing in North Queensland. In particular they are to note that the ghost town of Coolgarra no longer exists. It was deserted by the first time the author visited the place in 1969 and since then it has been all but obliterated by the white ants, bushfires and the tin miners. During the 1970s a tin dredge worked its way up the valley, leaving a changed landscape in its wake. If you visit Coolgarra now you will certainly find evidence of the tin dredging but apart from a few pieces of glass and rusty tin nothing remains of the township.

I included Coolgarra because that is where the first glimmerings of the plot came to me and because it really suited that part of the story. If it had not existed I would have invented a fictional place just like it.

The country in the Irvinebank, Montalbion and Stannary Hills area is as described at the time of writing. I must however make the disclaimer that, as far as I am aware, none of the people who live in that interesting part of the world have broken any laws, nor are they rebels agin the government. The area is well worth a visit. The maps should assist.

The characters in this story are fictional but readers are urged to make the effort to enjoy the unique experience of a country race meeting. 'Newman Park' near Mt Garnet is a great venue for such an interesting experience.

The steam trains are a different matter. When the author began detailed planning of this story on an Army Cadet exercise in 2000 the steam trains of 'RailCo' still ran from Atherton to Herberton. Unfortunately since then they have not. It is sincerely hoped that, at some time in the not-too-distant future, that they may run again. Money for the upgrade of the track and for repairs to the rolling stock is what is needed. But rail enthusiasts are also reminded that there is a steam train at the southern end of that line, at Ravenshoe (a D17 tank loco named 'Capella'). If readers want a delightful steam experience, they should make their way to the area.

In 2023 the Ravenshoe steam train is not running because track and bridge replacement are needed, as well as funds. The Atherton to Herberton line is closed but in Herberton a 'new' steam locomotive (a 1905 'Peckett' 0-4-0) is operating on a short section of track between the Railway Station and the Herberton Historical Village. Go to www.athrail.com (Atherton Herberton Historical Railway Inc.); and www.ravenshoesteamrailway.wbs.com (07) 4097 6005

Enjoy more C.R. Cummings stories

The Air Cadets

The Navy Cadets

The Army Cadets

www.ingramcontent.com/pod-product-compliance
Lightning Source LLC
LaVergne TN
LVHW040824090826
845145LV00001BA/148